ANNIE MURRAY

Chocolate Girls

PAN BOOKS

First published in Great Britain 2003 by Macmillan

This edition published 2012 by Pan Books
an imprint of Pan Macmillan, a division of Macmillan Publishers Limited
Pan Macmillan, 20 New Wharf Road, London N1 9RR
Basingstoke and Oxford
Associated companies throughout the world
www.panmacmillan.com

ISBN 978-1-4472-0646-0

1 3 5 7 9 8 6 4 2

A CIP catalogue record for this book is available from
the British Library.

Typeset by SetSystems Ltd, Saffron Walden, Essex
Printed and bound by CPI Group (UK) Ltd, Croydon, CR0 4YY

Visit www.panmacmillan.com to read more about all our books
and to buy them. You will also find features, author interviews and
news of any author events, and you can sign up for e-newsletters
so that you're always first to hear about our new releases.

*Margot and Jane – for warm welcomes,
comfortable beds and wonderful conversation
Thanks for everything*

Prologue

November 1940

It would be remembered as one of the worst nights of the Blitz on Birmingham. The city was already heavily scarred from more than two months of regular bombardments. Houses and factories had been smashed open, unexploded bombs, incendiaries and shrapnel littered the city and the Market Hall, a favourite shopping haunt in town, was now a smashed shell.

Exhausted city dwellers spent cold, terrifying nights in shelters and cellars or crowded into the cupboard under the stairs, wondering who would be next as the planes droned overhead. Explosions shook the houses, blasting the glass from windows, knocking plaster from ceilings. A few people, too worn out even to wake to the sirens, slept through the raids: others defied the dangers and also stayed in their beds.

The Luftwaffe were back tonight, in strength. By seven thirty they were dropping flares and incendiaries, igniting a path lit by tongues of flame for the bombers. And when the bombs did begin to fall it was one of the longest, most intense raids the city had yet seen. House after house was hit, major firms suffered serious damage, wave after wave of planes came over until it seemed the whole city was ablaze: too many fires for the Fire Brigades as they fought to save factories and warehouses.

In a residential street not two miles from the heart of the city, a bomb fell on a solid Victorian villa, just one in a row of such houses. It was a direct hit, plummeting through the roof, its explosion causing the floors of the house to collapse, the whole building caving in on itself. For a long time the smashing of glass, the crashing, groaning fall of timbers went on, the rattle of plaster, trickle of dust, clouds of it, thick and choking, billowing through the chill air before silently settling.

The wardens were not there. Not yet. No one was in the street to hear the faint, anguished voice of a dying woman calling out from the rubble.

'Oh God help me! . . . Where are you my poor darling? . . . *Mein Liebling! . . . Mein Herzensliebling . . .*'

And then these last, desperate cries faded away, unheard by anyone but a petrified cat, hiding squeezed behind a shed in the garden next door.

PART ONE

1939

One

July 1939

'There she goes!'

'Time's up, girls!'

The siren, known as the 'bull', blared out across the imposing brick buildings of the Cadbury Works, through the surrounding trees and wide swathes of lawn, signalling to the neighbourhood that the afternoon shift was over. The workers moved in chattering streams through the various factory blocks, down to the cloakrooms to retrieve their belongings.

Edie Marshall peeled off her cap and white overall. At last it was time to go home. There'd been an aching lump in her throat on and off all afternoon as she worked on the line in the wrapping department. Beside her moved an endless purple and gold river of wrapped chocolate bars to be counted and packed, but her eyes kept misting over, blurring her vision so she could scarcely see to count the six, then another six bars into a box. For Pete's sakes pull yourself together! she kept telling herself. In the break she'd gone and had a sharp little weep in the lavatory. But even after that she still kept filling up.

'Edie, over 'ere!' Her friend Ruby, picking out Edie's coppery red hair among the crowd, waved a plump arm. 'Get a move on!' She'd already got her bag and cardi and was ready to go.

The two girls walked out through the gates and past the Bournville swimming baths as they did every day. It was a bright, sultry afternoon, the gardens full of flowers, though the scent of roses and lavender was never as noticeable to an outsider as the tantalizing smell of liquid chocolate which wafted from the works and along the streets. Edie and Ruby worked with the smell so constantly that they hardly noticed it any longer.

As soon as they were out through the gates Ruby pulled out her little mirror and squinted into it to coat her full lips in bright scarlet lipstick. Once satisfied with the effect, she looked round at Edie.

'What's up with you?' Ruby nudged her. 'Got a face on yer like a wet week in Bognor.'

'Ouch – Rube!' Edie felt small and quite dainty next to buxom Ruby. The other girls had nicknamed them 'Ginger' and 'Cocoa' when they first started at Cadbury's, and Edie's freckly features and head of long auburn locks and Ruby's full-moon face and thick brown hair had drawn close together at every opportunity, whispering and giggling. Five years later they hadn't changed. Except, Edie thought dismally, now nothing was ever going to be the same.

'Come on – you're the one getting married on Sat'dy. You're s'posed to be happy!'

'But I *am* happy!' Edie wailed, at last bursting into tears. 'I want to marry Jack and get away from home and Mom and everything – I can't wait. Only I wish I didn't have to give up my job. I don't know how I'm going to stand it – no more swimming and the Art Club, and it's been like family, being here, with you and all the others, and I'm going to miss you all so much . . .'

'Oh Ede . . .' Ruby put her arm round Edie's shoulders and squeezed her tightly. 'It ain't going to be the same here at all without you—'

'. . . and all afternoon I've been thinking – Oh Rube,

I'm so worried Jack and me'll end up like our mom and dad!'

Ruby's face soured at the thought of Edie's mom, Nellie Marshall, the vicious old witch!

'Never, Edie – in a million years. Course you won't!' As encouragement she gave Edie another playful poke in the ribs. 'You and Jack'll get on all right. And I'll be round to keep you up on the gossip. But I'm fed up with yer for going and finding a husband before me! You could've flippin' waited!'

Edie ended up laughing through her tears. Ruby had always been able to cheer her up. They reached the corner of Kitty Road.

'I've got to go into town for Mom,' Ruby said. ''Er wants me to go down Jamaica Row – get a few bits of meat and that. We ain't got nothing in for tea.'

Edie felt so sorry for Ruby these days. Until close on a year ago the Bonners' house and Ruby's family had been the happiest place Edie knew and she'd spent all the time she could round there. The Bonners had begun to make her believe that family life didn't have to be the hard, bitter thing it had always been for her. But Ruby's dad dying had changed everything. Ethel, who'd been a jolly, plump woman with peroxide hair, forever singing and laughing, was a sad, grieving widow now. She'd sunk into herself and didn't seem to be able to snap out of it. She was finding it hard to cope with anything and Ruby, the oldest and the only girl, had had to take up the slack. Most Saturday nights now she was in town, late night shopping in the Bull Ring, the stalls lit up with flares as she sought out the last of the chickens and knock-down meat and fruit, the bags of broken biscuits. Poor Ruby was having to be the mom to her five brothers as well as the main wage-earner at the moment. Ruby always looked tired out these days. Mostly she made the best of it, but just occasionally she'd say, 'I wish she'd be a proper mom to us again,' in a way which wrung Edie's heart.

'I'll walk yer to the bus stop,' Edie said. 'Shall I take your bag home, save you carrying it?'

Ruby handed it over. 'Ta.'

As they waited to cross the Bristol Road she reached in her pocket and pulled out a couple of squashed-looking chocolates. Even after all this time at Cadbury's she still couldn't resist eating chocolate. Most people soon tired of it when surrounded by the smell and sight of it day after day.

'Here y'are.'

Edie's blue eyes narrowed with reproach. 'You'll get it in the neck you will, one day. No wonder you've got spots.' She took one of the marzipan diamonds, knocked a few fluffy bits off from Ruby's pocket and popped it in her mouth. Cadbury employees were allowed to eat chocolate so long as they remained within the factory, but taking it home was strictly forbidden.

Ruby gave a shrug which made her large bosom rise and fall. 'Who's going to know? They never notice.'

'Oh, you're awful,' Edie said, chewing guiltily as they crossed the road.

The two of them stood side by side as a queue of people built up for the bus to town. Edie enjoyed the feel of the sun, bringing out the freckles on her bare forearms. She kept her cardigan on though, the sleeves pushed up to her elbows. It came as second nature, never uncovering her left arm above the elbow unless she had to. Arms folded, her right hand fingered the triangle of pale, scorched flesh which looked so ugly to her. Such a terrible accident, Nellie used to tell people. Edie's so

8

clumsy – walked straight into me when I was bringing the iron from the fire. Such a shame. That was her mom: Mrs Marshall, prim stalwart of the Band of Hope temperance society, never a pin out of place in her home, clothes starched and ironed into hard lines. That same correct, upright woman who'd come at her across the back room that day when she was seven years old. She was ironing on a blanket on the table, elbows sticking out, thin body taut with fury. Edie never understood what she'd done to provoke Nellie that day, except that she was late home from school, had stopped to play on the way home. A few minutes after she got home Nellie snatched up the iron from the fire, teeth bared, eyes burning with loathing.

'That'll teach yer!' she spat at Edie as the iron hissed on her flesh. 'Hurts, don't it, see?' No accident. And afterwards, missing school in a blur of pain and fever. Making excuses. The shame of it. She uncovered the arm only when she went swimming. Nothing was going to stop her doing that, especially not her mom.

She started to feel better. What did she have to cry about – she was getting married! Getting out of home at last! She and Jack loved each other, and love always won over, she told herself. Like in the pictures. For a moment she saw herself up there on the big screen in Jack's arms, their lips moving closer and everything else fading except the two of them kissing, the violins playing louder and louder . . .

She was jerked out of her reverie by the sound of a stifled sob coming from the woman who was standing in front of Ruby. Edie felt she recognized her. It was hard to tell her age, but she'd be a bit older than herself and Ruby, with curling chestnut hair fastened in a bun, but from which uncontrollable corkscrews of hair had escaped and curled round her forehead and ears. The woman had a curvaceous, motherly figure, rather busty, and was dressed in a neat tweed skirt, a black cardigan buttoned over her white blouse and low-heeled, though stylish brown shoes. She was weeping quietly and intensely into her handkerchief. Edie watched her shaking shoulders, pitying her. She could tell the woman was mortified at having broken down in the street. She wore round, tortoiseshell spectacles and every so often pushed them up to wipe her eyes, but even as she did so the tears were replaced by more. Edie nudged Ruby.

'She's at Cadbury's, ain't she? Clerical, or accounts or summat?'

Ruby shrugged. The bus had just pulled into view and she was sorting out her pennies.

The weeping woman fumbled to find her purse and her handkerchief dropped to the ground at Edie's feet. As she didn't appear to notice, Edie picked up the sodden little square of cotton and cautiously touched the woman's arm.

''Scuse me – you dropped this.'

'Oh!' Startled, she turned round, obviously embarrassed, trying to keep her head down. 'So sorry. Thank you.' She had a nice face, Edie thought. Not a looker, just kind and friendly, even though her eyes and nose were red and blotchy.

'If I had a clean one I'd give it yer,' Edie said.

The woman glanced up and tried to produce a smile on her distraught features.

'Oh – not at all. But you're very kind.' The bus growled to a halt beside them and she turned away and climbed inside.

Ruby, one foot on the step said, 'T'ra then.' As the bus moved off, Edie saw Ruby's plump features, thick hair scraped back from her face as she leaned towards the window to wave.

Janet Hatton climbed down from the bus in Navigation Street, her damp handkerchief still clutched in one hand. Heading for New Street in the soft evening light, she fumbled in her bag for the packet of Players with shaking fingers. The packet had long been crushed deep in the bag with a box of Swan matches, under her little make-up bag, hanky and purse.

'Oh no, I never smoke,' she would tell people when cigarettes were offered round on social occasions. And she didn't smoke, at least not in her real life. She lit up, praying there was no one about who would recognize her.

She was early. Six o'clock sharp, he'd said. It was a quarter to. She lingered near the Council House, trying to make the cigarette last. She always tried not to inhale much of the smoke as it burned her throat, but she had come to find comfort in the habit of smoking, the smell of the unlit tobacco, and in what she felt was its vulgarity. It would appall Mummy, and that was all part of the attraction. It made her feel seductive, a woman of the world suddenly, which even at twenty-five she had never succeeded in feeling before. Alec's kisses, the admiration in his eyes, the way he laughed at things she said, the way *she* laughed now, more than ever before, the helpless, shameful excitement of it all – all these things had become tied into the smoking of a cigarette, which she had also never done before she met him, and until . . . Oh Lord, but tonight she despised herself bitterly for it. For all of it. Tonight all the tobacco tasted of was fear and dread.

The spindly arm of the museum clock said five to six.

The cigarette had made her feel sick. Throwing away the butt, she took out her powder compact, dabbed her nose and put on some lipstick, peering into the little mirror, holding it close as her spectacles were not quite strong enough. At least they hid her red eyes. She smoothed her cardigan over her hips, patted her hair, turning to look at her reflection in one of the shop windows. Her shadowy face looked back, bespectacled, topped by her foolish mop of curls, the picture completed by her dismal, glamourless clothes. And she saw what no one else could yet see: a silly, cheap little secretary, duped into carrying a bastard child.

'That's what they'll all say.' Her lips actually moved. 'You stupid, ridiculous little fool!'

The despair which had brought on her tears after work rose up and swamped her again. Janet was so appalled at herself. Here she was, a respectable young woman, a Quaker who was supposed to have high ideals, throwing everything away to run helplessly after this man. This man whose eyes and words and hands shocked her into an excitement she had never known before, aroused such desire in her, and whom she had to creep about to meet, to lie and pretend because she was not part of Alec's real life with his wife and small son.

In the shop window, another reflection came and stood beside her own and she jumped.

'Alec!'

'Kitten!' He smiled, handsome as ever, and there was no doubting the warmth in his smile, but at the same time his blue eyes were flickering beyond her nervously, to see if there was anyone who might see them, who might reveal his secret to Jean, his wife.

'How's tricks?' Alec steered Janet gently but firmly back along the street. 'Come on – got a surprise for you.'

'Oh,' she said helplessly, while her mind screamed, 'No! You've got to tell him now!'

'Just round the corner. Come on!'

She followed, looking up at the profile of this man who in his need had picked her out, had made her feel desired and honoured. He had a sturdy build, clipped black hair and moustache and a ruddy, cheerful complexion.

Round in Margaret Street he stopped suddenly. 'There!'

Janet looked, trying to get her breath. 'Where? What is it?' There was nothing extraordinary, a couple of cars parked at the kerb, a scattering of passers-by.

He pointed at one of the cars. 'John Spiller's lent me his Austin. I told him I had a few errands to run this evening. Hop in quickly, will you?' In case anyone saw, of course.

'But Alec, no! Look, there are things I need to say to you. And I said to Mummy I shouldn't be back very late.'

'And you won't be.' He slipped off his jacket and smiled reassuringly at her across the roof of the car, fingers tapping, wanting to be off and away. 'Come on, kitten – we can talk on the way.'

Two

Edie walked down Charlotte Road, one of a little grid of streets tucked, along with the infirmary and the Alliott engineering works, into a pocket of land between the main road, the wharf and the railway. Each of the four streets was long enough for two rows of forty or more tightly packed terraces facing each other, their tiny strips of back garden with outside lavatories and wash-houses, each one shared between two houses. When the builder, a Mr Glover, had put up this sturdy neighbourhood soon after the turn of the century, he named the streets after his family. The side road was Kitty Road, and off it fed Charlotte, Minnie and Glover.

Charlotte Road sloped gently downhill in the direction of the works and the wharf behind it. The Marshalls' house, number twenty-seven, was about half-way down. At the very bottom of the street two shops faced each other: on the other side was Higgins' hucksters shop, which sold everything from gas mantles to mops and buckets, and on their side was her dad's business, Dennis Marshall: Gentlemen's Barbers. Dennis Marshall was a short, barrel-chested man, spruce and upright, nails always scrubbed clean, absent from home as much as possible. As a small girl Edie had sometimes had to go and deliver a message to him, self-conscious as she stepped in her buttoned boots through the door, into that mysterious aura of sweat and shaving cream and male banter, of fuzzy little piles of hair sweepings on the floor. Some of them would say, 'Awright bab – Dennis, 'ere's yer littl'un come for yer!' and tease her or chuck her cheeks. This was her father's little kingdom. The one place he seemed happy.

Jack's family, the Weales, lived at number forty-seven. The front of the house badly needed a lick of paint, and as she passed, she could hear Mrs Weale's voice raised, moaning as usual, along the entry. Jack wouldn't be back in yet. Edie hurried past, threads of her prospective mother-in-law's voice trailing after her down the road. She and Jack were rescuing each other.

Rodney, her ten-year-old brother, was out playing on the pavement with a bunch of other kids. You could see his carrot-topped head a mile off, flying after a 'cat' – the little block of wood used for 'tipcat', their game craze of the moment. Seeing Edie they shouted, 'Eh, Rodney's sister – gorrany choclit for us?'

'You know I ain't, so why bother asking?' she retorted.

Rodney, playing the big man in front of his pals, thumbed his nose at her.

'Same to you.' She went down the entry and along the little path to the back of number twenty-seven, then realized she was still carrying Ruby's bag. Sticking her head through the open back door, through which drifted the smells of boiled greens and Bisto, she shouted, 'Mom – I'm back! Just dropping Ruby's overall round.' She didn't expect a reply and didn't get one.

Ruby lived in Glover Road. When she and Edie had met at their first Cadbury's interview, aged fourteen, Miss Dorothy Cadbury, with her kind eyes, old-fashioned clothes and hair coiled into 'headphone' plaits above her ears, had set them some little puzzles to do, then checked their hands and nails. No one would be taken on at the works if they had warts or other blemishes on their fingers. Then she asked them questions, starting with when were they born?

'October the nineteenth, nineteen-twenty,' Edie said.

When Ruby, next in line, offered the same answer, Miss Dorothy frowned. 'I mean *your* date of birth,' she said. 'Not hers.'

'That is mine,' Ruby said, going red. 'It's the same.'

Being accepted by Cadbury's was a coveted position in the area, a cause for celebration. It meant good, steady work in a clean atmosphere with holidays, education, medical and dental treatment and all sorts of sports and clubs available to the staff. For Edie, getting her place there was like the great miracle of her life. It was the one and only time she could ever remember her mother being obviously pleased with her. 'Of course our Edie's going to work at *Cadbury's*,' she boasted snootily to the neighbours. And Ruby got a place as well. Their lives had revolved round the works for the past five years: scrubbing round their work station every Friday, one Saturday off in four, the trips and picnics.

Next door to the Bonners lived a Mr Vintner, who'd been wounded and shellshocked in the war. He was sitting in the doorway of his house, staring at the street with his vacant, childlike eyes. With his one arm he liked to offer sweets to anyone who went by. As kids they'd been warned off ('Don't go taking sweets from that Mr Vintner'), but now Edie thought, poor soul, and went and accepted a humbug from the little white bag he held out.

'Thanks, Mr Vintner,' she said. 'You keeping all right?' He nodded at her solemnly.

Smudge, the Bonners' mongrel, was panting in a patch

of shade in the yard, and the back door was flung open. The smell that came out was a rank mixture of damp, stale cooking, a hint of booze. Ethel had always liked a tot of the hard stuff. These days it was more than a tot. Edie dreaded going there now. Every day when she was younger, she'd run round there as soon as she could. There was always something going on at the Bonners' house – the five boys up to all sorts: football, marbles, roaring up and down the street on home-made go-karts. Sid and Ethel had worked in the theatre, in variety, before they married. He was a pianist and she sang and danced. Ethel gave it up when the kids came along, while Sid earned regular money playing irregular hours for pubs, tea dances, ballet schools, and, like his father, by tuning pianos. Often, when Edie arrived at the house, she heard music floating out, jolly popular songs and dance tunes, and Ethel singing along, *No, No, Nanette* or songs from *Hit the Deck* in her strong, gravelly voice. Not now though. Edie tapped on the door and heard Ethel shout, 'Who is it?'

'It's only me – Edie!' She feared that Mrs Bonner might ask her in and sit staring at her with her sad, bloodshot eyes, hair streaky grey now the bleach had grown out.

Ruby's six-year-old brother, the youngest of the family, appeared in a filthy, torn vest and a pair of shorts which reached half-way down to his ankles.

'Awright Edie,' he grinned.

'Can't stop, Alfie,' she said quickly, putting the bag on the floor just inside the door. 'Just dropping off Ruby's swimming things. She's gone into town to get you all some tea. She'll be home soon.'

Edie walked sadly up the road, dodging the kids who were playing out. It felt terrible slinking away from the

Bonners as fast as she could. Not long ago she'd have done anything to be round there where it felt safe and everyone was kind! Everything she did this week hammered home the message that her life was changing and how much she was about to lose. In marrying Jack, she'd gain a home and independence of a sort, but ... Their swim today had been what set her off this afternoon. Memories kept flooding back.

She and Ruby had been together through the Cadbury's Continuation School until they were eighteen. One day of the working week they spent in the school on Bournville Green, extending an education that would otherwise have ended when they were fourteen. As well as subjects like arithmetic and history, they'd put on plays, been taken on outings – trips along the Cut, camping at Holyhead – and got plenty of physical exercise. It was because of Cadbury's that Edie had learned to swim. Tuesday lunchtime was Ladies' Day at the Bournville baths. There was time to swim, luxuriate in the showers which lined the gallery above the pool, and then eat a bit of dinner. Today they'd eaten their buttered cobs out in the sun. Ruby was the one who'd taught her to swim. Cadbury's had an instructor, to teach their employees. The initiate would go into the water with a rope round their middle and she held the other end and shouted instructions, hauling them along the pool. Ruby was one of those people who just took to it like a fish, but the instructor, Miss Proctor, scared the wits out of Edie.

'She just lets you go under all the time,' she'd complained after one of Miss Proctor's gruelling sessions. 'I'm not going back to her. I'll never learn to swim.'

'Oh yes you will,' Ruby said. Both of them were fifteen then. Patiently, week after week, Ruby had held

Edie's chin and told her what to do, gently towing her up and down the pool until her limbs started to cooperate and she gained the confidence to go on her own. By the end of the year she was happily swimming lengths. Edie adored swimming, the glowing feeling it left you with. Part of it was the lovely showers, with their half-moon-shaped enclosures and endless supply of hot water.

There were all the other activities too. Ruby was part of the Bournville amateur dramatics group and Edie had discovered she could draw quite well and joined the Art Club. It had been her favourite thing. Now she was getting married, she'd have to give all that up.

'You can still come – you can be my guest,' Ruby had told her recently.

But already Edie could sense a distance between them and her heart was heavy. If only she didn't have to give up work things would be perfect.

Seated beside Alec in the car, Janet watched his deft hands with their little tufts of dark hair as they turned the wheel, shifted gears.

He glanced at her. 'You're quiet. Everything all right?'

She nodded, staring out through the windscreen. Tiny flies kept colliding with it, pinned there, helpless. She tried to arrange words in her mind. She'd wait until they'd cleared the middle of town and get him to stop somewhere. By the time they passed the Moseley Baths Alec was talking fluently about Herr Hitler and Germany. Was there going to be a war as so many were saying? He thought not. Of course we were wrong to let them take Czechoslovakia, but sometimes a price had to be paid to keep the peace. No one would be so foolish as to start another war like the last lot.

'It's such a nice evening, I thought we'd go out into the country. Henley-in-Arden maybe. See what we fancy.' When Janet didn't reply, Alec looked at her again. 'Are you sure you're all right? You look a bit off-colour.'

'I do feel rather queasy.' This was the truth. She'd felt queasy on and off all day. 'Look—' He was driving through King's Heath. 'Let's go into the park. It's lovely at this time of year.'

'But darling, I was hoping we could be a bit more private.'

I know what you were hoping, she thought. Every time they met now was an excuse for lovemaking. As soon as they had crossed that threshold, the talking had stopped.

'Please.' She spoke sharply. 'I need to get out.'

He sighed impatiently and parked the car at the edge of the park. That sigh of his decided her. She would not tell him. If she told him everything he would have to be involved. He'd take over. And her mother might have to know. Better just to deal with it herself, somehow.

In the park he took her arm. 'Well, this is nice,' he said grudgingly, as they walked up towards trees. He moved his lips close to her ear. 'But I was hoping to have you tonight. I need you so badly, darling.'

'Alec—' Janet stopped and stood square in front of him. 'Please. Enough. We have to stop this.'

His dark brows pulled into a frown. 'But I thought . . . You've enjoyed yourself, haven't you? I thought we were in this together?' He tried to take her arm again, saying resentfully, 'You've certainly *seemed* to be enjoying yourself.'

Janet blushed. 'Don't, Alec.' She looked at her feet in their white summer sandals. 'What we are doing is wrong.

We have to stop it and if you're not prepared to do it, then it'll have to be me.'

'But—' He put his hands on her shoulders.

'What if I was to fall pregnant?' she flared at him. 'Have you thought about that?'

'But darling, I've always been careful!'

'Not always.'

They looked into each other's eyes. That one time, their only whole day out together, in Wales, which extended late into the evening, into making love on the sand in the dark. 'It's so much nicer without,' he'd said. 'It'll be all right, darling, just this once . . .'

'You're . . . not – are you?' he said now.

Janet swallowed. Oh, if only she could tell him, have him take everything on, take away the terror that came over her at night when the reality of what was facing her chilled through her. She had no idea what she was going to do.

'No. But I want an end to this.'

He heard her coldness. His hands slid from her.

'Oh. I see.' He sighed again, looked up at the pale sky above the trees. 'Well – I suppose, all good things . . .'

They stood there, at a loss for a moment.

'I'm sorry,' she said. Her chest ached with tears but she remained dry-eyed. It had to be like this. She had to face the future herself, without entangling him, his family. That was unthinkable. And she didn't want him deciding things for her.

'I'd better drive you back then.' She was silent. 'Janet – d'you really mean this?'

Her eyes met his, steadily. 'Yes.'

Three

Edie leant up on her elbow and looked down at her husband. Husband!

It was the morning after their wedding and she had woken in utter bewilderment when she saw the beams above her, and the lopsided slant of the room. Where in heaven was she? The room over the Pack Horse out at Kidderminster! Her wedding night. Everything felt strange: the lumpy mattress, the stiff cotton of her new nightdress, the unfamiliar rhythm of doors opening and closing downstairs and the hot heaviness of another body the other side of the bed.

She slid her hand across and touched Jack's back, hard and flat, like a wall, just as it had felt last night when he'd been on top of her, leaving that sticky mess behind. She flushed with shame. Surely it wasn't supposed to be like that?

She pushed herself up to look at him, over his pale, thin shoulder, naked except for his singlet. All she could see was the bruised portion of his face.

Tuesday, the evening they'd gone looking for lodgings, she'd called at his house. Mrs Weale, his sickly, complaining mom, called him down. There was a pause, then Jack appeared, tall and lanky in the doorway. Edie's hand went to her mouth.

'Oh my God, Jack – what've you done?'

The right side of Jack's normally impish face was barely

recognizable. His eye had almost disappeared into the swelling and his cheek was a swollen purple mess. The other side of his face, Edie could see, wore a decidedly sheepish expression.

'Bit of a fight,' he admitted indistinctly, looking down at his grubby boots.

'And it's worse than that,' Mrs Weale complained, folding her arms in a way which immediately made Edie feel like taking Jack's side. 'Go on then – are you going to tell her, or am I?'

Jack suddenly strode over, hoiking Edie's arm. 'Come on, Ede – we're going out.'

'Jack – just tell me!'

'Come to the park and I'll tell yer.'

'But Jack—' She stopped outside, exasperated to the point of fury. 'We're s'posed to be going over Fordhouse Lane – to look at the rooms.' She peered more closely at him. 'What a sight you look,' she said tearfully.' You've got to go to our wedding Sat'dy looking like that.'

'Thing is, Ede . . .' Jack began. 'It were that bastard Scottie MacPherson.' She could hear his anger, feel him tense up at the very mention of his name. He'd had a long-running feud with Scottie. Whenever Jack, Frank and the other mates he knocked about with ran into Scottie, it was like a red rag to a bull. Edie even suspected they'd forgotten what the original grudge was about. If it hadn't been Scottie it'd be someone else – that was just how they were.

'We 'ad a set-to outside the Dog last night. And then I were late for work this morning. Very late. And they took one look at me and said I'd had enough warnings . . .'

Edie's heart sank even lower. 'They let yer go, daint they?'

He nodded, wincing at the pain in his head.

'Oh Jack, how could yer?' Edie was enraged by seeing her mother's predictions coming true even before the wedding! 'You know my job finishes as soon as I'm a married woman. I've got enough to put down for that Mrs Smedley for the rent, but after that it's up to you 'til I can find a little job somewhere. What're we going to tell her?'

'She don't need to know I've lost my job – I'll soon find summat else. I always do, don't I? Don't fret, love. We'll soon be on our own without them all nagging all the time. It'll be all right. You've got to trust me.'

'*Trust* yer?' Edie exploded. 'I could bloody *kill* yer! Look at the state of yer!'

Jack nudged her as they walked slowly, side by side. Edie faced forward, refusing to be appeased. He tried tickling the back of her neck as she dragged him off to catch the bus to Stirchley.

'Aw, Edie – don't be like that. I won't be out with my pals once we're married. I'll 'ave to settle down then, won't I?'

'It ain't funny Jack. And yes, you have got to stop fighting – be more responsible. Yer like a great big load of babbies, all of you lads, that you are.'

'Come on—' He slipped his arm round her and she flung him off, but he could see she was beginning to come round. 'Let's go and see that Mrs Smedley – get our little nest sorted out, eh?'

'No thanks to you,' Edie grumbled.

'You're getting wed on Sat'dy. Look on the bright side, eh.' He leaned round and his one wholesome eye peeped cheekily into hers. He pecked a kiss on her freckly nose.

'I'm gunna 'ave to look on the bright side of your face an' all,' she said. 'You great big Charlie.'

The swelling had subsided completely by their wedding day, but the whole area had turned a rainbow mixture of blue, mauve and yellow and she'd felt embarrassed and disappointed in him, especially when Jack's friends made ribald jokes about his exploits. And her mom had loved it of course, sweeping into church all dressed up, peering snootily down her nose at the Weales from under the brim of that big hat. The photographer had arranged it so that Jack and Edie stood sideways on in the wedding picture, so the good half of his face was showing, she looking up at him, as she only came up to his chest.

The day had gone well enough. Edie's mom and dad had concealed their differences, or at least ignored each other all day. Her mom had made a great to-do over Edie's wedding dress, forcing her into an elaborate crêpe and lace creation with a long skirt and a short overskirt, when Edie would rather have had something pretty and simple. But, oh no, Nellie was going to make sure things were done in style, even if Edie was marrying a Weale. Otherwise Nellie hadn't said a word to her, not even her last night at home before the wedding. No motherly advice, nothing. Thank goodness for Ethel Bonner. Ruby's mom had roused herself enough to advance Edie's education on the intimate realities of married life.

'I don't s'pose Nellie iron bloomers will've said a word to her, poor wench,' Ethel said. So at least Edie had been prepared in theory, even if the reality turned out to be a mortifying disappointment.

Edie had wondered if her mother was reconciled to her marrying Jack, but as she processed back along the aisle of St Andrew's church as a married woman on Jack's arm, proud of how smart he looked in his wedding suit (except for his black eye) and holding her little bouquet of roses and carnations, she caught her mother's eye and saw a hard, dry-eyed expression on her face which chilled her. Then she thought, Oh well, Mom, it's done now and even if you can't be glad for me, you can't stop me. You never wanted me really, either of you, so now you've got shot of me. She tried to forget her bitterness a moment later when she was out in the warm sun, being pelted with rice by the cheering Cadbury girls. A lump rose in her throat as she thought how they'd been more of a family to her over the years. She had been given a gold-edged bible by Miss Dorothy Cadbury as a gift when she left the firm, which was a lovely gift, but getting married meant she was losing all these pals! But now she had Jack, Edie told herself. Her new life was beginning. Having her own husband and home would be worth everything. Jack's best man, Frank, gave her a moist peck on the cheek. Ruby, stately looking in her yellow bridesmaid's dress, managed to catch the bouquet, which Edie made sure she threw in her direction. Ruby's fleshy features broke into a beam of delight and Edie saw her wink at Frank.

'Oooh,' she chuckled, 'I don't think that's going happen in a hurry!'

After all the chatter and good wishes, everyone cheered them off for their wedding night. Edie and Ruby embraced tightly, both with tears in their eyes.

'Yer look lovely, Edie,' Ruby sniffed. 'I 'ope yer have a lovely time with Jack. I ain't half gunna miss yer though.'

'Oh Rube—' Edie kissed her, laughing and crying at once. 'Your make-up'll start running! And I'm coming back tomorrow – we're not going to Australia! You come and see me as soon as Jack and me are in our new place.'

'You won't keep me away!' Ruby sniffed, trying to smile.

They hugged each other tight and Edie felt a deep pang on parting with her as she and Jack left to catch the train. This was the end of an era for them and Ruby was the one being left behind. The next morning, lying beside her new husband, Edie wondered if Ruby felt even half as desolate as she did.

Easing herself up in bed, she sat with the bedclothes over her knees, her fiery hair loose over her shoulders. Arms folded, she instinctively stroked the scar on her arm with her fingers, as she did whenever she felt ill at ease. There was a little gabled window from which she could see a sward of grass, a gate, and sheep dotted in the distance. A dog was barking somewhere and drifting up the stairs came the smell of frying bacon.

Jack stirred slightly in his sleep. He looked very young, with his eyes closed and face relaxed. He was tall and thin, malnourished-looking, with hard, knotted muscles and very pale skin. Edie watched him, dreading him waking. He seemed such a stranger lying there. And now she had to spend the rest of her life with him! What on earth had she let herself in for? And what could they say to each other after last night's fiasco?

When they had reached the pub the evening before, the landlady led them through to a dark little room with a beamed ceiling, laid before them bowls of oxtail soup and pulled a pint of bitter for Jack. She looked rather knowingly at him, seeing his bruised face, and Edie was embarrassed. The glass of cider she requested also went straight to her head and made her feel muzzy. She'd changed out of her wedding dress and into a new shirtwaister she'd also made for herself in pretty swirls of blue and green, and was very pleased with the way it looked, the soft poplin seeming to caress her slim waist, falling in soft, flowing folds. She wanted Jack to say how nice it was but he didn't seem to notice. He drank his pint with more enthusiasm than he looked at her.

'What did yer think of my wedding dress, Jack?' she whispered. There were only a couple of men besides them in the room, drinking at the bar.

Jack looked up from his soup and smiled. 'It were lovely, Ede. Did you make it?'

She beamed back at him. 'It took me weeks. I was ever so pleased with it – and the veil.'

Jack frowned. 'Veil? Oh ar – veil. It were a good day. Now we can get down to it can't we – being married, like?'

Both of them were suddenly full of nerves and ill at ease, with scarcely a word to say to each other. They were both nineteen and Edie realized it was the first time they had ever been properly alone. Oh, there'd been those walks round the back streets in the evening, keeping out of everybody's way. Stolen kisses in doorways or down by the Cut. Even the odd few moments indoors when Nellie allowed them to use the front room, but Edie could never relax at home, feeling her mom's disapproving presence from the next room. Courting had been one long battle to snatch a few minutes away from everyone else. Now they had all the time they wanted, neither of them knew what to do with it. And in Edie's mind all the time was the thought that soon they'd have to go upstairs.

Thanks to Ethel's foresight, she knew, give or take, what was supposed to happen. Certainly things hadn't progressed that far before, she'd seen to that. She couldn't say she'd wanted them to either. A kiss and cuddle was nice enough.

They latched the door behind them and Jack stood grinning at her. Edie's hands were cold despite the warmth of the evening and her legs felt peculiar, a condition not made any better by the cider. She was certain it was the first time for Jack as well. She didn't think he looked nervous, but when he came and put his hands on her shoulders, she could feel he was trembling.

'Oh, Jack.' She smiled, touched by this, and waited for him to sweep her into his arms like they did in the pictures and for everything to melt into a rosy haze. Even Ethel had suggested things might feel rather nice. She closed her eyes and raised her face to him.

'Now then,' she heard him say. ''Ere's the moment we've been waiting for.'

She was reassured by the way he put his arms tightly round her, just held her, warmly, for a moment.

'We're married, Jack – can yer believe it?' she said. 'And I do love yer.'

Suddenly he picked her up. Edie opened her eyes, letting out a squeal of shock, as he carried her to the bed and half threw her on it. 'We can do whatever we like now!' he said, with relish, and more or less flung himself on top of her. His hands were everywhere, no holds barred, squeezing her breasts through her dress. He quickly became very excited. After a short time he jumped up and tore off his shirt and trousers. Seeing him suddenly naked, Edie didn't know where to look.

'Eh, Ede, let's get yer frock off.'

Carefully she unbuttoned her new, so lovingly sewn dress and began to pull it over her head, but suddenly she felt it yanked from above and heard the stitches rip in one sleeve. A second later she was on the bed in her little camisole and bloomers, her flesh covered in goose-pimples, arms folded because she felt so exposed. Wasn't she suppose to *feel* something? The only emotion sweeping through her was mortifying embarrassment.

'Come on, Edie—' Jack stood over her, his desire all too visible to her eyes. It made her want to giggle with nerves, but she stifled her laughter.

'You're in a great hurry, I see!'

She pulled her vest over her head and reluctantly slid her bloomers down, exposing her white body, the scar, her lightly freckled arms and shoulders. Her hair licked in russet flames down her back. She was looking up shyly at him, waiting for him to do whatever those loving things were that men were supposed to do, but he pushed her back clumsily on the bed, frantic with excitement. He hardly even seemed to see her. Edie felt nothing, except pawed at. Just once he looked into her face and said again, 'Come on, Ede!' as if she was supposed to be doing something, but she couldn't make out what it was. In any case a moment later, tense and flushed in the face, he dragged her legs apart and tried to push up into her. But it was all too late. She heard him cursing and felt the patch of damp stickiness spreading between them as he collapsed on to her.

What seemed like an age later he climbed off her, cross and out of sorts, not looking at her. They cleaned themselves up, then lay side by side in silence. After a long time, in which Edie felt a lump come up in her throat, she whispered, 'Jack? You still awake?'

But there was no reply, even though she didn't think he was asleep. There was nothing for it but to try to settle for the night. But Edie couldn't sleep for ages. What had gone wrong? Wasn't he supposed to have got a bit, well, further *in* than that? Was there something wrong with her that meant Jack couldn't function properly with her? Some blockage? Did that mean she wasn't a proper woman and wouldn't be able to have a babby? If only he'd say something! Her mind spun round and round and she felt very tearful and lonely as Jack slept, oblivious, beside her.

Now daylight had come she felt a little more cheerful. It was some time before Jack woke. She watched him open his eyes and register where he was, looking over his shoulder at her as if to check it wasn't all a dream.

Edie smiled. 'Morning, sleepyhead.' She leaned over and kissed him, trying to inject some warmth and intimacy into the day.

Jack kissed her back, rather abruptly, still without looking at her. She tried to tell herself that he was embarrassed, sulking after last night, but his rejection still felt like a slap, bringing tears to her eyes. Instead of pulling her into his arms as she'd hoped he might, he flung the covers back, yawned, stretched, then sat up.

'Right,' he said. 'I can smell cooking. Time for a bite to eat.'

He sat on the edge of the bed so that she could only see his white, sinewy back as he pulled on his trousers. She might as well not have been there.

Four

Ruby came round to Edie and Jack's new lodgings the next week, and Edie laughed with delight at the sight of her.

'Hello! It's nice to see your big grin coming round the door! You out today then?'

Ruby sat down with a groan, kicking off her shoes. 'Oh, my feet're killing me! Yes, we're out today. I've been on coating caramels – it's so warm it was coming off again as fast as we could get it on.' Cadbury's sometimes had to send workers home on summer days when it was too hot for the chocolate to set.

'Hey, look at you, Ginger!' Ruby let out her big, generous laugh and gazed enviously round Edie and Jack's humble lodgings. 'Married woman, eh! 'Ow's life with Jack the Lad then?'

'It's awright,' Edie said.

'More than awright by the look of yer. Ere y'are – brought yer some oranges.'

'Ta,' Edie grinned. She had her hair pulled into a high ponytail to keep her neck cool and it swung round jauntily. 'Look, 'ere's a tanner for 'em.'

'No, yer awright. Tuppence'll do. They've ate half the bag at home already. I 'ad to stop Perce and Alf polishing the lot off. I said, 'ere, save some for Edie, they're her favourite.'

Oranges, already peeled, were sometimes sold in the

Cadbury's reject shop, twenty at a time, along with brown bags of misshapen chocolate, priced cheaply for the workers. The fruits were leftovers from making orange creams, and a real treat when they were available. Edie put the kettle on and tipped the old dregs into a square of newspaper.

'Don't want her downstairs to see me throwing this lot out. She's a miserable old bitch. Told me I should re-use my tea-leaves two or three times to be eco-nomical!' Edie imitated her landlady, Miss Smedley's, pinched features and affected voice.

'None of her business what you do, is it? But it's awright, this, ain't it?'

'It'll do us,' Edie said, defiantly spooning fresh tea into the pot. 'Least it's ours.'

She and Jack had had to keep their sights low when they were looking for lodgings. Edie's dream of a house had shrunk to two rented upstairs rooms in Fordhouse Lane. You came straight in from the street through the dark hall and upstairs. All the floors were covered with brown lino, so thin and worn you could see the line of every floorboard through it. At the back was the bed-room, containing two single beds which Edie and Jack had moved together, lifting them across the floor so Miss Smedley wouldn't hear and then setting the springs screeching as they collapsed on them in fits of laughter at the thought of her eavesdropping below. The kitchen looked out over the front. Apart from the table and two chairs there was one ancient leather easy chair, horsehair bulging through holes in the arms, a tiny stove with two gas rings, a cupboard and a battered old meat safe tucked in the corner.

The two of them sipped tea. Edie kicked her shoes off as well. The window was open and warm air floated in from the street bringing dust and factory smells as they laughed and chatted together, remembering old jokes, catching up on news. Ruby's loud laugh filled the room. Charlotte Road had been supplied with Anderson shelters and George, Ruby's brother, had said he'd put theirs up but he hadn't got round to it. The lads had spent most of the last two days at school filling sandbags to pile up outside. Barrage balloons hung over the city like bloated fish.

'You seen our mom?' Edie asked.

'No. Oh ar, I did once – in Mrs Higgins' shop. Why – ain't she been round 'ere?'

'Once,' Edie said, refilling Ruby's teacup. She'd given her the one cup that had a saucer to match. 'Just after we moved in. Turned her nose up and went off again.'

Edie had seethed with resentment at the intrusion and at Nellie's cutting remarks. Seeing her mother outside her usual home, Edie was struck afresh by how peculiar she was. How she seemed permanently to carry a fierce inner tension that was written in every line of her body. She was always in search of some imagined perfection in everything – houses, furniture, people – and was always destined to be disappointed. The very air she breathed appeared to make her furious with resentment.

'D'you want a cup of tea?' Edie had asked.

Nellie made a dismissive gesture, her nose wrinkling. 'Oh no, ta,' she said, as if drinking poison would be a preferable alternative. She gave a last look round the room.

'Well, I s'pose this'll 'ave to do yer,' she said harshly, running a disdainful hand over the table to check for dust. 'Though I did expect my daughters to start their married life in a proper house at least.'

She left with an air of washing her hands of Edie.

'Mom's just glad to get another of us off her plate, even if she will miss my wages. I ain't been home to visit. Sod them all, I say.' She stirred her tea.

'And how's life with Jack?' Ruby asked, with a suggestive look.

'All right,' Edie blushed. Not that she'd tell Ruby anything. Not *private* things. Since their ill-fated wedding night things had improved a great deal. The next day had been awful: silence between them, Jack sulking, full of hurt pride. Edie was as relieved as anything to get back into Birmingham and have practical things to do, setting up home. Jack hadn't even attempted to try again the next night, but by the next day they'd made up. It was helped by Jack getting a new job on the Monday, in a bicycle repair shop. Edie said give it a few days and she'd get a little job, probably in a shop as well. They were in the mood for celebrating that night and more relaxed with each other. Bedtime went a lot better. She couldn't say she found married intimacy exciting – it all seemed rather messy and undignified – but it seemed to please Jack. At least it meant she was normal. Edie was convinced from that first time that she'd be expecting a baby straight away.

'The only thing is,' she told Ruby, 'he's getting back into his old habits. He come in, Sat'dy night, stinking of beer and chips and with a great big shiner. I don't understand him, Rube. I had a moan at him and he says, that's what makes a Sat'dy – a few pints, a bag of chips and a good fight. I mean can you believe it? When he's married?'

'Well, you didn't think he'd just change overnight, did yer? You know what he's like.'

'I know,' Edie sighed. 'Still, we're all right. I miss you lot though. I'm going to have to get myself a little job at the Co-op or somewhere. I've cleaned this place from top to bottom I don't know how many times. I even went to see our Florrie in Coventry last week. Her little lads're lovely,' she added wistfully. How she longed to have her own baby so she could love and care for it!

Edie had hoped that although Florrie was so much older, her having married might have bridged the gap, but Florrie was just as bossy and superior as ever. Edie loved to hold little Ian, though, who wasn't yet two, squeeze his smooth, plump arms and play with his warm toes. She remembered her brother Rodney at this age, before he became a millstone round her neck as she was the one expected to mind him all the time. Her mom was never interested in looking after him.

Refilling the teacups, she said, 'How's your mom, Ruby?'

'Not too bad – you know 'ow it is . . .' But Ruby's face fell. 'Truth is, she had a bad do Monday night. I've never seen her that far gone before. She got up to go to the lav and fell over. Couldn't budge.' Ruby fanned herself with Edie's little sketchbook, which had been on the table. 'Me and George and Perce had one hell of a job with her. I said to 'er when 'er come to the next morning, "Mom, yer can't go on like this. You're making yourself really bad."' Ruby shook her head. 'It was terrible to see her, Ede. She started crying, saying she was sorry. I think it brought her to her senses a bit actually. She was vowing she'd never do it again. But all this talk about war's getting her down an' all. She says she can't stand the thought of all that again.'

Edie's heart ached for her. Mrs Bonner had been such a happy, sweet-natured woman before she lost her husband Sid and fell into the clutches of melancholy.

'So, tell us then,' Edie urged. 'If everything's so bad, how come you look like a cat that's 'ad the cream?'

Ruby laughed, bosoms quivering under her pink frock. 'Thing is, Ede,' she giggled, 'well – you know Frank?'

'Ye-e-es . . .' Edie said, laughing at Ruby's sudden coyness. Of course she knew Frank, Jack's best man. He and Jack had been at school together and Ruby had walked out at one time or other with most of the lads in Jack's group of friends. Frank had got one of the best apprenticeships of them all, at the Austin works. He was a strong lad, with a kind of restlessness about him that Edie had never been comfortable with, but he was all right.

'Well, when you'd gone, after the wedding, Frank asked me out for a drink with 'im, to celebrate like. And, well, I've seen him a few times since. I think he's changed, Edie. I mean last time I walked out with him we were much younger . . .'

'You cheeky so-and-so!' Edie laughed. 'Well, you're a fast worker!' She was pleased for Ruby. She thought how bonny Ruby had looked at the wedding. Frank had seen her at her best.

Ruby leaned forward with relish, seeing Edie's freckly face smiling at her expectantly.

'And I'm going out with him again – tonight. We're going to the pictures.'

By the first weekend in September there was no subject on anyone's lips except war. On the Friday, the Germans invaded Poland. Children were evacuated from the centre of Birmingham in large numbers the next day and all the houses had to be shrouded in blackout material.

The day before war broke out, Edie was only dimly aware of what was happening. On the Saturday morning she started with a violent bout of sickness and diarrhoea. After hours of being sick until her stomach felt as if someone had trampled over it in hobnailed boots, and dragging herself groggily down to the cobwebby outside toilet, she felt weak and wrung out. All other life felt distant. On Saturday night, lying in bed too exhausted to move, she turned to Jack and said tragically, 'Just put me out of my misery will yer? I've never felt so terrible in my life.'

'You'll be awright,' Jack said. 'You must've eaten summat bad. It's probably the heat. You look a bit better now though. D'yer want a cuppa tea?'

Edie groaned. 'Awright – but I don't think I can stomach stera in it. Just leave it black.'

She was touched by how kind and gentle he'd been with her while she was ill. Surprised by it. It had brought out the best in him. Seeing how ill she was feeling, Jack had even promised to sacrifice his Saturday night out with the lads. All right, he may not be perfect, Edie thought, but he's been good when I've needed it. She basked in the unfamiliar feeling of being loved and cared for, listening to his movements as he brewed the tea next door. He brought two cups through and put hers on the chair by the bed. The tea was so strong you could have stood a spoon up in it. Sipping it, Edie wished she'd had sterilized milk in it after all, but she didn't want to complain and tried not to make faces at the bitter taste.

'Stay with me and drink it,' she asked. 'Tell me what've I missed? There's everyone glued to the wireless and talking about war and I 'ave my head stuck down the pan!'

Jack sat down on the bed with his tea. 'We've got to

make sure them blackout curtains are closed proper. They're talking about gas attacks and all sorts. Things ain't looking very good.'

'Jack?'

'What?'

'Give us a kiss.'

He grinned and leaned down to kiss her cheek. 'That better?'

'Yes,' she said happily. 'Much.'

She felt well enough to sit up and drink her tea. The next morning Mrs Pattison, the lady next door, came running in just before eleven to invite them all to listen to their wireless. Miss Smedley didn't possess such a thing, of course. Edie felt well enough to go. So she and Jack were sitting in the Pattisons' cosy back room when they heard Neville Chamberlain announce that Britain was now at war with Germany. After the broadcast, Mr Pattison switched off the wireless. There was a pause.

'Oh well, there it is,' he said gloomily. 'Here we go again.'

Five

'Janet dear, are you ready?'

Janet rummaged frantically through the little white chest of drawers in the bathroom.

'Coming!' she called, in what she hoped was a light, normal tone, then muttered, 'Oh thank goodness!' as her trembling hands at last uncovered a last few remaining Dr White's sanitary towels. She already had her white summer hat pressed over her thick curls, ready to go out to Weekly Meeting. But just as they were about to go, she went to the lavatory and noticed that the few brownish spots of blood which had started yesterday were turning into something heavier. She'd gone all clammy under her arms and her legs felt wobbly as she fixed the towel to the little belt. What was happening? She must be losing the baby? Oh, please let her be losing it! Her mind sent out this terrible prayer without her even thinking about it. Please God, get me out of this . . .

'We're going to be late, my love!' Her mother, Frances Hatton called from the hall.

Janet took a second's glance in the looking-glass, thinking, my goodness, do I look normal? Won't they be able to see? Then she chided herself. How ridiculously self-centred of her. To everyone else she was still reliable old Janet. No one else knew about her sordid transgressions other than herself. Goodness knows, they'd be appalled, but now there were far graver things on people's minds. This time a week ago Neville Chamberlain had announced the outbreak of war.

'Are you sure you're all right, dear?' Frances held out the box with her gas mask in it. 'You're still looking very pale. You don't seem quite right at all at the moment. I think we'll definitely get you along to Dr Hartley this week.'

'No need, it's just my monthly visitor. I feel ropey with it this time.' She forced a smile, then busied herself buttoning her cardigan. 'Sorry, you could have gone on ahead.'

They set off along Linden Road towards the Friends' Meeting House. The war had started changing things straight away. Windows of houses were criss-crossed with tape against blast and the postbox along the street was now painted yellow.

'Something to do with gas,' Frances told her. 'I believe it changes colour if there's a gas attack.'

Frances was a well-preserved woman for her sixty years, who had once been rather a glamorous beauty, her friends told Janet. The great suffering of her life, the death of Janet and Robert's father in France in 1916, had caused her abhorrence of both war and religious dogmatism, and she had since adopted the Quaker way of Christianity and pacifist beliefs. Though she dressed now with a simplicity consistent with the beliefs of the Society of Friends, it was nevertheless simplicity with flair. She had an eye, which Janet had inherited, for choosing sensible yet stylish shoes. Her clothes were certainly free from fripperies, but with the cut of a collar, an unusual row of buttons, the most sober feather gracing a hat slanted just at the right angle over her thick salt-and-pepper hair, she was still a woman who could turn the heads of older men. Janet had grown up wishing she had inherited more of her mother's looks than just her thick head of hair, and that she didn't have to wear her beastly specs.

They exchanged greetings with a few people on the way into the Meeting House. Mrs Bowles from Edgbaston, the Maylands from Selly Park. With relief, Janet settled into her place in the Meeting, welcoming the silence and lack of intrusion. She felt horribly self-conscious, as if everyone there must be able to see into her mind. It had been the same ever since she knew she was carrying Alec's child, but she had done nothing about it. The fact that nothing was showing yet had paralysed her, as if she just could not face this reality. No one would guess yet. She could put off facing up to what was happening to her. But now she was horribly aware of the towel between her legs. Why was she bleeding? Was she losing the child? Oh, if only she could ask someone for help! Frances had been a midwife before she married, but she couldn't tell her. She mustn't know, Oh heaven, what was she going to do? Panic rose like bile at the back of Janet's throat and she forced it down. So far she could feel only a very light griping in her stomach. Otherwise she felt all right. The need to behave normally kept her calm. She fixed her eyes on the bowl of white roses on the small table in the middle of the room, trying to settle amid the gentle presence of the other Friends and bring herself into the right frame of mind for worship.

But chaos reigned in her. Ever since that day when Alec Storey had walked with her brother Robert into the garden, Janet's life had run off the rails so that she could barely recognize herself. The men had been playing tennis and were still in their whites. It was already autumn and they'd complained of leaves drifting all over the court. Robert worked at the bank in Colmore Row and Alec had recently arrived to work there. The two of them were much of an age. Alec had charmed both Janet and her mother over cups of tea and sponge cake. Only a week later a little note had arrived from him, in a sealed envelope. 'I'd very much like to see you again.' He hadn't mentioned his little family during tea. She realized only later how odd this was, since it was only a few days before Robert's own wedding and that had made up not a small part of their mother's conversation.

Alec kept Janet in the dark about it until she asked, straight out, one autumn evening. They were sitting in St Paul's churchyard in the chilly dusk, his arm round her shoulder.

She didn't prepare him, just came out with it. 'Alec, are you married?'

A long exhalation of breath was all that followed. Alec seemed to slump down into himself, deflated. She gripped his arm as if to comfort him through the admission even though her nerves were screaming with dread at what he'd say.

'The thing is, Janet . . .' He didn't look at her, but stared ahead at the row of gravestones across the path. 'Once you have children . . . I have – we have – a son, Edward. He's three. Lovely little chap. But so far as Jean and I are concerned, the, you know, the loving side of things sort of died out after he was born.'

'Was the birth very difficult?' Janet asked, trying to be sympathetic, though she was withering inside. She withdrew her arm from his.

'Not especially I don't think. She just lost interest. Thinks of nothing but the boy. When I saw you I just knew you had a loving disposition – that you are what I need.' Coaxingly he added, 'You mean so much to me, the way you've been such a friend over these last weeks.'

His brown eyes were full of that longing which wrung

43

her heart, and he leaned forwards to kiss her, but she pulled back. The truth of what she was doing appalled her.

'But Alec, this is so wrong. You're a married man with a child!' She got up, backing away from him. 'I don't want it to be like this. You've been most unfair – you should have told me. How could we have any sort of future together? I want to get married myself, not steal someone else's husband. You should never have asked to see me . . . led me on. It's not fair . . .' She began to cry and he stood up and came to put his arms round her.

'No!' She pushed him away. 'I'm sorry. I can't carry on like this. It's terrible . . .'

She ran away from him that night, went home and made herself believe it was over. They didn't see each other for two miserable months. With Robert married and gone and now no Alec, life felt desolate. Then one evening in the depth of winter, he called at the house, very late. Her mother was in bed and Janet was already in her nightclothes. She fixed the chain across the door and squinted out through the crack.

'Oh Alec!' She was tearful even at the sight of him. 'For pity's sake, what on earth are you doing here?'

'Let me see you. Please, Janet.' He came right up close to the door so she could feel his breath on her face. He looked cold, a scarf in the neck of his gaberdine coat, the shoulders wet with rain.

'But I can't. It's useless. I can't let you in. What if Mummy hears? And I'm undressed for bed!'

'Dress again then. *Please*, darling.'

And she did. Stupid, desperate, longing fool that she was, she went and put her slacks and sweater on under her coat and went out to him. In the back garden he pulled her close and kissed her with more insistence than

44

he ever had before, his hands pressing her hungrily to him, urgent on her breasts. He left her weak with desire, unable to say no to his caresses, or to meeting him again, or to stand by her principles or her common sense. And that was how it had been all through the spring, furtive meetings and kisses, drinks in public places, until one evening when she'd lain back under his insistent body among the crackly leaves in a patch of woodland near Kenilworth. Even then she'd managed to delude herself that she wasn't really doing anything so harmful. She was giving companionship to a lonely man. She'd tried to block out thoughts of his wife, his other life.

Now, in the Meeting, she cleared her throat and shifted a little in her seat. The pain in her stomach was becoming more insistent, a low, burning gripe. After a time of silence people were getting up and ministering. Sharing the direction the Spirit was pointing in their lives at this time of crisis. But she couldn't discipline her distracted mind. Over and over she remembered their lovemaking, that first time on that sultry evening.

He led her under trees, their feet making fallen leaves rustle, stepping around branches and ferns and tree roots. The light was shadowy, and the little wood gave the feel of a fairy story. He looked for the driest spot near the trunk of a tree which was scattered with brown leaves, kicked some pieces of branch aside and laid out his coat. He reached for her hand. Janet hesitated, but his eyes beckoned her on. Slowly, hardly believing what she was doing, she raised her hand to meet his, knowing as she did so that she was saying yes to more than she had ever agreed to before.

'Oh darling.' He drew her into his arms, feeling her shaking. 'I've been thinking of nothing but this all day.'

She closed her eyes and raised her face to him. He

removed her specs and laid them on his jacket. His warm lips closed on hers and she felt him begin to unbutton her dress. She had the presence of mind to pull back, her brown eyes stretched wide.

'But Alec, no! What if I was to bear a child? I can't . . .'

He smiled, laughter lines appearing at the corners of his eyes in the way she loved. He caressed her face with his fingertips to quieten her. 'You won't, my darling. Look—' Reaching in his pocket he produced a French letter. He had to explain what it was, as she'd never seen one before.

'Oh Alec!' She put her hand over her mouth, a blush spreading right across her body.

She should have got up then, said no, never, she'd never . . . and run back to the road, run from him for ever. Her common sense told her this over and over again, but then he said how much he wanted her, needed her, and with that hungry look on his face he'd teased the front of her dress open. She'd always been bashful about the ample size of her bust as a girl during games at school, when she'd felt self-conscious and cumbersome beside some of the others. Now she heard a man gasp with pleasure at the sight of her, saw Alec bury his face in her pale flesh. She looked down at him, stroking his black hair, feeling herself go limp with desire.

'We have tried to keep the peace,' the voice of an elderly man was saying behind her. For a moment her mind was hauled back into the Meeting. She'd all but given up trying to centre her mind on worship. Fragments of his speech reached her.

'We have failed and the darkness of war is upon us again after a brief interval . . . In rejecting violence, do we give the aggressor leave to do his worst? . . . No clear, comfortable answer is forthcoming . . .'

Janet couldn't keep her mind on the moral dilemmas posed by the war, even though she knew how urgently it affected the Friends. John Steven, a boy she'd grown up with, was sitting across from her. Surely he wouldn't go to fight? He felt very strongly, she knew. He'd be a Conscientious Objector, like the others. To her shame her mind was still full of Alec. She had not been able to resist him. She had responded with all the passion of her nature. Alec had been highly excited by her. She burned with shame. She was a sinner, a hussy. Surely they could all see it! And as well as that sin, there were all the lies she'd told her mother. That she was going out with Joyce, one of the other typists. That she'd worked late. All the time she was haunted by the deceptions, by her mother's trust in her, sitting there beside her with her hands in her lap, her eyes closed. During her upbringing Frances had read her selections of the writings of George Fox, founder of the Society of Friends, and fragments of it haunted her now.

'Friends, whatever ye are addicted to, the tempter will come in that thing . . .'

Well, now she was reaping the consequences all right. She'd rebelled against being dear, sensible Janet, but dear sensible Janet, she could see now, might well have been a much more impressive person to be.

Never had she been so relieved to see the Elders shake hands, signalling the end of the Meeting. She felt queasy, and wanted to get home, curl up in a ball and sleep, but people needed to stay on and talk, to encourage each other. All the way home Frances talked about the war and pacifism. At last they walked back into the house to the smell of a small knuckle of beef roasting in the oven.

'A number of the Friends have taken in refugees now,' Frances said, stirring the gravy. 'The Pilgers and Mrs

Bowles each have someone. Some are the Jews one sees advertising in the papers of course, and those poor Belgians. I do feel it's perhaps something we could do – offering hospitality. Oh, my dear, are you all right?'

Janet had gone deathly pale and was sitting at the table clutching herself in agony.

'Oh . . .' She gasped. 'Oh Mummy, I'm so very sorry. There's something I'm going to have to tell you.'

Ruby was so late for work that day that she did something she and Edie used to do when they were fourteen. She raced down to the Dingle, the little path down to the Cut by the wharf, and ran along the towpath by the canal's pewter-coloured water. She wasn't sure if it was really quicker but it always felt like a short cut. She might just make it to clock on in time! She was carrying two dry cobs in a bag for lunch. For a penny you could get a bowl of thick, delicious soup in the works dining-room and she and Edie used to have one together, usually after a swim.

Oh Ede, I don't half miss you, she thought. But a smile appeared on her face at the news Edie had told her on Saturday. They'd gone out for a drink, she and Edie waiting at the beery table while Jack and Frank were at the bar. Edie put her lips to Ruby's ear and whispered, 'I'm expecting, Rube!' Her heart-shaped face was glowing with happiness and even though Ruby felt a pang of jealousy, she couldn't but be pleased for her. Edie beckoned Ruby close again. 'I'm two weeks late and I've started feeling ever so peculiar, sick of a morning and that.'

'Oh Edie!' Ruby hugged her, brimming with excitement. 'Fancy – already! Oh, I'm ever so happy for yer. Does Jack know?'

Edie shook her head, eyes dancing. 'No, I'll tell him when we get home tonight. I'm counting on you and Frank to make sure 'e doesn't go off getting into his Sat'dy night mischief!'

The presence of Frank and Ruby kept Jack in order, keeping him out of the company of his rowdier drinking pals, and the two of them saw Edie and Jack to their front door.

'Better not invite you in,' Edie said. She gave Ruby's arm an affectionate squeeze. She nodded towards Miss Smedley's front room. 'The old witch don't like anyone enjoying theirselves!'

After all the 'goodnights', Ruby and Frank were left. Frank immediately put his arm round her shoulders and pulled her close. Ruby smiled with anticipation in the darkness.

'This is the moment I've been waiting for,' Frank breathed into her face. She could smell beer, hair cream, the hot breath of desire. They turned into a side street and he pulled her into his arms.

'Wish I could see you better,' he said. 'I couldn' t take my eyes off you all evening.'

Ruby's large body shook with surprised laughter. 'That's the first time anyone's ever said that, I can tell yer!' She narrowed her eyes in the darkness, straining to make out Frank's chiselled features. 'Fatty's the only thing I've ever got called!'

'No.' His hands moved down her arms, encompassed her hips. 'Not fat. You're a real woman, you are. I've always thought so. Like one of them big ships. *Majestic.*'

'HMS *Majestic.*' Ruby let out her loud laugh. 'You

cheeky sod.' But she was as chuffed as it was possible to be.

She felt all churned up inside, thinking about the kisses which followed, the way Frank touched her. He'd pressed against her, sulky with frustration when they had to part. She'd allowed her thoughts to race ahead. They could get married soon. She could have all the same things as Edie. They could even be neighbours, bring up their babbies together! She chose not to think for a moment about what would happen to her mom, to George and the boys if she wasn't there. She was full of desire and expectation.

Until yesterday. Trotting as fast as her plump legs and ill-fitting shoes would allow, she raced in at the back of the factory. Last night Frank had told her he'd received his summons to register for active service and attend the medical check-up! Ruby was horrified.

'Never mind, Rube.' Once again they were in the dark street. There was no privacy either at Ruby's house or with Frank's large family in Heeley Road. He stroked and kissed her. 'If I'm one of the first I might get the best jobs, eh?'

'Oh, please don't go!' She was surprised how aggrieved she felt. There was no need to turn on any tears, they came pouring out of her. At home she had kept her feelings down, but suddenly at the thought of Frank going it was as if all the grief about Dad's death, all the struggles they'd been through since, came pouring out at the same time. She couldn't stand another loss.

'I don't want to go,' Frank was saying, his hands pressing her close to him. 'I don't want to let you go of an evening, never mind go away and leave yer.'

With a cry she flung her arms round his neck and pressed her wet face against his. She heard him say solemnly, 'I love you, Ruby Bonner. I want to make you my wife.'

'Oh!' She pulled back from him. 'Oh Frank – d'yer mean it? Oh, I love you too!' She was laughing now.

'Course I mean it. You're just – well, you're everything to me! So, will yer, Ruby? Will yer marry me?'

'Yes!' She'd wept with happiness. 'I want to stay with you for ever. I want to be your wife!'

It had been the happiest moment of her life and she told him so. But when she'd had time to catch her breath and come to her senses, she'd told him they'd have to wait. She wanted to marry him more than anything in the world, but how could she? If she married, she'd have to give up her job, and she'd have to watch her brothers struggle on alone to support her and their mom. And Frank wasn't even going to be here, not now he'd been called up.

Frank took this badly to begin with. 'But I want you, Ruby. Why can't we at least get wed even if I'm going away? You could still live at home.'

'I'm worried about my job,' she told him. 'I can't rush into it just yet, even if it's what I want more than anything. Oh Frank, if only we could go and live on an island somewhere where there's no war and no families – just you and me!' She clung to him. She was frightened he'd go and find someone else!

In the end, Frank came round reluctantly to her way of thinking. 'You're worth the wait,' he said, kissing her.

This morning, as she panted through the aroma of chocolate and into the crush hall where they all gathered in the morning, she felt down, and resentful about it. Why did Frank have to be one of the first called up? Damn their wars! This time it was that rotten, bloody Hitler spoiling everything!

Six

Edie sat in the little room overlooking Fordhouse Lane, cuddled up in the old armchair, hair loose, an old crocheted blanket laid across her lap and a cup of tea on the table by her elbow. She was waiting for Jack to come home, her sketchbook in her lap, drawing the fireplace, trying to capture the life in the flames. Outside it was almost dark, cold rain lashing against the rattling, draughty windows. Every so often a gust howled down the chimney, making the coals hiss and flare up.

'Come on, Jack,' she whispered impatiently. The smell of mutton stew laced with carrots and onions curled round the room, along with the steam from the gently boiling potatoes. 'If yer going to be much longer I'll 'ave to start in on them taters. Me and Little'un 're starved!'

She sat with her hand over her stomach. There was nothing to show yet, as she was only a few weeks gone, but she loved the idea of the child inside her. She felt very grown up and proud. She was making a life for herself. She and Jack had overcome their problems as a married couple and now she was to be a mother. Even Florrie was showing her a bit more respect. I'm not just the kid sister any more, Edie thought, chewing the end of her pencil and watching the licking movements of the fire. And there isn't much sign of anything happening with this war. Not to us anyroad. No wonder they're calling it 'phoney'. And I've got two little jobs and a babby on the way!

She'd found two cleaning jobs, one up at the Oak Inn in Selly Oak, and one for a family in Cartland Road. She and Jack could manage. She felt warm and contented. She wasn't even being sick as much as Florrie had assured her she would. She felt quite well in herself, although more tired than usual.

The potatoes must be ready by now. She pulled herself out of the chair, poked them with a fork and turned off the gas. Going to the window, she looked out between the criss-crosses of anti-blast tape.

'Nowt to see out there,' she said. 'Black as a bear's backside.' She pulled the blackout curtains, shutting out the night, and lit the gas mantle. As she did so she heard the door open downstairs and smiled. Here he was, just in time! They could have their tea and turn in early, cuddle up in bed together. She turned to the door, smiling as he came up the stairs.

''Allo love,' she called as he came in. Water was dripping from his cap and his face and overcoat shone with it.

'It's coming down in torrents out there,' he said, stripping off his outdoor clothes.

''Ere.' She handed him a strip of rag. 'Dry yer face and give us a kiss. I've made us a nice stew for tea.'

'Smashing.' He obliged with the kiss. His cheeks were cold and damp. 'Smells good. But before we 'ave our tea, Ede, I've got summat to tell yer.'

Edie looked up at him anxiously. His face and tone were solemn.

'What, Jack? You've not lost that job, have you?'

'No – not exactly. Look, sit down, eh?'

She sank into the armchair. Another, much more alarming thought struck her.

'You've not been called up? They can't've done yet, surely – you're a married man . . .?' Her mind was awhirl with worries.

'No – they ain't called me up.' He stood over her, seeming so tall. 'I went in today and volunteered.'

'You! What d'you mean, you volunteered? For . . .?'

Jack nodded. 'The RAF. I've volunteered to train as a flyer.' He held up his hand to silence her outburst of objection. 'Thing is, love, you know Frank's had the call-up. And a couple of other lads from the dairy, and Lol and Patsy.' Of all Jack's pals, he was the first to marry. All the others were footloose, if not fancy free. 'They'll call me up in the end. I want to go now, with the blokes I know.'

'But Jack,' Edie felt herself becoming tearful. She was terribly hurt that he had volunteered to go away and leave her, just when she felt so safe and happy. That was far worse than getting the call-up! 'We've got the babby on the way. Your pals ain't got families and responsibili-ties like you have. You could get a reserve job – in a factory. You might never have to go. Oh Jack, please don't go away and leave me on my own 'ere!' She broke down.

Jack gave a heavy sigh. Guiltily he squatted down and put his arm round her shoulders. 'I'm sorry, love, but it's too late. My name's already down, this afternoon. It's not that I want to leave you, Ede, and I know it's a bad time. But you've got Ruby, and yer mom.'

'Mom!' Edie exploded. 'What the hell good's *she* ever been to me?'

'It's just,' Jack continued, 'they say it's not going to last all that long. And when they're all chewing over their exploits after it's over, I don't want to be the only bloke left on the sidelines.'

The days before Jack was due to leave for training went terribly quickly, and there was little pleasure in them for Edie because she was so desolate about him going. On the last evening, he and Frank wanted to go out for a farewell session in the pub.

'Anyone'd think they were never going to see another drink again in their lives, the way they're carrying on,' Edie grumbled to Ruby, watching the little knot of lads walk away along the Bristol Road, in high spirits and full of bravado.

'Come on, eh? Come round ours for a bit. They won't be late. Frank said 'e'd get everyone out by ten.'

'Huh,' Edie said. 'I'll believe that when I see it.'

Nervously, Edie went home with Ruby, but she was relieved to find Mrs Bonner moving slowly round the back room, gathering the plates up from tea to wash up and shooing Billy and Alf from the table. Perce, who was fourteen and had just started work, was round at a pal's house. George, who was helping clear up, smiled at her. There was washing dangling from the backs of the chairs and from a string across one corner of the room.

Mrs Bonner was wearing a voluminous cream frock dotted with big red poppies and flat shoes so worn out that their sides had collapsed and she was forced to slop along in them to keep them on. She had a bad cough, which doubled her up, her chest rattling.

'Awright Edie?' she said. 'Ain't seen you for a long time. How're you getting along? Keeping well?'

'I'm awright ta, Mrs Bonner,' Edie said, trying not to wrinkle her nose at the smell of the house. Ethel had never been the most attentive housewife at the best of times. 'And yourself?'

'Oh, going along,' Ethel Bonner said. 'Not so bad.' But there was a dull listlessness about her speech which wrung Edie's heart. She'd had the stuffing properly knocked out of her and it was terrible to see. Her skin was bloated and spongey and her hair had a sickly yellowish tinge to it from her smoking.

'Rube, can you get Alf up to bed?' Ethel said. Ruby didn't need telling. She was usually the one in charge anyway. 'Let's put the kettle on and you and Ruby can have a chinwag. It's nice to have some company in the 'ouse. Your Jack's on his way tomorrow with Frank, is 'e?'

'Yes,' Edie said, a surge of pride mixed with her anguish that Jack was leaving her behind. 'Out for their last night on the tiles.'

'Terrible, them lads 'aving to go back into all this again. Criminal I call it . . .' The cough cut her off again.

'I've told Frank to bring 'im back in good time,' Ruby shouted from the stairs as she shooed little Alf up to bed.

'On a lead!' Edie found herself laughing in spite of her misery.

Even Ethel Bonner gave a chesty chuckle. 'That's where yer want to keep 'em, bab, take my word for it!'

Once Alf was bedded down and the clearing up done, they settled in the back room, Mrs Bonner in her sagging chair, lighting up a cigarette. Billy, who was nine, was absorbed at the table with the *Sports Argus*, copying out football scores. Ruby and Edie sat either side of him, the big brown teapot between them. Edie thought sadly of the long silent piano in the front room.

Ethel went to the sideboard and brought out a bottle

of Gordon's. 'Just have a tot to go with my tea,' she said apologetically.

'Go easy with it, Mom, please,' Ruby said, pouring out tea into the family's motley collection of chipped cups. 'Frank's got summat to say to yer tonight.'

Edie looked closely at her, hearing the urgency in her voice. She looked questioningly at Ruby, and saw the excitement in her eyes. She had a glow about her. Were she and Frank going to announce that they were to marry as well? Edie wondered, hoping that was the case. If only they'd met and married earlier, she thought, then Frank wouldn't have been called up either, and probably Jack wouldn't be leaving tonight ... But it was no good thinking like that. She realized Mrs Bonner was saying something to her.

'I said 'ow's yer mother?' She repeated. 'I ain't seen 'er in months.'

'Oh, awright,' Edie said. She and Jack had called in earlier. It was the first time Nellie had heard that Jack had volunteered. She looked at Edie stony-faced and said, 'Well, you needn't think yer coming back 'ere, yer know.'

'What makes yer think I'd want to?' Edie snapped, but the bitter words sunk deep into her. She was very anxious about how she was going to cope on her own when the baby arrived. No help from this quarter though, obviously. She'd told Ruby what her mom had said.

'Don't you get all in a state. I'll 'elp yer, Edie, any way I can, you know that.'

'You've got enough on yer plate already, Rube,' Edie said gloomily. 'Without adding me to the pile.'

'Don't talk daft.' Ruby flung her arm round Edie's shoulders. 'You're me best pal. You'll never be on yer own with me around – there's a threat, eh!'

Edie knew that despite Ruby's kind words she wouldn't be able to help much. She couldn't help worrying. If only there was someone she could really turn to and rely on!

They sat drinking their tea in silence for a while. The broken clock watched silently from the mantle and Billy Bonner put his head down on his scrap of paper, eyes closing. Ruby sent him off to bed. Mrs Bonner finished her tipple and dozed by the fire. Edie looked at her, trying to imagine the young woman she had once been, when she'd looked very like Ruby. Edie laid her hand over her stomach. The sight of Mrs Bonner and the thought of Jack going in the morning made her feel so emotional she felt a lump rise in her throat and she tried to snap out of it and talk to Ruby and George.

'Wonder what they'll be doing in that camp when they get there,' she said, doing her best to sound bright and cheerful. She was sure Ruby's mind was running ahead with Frank and Jack the way hers was.

'Must 'ave to learn everything there is to know about planes and that,' Ruby said. 'Another drop?' She topped up Edie's cup.

'Jack doesn't know one end of a plane from another,' Edie grinned. 'Can't imagine why they took him on. 'E's just as likely to sit on the tail bit and fly it backwards!'

That set the two of them off, thinking of more and more ridiculous exploits their beloved fellers might get up to. 'Heaven help the RAF when those two nutcases arrive,' Ruby laughed. 'They won't know what's flippin' hit 'em!'

'You sorry you're not going, George?' Edie asked him.

George considered the question in his usual quiet way. 'No,' he said eventually. 'It don't appeal to me, fighting, like. And anyroad, I wouldn't want to leave Rube to 'ave to cope 'ere on 'er own.'

'He's a home-boy, our George,' Ruby said fondly. 'Anyway – 'e ain't eighteen 'til January. I s'pect Cadbury's'll find plenty to keep 'im busy.'

They talked on in a desultory way and Mrs Bonner continued to snooze. Edie felt more and more uneasy. She'd lost track of time and it felt very late. She found herself listening out now, for the sound of the men coming back, but another half-hour passed and still there was no sign of them. She started to feel very tense with anger and a sense of rejection. Jack ought to want to be with her tonight!

'Oh, this is the limit!' she burst out eventually, unable to contain her feelings. 'They're the bleeding end, the pair of 'em! They're going off tomorrow for God knows how long and they can't even get themselves out of the pub in time for this once. I could crown Jack when 'e goes on like this, that I could.'

Ruby was looking strained as well. She wanted to break the news to her mom that she and Frank were planning to get engaged, but her mom was fast asleep and it felt as if the moment had passed.

When they could stand sitting waiting no longer, Edie and Ruby both went back and forth to the front door to look out and see if there was any sign of them. It was pitch black and they had to close the front door behind them so as not to show a light. Each time, the street was deserted. Mr Vintner next door had long ago been wheeled back inside.

'Oh, blast them!' Ruby said. 'Where the hell are they? I don't even know which pub they was going to.'

'All of them, knowing them,' Edie said.

Ruby went out again a bit later, pulled the door closed behind her and stood listening. A sound at the bottom of the street caught her attention. Footsteps!

'Edie.' She stuck her head in through the door. 'I bet that's them!'

They waited on the step, suddenly lighthearted.

'What time d'yer call this?' Ruby called down Glover Street.

Edie shushed her, giggling.

But there was only one set of footsteps hurrying towards them. Frank emerged through the gloom.

'Awright,' Edie laughed. 'What've yer done with 'im? Don't tell us 'e's too far gone to walk home?'

Slowly Frank came in through the gate, and then, in the dim light from the door, they caught sight of his face.

Seven

All Frank could say was, 'Oh God, Edie, I'm sorry. Oh Edie . . .' Over and over again.

Somehow they all got inside. Edie was shaking so much that Ruby had to catch her before she fell to the floor and sit her down at the table.

Mrs Bonner woke with a start. 'Wha—?' She struggled to sit upright. 'What's going on?'

'Tell me!' Edie cried. 'Frank, tell me what's happened. Where's Jack? Oh, don't look at me like that!' She flung her arm across her eyes to shield herself from the expression in his. His face seemed sucked in on itself, gaunt as a greyhound's.

'Summat terrible's happened . . .' Words choked out of him.

'He's not dead . . . Jack's not dead, is he?'

There was an awful silence. Edie slowly brought her arm back down and there was no escaping Frank's look now, the ghastly whiteness, shadows under his eyes as if he'd been punched.

'He can't be,' she whispered. 'Are you sure?' But she could see from the expression in his eyes that it was true. 'How can 'e be dead? He was with you – he was . . .' She ran out of words. Full of life, he'd been. Going off with his pals in the prime of life!

'Oh,' she kept hearing herself saying. 'Oh no, what've you *done* to him? Where is he?' And those wailing noises must be coming out of her and she had no control over them! She heard Ruby say, 'She's gone as white as a sheet – oh Lor', I 'ope this don't bring the babby on . . .'

Edie felt herself jerking about, her hands moving convulsively in her lap. Then her whole body rebelled.

'I'm going to be sick!' she cried, a hand going to her mouth. Ruby ran from the scullery with a pail just in time, and orange tea gushed out of her. She whimpered over the bucket, wiping her mouth.

Ruby stroked Edie's back, took the bucket away. Edie looked up at Frank.

'Where's my Jack?' she moaned. 'What's happened, Frank?' She reached for his hand as if he was a living link with Jack, and he came and took it, standing beside her, both of them shaking.

'It's my fault, I should've got him out of there earlier . . .' Frank sagged and fell abruptly to his knees beside her. 'I should've stopped him, I should've . . .'

Edie found Frank's head bent over her lap, the usually slicked-back hair flopping sadly down now. She laid her hand on his head and heard his sobs and the room seemed to come back into focus.

'Frank, don't. Whatever's happened, I know it wasn't your fault. I know you'd've done anything for him. Just for God's sake tell me.'

Frank raised his head, tears streaming down his contorted face. 'Oh Edie, I'm sorry,' he sobbed. In the gaslight she could see the wet of his tears shining.

'We'd come out of the pub, I'd got him to leave and we was only down the road. Jack was tanked up but we was on our way home – me and Patsy and Lol. We'd just gone under the railway bridge when we run into Scottie MacPherson coming down over the Cut . . .'

Edie's left hand came up to her throat, clenched in a fist. The others all stood and sat in silence.

'Course – it was red rag to a bull. I tried to get Jack past, but course Scottie'd had a skinful an' all and he wasn't going to leave it there and they started the usual old argy-bargy. The rest of us tried to pull Jack off. We was saying, come on, pal – Edie's waiting for yer. He started coming with us – we'd got up on the bridge over the Cut by then and we thought it was finished, but then suddenly Scottie comes up again and Jack – I don't know why 'e did it, I mean 'e couldn't even walk straight – jumps up on to the ledge of the bridge—'

'Oh Frank,' Edie gasped. 'Did Jack drown himself?'

'No – 'e daint fall in the Cut, Edie,' Frank said gently, his eyes filling again. 'He was up there dancing about on the wall and the three of us were all telling him, come on mate, just get down off there and trying to cop 'old of his hand – 'cept Scottie was leading him on, shouting about how he couldn't walk along the edge and he was yeller and all that, so Jack starts trying to walk along the bar on the top. And . . .' Frank could hardly speak now for tears. Ruby was crying as well. It was Edie for now who was dry-eyed, her face set and white.

'Course he couldn't do it – too much ale inside 'im—' Frank pulled away from Edie and raised his arms in the air. ''E were like this, he just seemed to hang there, and then he went over the side – backwards.' Frank broke down again and covered his face. In between sobs he said, ''E just . . . vanished.'

Edie sat like a stone.

'We daint hear a splash from down there. We just – I thought he'd jump up, that he was joking. But he daint. We ran down to the Cut to see. Jack was lying there, right on the edge. He must've given his head a hell of a bang. Patsy ran back to the pub to get an amb'lance.' Frank managed to speak more calmly now, as if infected by Edie's stillness. 'They took ages coming, in the blackout and everything ... When they got there, they said he'd – gone.' His face crumpled. He bent over Edie's hands in silence.

'Where is 'e?' she whispered.

'They took him.'

Tears running down her face, Ruby came and knelt the other side of Edie and wrapped her arms round her.

They tried to persuade Edie to stay in Glover Road that night, or at least to go to her mom's in Charlotte Road, but she was adamant.

'I want to go home.' She got up and paced around the room, ready to walk straight out of the door. 'I want to sleep in my bed – Jack's and my bed, in our room where we live ...' She spoke distractedly, her eyes glassy with shock.

Ruby tried arguing that it was pitch black out there, that she was in no fit state, but it was no good.

'We can't leave her like this,' Ruby whispered to Frank. 'We'll have to go with her.'

She went to her mother, who was shocked and tearful.

'Mom, Frank and me are going to take Edie home and stay with her. You and George're going to have to see to everything for tonight. I'll 'ave to go straight to work from there tomorrow.'

'It's all right, sis,' George said, his fragile features pale and serious. 'We'll be awright, won't we, Mom?' He looked appealingly at Mrs Bonner, who struggled out of her chair.

'Course we will.' Weeping, she gathered Edie into her arms for a moment. 'Edie love, I don't know what to say. I couldn't be more sorry for yer.'

Edie nodded. 'It hasn't sunk in, Mrs Bonner. I just can't . . . I just need to get home . . .' She trailed miserably into silence.

'I'll run home and let our mom and dad know what's happened,' Frank said.

While Frank went round to Heeley Road, Ruby made another cup of tea.

'Get this down yer, kid,' she said to Edie. Edie sipped obediently. When Frank was back and the tea finished, they put on coats and hats and set off into the damp, cold darkness. Frank had a tiny torch which shone a pencil of light at their feet, and he and Ruby walked either side of Edie, each with their arms linked with hers, in grief-stricken silence. Afterwards Edie could never remember walking back there that night. There was almost no traffic on the road except for a last bus of the night, crawling slowly along, lights shaded. The streetlamps were blacked out and gave off the barest sheen of light. They passed the darkened Cadbury works and just as they were turning off an ARP warden loomed out of the darkness, holding a tiny torch of his own.

'On yer way home?' he asked importantly.

'Yes,' Frank said. 'Nearly there.'

Edie let them into the house, all moving as quietly as they could so as not to rouse Miss Smedley. When she opened the door of their two little rooms, Edie moved about for a few moments, automatically pulling the curtains and blacks, lighting the gas mantle, poking at the dead remains of the fire.

'Come on, love,' Ruby said. 'I'll bunk up with you tonight. Can you manage in the chair, Frank?'

'Course,' he said wretchedly. He would have slept naked on a bed of nails if it would bring Jack back.

Edie pulled away from Ruby and walked slowly to the door of her bedroom. She leaned against the doorframe in the dim light, looking in at the unmade bed. The bed where she and Jack had made love last night and talked about the unborn life that was growing in Edie. The bed with the covers open on Jack's side, thrown energetically back as he got up this morning, full of the vigour and expectancy of his twenty-year-old body. The body which would never now lie beside hers again.

Unsteadily Edie went to the bed and lay down in his place, burying her head in the dip where Jack's head had lain, to muffle the howl of anguish which broke from her.

Eight

'Don't forget your gas mask, dear!'

Frances Hatton dangled the battered box on its piece of string out through the door as Janet reached the gate, and she turned back to fetch it.

'Blow it! Do we really need to carry this stinking thing about all the time?' she said impatiently. 'We haven't needed it once yet.' There were so many things to remember now the war was on. Gas masks, her identity card, which was forever dropping out of her purse until Frances had bought metal identity necklaces they could hang round their necks instead.

Frances's serene face smiled back at her. 'Never mind. Best be on the safe side. Are you going to Joyce's house or meeting her in town?'

'I said I'd meet her in Corporation Street – outside Lewis's.' Janet backed down the path. She quite often spent an afternoon in town or playing tennis with her friend Joyce.

'Have a nice afternoon then—' Frances, about to close the door, opened it again. 'Oh, Janet, don't forget to buy a little something we can send to Auntie Maud while you're there, will you? Perhaps a nice soap. And love, your hat isn't straight.'

'Righty-ho,' Janet called back, absent-mindedly pulling her gloves on and levelling up her hat. 'All right. I'll see what I can find.'

She headed for Bournville Station to take a train into town, dressed, under her coat, in her favourite winter skirt, in a soft sea-blue, with a white blouse and crimson cardigan, and navy court shoes which toned in nicely. Frances had made the skirt for her after the miscarriage, in September. It was, Janet saw, part of her mother's way of comforting her, of marking a new beginning. Frances's emotions sometimes expressed themselves through clothes.

Janet brushed her hand across the front of her body for a moment in an almost unconscious gesture. She'd found herself doing that in the three months since, checking she wasn't swelling out at the front. While she was still carrying the child she'd kept forcing the thought of it away, denying it to herself. Only after it was over did she realize how the fact of it had pushed into every corner of her mind, changed everything. Sometimes she woke, sick with dread, thinking she was still pregnant. Despite the scouring, the D and C she'd had in hospital, sometimes she thought maybe it was still in there, growing. She would have been six months gone by now, almost certainly too big to hide it. How had she thought she was going to hide anything much longer from a mother who had been a midwife? What dreamworld had she been living in?

Frances had been extraordinary. That Sunday, sobbing with pain and humiliation, Janet had sat at the kitchen table and gasped, 'I'm bleeding, I'm bleeding so terribly!'

Frances stared at her, still holding the gravy spoon, and in those seconds Janet saw her horrified mind asking itself questions, answering them and gearing itself to respond. And despite the appalled expression in her eyes, she did so as if out of a deep well of inner calm. Putting the spoon down, she came to the table.

'Oh my darling!' Janet would never forget the distress in her voice. 'We must get you to bed. I knew there was something . . . You're not . . .?'

Wretchedly, Janet nodded, beginning to sob.

'My dear – how long is it . . .?'

'Two and a half months – about,' Janet wept. 'Oh Mummy, I'm sorry. I'm terribly, terribly sorry.'

Frances didn't ask questions. Not then. She stayed with Janet, looking after her through all the cramps, the bleeding, as she expelled the tiny life that had begun in her. Discreetly she contacted Dr Hartley, and when she saw it necessary, took Janet to the hospital for the D and C. Janet shuddered at the contemptuous looks she had had from one of the nurses.

She stared out of the train window. A fine drizzle was falling. The railway ran close to the Cut and she saw the busy, colourful traffic of joeys and narrowboats hauling laden buttys along the sludgy strip of water, steered by men with their collars up, hats tilted forward against the wet. Many of them were bringing supplies to Cadbury's: cocoa beans shipped from Ghana to the docks, already shelled into nibs of chocolate, cocoa butter, and gallons of condensed milk from factories in Wales, Staffordshire and other counties, all moving along the waterways to the factory.

For a moment she allowed herself to think about Alec. How stupid she'd been, how naïve! And yet, despite everything, there came once again the old reflex of longing for him. The thought of his face, those dark eyes looking at her with such desire, could still fill her with a bitter ache. What a stupid fool she was, still hankering after him! But she couldn't help wondering what would have happened if she'd told him about the baby. She frowned and looked down through a blur of tears into her lap at her worn brown gloves, avoiding the eyes of the elderly woman opposite her. Her emotions were unstable: grief one minute, the next an overwhelming sense of reprieve from what might have been and of youthful freedom, as if she had been reborn herself.

She got off at New Street, slinging her gas mask over her shoulder, and walked through the Saturday afternoon bustle. The changes which had marked the beginning of the war, the sandbags shoring up buildings and laid over gratings, the new signs pointing to public air-raid shelters and warden's posts, had become almost commonplace now.

'Oo-ee!' Joyce greeted her, waving from near the front entrance to Lewis's. Her wispy fair hair, which she tried in vain to curl the ends of, was sticking out from under a flat, navy hat which sat precariously on top of it, like a tea-plate. Joyce was a straightforward, friendly girl who spent her days typing invoices at Cadbury's.

'Let's go and have a mooch and then we can have some tea and a cake somewhere, eh?' Joyce suggested. Janet smiled. Tea, cake and a sit down was always Joyce's favourite part of a shopping expedition. She really preferred chatting to walking round in the crowds.

'That's all right with me,' Janet agreed. It was good to be in company and to escape her thoughts. 'I haven't very much to buy now anyway. Mum's already bought me something to give Robert!'

The two of them strolled through the grand department store, smelling the perfumes and admiring the Christmas displays, wondering at the dolled-up assistants in the cosmetics department.

'I wish I could look like that!' Joyce groaned, self-mockingly. 'However long I take over my make-up it always looks as if I've put it on with a trowel!'

'No it doesn't,' Janet said. 'You look perfectly nice as you are.' She thought the girls behind the counters looked overdone and false.

'And who wants to smell like a polecat?' Joyce laughed. 'Well, I would, for one, if I could afford something really good!'

They went to the fabrics department, sighing over the exotic colours of satin and crêpe de Chine. Janet fingered the end of a bolt of peacock blue raw silk.

'Mother would *love* that for a skirt length,' she mused. 'I mean she'd think it was extravagant and she'd never buy it for herself, but she'd love to have it and make it up.'

She wanted to spoil her mother. She felt a general responsibility for her happiness, but now there was a new sense of debt to her and deep regard. After some agonizing she decided she could just afford a length of the beautiful silk for a straight skirt, and chose an elegant pattern for Frances to make. It was nice to buy a present she knew she'd be pleased with. Joyce bought a few reels of cotton and some hooks and eyes, and was just suggesting that they went out to the Kardomah, when Janet suddenly remembered the gift she was supposed to be buying for Auntie Maud.

'Toiletries, Mother said. I should have got them when we were down there before.'

They made their way back through the busy store. The war hadn't prevented the festive spirit. They saw a sign ahead saying, 'Come and visit Father Christmas today!'

'Ah,' Joyce said pointing, her crimson painted lips parting in a smile. In front of them had gathered a line of excited children waiting to go and meet Father Christmas, under the tinsel and dangling streamers. The two littlest children in the line were literally jumping up and down with impatience. 'Aren't they gorgeous? Oh Janet, don't you think it must be lovely to have kiddies of your own?'

'Yes,' Janet spoke lightly. 'It must be nice, with a good husband behind you. Otherwise it involves a lot of drudgery, I'd say.'

Joyce caught sight of a little girl with thick, blonde bunches dangling each side of her face. 'Ah!' she cooed. 'Look at that one!'

As she said it, Janet froze, horrified. She didn't hear more of Joyce's chatter because in that moment, joining the back of the queue, was a face she recognized. He was a head taller than the people in front, holding in his arms his young son, who was dark-haired like him. Alec. Right there in front of her. And beside him, through the huddle of people, she saw a small, delicate-looking woman with neat brown hair curling round her collar. Though not a raving beauty, she had a fresh-faced, timid look. Alec was leaning down to hear something she was saying.

Heart pounding, Janet seized Joyce's arm.

'I know, let's go and get that cup of tea. I'm parched.'

'But what about the present you were going to buy?'

'Oh,' Janet tried to sound casual, though sweat was breaking out under her arms. 'I'll get that somewhere else. I don't want to have to wade all the way through the shop again. Come on—'

Only once she was out in the street did Janet feel she could breathe easily again. As she and Joyce sat with their tea and cream horns, amid the tinkling of cups and saucers and teaspoons, Janet gradually felt her pulse return to normal. She listened to Joyce, who was running on about her latest prospect, Dickie, a worker in the print room at Cadbury's, and when the factory would be going over to war work and would Dickie have to join up? Janet

72

nodded and smiled, pushing her cake back and forth across the plate, wishing she'd only chosen tea. She felt as if she'd been punched. Slapped in the face by reality. She'd nearly come face to face with Alec and his wife and son. Real people. A marriage.

What would he have done? her horrified mind demanded. Pretended he'd never seen me before? What was I to him, after all? Mistress? Bit on the side? That's the truth of it. She had allowed herself for months to be part of that sordid, deceptive situation and had kidded herself that it was something more. He'd bought her with evenings out and trips. She'd been little less than a prostitute! And look how her life had almost been ruined – for what? For a lying, deceiving, sex-obsessed man! She felt herself turn rigid with anger, boiling inside. She wanted to rage and storm at him, to hurt him badly. How could she have been so naïve and stupid?

'You don't seem to be getting on with that cake very well,' Joyce observed, peering over, a dab of cream at the corner of her lips.

'I don't seem to have any appetite.' Janet just managed to jerk her lips into a smile. 'Don't know why. Would you like to finish it?'

1940

Nine

'Edie – are you awright? You've gone pale.'

Ruby mouthed the words to her along the bench where they were working, assembling gas masks.

Edie tried to smile back, but another griping pain tore across her innards. Sweat broke out on her forehead. She leaned against the bench, letting out a long, jagged breath. She felt hot, and nauseated by the warm day and the rubbery smell of the respirators.

As the pain passed she wiped her sleeve across her face.

'I'll be awright,' she told Ruby, whose plump face was also red in the spring warmth. No one on the shop floor except Ruby was supposed to know Edie was expecting, though a couple had guessed. But her stomach was very 'tidy' and she wore a loose overall. She had been desperate to have her job back. Straight after Jack's death it was all she could think about. She couldn't face the reality of what was going to happen after the baby arrived.

Ruby had sorted it out for her. 'I've spoken to Miss Dorothy,' she told her. 'You're not a married woman any more, you're a widow. She knows you're in the family way, and they don't like mothers working, but you are a special case, and with the war on things're changing anyway. She said you should come and see her. She was ever so nice, Edie.'

And Miss Dorothy had been very kind. Edie returned

to work at Cadbury's in the autumn to find things already changing because of the war. Some old familiar faces had moved to other factories for war work, and some blocks of the Bournville factory had been turned over to Austin and Lucas and other firms involved with war production, so the trains which passed through the site and the canal boats coming to the factory wharf were now carrying quite different components from cocoa butter and condensed milk.

By the spring of 1940, the Germans had moved across Denmark and Norway, and into the Netherlands and Belgium. The war was coming closer. The workers at Cadbury's were told that there was to be a new development. While there was still some chocolate being produced, especially for the forces, a new company had been formed called Bournville Utilities Ltd and another section of the factory was to be turned over to production for the Supply Departments of the British Government. Two thousand workers were to be transferred and Edie and Ruby found themselves among these. They were very happy to know that they were to work together, assembling the service respirators. Being back at Cadbury's was the one thing which had carried Edie through her time of most intense grieving for Jack.

She carried on working again for a few minutes, screwing the nozzles on the front of the respirators, but in a few minutes she was gripped by another excruciating pain and only just managed not to cry out. As it died away she was seized by panic. It had begun as a low grumble, like her monthly tummy-ache, but it was getting worse and worse. What could be the matter with her? She wasn't due until the end of June – that was another six weeks away!

Another half-hour passed and she became unable to

hide her distress. A pain came which was so agonizing that she doubled up over the work bench, sobbing in agony. Ruby immediately left her place and ran round to her.

'Ede? Edie – can yer speak to me?'

Edie shook her head, crying.

Other women were crowding round as well.

'You feeling bad, Edie?'

'What's the matter with her, Ruby? 'Ere, stand back, let the poor girl have some air!'

One of the older workers, a Mrs Fisher, who had been re-employed now the war was on, took Ruby's arm.

'Is she, you know, in the family way?'

Ruby nodded, frightened. 'Only it ain't due yet. I don't know why she's in this state.'

Edie gave another howl of pain, her knuckles white as she gripped the edge of the bench. 'Oh God!' she moaned. 'Help me . . .' Her words died out into a deep gasp.

The supervisor appeared, Miss Larkin, a rounded, calm woman.

'What's all the fuss?' she demanded.

'It's Edie,' Mrs Fisher said. 'Seems like her babby's on the way.'

Miss Larkin took one look at Edie and without batting an eyelid said, 'Ambulance. Mrs Fisher, could you and Ruby help Edith downstairs please?'

Ruby was very grateful for the older woman's concerned presence, because Edie was panicking and in a bad state. She doubled up when they were half-way down the stairs, panting and sobbing. Once she could speak again she cried out, 'Oh – it hurts, it hurts! Oh God, what's happening? This shouldn't be happening!'

'Come on, bab.' Mrs Fisher guided her down the rest

of the stairs, arm round her shoulder. 'You'll be awright – maybe the babby's decided to come a bit early, or you might've got your timing wrong. There's nothing the matter – this is just how it is when the babby comes.'

Ruby, squeezing her other arm, said, 'Just hang on, Edie, you'll be all right.'

When the ambulance drew up outside, Edie was once again gripped by the fierce contractions. She could think about nothing else. There was a woman driving the vehicle and she took one look at Edie and said, 'Oh, I see how things are. Well, not far to go. We'll get you into Selly Oak.'

'Can I go in with her?' Ruby begged.

The ambulance driver looked at Mrs Fisher.

'Well, I don't know,' she hesitated, looking at Ruby's pleading face, then tutted. 'Go on then – I'll tell 'em in there.'

It was barely a mile to the hospital, but to Edie the short journey seemed endless. She lay in the ambulance, waves of agony crashing over her, the sweat soaking her clothes, hair plastered to her head.

'I'm frightened, Rube,' she sobbed between contractions. Ruby gripped her hand, not knowing what to say. She was scared herself. Edie was in such agony, and why was the baby here so early?

The attendant in the ambulance made soothing noises. 'Soon be there,' she said. 'We'll get you comfortable and sorted out.'

When they rushed into the back of the Infirmary at Selly Oak, the thought of having to get up and move made Edie sob again.

'I can't,' she cried. 'Can't I just stay in here?'

Ruby and the ambulance woman helped her up, and as

she managed to get upright, a gush of greenish-brown liquid ran down her legs.

'It's all right – that's just your waters gone,' the attendant said, but her eyes met Ruby's and Edie saw it. Something was wrong, she sensed, though not really knowing or understanding. Ruby felt a chill go through her. She had been at home when her mom started off with Alfie's birth, and the breaking waters had been a healthy, pinkish liquid, not this murky, faecal brew.

'Come on, Ede,' she said gently, trying to sound calmer than she felt.

She wasn't allowed into the labour ward with Edie.

'I'll wait outside!' she called as they took her away through the doors. Ruby sat down shakily on a chair in the corridor. From inside the ward she heard snatches of cries from the women in their labour pains, which made her feel even more unsteady. For a second she thought about running round to Charlotte Road to tell Edie's mom, but realized what a stupid idea that was. Nellie Marshall would be no help or comfort at all. If anyone loathed childbirth and anything to do with it, it was her.

Inside, Edie floated on a sea of pain and confusion. Her distended stomach tightened like a drum and released with every contraction until they came so close together that she was awash with discomfort. Another woman across the ward was in hard labour as well and it got so that at times Edie could hardly tell which of them was crying out. She felt people tugging at her clothes. Mostly she kept her eyes closed, going deep inside herself, trying to fight the pain. She was barely aware where she was. There were voices, snatches of words, 'foetal distress . . . very premature . . .'

It felt as if hours had passed, though it was hard to tell

if it was more than hot, searing moments. Opening her eyes, she saw the dark windows but didn't know if they were blackouts or the sky. The pain mounted and burned and a voice floated past ... 'Should we think about opening her up ...?' She wanted to shout 'No! No!' and perhaps did, but nothing more happened than a pricking in her arm. More time passed and suddenly she was awake again and her body seemed to belong to someone else. Her head jerked up as her belly contracted, crushingly, and the people round her were saying, 'Push!' and she suddenly split apart with such pain that her cries became one long, high scream. At last she pushed the baby out with a terrible heave and a slither. She lay back, groaning.

There was a long silence. She didn't know if she'd slept. When she opened her eyes the doctor and midwife were shaking their heads over something lying between her legs.

'My baby,' Edie whimpered. 'Jack's baby ...' She held her arms out and the midwife's face swam into view.

'I'm sorry, dear. Your baby got into trouble. He was in too much of a hurry to get into the world. I'm afraid he hasn't made it.'

Edie heard a long, agonized whimper like a dog in distress coming from somewhere and only after a few seconds did she realize it was coming from deep within herself.

They came home from burying the little white coffin on a perfect spring afternoon. The lilac was in blossom and yellow laburnum swung like bells. The warmth and fertility around her only increased Edie's despair. She knew she was burying all hope of a living memory of Jack and of being able to share that with their child. She was burying her love, her future. She staggered out of the cemetery supported by Ruby, her mom and dad walking behind.

'I'm sorry for yer, wench,' Dennis had said gruffly, in the cemetery. He stood very straight, barrel-chested, not knowing what else to say, but Edie at least felt he had meant it.

'You coming in for a cup of tea?' Nellie said as they walked slowly back along the Bristol Road. 'I've made us a few sandwiches like, a nice tin of ham.'

Edie said nothing. She couldn't think about anything, least of all sandwiches and tins of ham opened for show.

'Thanks, Mrs Marshall,' Ruby said politely.

Nellie Marshall signalled to Ruby to move out of the way, and came up beside Edie and took her arm. She was dressed immaculately in black, face well made-up.

'It's a bad do losing a child.' She spoke abruptly. 'But in your case, with the war on and Jack gone, it's a blessing in disguise, you must admit.'

Edie stopped and violently pulled her arm free of her mother's.

'How can you say that? That's a terrible, wicked thing to say! It's not a blessing and I'll never say it was!' she shouted, hysterical with grief and fury. 'It might be to you, but then you never wanted any of us anyway, did you? Too much mess and trouble in your respectable little life, aren't we? But I wanted my babby, and I'd've loved him, not like you.' She took off fast down the road. 'You can keep yer perfect house and your sodding sandwiches!'

Ruby glanced at Nellie Marshall and chased after Edie, muttering, 'Hard-faced old cow,' under her breath. Edie's mom really was the limit at times.

'Edie, eh Ginger!' She caught up with her. 'Where're yer going?'

'*Home*,' Edie sobbed. 'To my place and Jack's. It's the only proper home I've ever had.'

Ten

'Here we are dear, sit down – you must be exhausted.'

As Janet settled herself wearily at the table, Frances Hatton laid a plate of chops, potatoes and greens, well lubricated with gravy, in front of her and poured from the pretty china teapot.

'Thanks,' Janet said, pushing a stray lock of her uncontrollable hair out of her eyes. 'This looks nice. I could do with it, I can tell you.'

It was eight-thirty at night and her day's work, which began at eight in the morning, had only just ended. Industries up and down the country were urgently gearing up for what the war might bring next, and twelve hours a day, seven days a week, had become commonplace working shifts. The Whitsun Bank Holiday had been cancelled. Since the retreat at Dunkirk the atmosphere had been tremendously tense. Who knew where the front line was to be in this war? Now the German planes which were attempting to break down the island defences were slugging it out over the Channel and Kent day after day in what was being called the Battle of Britain. There was talk of almost nothing else.

'What's happened?' Janet wanted to know. 'Have you listened in already?'

'Yes, we can hear it again later. They're evacuating the Channel Islands – thousands of them coming off.' Frances stirred sugar into her tea. 'And the fighting's still going on like mad. The news was full of tallies of planes shot down, as usual. I'm so glad Robert's not involved.'

The idea of her rather stodgy brother as a fighter pilot seemed quite absurd to Janet. Fortunately he was safe in a reserved occupation in the bank. She tucked into her meal with relish. Frances forgot the war for a moment and smiled at the sight of her. Janet had always had a good appetite. She looked so much better now, the colour back in her cheeks again.

'I had a letter from Auntie Maud today,' Frances remembered, getting up to fetch it. 'She wanted to let us know they're all right, so far anyway.' Janet raised an anxious smile. She liked Auntie Maud, with her flamboyant clothes and scatty ways. But she lived with her two daughters outside Maidstone, right under the fighting.

'It must be awful down there,' Janet said.

'She writes – well, here's a bit I can decipher: "They're trying anything to prevent German planes landing. You see all manner of things scattered over the fields, so that the countryside is beginning to look rather like an endless church bazaar, if you can imagine anything so depressing. The other day I saw a farm cart, a very nasty looking double bed, an old kitchen range and a pile of rotting railway sleepers all in one field! Everyone's nerves are in shreds – first bombs on Canterbury, now this. We've seen some snatches of it and it's terrible to think about the pilots up there . . ."'

'I do hope they'll be all right,' Janet said. 'They could come up here to us if it gets any worse.'

'I've already offered,' Frances said. 'But I don't imagine she'll come. Not while the house is standing – her pride and joy, you know.'

'Everything seems to be higgledy-piggledy these days, doesn't it?' Janet said, cutting up her chops. 'Beds in fields, men marching about in the park, no street signs . . . It all feels rather barmy.'

Frances folded up the letter when she'd finished and sipped her tea, asking Janet about her day. Cadbury's were pushing forward production of a whole range of things: tools and jigs for other firms, milling machines and parts for guns and aeroplanes and the shop floors and offices hummed with activity. Industry was on red alert to produce for the war effort.

'I do feel,' Frances said, 'that I'm being rather a useless item sitting here. Maud's letter brought it home to me. Of course I could volunteer for something, but Janet, I wondered—' She hesitated. 'A number of the other Friends have taken in refugees and I do feel put to shame. With all these people coming from Jersey and Guernsey they'll need billets, and I wondered whether we might think of taking someone.'

Janet smiled encouragingly. 'Of course. Why ever not? I know you mentioned it before and my – problems – got in the way. We've so much more space than some people.'

Frances beamed back. 'You wouldn't mind? Only it might mean quite a bit of inconvenience for us.'

'No, of course I wouldn't mind.' As she said it a weight seemed to fall from her. It was such a relief to do something right and good. 'Some of these people must have had a beastly time of it. It's the least we can do.'

'Well, I'm proud of you, my love.' She poured Janet another cup of tea and cut her a slice of cherry madeira.

'Cake's a bit dry, of course,' she apologized.

'No, it's lovely.' Shyly, she looked up. 'Mummy, look, you've been so marvellous. About everything.'

They had talked, of course, over the months since the miscarriage. Janet had explained about Alec, how she felt.

She'd said how sorry she was about it, about the untruths she'd told in order to see him. She knew how much grief it had caused her mother, yet she barely uttered a word of reproach. Janet had been astonished at her calmness.

'Well, you've learned the hard way,' Frances looked at her over the edge of her teacup. 'At least, I hope you've learned.'

'Some mothers would have put me on the streets.'

'I daresay,' Frances said dryly. 'Though I've never fathomed what good that does anyone.' She put her cup down.

'But what would you have done if I hadn't lost the baby?'

Frances's liquid brown eyes studied her face for a moment. 'Darling, it would have been difficult. There would have been tongues wagging furiously, but we'd have managed. You're my daughter, that's the most important thing, and I do think it's terrible to treat the arrival of a new being as if it's the end of the world. And you know . . .' A smile played at the corners of her mouth.

Janet was taken aback. 'What?'

'No, I really shouldn't say it.'

'Oh, you can't not tell me now!'

'Well, oh dear, this is terrible, but when you were so out of sorts and behaving rather secretively . . .'

So she had noticed something, Janet thought.

'I mean it'd been some time since you'd had a young man in your life – at least, that's what I thought. And you were always at the tennis club, and spending all that time with Joyce. Well, I did begin to wonder if you were perhaps more *that* way inclined. I mean you'd never shown signs of it before but then sometimes it comes out later. I'm a broad thinker in my way and I was trying to accommodate myself to the idea.'

Janet stared into her mother's face with its confiding expression for a full ten seconds in blank astonishment before bursting into peals of laughter. She pushed her chair back and laughed until tears poured down her cheeks. All this time, creeping about with Alec, their secret meetings and urgent, self-indulgent passion, and her mother thought she was mooning over Joyce! Seeing her, Frances began to laugh as well and it was some minutes before either of them could speak.

'Oh Mummy!' Janet spluttered at last. 'You are extraordinary, you really are!'

'Well, I know *now* that I got it all wrong,' Frances said.

They looked at each other, and began laughing all over again.

Eleven

Edie was working on the line, amid the stench of the respirators, when the unearthly wail of the air-raid siren tore through the hot afternoon. One of the the girls who'd gone to the pictures the night before was giving them a blow-by-blow account of the story. Edie loved to hear romantic stories and her deft hands could do the job before her automatically now. She had slipped into a fantasy world where everything turned out right, and the siren made her jump violently.

'Oh my God!' she cried, clutching at her chest. 'Not again! I feel as if my heart's going to give out every time I hear it!'

The factory bull had been silenced by the war, but in August the first bombs had fallen on Birmingham and the siren was going off in the daytime. They all had to troop out.

Shrugging off their overalls, the workers left everything on the benches and moved down the stairs, streaming like ants through the factory. Edie, like everyone else, strained her ears to try to make out the sound of planes approaching through the blue summer sky. Soon, they were all crushing into the gloomy basement.

'Ey-up, Ginger,' said a girl called Connie, plonking herself down beside Edie. 'At least we get to 'ave bit of a sit down. I've even remembered me knitting today.' She unwrapped her needles with a few curling rows of white wool on them.

'That's a good idea,' Edie commented. 'Help keep your mind off it. What're you knitting?'

'It's for me sister – 'er babby's due next month. I'm doing a matinée coat.'

'Ah.' Edie felt grief twisting inside her. 'That's nice.'

Ruby was in another part of the basement. She loathed the closed-in feel of the stuffy, dimly-lit basement, and had to fight against the panic that rose in her at the thought of being entombed in there by the building above. She tried to keep her mind diverted from listening for the sound of planes overhead, or worrying about what might happen.

Think about Saturday, she told herself. Just a few more days and Frank'll be here and we'll be married! He'd managed to get himself twenty-four hours' leave to come to Birmingham. Soon she'd be his wife. It was true that she'd carry on living at home for the moment, that nothing much would change, but she was so happy now she knew she could marry and keep her job. She sat thinking about seeing Frank, about the little cream dress she'd found in the rag market, which looked almost new.

It had been a long wait and she understood Frank's frustration over it. At times she'd almost given in and thought to hell with it, let him have his way, he wanted her so much. But all the warnings her mom had given her about 'letting them have their way' and 'being left holding the baby' rang in her head. In the end it was Ethel who persuaded her to get married.

'You mustn't let me stand in your way, Ruby. Your

Frank's a fighting man and he needs you.' And George's girl Dorrie came round often and helped out.

Over the months Frank had been home on leave a few times. After initial training as a wireless operator at Compton Bassett in Wiltshire he'd been posted over on the east coast, to Bomber Command. He was ranked as Sergeant now he'd completed his training. He told her about the other lads, their pranks and exploits, the entertainments on the base and talk in the bar during their hours off. She heard about Beaky ('he's got a great big conk on 'im'), Wally Wodgers (''cos he can't say his r's pwoperly') and Sam Corcoran, an air gunner who was his best pal on the base. Ruby would laugh, watching his face light up, though at times she felt wistful and a bit left out. But when he kissed her and held her close it all felt right. They'd go to the pictures and sit at the back. As soon as the lights went down Frank was all over her, hands exploring inside her dress.

He'd been home in May and they went out to the Lickey Hills. The tram was full to bursting with families having a spring day out to see the bluebells in flower on the wooded hilltops. When they were disgorged at Rednal the children scattered away from the road, which was lined with an assortment of tearooms, to dive amid the bracken and bluebells and gather bunches almost too big for their hands to hold.

'I remember doing that,' Ruby laughed, her arm looped through Frank's as they walked. 'And they're all wilted when you get them home!'

Frank leaned down and picked a couple of sprays of the mauvish blue flowers and threaded them through Ruby's top buttonhole, kissing her nose as he did so.

'There, Queen of the May.'

'It's lovely here,' Ruby said. 'It's hard to take in the war when you're somewhere like this.'

'Feels real enough in the Forces,' Frank said tersely.

She glanced up at him. They'd climbed until they could see the sweeping view of the surrounding counties. The air blew sharply in their faces with a tang of cold to it, and ragged clouds brushed across the sun. Frank seemed remote suddenly, and hard. Sometimes he frightened her, the way he looked.

'Frank?' she touched his arm. 'What's up?'

He looked round at her sternly. 'We don't know how bad it's going to get, do we? I just want to make you mine. Before it's too late.'

The look in his eyes and his tone brought the blood to her cheeks.

'You want to get married, straight away?'

'If that's what it takes. I want—' He turned and pulled her to him. 'I'll show yer what I want.' He kissed her hard on the mouth.

Clapping, accompanied by ribald comments, broke out from the picnickers seated round them.

'Frank!' Ruby pushed him away, pretending to be on her dignity.

'We're going to get wed!' Ruby shouted joyfully to them. 'How about that, eh?' She let out her loud, jolly laugh and more applause followed. She felt foolish now, not having said yes before. How could she deny Frank when he was a fighting man?

She sat in the basement, trying to ignore the air-raid and dreaming of her wedding night.

'They're coming, listen,' someone said, shushing everyone.

The droning sound of planes grew louder and closer.

Ruby looked at the faces around her, waiting tensely in the sudden quiet. The first wave passed over and everyone let out a long breath of relief.

Edie watched Connie's fingers twining the wool round her needles. The sight of the half-knitted matinée coat, so like the one she had laboriously made for her little baby, brought all her emotions to the surface. Though months had passed, sometimes it all came back harsh and raw as if Jack had died only yesterday. She'd seen his cold body before they fixed down the coffin lid. His face was grazed from where he had hit the ground. Edie had leaned down and stroked his dark brows with her finger. She kissed the unblemished part of his cheek. He looked younger, more as he had when they were fifteen and the Weales first moved into the area.

'Oh Jack,' she whispered, her tears falling on his cold, still face. 'I love you so much. Why did you have to go and leave us?'

Ruby had seen her through the funeral, had spent all the time she could manage with her. After the first shock of grief all the worries about practical things assailed her, adding to her pain. She felt horribly lonely. The emptiness of their rooms without Jack coming home was almost unbearable. She knew it would be cheaper to rent only one room, yet she couldn't stand the thought of moving anywhere unfamiliar. Once inside she could hide away in their little nest and remember the sound of him coming through the door, the feel of him lying beside her at night. She'd imagined telling their child, 'That's where your dad used to sit, and he stood and shaved by the little mirror over there, that speckled mirror which he said gave me even more freckles on my nose than are really there . . .'

After she lost the baby, little Jack as she called him, weeks of numbness were followed by acute pain and and misery at the double loss. She felt so alone. Everything had been taken from her. Many an evening she sat crying, holding the little white matinée coat and bootees, stroking them, aching to hold the child, and to be held in her turn and comforted by Jack. She had to endure her breasts producing milk when there was no baby to feed and at times she felt beside herself, as if she just couldn't go on. As the spring turned into summer, she saw that in one way at least, her mother's harsh comments had been true. How on earth would she have managed if her baby had survived? She had never faced up to the reality of what was happening. And now it was all over.

She was so glad to be able to go back to work and be amid the camaraderie and busy atmosphere. Neville Chamberlain had resigned as Prime Minister and they were becoming used to the sound of Churchill's growling voice on the Pattisons' wireless. The war was coming to their doorsteps, quite literally, as a trickle of the uninjured lads from Dunkirk turned up at their homes. Fear and tension permeated everything.

And now I'm sitting here waiting for them to drop bombs on us! Edie thought. Everything welled up inside her and she leaned forward and shielded her face with one hand to hide her tears. Another thing which was setting her off was the thought of Ruby and Frank's wedding that weekend. It was lovely that they were getting married. Ruby had been so good to her and Edie was genuinely delighted for them, but the imminent wedding only made her feel more lonely. She felt sobs rising in her.

The planes moved overhead and everyone waited, as if holding their breath. There was a sigh as they passed, then an outbreak of cheering.

'Let's 'ave a sing-song!' someone called from the other end, and after several ragged attempts, launched into 'Kiss Me Goodnight Sergeant Major'. Edie kept her head down, glad that her crying would be hidden in the raucous noise.

After a moment she felt a hand on her shoulder. Someone was budging the others up to sit beside her, and then a pretty cotton handkerchief, embroidered with a curling 'J' in the corner, was pressed into her hand.

'I owe you one, sort of, don't I?' a gentle voice said. The woman smiled at Edie's bemused expression as she turned to see a face framed by frizzy, curling hair which seemed determined to escape from any restriction imposed upon it in the form of hairpins.

'D'you remember, the bus stop? I was rather upset that day and you said you'd give me a hanky if you had one?'

'Oh!' Edie tried to smile, wiping her eyes gratefully. In contrast to the last time they'd met, the young woman's face was smooth and untroubled by tears and the brown eyes behind her spectacles were full of warmth and sympathy. 'I didn't recognize you.'

'You seem upset,' she said.

'Yes, well . . .' Edie said shyly. 'I'll be all right.' But in the face of such kindness, more tears ran down her cheeks. 'Thing is,' she blurted out, with no idea why she was doing so except the woman looked so kind, 'I lost my husband and then our babby, all since September.'

'Oh my word, how dreadful, you poor girl!' Janet immediately put her arm round Edie's shoulders. 'You don't look old enough to have had all these awful things happen to you.' Edie was a little embarrassed, but she welcomed the comfort. There was still plenty of noise around them: the singers moved on to 'Ten Green Bottles'. 'I do hope you've the support of your family to see you through.'

'Not really.' Edie stared down into her lap. She wiped her face fiercely. 'Still. No good moaning. There's nothing can be done. Just 'ave to get on with it.'

'You haven't been moaning, far from it. Look, I don't even know your name. I'm Janet Hatton. I work upstairs: typist, in the buying department.'

'Edie Weale. My pals here call me Ginger. I'm on the masks at the moment.' She found herself telling Janet a lot about herself, how she lived alone above Miss Smedley. She told her she didn't see eye-to-eye with her mom, but she didn't elaborate much on that. She couldn't explain Nellie even to herself, let alone a stranger, even though, within minutes, Janet didn't really feel like a stranger at all.

'I suppose I'm lucky with my mother,' Janet said. 'We've always got on quite well. My father died in the last war and she's looked to my brother and me really. She worries about things too much, but she's very good to me.'

'You ain't, I mean, you're not married then?' Edie wondered if she was being too nosey, but she found Janet remarkably easy to talk to.

'No,' Janet said, with a faint smile. Edie thought she also saw her blush, though it was hard to be sure. 'Not yet. There was somebody, but it would never have worked.' Edie heard the sadness in her voice and wondered if that was why she had been crying that night at the bus stop. She didn't feel she could ask any more. 'Actually,' she added gloomily, 'I don't think I'm a very good judge of men.'

'Oh well, you'll find someone, I'm sure,' Edie said.

Janet smiled wistfully. 'We'll have to see, won't we?' She removed her arm from round Edie's shoulders and they chatted for a while. The singing behind them came and went in waves. Janet told her that she and her mother had had two evacuees from Guernsey staying with them.

'Mum thinks she ought to be doing more, so we said we'd have them. One of them's still with us,' she smiled wryly. 'They were cousins, two girls. Very different characters. The quiet one, Marie, who's stayed, has got herself a munitions job and she's getting along fine, but the other was a right little madam. She's twenty-one. I think she found our household a bit staid for her – thought her wings had been clipped. She's gone up to Manchester to a friend of hers who's come over as well. I'm not sure she'll find the bright lights in Manchester either, at the moment!' Janet looked carefully at Edie for a moment as if wondering whether to say what was on her mind. 'I was wondering, have you volunteered for anything yet?'

'Me? No. My dad's in the Home Guard and my pal Ruby, her brother's on firewatch here. D'you mean the ARP?'

'Yes, of course. There are all sorts of things to do, especially if there's going to be a lot more of this.' She rolled her eyes to indicate the planes overhead. 'I've joined up as an ambulance driver for the ARP – but you could do First Aid or work with the WVS.'

I *should* do something, Edie thought, hearing the urgency in Janet's voice. Why haven't I done it before? I'm just sitting there night after night.

'What do they do, then?' she asked.

'The WVS? Oh, all sorts. Almost everything. A lot of the time they run canteens. I saw them at New Street Station, after Dunkirk. They were handing out tea to the wounded chaps.'

'Well, I think I could hand out tea,' Edie said, feeling a sudden surge of enthusiasm. 'I don't know what to do with, you know, blood and bandages and that sort of thing.'

'There you are!' Janet gave Edie's hand a squeeze. 'There's nothing like getting out and lending someone a hand to cure the miseries. And believe me, I should know! Tell you what, Edie, would you like me to come with you if you go to volunteer?'

Edie was astonished. This woman, whom she barely knew, seemed ready to befriend her. Coming from some people that would have seemed pushy, but she had warmed to Janet immediately and seen how kindhearted and jolly she was. And it would be nice not always to have to do everything alone.

'Well,' Edie laughed. 'I don't know why you'd want to spend your time sorting me out! But yes, that'd be very nice, if you would.'

'I'd love to!' Janet said. 'Sounds as if you've had a rough time of it. You could do with a bit of help.'

By the time the 'All Clear' sounded, Edie felt she had made a new friend, and she felt warmed and more cheerful.

The next day after work, Janet took her to volunteer for the Women's Voluntary Service.

Twelve

The first time Ruby saw Edie in her WVS uniform in her room at Miss Smedley's, she roared with laughter.

'Sssh!' Edie urged. 'Or *she'll* be up here carrying on!'

'Oh Edie – you don't half look a sight!' Ruby came over and snatched the schoolgirlish felt hat from Edie's head to try it on, clowning in front of the mirror. Her eyes danced with mischief. It looked too small, and ridiculous perched above Ruby's moon face, and Edie laughed as well. 'Eh, I thought it was only them posh ladies from Edgbaston and that went in for the WVS?'

'Well, some of them are,' Edie conceded, coming over and trying to grab the hat back. 'Come on, Rube, give us it, you're making a mess of it!' She got it back from Ruby's clutches and smoothed it out. 'They're not all, though, there's all sorts. And Janet said . . .'

'Janet said, Janet said . . .' Ruby mocked, sitting herself down at the table.

Edie sat opposite her. The kettle steamed on the hob. 'You're not jealous, are yer? She's ever so nice.'

'No,' Ruby conceded with a grin. 'Course not. And you're right, she *is* nice. Seems very kind, the sort who'd mix with anyone and treat yer all the same.'

Janet had been amazingly good to Edie. She'd invited her home for tea, and gone with her to the WVS. Edie appreciated her kindness so much that she asked if she could bring Janet along to Ruby and Frank's wedding, as quite a few Cadbury girls were going. Janet had come in a lovely sunflower-yellow dress and helped keep everyone calm when Frank was dreadfully late arriving from the east coast and Ruby was convinced she'd been jilted at the altar and would never become Mrs Gilpin. In the end the day went off very successfully and Edie felt honoured that Janet seemed to want to be her friend.

'She said I'd be better off in the WVS than in the Red Cross if I didn't want to be dealing with blood.' Edie got up to see to the kettle. 'I still feel funny in these clothes, though.'

'I'm not surprised,' Ruby chuckled.

In fact Edie found she was proud of her uniform, with its green and grey tweed suit and beetroot-coloured jumper. Even the hat wasn't too bad, and with her hair tied back neatly, its colour toning nicely with the green, she thought she looked rather fetching.

'Mom told me she thought it was ridiculous, me working and volunteering nights as well,' Edie said.

'You asked her opinion then, did yer?' Ruby asked wryly.

'No, but I got it anyway.' She winked. 'You know, you could join up as well. Even though you're a married woman now.' Only half joking, she looked across at Ruby, who with her elbow on the table and head resting against her hand was eyeing her with what Edie suddenly realized was a wistful envy.

'Can't really, can I? With George firewatching nights in the Home Guard someone's got to be at home with our mom. She won't cope on 'er own.'

'I thought you said she was better? She looked much more herself at the wedding.'

'I know. She tried so hard, really pulled herself together. She's trying the best she can but it's hard for 'er and some days she's still ever so low. I daren't leave 'er, not at nights when George ain't there. She hates the shelter and she'd be frightened to death. I mean anyone would – on their own with kids in all this.' She sighed heavily.

'Sorry, Rube.' Edie lifted the kettle off the gas as it gushed steam, and mashed the tea.

'What for?'

'That thing's're so hard.'

'No.' Ruby sat up, rallying herself. 'I'm all right. It's just—' She blushed. 'I just feel a bit down today. I know it's silly of me, but after Frank went back . . . well, my monthly was late so I thought, I hoped . . . I mean it's stupid even to think of it in the middle of all this. Anyway, I came on today, so that's come to nothing. I s'pose it's for the best though really.'

'Ah, shame for yer.' Edie came up behind and gave her shoulders a squeeze. 'Never mind, you'll 'ave plenty of time for babbies when this is over. And if you had one now Frank wouldn't be 'ere to see it, would he?'

'No, I know.' Ruby sniffed. 'Only I really started thinking I was . . . Anyway I feel better just 'aving told yer.'

Edie emptied a bag of misshapen chocolates on to a plate. 'Come on, cheer up – have a caramel and a cuppa.'

They sipped their tea. Ruby lit up a cigarette. Her grey eyes, suddenly full of laughter, looked at Edie over the rim of her teacup.

'What?' Edie demanded.

'For God's sake take that hat off, will yer? You're putting me off my cuppa!'

*

After a time, that August, there were so many raids during working hours that they just had to carry on through most of them. But the last week of the month, the Germans turned their attention more to night bombing. On the last Sunday night of the month clusters of planes came over, showering the centre of the city with high explosives and incendiaries, and one of Birmingham's favourite landmarks, the Market Hall, was gutted. The big clock inside, with its carved oak knights which had always fascinated Edie as a child, was destroyed as well.

It was the beginning of the nightly routine of the Blitz, which was to affect them for months to come. Ruby and Ethel Bonner made sure the boys had something warm to put on, piled ready by their beds at night. After each night cowering in the shelter they soon found out the things they would most need – a tilly lamp, candles, a flask of hot tea, and on the nights he was with them, George's penny tin whistle to give them a tune and keep their spirits up. Ruby sat up most nights, unable to sleep in the cramped shelter, Smudge whimpering at her feet, listening to the drone of the engines coming over, the whistle and crump of the bombs, longing for Frank and wondering where Edie and Janet were on the nights they were on duty.

Later, Edie would always describe her first night with the WVS as a 'proper baptism by fire'. She was sent to St Matthew's church on Bristol Street, which was being used as a rest centre for people who were bombed out. St Matthew's school next door was also a first-aid post.

Edie turned up for her evening duties flustered and

afraid she was late, feeling very self-conscious as she travelled into town on the bus, the tweed suit hot and itchy on the mild evening. She'd been at Cadbury's all day and wondered how on earth she was going to manage to stay awake all night, and what the other WVS ladies would be like.

When she reached the school it was dusk and the place was already blacked out. She pushed the door open timidly and immediately set eyes on another woman in WVS uniform, bustling away from her down the main corridor. She was short, plump and rather fearsome-looking, with what could only be described as an officiously wiggling backside.

A young, blonde nurse came out of a classroom and smiled at Edie.

'Looking for the other WVS volunteers?'

Edie nodded.

'They're in the kitchen, along there. I think Mrs Lordly's there – she's in charge.'

Edie rounded the corner of the kitchen to see Mrs Lordly, the plump woman, at the sink, tapping her hand against the faucet in frustration as water trickled with exasperating slowness into a metal jug. Behind her were two rickety trolleys on to which a tall, very thin woman with a tragic expression was stacking tottering towers of white cups and biting her lip as if to prevent herself saying something she'd regret. The pair of them immediately reminded Edie of Laurel and Hardy.

'Ah—' Mrs Lordly caught sight of Edie. 'About time! The others are late as well. What are we to call you?'

Edie hesitated for a second. First names seemed far too informal for Mrs Lordly.

'Mrs Weale,' she said, hoping her once-married status

104

would give her weight in this rather frightening woman's eyes.

'Well, let's hope you've got a bit more about you.' Her eyes strayed scornfully towards the thin, tragic woman. 'Come and fill these jugs and get them in there, fast as you can—' She indicated the tea urn, which was heating over a miserable-looking flame on the range. 'Miss Hansome *forgot*' – this with much scorn – 'to put the water on when she arrived. At this rate we shan't have any boiled water before midnight.'

Edie jumped to do as she was told.

'Now,' Mrs Lordly said, waving an arm briskly at the trolleys, 'one of these is going to the table in the hall here for the first-aid lot. We'll take the other into the church once it's ready.' She picked up two large tins from the side. 'I've baked a number of biscuits in my own time – rather dry I'm afraid, but needs must. Don't fill that beyond the mark—' she said to Edie, and bustled out.

Edie poured another jug of water into the urn. There was a clear plimsoll line up to which it was obviously normally filled. When the jug was under the dribbling tap again she turned to look at Miss Hansome.

'Hello,' she said, cautiously.

'Oh—' The woman looked up at her in a vague sort of way. Edie tried to guess her age. Sixty? 'Hello, dear.'

'I'm Edie.' She wanted to be friendly, feeling pity for this sorry specimen with her red nose and wispy grey hair. To her surprise, Miss Hansome left her post, came over and offered a thin, veiny hand.

'Deirdre Hansome – Oh! Oh, goodness me!'

One of the cups which she had put at the top of an already teetering pile had fallen and smashed loudly on the tiled floor.

'Oh heavens—' Miss Hansome wrung her hands help-lessly. 'I *shall* be in trouble now.'

Edie ran to one of the cupboards. 'There must be a brush in here somewhere—' She found an aged dust-pan and a brush with a thin row of remaining bristles. 'Here – come on – we can clear it up before she gets back!'

Edie energetically swept up the pieces while Miss Hansome dithered behind her. She tipped the broken china into the bin, concealing it under some of the rubbish, and was just stowing away the dustpan as Mrs Lordly reappeared. Miss Hansome jumped guiltily at the sight of her plump calves striding in.

'What's the matter?' Mrs Lordly said suspiciously.

'Nothing.' Edie smiled, shutting the cupboard. 'I was just wondering what was in the cupboards. The urn's almost full now.'

'Right. About time.' She peered into it. Edie winked at Miss Hansome, whose eyes widened in astonishment and then she smiled back.

'I don't know what you're finding to smirk about,' Mrs Lordly snapped, turning on her. 'It's taken you half the evening just to set out a few cups. Come along – get this trolley over here. When the urns *finally* boil it'll be no good having it left in here, will it? The first-aid staff want their drinks.'

The sirens went soon after nine o'clock. Edie felt her heart pounding immediately with dread. In this part of town they were much nearer some of the big works like the BSA which were prime targets for the bombers. She thought of her mom and dad and Ruby out in Selly Oak and wished for a moment she was there with them.

*

Janet was also on duty that night. She arrived slightly late, running into the depot in Selly Oak.

'Oh, *bother* it.' She banged her bag down on the table where a group of other volunteers were sitting enjoying a cup of tea. Her tin helmet, with the red cross on top, was reluctant to settle on her head with its wayward mop of hair.

'Hello, Janet,' the others greeted her affectionately.

'Running a bit late are yer?'

'It's all right, you've got time for a cuppa. No sign of Jerry yet.'

'Ah—' Janet smiled, flustered, still trying to stuff her hair under the hat. 'The night is young yet.'

Among the mixed group of young men and women whom she was coming to regard as friends she saw a new face. A very tall man was also making for the table with his cup and saucer. He sat his lean frame down with an easy, relaxed movement. All Janet took in at a first glance was dark, neatly cut hair and a rather prominent nose, but once she had fetched her own cup of tea and joined the others at the table she found her eyes drawn back to his face. He was at the other end of the table, listening to two of the older volunteers talking. None of his features was especially attractive individually, but there was something about the overall set of his face which kept drawing her gaze back to him. It was a strong face, almost hawkish. He seemed to be a quiet person, listening amid the chatter, sometimes giving a smile which showed a wide, sensuous mouth. Janet nudged the girl next to her.

'Who's that then?'

'Oh, he's a new one. Martin something or other. Shame about the conk, eh?' she laughed.

A moment later she saw the man look at her for a moment, then away when he saw her return his gaze.

When they'd drunk their tea, Janet took a couple of the cups back.

'Thanks ever so much,' she smiled at the WVS women. 'I needed that.'

Passing the end of the table, Janet noticed that the man's arm was resting on the table, his hand toying with the salt cellar. For a second she took in long, agile fingers, a sprinkling of dark hair, and caught a snatch of his conversation.

'. . . So yes – we did have to despatch the children – the older two at least . . . The little one's still at home, running us ragged! . . . And she doesn't enjoy going down in the cellar during the raids . . .'

She'd only been sitting down again a few minutes when the air-raid warning went off, its wail causing the usual sensation of sick panic. She wondered whether her innards would ever quite feel normal again after this combination of lack of sleep, snatched eating and frightening rushes of activity. They waited, first hearing the planes go over, hearts seeming to fail as they passed overhead, then muffled bangs from the distance.

'Oh God,' someone murmured. 'There's a lot of them. This is a bad 'un.'

When the calls started to come through, thick and fast, Mr Coggane, in charge of the depot, started to send them out. Janet was one of the later ones to go.

'Right—' he ordered. 'Highgate.' He gave more details. 'You can go with – Mr Ferris!' he called. Janet looked round. She was disappointed, had hoped to go with one of her friends, someone familiar. Who was Mr Ferris? The tall man jumped to attention and hurried over.

'Get over to Conybere Street area . . .' Mr Coggane said again. 'Off yer go.'

Janet looked at her new colleague. 'Everything's ready.'

'Very good.' His voice was rich and deep. He gestured to her to go ahead. 'Lead on – this is my first time.'

Outside was a chilly, clear night, the smells of fallen leaves and smoke in the air. The siren was still howling and there were shouts in the street as the wardens went about their duty.

'Looks as if this is ours!' Janet shouted over the din as they ran to the leftover transport. Their 'ambulance' for the night turned out to be a carpet fitter's van with a green and gold livery, loaned for the purpose. As Janet pushed the first-aid kit into the back the man waited behind her.

'I'm Martin Ferris, by the way.' He held out his hand.

'Janet Hatton. Pleased to meet you,' she said briskly.

It was a hurried handshake, both of them immediately moving away towards the van doors. She got into the driver's seat.

As they rumbled off along the main road she wound the window down slightly, better to hear what was happening outside. The straight beams of searchlights jittered about the sky and there was a glow ahead, fires burning. The night felt chaotic and unsafe. She felt the usual combination of fear and exaltation, a kind of purity of purpose, surrender to the unknown. And the physical symptoms of fright – cold hands and feet, her breathing shallow, heart racing. She glanced at the figure beside her in the shadows, features eerie in the gloom. She was listening for more planes, and thought she could hear them faintly against their engine, but with half her mind she assessed him. Interesting. Rather attractive, actually, she realized. But it was no good thinking about that.

She'd just heard him talking about his children: she wasn't ever going down that road again. For a moment she wondered how Alec was, whether he ever thought about her. He'd be carrying on his life with his sweet-looking wife and that little boy, perhaps ashamed now of what she had been to him. Was she ashamed? she asked herself, and decided again that she was, only she was more sorry than ashamed.

'Been doing this long?' Martin Ferris asked, loudly over the engine, and she jumped, her thoughts disturbed.

'Yes,' she shouted back. 'Well, since the spring. That's when I trained in first aid.'

'Brave of you!'

Perhaps she didn't catch his tone perfectly, but his words seemed to contain mockery. Was he another of these who didn't believe women should be doing anything, or could do anything?

'Not really,' she replied stiffly. 'Someone's got to do it.'

She saw him nod. After a pause he said, 'What do you do in the daytime?'

'I'm at Cadbury's. Secretarial.'

'Ah, very nice. Marvellous place to work, I gather.'

Carrying on a conversation at the top of your voice was a discouragement to being too expansive. She tried to think of a brief reply to shout back. 'Yes. Kind people. Very good employers.'

No doubt, she thought, he's saying to himself. 'Ah yes, a little clerk,' in that condescending way Alec had about people in the bank. Quite a number of men of her age seemed to have this superior attitude. For a second she thought about John Steven, her friend from the Meeting House, now on a farm somewhere. He was never

110

superior like that. Why had she and John never grown closer, more than friends? The thought startled her. She realized it had never occurred to her to think of John in that way.

'Cadbury's haven't been bombed?' Martin Ferris was asking.

'No, thank goodness. Course, there's a lot of green space round it, and it's mostly covered over now. You know, camouflage.'

Again, the nod. They were quite close to the middle of town now and the atmosphere of chaos increased. A fire engine overtook them, its bell clanging, and there were fires ahead. She felt coiled like a spring, ready to leap into action, and the tension distracted her from the conversation. Perhaps she should ask him about himself, his work. Let me guess, she thought. Bank as well? Engineer, something in an office?

She was just about to ask when he cut in, 'Here, this must be it.'

'Yes, looks like it!' she replied hoarsely, pulling up.

A warehouse was on fire and further along the middle of a row of houses had been hit and were also burning. There were men moving about like shadows in front of the flames, and the hoses snaked like intestines along the street. When they climbed out, the smoke and dust in the air set both of them coughing. Janet felt her eyes begin to smart. From further to the east they could hear explosions.

'Over here!'

The ARP warden beckoned frantically. A man and woman who had been rescued from the least damaged of the houses were sitting hunched in the road and Janet and Martin were soon bandaging their injuries and trying to

111

reassure them. Another man was brought to them and they loaded them in the van to take them out to the hospital.

'We'll be back,' Janet said. It was clear they were going to be needed again. She stayed in the back with the injured while Martin Ferris drove back to the hospital, then rejoined him in the cab as they returned to Highgate. This time the sound of planes was close overhead. In the street one of the wardens seemed to be arguing with a policeman about who was in charge.

'Well, that's a lot of help,' Janet snorted at the sight of them.

'I'm not bloody standing here talking to you, yer blithering idiot,' the warden was shouting, 'when there's people injured in there still . . .' He turned away, then stopped, suddenly became aware of the growling engines above them all.

'Get under cover!' he roared.

'Quick!' Janet felt Martin tug her arm. 'Under the van!'

They moved so fast that afterwards she couldn't remember it, just finding herself squeezed face down under the van amid the ash and rubble of the street, in the stink of brickdust and drains. Her tin hat had slid over one ear, so she turned her head away from it and found that, in a position of strange intimacy, she was lying with her face up close to Martin Ferris's back.

Thirteen

They left a dim light on in the school corridor and huddled together under the staircase with the nurses and auxiliaries. Miss Hansome began muttering to herself, very quietly, and Edie realized she was reciting the Lord's Prayer. Snatches of '... daily bread ... not into temptation ...' came to her. Edie reached out for a second and touched her hand. Miss Hansome jumped, then looked back at her with nervous gratitude.

The explosions began. Some of them were very close. Edie had never been so near the heart of the bombing before and her mouth went dry. One landed so close that the whole school shook and rattled and they heard the sound of breaking glass.

'Jesus Christ Almighty,' one of the auxiliaries said, with too much sincerity to be accused of blasphemy.

The ack-ack guns started up, blasting out from their emplacements round the city. They let out a small cheer.

'Go on, get 'em. Get the buggers!'

Every time there was a bang everyone flinched, instinctively. The noises went on and on. Some time later the front door burst open and for a second the two people who came through it were silhouetted against the glowing world outside. Edie made out an ARP warden, supporting an elderly man on her arm. Both looked pale and strange, coated in dust, except for the deep red gash on the man's head.

'He was out in it,' the warden said. 'He's had a blow on the head – doesn't know what he's doing.' And she was off again, out through the door.

The nurses jumped into action. Edie followed the warden to the door, impressed by her bravery, and stepped outside for a moment. The air was acrid with smoke and she could see that there was a fire burning not far away, behind the houses opposite. The night was coppery-red and alive with the sound of shouts and fire-engine bells and the stern rattle of ack-ack fire. The sound of the first lot of planes was receding. Edie heard voices moving closer and saw two women supporting each other along the street.

'That the first-aid post, bab?' one of them asked shakily.

'Yes – d'you need some help?'

Both of them looked dazed and were covered in cuts. Edie helped them inside.

'Mrs Weale?' Mrs Lordly's voice rang out. 'Would you please come and help me with this urn? I think we shall soon be needed in the church.'

Between them they lifted the heavy urn on to the trolley and wheeled it into position. Edie tried to concentrate on what she was doing and block from her mind the unmistakable drone of planes moving closer outside. The nurses were doing their best to make the growing queue of injured comfortable in the first classroom. Edie had been sent back to the kitchen for the sugar and was on her way back when once more the door was flung open and a girl of about nine years old ran in, wide-eyed, lank hair hanging either side of her cheeks. The first person she saw was Edie and she ran to her, panting so hard she could barely speak.

'Help, help me!' she gasped. 'It's our mom. 'Er's come

over poorly and Mrs 'Iggins ain't at 'ome and I dunno where to find 'er . . .'

'What's the matter with the child?' Mrs Lordly demanded.

'She says her mother's poorly,' Edie told her. 'What's your name, love, and where've you come from?'

'My name's Lizzie: I'm from down the road. I think it's the babby coming 'cos Mom's shouting out and there's only me and me brother in the 'ouse with 'er.'

'Could one of the nurses go?' Miss Hansome wondered over Edie's shoulder.

'No need for that.' Mrs Lordly untied her apron. 'We can't spare them from here. Too much going on. I shall need some help.' She eyed Edie doubtfully. 'Don't suppose you've any experience of childbirth?'

'Well – yes. I have,' Edie admitted. 'I mean . . .'

'Right. Needs must. You'd better come along.' Mrs Lordly jerked her head at Miss Hansome. '*You'd* be no use at all. I hope you can at least manage to man the urn without creating chaos? Come along.'

Edie trotted obediently after her. 'But aren't we s'posed to stay here?' she asked as they both plunged out into the mayhem of the streets.

'Our role is to go wherever we're needed.'

Outside was almost as bright as day. As they marched along the street of mean, closely packed terraces behind Lizzie's frantic figure, Edie began to feel a reluctant admiration for Mrs Lordly. She might be bossy and rude but she was certainly brave. How on earth was she going to know what to do, though? Edie felt terrified at the thought of dealing with this unknown woman, labouring alone in her house. But this anxiety was blocked out by fear for her own life as the planes drew closer and roared overhead. She prayed with every fibre of her being for them to pass over. A moment later she and Mrs Lordly plunged after Lizzie along a dark entry and in at the back of a house. As they did so, there were muffled explosions in the distance.

At the back they found a neat, homely room with an oil lamp burning on the table amid the remains of a meal. The woman of the house, in her mid-thirties with bobbed, dark hair, was kneeling over one of the chairs, gasping with pain. Beside her was a little boy of about seven, watching her with frightened eyes. He had one hand on her shoulder.

'It's all right, Mom,' Edie heard him say, with surprising composure. 'They've come to 'elp yer.'

The woman looked up in the midst of her pain, saw the two women in their uniforms and started sobbing with relief.

It was pitch dark under the ambulance. Janet lay tensed beside Martin Ferris, eyes clenched shut as the planes passed over them.

'Thank God.' The words escaped her without her even willing them. Only then did she become aware of a sharp piece of masonry digging into her ribs.

'Are you all right?' Martin shouted.

'Yes. You?'

'Perfectly. I think it's safe to move now.'

Occupants of the street resumed their search amid the rubble. Someone had heard cries from under the ruins of one of the houses. A woman, by the sound of it. The warden was shining a torch over the wreckage. Janet and Martin pushed through the knot of people who were watching.

'Anything we can do?' Martin asked.

'Stay here and keep her talking for a few minutes, will you? We'll need reinforcements for this. Christ knows when they'll turn up.'

'Can you see anything?'

'No – not a thing.' And the man was gone.

'Is anyone there?' the voice wailed from under the rubble. It was a petrified, sobbing voice, neither very old nor very young. 'Don't leave me!'

'It's all right,' Janet called out. 'There's someone here – you're not on your own.'

'It's Mrs Rossi,' a woman said behind them. 'Poor soul. Her legs ain't so good.'

'Oh, help me! Please help me! Am I going to die . . .?'

Martin glanced sombrely at Janet and squatted down as near as he could get to the voice.

'Hello?' He said hello a number of times, trying to calm the woman, to make her listen. 'Can you tell me your name?'

'Mrs . . . Mrs . . . I can't remember. Oh, Mrs . . .? I don't know my name.'

'Don't worry. You're not alone here, and we shan't leave you. They've gone to get help to lift some of this off you and then we'll get you out. Are you in much pain?'

The woman said that her back was hurting and her legs and please, please would someone get her out of here, it was horrible, and she started to cry again. Janet squatted down beside Martin.

'Will you fetch something from the kit that I can give her?' Martin said. 'A sedative.'

'D'you want me to . . .?' Janet asked. After all, it was his first time out!

'I'm a doctor.' He said it quietly, patiently. 'Almost, anyway. Good practice for me.'

'A *doctor*?'

'Medical student. Final year.'

'Oh, I see.' She heard herself sounding abrupt. Why hadn't he *said*? 'I'm sorry. I'll bring it over.'

When she came back she heard his voice talking on and on to the woman, and found its low, assured tone comforting herself. She felt a new, reluctant respect for him.

'The main challenge is going to be getting close enough to give it to her,' he said. 'A little phenobarbitone should calm her down for a while.

'I'm going to try to reach you to give you something to help the pain,' he called into the darkness. 'Tell me if you feel me touch you, all right?' To Janet he said, 'Give me a hand, will you? We'll have to be damn careful not to shift anything and make it worse.'

Janet didn't really think they would be able to reach her. Her voice sounded clear, but too far away. Even with her arms stretched to the fullest extent, all Janet's hands met were rough surfaces and pockets of air.

'It's no good,' she gasped. 'I can't feel anything.'

Martin let out a grunt with the effort of stretching. 'Is that . . .? I can feel something . . .' After a moment he seemed more sure. 'Can you feel that, ma'am?'

'Mrs Rossi! I'm Mrs Rossi!'

'Well done,' Martin said. 'That's good. Now, Mrs Rossi – is that you I can feel down there? Can you feel my hand?'

'No – where? I can't feel anything. Oh, Lord God.' She set up a rhythmic muttering. Janet realized she was saying the rosary.

He frowned. 'It's no good, she's too far away. *Damn.*' She was moved by his anger and frustration at himself for not being able to help.

'It's all right—' She tapped his arm. 'Look – they're coming now. We ought to go and see if there are others.'

They found one other casualty who needed to go to hospital and left before Mrs Rossi had been brought out from under her house. They fetched her the next time. By then she was barely conscious.

By the time the raid ended and the calls stopped coming the night was almost over. They drove back to the depot in silence, suddenly dazed with exhaustion. Janet could feel that her face was thickly coated with dust and the inside of her nose and mouth felt clogged with it as well. Martin drew the van to a halt outside and switched off the engine.

'Phew.'

'Yes,' she said. 'What a night.'

'Well—' he gave a wry smile. 'D'you think I made the grade?'

'Oh yes.' Janet thought of the gentle, reassuring voice she had been listening to through the night. 'Very much so.'

'Thanks.' He stared out into the darkness for a moment. 'It's funny, I'm exhausted but the last thing I feel like is sleep. It feels as if we ought to go and have a drink or something. Live it up.'

'Well—' Janet laughed, nodding towards the depot. 'At this time of night I think the best you'll manage is another cup of tea.'

'That would certainly be welcome.' He looked round at her. 'Would you care to join me?'

Common sense told her to get to bed as fast as possible before work tomorrow. But her stomach was rumbling and the thought of the walk home without even a drink was dismal. Stiffly, she said, 'Yes, all right then.'

They took off their coats and sank down at the table with their tea. Martin passed her the sugar.

'This is some well-brewed stuff. Still, I'm ready for anything after that.'

'Me too,' Janet stirred in the lumps of sugar then slumped back in her chair. 'Actually, I'm ravenous.'

'I'm sure they could provide you with a bun or something here, couldn't they?'

'I'll skip it. It'll only sit in my stomach like a lead weight at this time of night.'

'Cigarette?' He held out a packet.

'No. Thanks.'

Martin seemed to think the better of lighting up himself and put the packet back in his pocket. He looked across at her in what seemed to her an appraising way which raised her hackles. She felt as if her skin was prickling under his gaze.

'Where d'you live?'

'Linden Road. Bournville.'

'I'd be happy to give you a lift home.'

She looked at him over her teacup, one eyebrow raised. 'Have you got a car?' She couldn't keep the sarcasm out of her voice. 'I thought all students were terribly poor?'

'No, motorbike and sidecar. Would that be acceptable?'

Her mouth twitched into a smile. 'That sounds rather fun. Yes, thank you. It would be very nice not to have to walk. But tell me, I didn't get round to asking you before, about your training?'

Martin sat forward, animated. 'As I said, I've almost finished. They've let the last of us stay on to finish qualifying and then, if this is still all going on, I suppose I'll be an army medico or something – thank goodness. It's such a relief to have a justifiable reason not to bear arms. The thing is, I'm trained to try to save life so it doesn't seem consistent then to go out and take it. Although now we're up against someone like Hitler, and all those other chaps are out there fighting, well . . .' He shrugged. 'I'm just glad I'm a doctor and I can carry on doing that. Perhaps that just sounds cowardly to you?'

'Not cowardly, no. I'm a Friend, a Quaker, you see.'

'Are you?' He considered her with apparent respect. 'Well, that's interesting. A very serious body of people the Quakers. And hence your working at Cadbury's.'

'Well not hence, no. Most people who work there aren't actually Friends.'

'True. But they've had such an impact haven't they? I mean it's extraordinarily pleasant round there considering it's a factory – all the trees and gardens. And aren't I right in thinking they endowed the Woodlands Hospital?'

'Yes, it was the Birmingham Cripples Union originally. And they gave a lot of the schools and colleges in the area – and the park in the Lickey Hills.'

'No pubs though?'

She smiled, feeling the mask of dust on her face. 'Definitely no pubs.'

She told him she lived with her mother and Marie Falla, the young woman from Guernsey, and Martin offered the information that he lived in a shared house.

'That must be quite a squeeze, with children and everything?' she asked.

'It can be. Of course I'm out a lot, and now the boys have been sent out into the country. It's rather desolate without them really. Doesn't feel as if we're a family any more. But yes, never a dull moment normally. I have to stay in the library if I want to get any work done!'

He stretched and got to his feet, yawning. She was suddenly conscious of just how tall he was. 'It's horribly late. We should really try to fit in some sleep. Are you ready?'

'Yes,' she said sleepily. She felt suddenly warm and drowsy and wished she could curl up and sleep in the depot. But she soon woke up again when, tucked into the sidecar of his motorcycle, she was whizzing along in the very cold, smoky night air, his scarf, which he had gallantly lent her, wrapped round her neck. The sky still glowed pink. It was half past five when he deposited her outside her mother's house, reaching for her hand to help her climb out. His gloved hand dwarfed hers. She was conscious that she must look a frightful mess, covered in dust and hair all over the place. Good job it's still dark, she thought. Then she chastised herself bitterly for being so ridiculous. He's married, and in any case I am not interested in men. They're too much trouble altogether.

She stood on the pavement, unsteady with tiredness.

'Thanks so much,' she said, in formal tones. 'I'm very grateful.'

Martin gave an amused smile which grated on her. What did he want her to do? Grovel with gratitude?

'A pleasure,' he said.

There was an awkward silence and she was about to turn away, but then the voice came again through the darkness.

'It sounds awful to say it, but I've enjoyed tonight.'

'Good. Well, I'm sure it won't be the last time.'

'I hope that Mrs Rossi is all right.'

'Yes,' Janet said more softly. 'Horrible.'

'Anyway, see you again perhaps.' He revved up, gave her a brief wave, and was off.

'Goodbye – Oh! I've still got your scarf!' But he was gone, the roar of the motorcycle receding in the distance. She turned to go inside, reaching into her pocket for her key. She felt overwhelmed by exhaustion, and a sudden sense of anticlimax.

Edie settled Lizzie and her brother to sleep under the table in the front room. She brought a mattress down from one of the beds and they covered it with copies of the *Birmingham Despatch* for the woman, Alicia Jewel, to settle on. Mrs Lordly, who seemed to be in her element, rattled pans in the scullery, prepared water, found a sharp knife, string. She looked out two candles and stood them, lit, in saucers on the table with the lamp. Every so often there came a thump from outside and the windows rattled, but Edie found she had almost forgotten the raid, so caught up was she by the drama going on inside.

Mrs Lordly, hands on her broad hips, had ordered Alicia to lie on her back. But as soon as another bout of pain swept over her she scrambled on to her knees again. Edie was very nervous. Memories of her own labour came flashing back to her, raw and terrible. The agony, the fear. This was not Alicia's first time, and she was older than Edie, but the pain was the same. All it would take to make it easier would be a little kindness. She found herself drawn to the woman's side, kneeling down, taking her hand as she wished someone had done when she'd birthed and lost her baby.

'We'll help you, bab.' She was surprised at the tender motherliness she heard in her own voice. 'Don't worry, we won't leave you. It'll be all right.'

She felt an answering squeeze. 'It's getting close,' the woman panted. 'My waters went ages back.' She gave a sob, released by Edie's kindness. 'Oh God, the pain . . . I can't do it again, I can't!'

'You can,' Edie said, touched. 'You've done it before, haven't you? You *can* do it.'

Edie stroked her back. She was wearing a threadbare navy dress with tiny white polka dots all over it. Edie could feel the heat coming off her and she smelt pungently of sweat. Edie found her own breathing tuning in with Alicia's.

'What are you *doing*?' Mrs Lordly appeared again, her pudgy face furious. 'Lie down again – you can't carry on like that, it's a disgrace!'

Alicia, who was at the height of her pain, took no notice.

'What's the matter?' Edie said, worried. 'Does she need to lie down? Will she hurt herself?'

'I'm not having her on her hands and knees like ... like an animal! I said *lie down*, Mrs Jewel.'

Leave her alone! Edie wanted to scream. Can't you see she's in pain?

'You must lie down,' Mrs Lordly commanded afterwards. Edie loathed her bullying tone. Why did she have to carry on like this?

'I couldn't 'elp it,' Alice said, turning back on to her back. She was frightened of Mrs Lordly. 'Only when the pain starts it's just what I do.'

'Well, you must try to control yourself,' Mrs Lordly said, tight-lipped.

The pains were coming even closer together now and Edie found it almost unbearable to watch. Alicia groaned through two more on her back, seeming in even greater pain, as Mrs Lordly stood over her. With the next one she cried, 'I'm not doing what you say!' and twisted back on to her knees.

'Disgusting,' Mrs Lordly commented. She was sitting

on the chair now. 'And do stop smothering her, Mrs Weale. None of that is necessary. She's only in pup.'

Edie could feel her temper rising, but she tried to choke it back. 'I'm just trying to help,' she muttered.

'Oh God,' Alicia moaned, falling forward in exhaustion. 'I can't . . .'

'You can!' Edie urged. 'You're nearly there.'

'Do try to control yourself,' Mrs Lordly instructed.

'Have you got children yourself?' Edie asked, only just succeeding in keeping a civil tone. God help them if you have, she wanted to add.

'I've two sons, thank you. And I certainly didn't make all this fuss bringing them into the world. Nor did my sister, and I delivered both of hers.'

Edie bit her lip and tried to block the woman's heavy body out of her view. Dried-up old cow! Why were people so nasty?

She lost track of time, of everything except the events of the birth. At last, after what felt like days, the intensity of it reached a peak.

'It's coming!' Alicia shouted. She braced herself on her hands and knees and, short of physically throwing her on her back, there was nothing Mrs Lordly could do about it. After several more acute waves of pain the woman began to push the baby out. Mrs Lordly, Edie had to acknowledge, seemed to know what she was doing, and with a final groan Alicia had delivered herself of a little girl. As she slithered out, Edie watched, mesmerized, completely possessed by the moment.

'Breathe!' Fists clenched, she entreated the tiny figure, hardly realizing the thought had escaped through her lips. 'Oh, breathe and be all right – *please* . . .'

The tiny infant made a small choking sound and Mrs

Lordly cleared something out of her mouth. There came a thin, but full-throated wail.

Edie sank down on to her knees again, the tears pouring down her face.

'My baby,' she sobbed. 'Oh my little baby.' Grief poured out of her sharp and raw. She had barely glimpsed her little boy, her poor, dead child, had never held him before they whisked him away like something dirty. How could they have just snatched him from his mother without even letting her see him and say goodbye properly?

Walking home that night, leaving Alicia lying with her sweet daughter, and the smoke-filled sky quiet at last, Edie wept and wept. Living with Alicia through the intense, primal birthing of her child had ripped the surface off her inner wounds, leaving her raw and hurting. She sobbed her pain to the empty streets. Oh God, would she ever get over the ache of wanting to hold a baby of her own in her arms?

Fourteen

One evening in early November, after dark, Ethel Bonner heard a knock at her door in Glover Road.

'Blast it, who can that be? And calling at the front an' all.' She'd just settled in her chair with a steaming cup of tea and didn't have the energy to get up. 'Get the door, Alfie.'

Eight-year-old Alf scampered along and tugged open the door on its stiff hinges. Outside in the dusk stood a short man with a neat little moustache, wearing a natty pinstriped suit with flamboyant lapels, his hat held against his chest as if in preparation for making a speech.

''Ello there, sonny.' The man spoke in the tones of a Cockney bus conductor, though Alf was quite oblivious to this fact and just stared, mouth agape, at this apparition on the doorstep. 'Is your muvver in the 'ouse terdie?'

Ethel, ears pricked in the back room, felt her heart beat quicker. There was something familiar about that voice and she struggled to place it. Surely it couldn't be . . .?

'Mom – there's a man . . .'

'Well, didn't yer ask his name?' she scolded, hauling herself exhaustedly up from the chair.

At the front door she stood looking at him for a few seconds as the years peeled back.

'Mimi! It *is* you, isn't it?' The visitor cried melodramatically, throwing out his arms as if to embrace her. The

Cockney bus conductor had transformed into a lovesick Clark Gable. 'My darling, at last I've found you!'

Ethel's knees went weak on hearing her old stage name and her hand went to her heart. 'No,' she managed to say at last. 'Surely not, Ernie Dempsey?'

'The very man! Mimi has not forgotten me!' Now there was a touch of the tragic Shakespearian. 'Oh, to be so remembered by posterity!'

'Ernie – what're . . .? My God! Well I never . . .' Ethel spluttered. 'What in heaven's name're *you* doing here?'

Switching to a roguish Dublin brogue he protested, 'Sure, are you not going to invite me in, Mimi sweetheart, now I'm after coming all this way?'

Chuckling, Ethel held the door open. 'You'd better come through to the back,' she said, thanking her stars she'd just tidied up. 'There's tea in the pot. Billy, pour Mr Dempsey a cuppa will you?' Up close to his ear she added, 'And make sure the cup ain't chipped.'

'These are your boys?' Ernie Dempsey asked, laying his hat in the table.

'This is Alfie, my youngest. Do sit down, Ernie, yes, take that seat, by the fire and warm yourself up. That's Billy in there, he's ten.' Billy brought Mr Dempsey his tea and the two boys hovered in the background listening, fascinated.

Ethel brought a chair up close. She felt horribly conscious of the rough state she'd allowed herself to get in since she'd last seen her former colleague. When would that have been? Fifteen years or more ago. Ernie Dempsey! Still looked just the same, only older of course. How old must he be now? Let's see, she was forty-two, which put Ernie well on into his fifties. He was still full of his sweeping theatrical gestures and bewildering way of talking in different accents, as if he consisted of a whole array of people occupying the same body. It was his way of covering up his shyness. He'd settle down, she remembered, once they got talking, into his usual soft Brummie accent. She ran her hand over her hair. What a colourless mess it looked! She'd have put a touch of rouge on, if only she'd known he was coming!

Ernie sat, rubbing his hands along his thighs. 'But by my recollection you had a daughter, did you not?'

'Ruby's the eldest, Ernie. She was just wed a few months back. A nice young man – away now of course, RAF.' She felt proud saying that. 'Ruby was given a position at Cadbury's. Still there, she is, and her brother George who came next. Then there's Perce, 'e's fifteen now so 'e's at work. Thing is, Ernie – we've had a bad couple of years. I lost Sid just over two years ago and I've found it hard to pick myself up. Got in a right state to tell you the truth.' Tears welled in her eyes and she wiped them away. 'We was very happy together, me and Sid, all these years. He 'ad a growth, you see – only lasted a few months.'

'Poor Mimi.' Ernie reached out and clasped her plump hand with genuine tenderness.

She squeezed his, then withdrew her hand. 'Don't, Ernie. Don't get me started.' She wiped her eyes. 'Tell me about yourself. How're you both – Edna well?'

'Edna's in very good health now. We had a bit of a bad do, oh, three years back, but she seems to be over that now.'

'And—' she asked hesitantly. 'You didn't have children?'

'Alas, no . . .' For a moment Ernie retreated again behind one of his theatrical personae. 'The fates decreed that it was not to be . . .' Ethel saw a glimpse of the pain this had given him in his face, then he smiled chirpily.

'But it has meant that Edna and I have had a marvellous working life together. We've been touring a great deal – settling for a time here and there. Blackpool, the south coast, vistas of windswept grey sand ...!' He picked up his cup and saucer and sipped his tea. 'Times were getting very lean though, the last few years. I'm afraid Edna and I had had our heyday.' He laughed self-mockingly, looking up at her, and Ethel realized she was being sized up. She felt herself shrink under his gaze. What must he think of her? She tried to tuck her feet back so that her skirt hid them. Her ankles were swollen and she was wearing her awful old shoes! She'd let herself go badly, and it hurt her. She was nothing but a fat, blowzy old woman.

'I've been a bit any'ow lately, Ernie,' she said, miserably.

'Not a bit of it, Mimi love.' Again, he touched her hand. 'You've been through a difficult time of it. Now – you listen to me.' For a moment he was back to the Cockney bus conductor role. 'Uncle Ernie's got just the ticket to lift you out of yourself. How would you like,' he leaned back and paused, to maximize the dramatic effect of his words, 'to work again? With me?'

Ethel stared dumbfounded at him. 'Work? *Me?* What on earth are you going on about, Ernie? I'm on my own here with five to look after, no husband ...'

'Well, surely that's all the more reason to earn some money, although I can't promise fabulous wages ...'

'But look at the state of me!'

'Ethel, Mimi,' Ernie put his cup down and sat forward, speaking urgently. 'War's a terrible thing, but it does bring with it certain opportunities for people like us. Two years ago I was put out to pasture, finished, and I knew it. Edna gets the odd character role here and there, but we knew we'd had our time. Suddenly, bam!' He punched his left hand with his right fist, 'Mr Hitler. Things look even worse. They close all the theatres and picture houses so it's looking bad for everyone. Curtains. But what we've got now is factories full of people, overworked and blue and hungry for any kind of entertainment. And old Ernie Dempsey manages to land himself a nice little job with ENSA.'

Ethel gave a faint smile. 'The entertainment people?'

'That's us – Every Night Something Awful. Anyroad, they have all the bands in and the professional troups, but Joe Loss and Geraldo can't be everywhere – nor the pros from the Rep and the Alex. They can't keep up with the demand for concerts and shows. So, I'm getting together a little variety group of old hands. So far I've got Alf Lonsdale—'

Ethel let out the most full-hearted laugh any of them had heard from her for a very long time. 'Not that old devil, oh deary me, his jokes were out of the ark back in nineteen twenty-five!'

'Well, he's aboard, and Dot O'Sullivan, remember her?'

'Oh yes, God love 'er. Still doing the same old character pieces?'

'Variations on a theme, let's say. And a few younger ones. But you were a real goer in your day Ethel, and you still could be. Why don't you come and join us?'

Ethel stopped laughing, seeing he was serious. 'But Ernie – look at me! I can't dance any more! I ain't had a pair of dance shoes on for as long as I can remember.'

'No, but I bet you can still sing given half the chance. You used to be able to belt them out like no one else I know. None of us is a spring chicken any more, but I bet you could do a few moves. Bit of a song and dance routine – they'd love it.' He went over to the long-silent

131

piano and lifted the lid, teased out a few chords. 'That's what they want, a good sing-song with someone who knows how to jolly 'em along!'

'Oh Ernie—' Ethel smiled at the sound of the old piano. She could barely trust the flicker of hope that ignited in her. Could she have some sort of life again after everything had felt so dead and buried for so long? 'Oh no – I couldn't!'

'Mimi love—' He came over to her again. 'Once a performer, always a performer. It's in the blood. What I'd like to say to you this evening is, welcome aboard the troupe to my old pal Mimi Cohoon. We'll have a ball, you and me and Edna. Like old times.'

'But, Ernie.' Ethel tried to keep her excitement within bounds. He didn't think she was past it, past everything, the way she'd felt for months now. He really thought she could do it! A flush of pleasure rose in her cheeks.

'Go on, Mom,' Billy said from behind her, and Ethel jumped.

'Oh Lor' – I'd forgotten you two were listening in!'

'Would you be on the stage again, all dressed up and that?' Billy asked.

'She would indeed, young man,' Ernie said. 'And wouldn't that be fine? Your mother,' he added solemnly, 'has the voice of a nightingale.'

'More like a foghorn,' Ethel chuckled. 'Look, Ernie, this is all very well, and I'm more grateful to you than I can say. But I can't just launch into summat like this. I'd have to speak to Ruby, and George. They've been golden, the pair of 'em, while I've not been myself, and if this is going to make life too difficult for them I'll have to let it go.'

'Oh, go *on*, Mom,' Billy said. 'Our Ruby won't mind.'

'When will she be home?' Ernie asked.

Ethel looked at the clock. 'George is on firewatch tonight, but our Ruby'll be back within the next half-hour I should think. I mean you can wait if you want but if there's a raid you're going to get stuck here.'

'Well, that wouldn't be an entirely tragic occurrence, would it?' He lapsed back into his Shakespearian mode of speech.

'How about I put you out a nice bowl of parsnip soup while we wait?'

'That, my dear,' Ernie gushed, 'sounds like the nectar of the gods.'

So, each with a bowl of heavenly nectar, which was in fact rather pale and stringy, they sat at the table reminiscing over old times. Billy and Alfie grinned at each other, hearing their mom's unfamiliar laughter ringing round the room. She was like a woman reborn.

At last they heard the back door opening, and Ruby appeared, pink-cheeked from the cold. Ethel laughed again at the astonished expression on her face as she came in.

'You awright, bab?' Ethel asked her.

Ruby nodded wearily, but with a smile playing on her lips at her mother's obvious jubilation. 'Who's this?'

'This, Ruby, is my old friend Ernie Dempsey, and he's come tonight to offer me a job.'

An hour later Ernie Dempsey arranged his hat jauntily on his head, stepped out of number six, Glover Road, and walked off along the dark road, whistling.

Well, that had gone very satisfactorily! Seeing Mimi again had done him the power of good, even though he'd had to conceal his sense of shock on first seeing her. That daughter of hers, Ruby, looked more like the Mimi he remembered – buxom and full of fun. She'd only hesitated a few seconds before saying excitedly, 'Go on, Mom.

You'd *love* it – you know you would.' He'd always had a soft spot for Mimi. She'd gone to seed a bit now, of course, but she wasn't past redemption. There was something about her still, an earthy appeal, and a good costume and plenty of make-up could remedy a great many ills. His little band of followers was growing. Now all they needed was to find a name for themselves.

He turned on to the Bristol Road to get the bus home, a lighthearted spring in his step. Oh yes, the war wasn't proving half bad for Ernie Dempsey. He felt as if years had been lifted off him. He and Edna were looking at being able to work again and having a few quid in their pockets. And after seeing poor old Mimi, he felt the glow of knowing he'd given someone else a chance as well.

Fifteen

Edie sat on the 61 bus, on her way to the rest centre at St Matthew's, gas mask on her lap, arms hugging her coat round her. She was cold, tired and miserable. All day she'd been on the line at Cadbury's and another long night on duty stretched in front of her. This in itself did not bother her. Being busy and among other people was better than sitting at home on her own.

Since the night last month when she and Mrs Lordly had help deliver Alicia Jewel's baby (which was, she had heard since, thriving), her own grief for the loss of her child had been opened up, more deeply and painfully than ever. Watching the other woman labour and bring forth her child made her ache for the baby she had never been able to carry in her arms. It was no good saying anything to anyone. Everyone had their problems these days and hers was past history to them. She was expected to put it away and get on with life.

She'd just come from her mother's house. To her astonishment, Rodney had come round yesterday with the suggestion from Nellie that Edie go round to Charlotte Road for her tea that day when she'd finished work. Edie was briefly cheered by this suggestion. Perhaps her mom was waking up to the fact that she was suffering – that she was so sad and lonely. But when she arrived she found out soon enough why she was suddenly welcome back home. Florrie and the two boys had landed on her suddenly. They'd come two days ago after the horrific nights of bombing on Coventry. The *Gazette* was still in the house with its banner headline, COVENTRY – OUR GUERNICA.

Florrie had not been bombed out, but seeing the devastation of the city the day after had sent her, and many other people, into a panic. She'd managed to get a lift in a neighbour's van and join the slow-moving trail of people escaping from city. Her mom's was the only place she could think of to go.

'It's all very well, wench,' Dennis Marshall said to her, 'but I reckon you've climbed out of the frying pan into the fire coming 'ere.'

'But I had to leave, Dad,' Florrie said. 'I were that frightened. You've never seen anything like it. There was so many dead they 'ad to pile them up in the swimming-pool.'

Dennis frowned. 'What – with the water in?'

'Oh, don't be so dense, Dennis!' Nellie snapped. 'Of course not with the flaming water in.'

Edie could see how much her mother resented having the mess and noise of young children in the house again. So that's why she'd been invited. Nellie wanted another pair of hands to do the work! She was soon slaving away, helping feed the children, washing up, do this Edie, do that. Dennis had his Home Guard uniform on and was hurrying his meal to get out in time. Once tea was over Edie sat in the corner with Rodney. He'd given Eric, the older boy, a couple of old comics, *Boys' Own* and the *Hotspur*, and was being unusually cooperative in helping him look through them. Edie watched his freckly profile. He was getting big now as well – he'd be out to work next year. She felt sorry for him being left on his own at home, but Mom and Dad had more time for him than their daughters. They should've only had him, she thought bitterly.

'You awright, Rodney?' she asked softly, trying to establish contact with at least someone in her family.

He looked round, briefly. 'Yeah.'

'That's good.'

By the time she had to leave Edie felt more cast down than she would've done going home on her own. Talk about lonely in a crowd, she thought.

'Bye, Mom, Florrie,' she said, going to the door with her coat on.

'T'ra Ede, see yer soon,' Florrie called.

Nellie, who had Florrie's youngest on her lap, barely looked up.

She didn't even remember I was going on duty, Edie thought, on the bus. Even with this garb on. Mrs Hatton wouldn't have been like that, she'd've been worried, shown a bit of interest. Of course, comparing her mother with anyone else's had always been a waste of time. She wasn't going to change now.

The thought of Janet's mom warmed her. Janet had asked her and Ruby round for tea on several Sunday afternoons, to their cosy house owned by the Bournville Village Trust. Edie thought Frances Hatton was the most wonderful person she'd ever met. She'd baked scones and little cakes and they'd sat in the parlour with Marie Falla, the shy girl from Guernsey, and been made as welcome and comfortable as anything. Edie was impressed by the graceful room with its chintzy chairs and the piano open and ready to play. And what was it about Mrs Hatton? Edie thought, as the bus crawled along in the darkness. She had lovely clothes, not fancy, but beautiful. Some of them looked quite old and worn, but the soft skirts, stylish blouses and woollens of soft autumn colours captivated Edie. Her mom was very particular and clean, of course, but she always dressed her tiny frame in hard colours: navy, black, and royal blue, stiff shirtwaisters and tight pleats. There was no *give* in her clothes: they all looked starched. Whereas last time she'd seen Janet's mom, she'd been wearing a dark green velvet skirt and a lovely thick cardigan in a warm rust colour, a little silk scarf patterned with leaves at the neck. Everything she wore was simple, but it looked so nice on her, and add to that Frances's thick hair, those lovely dark eyes and her – what was it? Edie thought. Her *interest* in everything, that was it. The way her eyes lingered on your face, drinking you in. Everything they told her seemed to be of great concern to her, the way it was with Janet. Edie had never experienced anything quite like it before.

Both she and Ruby had found themselves telling Frances Hatton all about their lives, especially Ruby. When she talked about her father's death and how her mom had been, Frances nodded with great understanding.

'Poor dear,' she said. 'It is the most terrible thing. I lost my husband in the last war and I felt as if I'd lost half of myself for a long time afterwards. Your mother has had a terrible amount to contend with, and of course,' gently she touched Edie's shoulder, 'dear Edie as well.' Edie flushed, gratefully. 'What a lot of sadness. But you know, all we can do when things are sad is gather together and help each other through. And your husband sounds marvellous, Ruby dear.' She held out a plate. 'Another scone?'

Mrs Hatton was so kind and just accepted everyone as they were. Edie imagined what her mom'd be like if she had a refugee living in the house. She found her own family enough of a trial.

A wail cut through her thoughts. The air-raid siren. A groan passed through the bus and people started cursing.

''Ere we go again. 'Ow're we ever s'posed to get to work on time in this bloody lot?'

The driver braked. 'Anyone want to gerrof 'ere? I'm gunna keep going, see if we can crawl through to Navigation Street, or as near as I can get.'

Several people got off and they moved carefully on. By the time Edie reached St Matthew's, the raid had still not begun.

Back in the Selly Oak depot, Janet was also reporting for duty as the sirens began to howl out their warning. She met Joyce on her way in. They'd gone and volunteered together in the beginning but usually worked different nights.

'Oh – you're on tonight as well, are you?' Joyce said thankfully. 'Jolly good. Feels to me as if it's going to be a bad one.'

'Well, let's see if we can get a cuppa inside us before all hell breaks loose,' Janet said, pushing the door open. She glanced round as they waited at the counter, pretending to herself that she was just generally seeing who was on duty. Of course Martin Ferris may or may not have been among them, but she wasn't looking *especially* to see if he was there. Since the night they had been sent out together they had coincided three or four times, but had not worked together again. Janet had tried to make sure she worked with other people, had kept away from him. She knew it didn't matter: he was obviously a happy family man and she ought to have been able to relax with him as a friend. But she could not be near him without his presence affecting her. While they waited in the depot for the call-out she always had a prickly, restless sensation of being aware just where he was and who he was talking to. Now and then she caught him looking her way and sometimes he smiled. For politeness' sake she'd give a faint smile back, then look away. The effect he had on her annoyed her hugely but she couldn't seem to prevent it.

He's not here tonight, she thought, beginning to relax. No risk of being teamed up with him. She sipped the weak, sugary tea and tried to pay attention to what Joyce was saying, wondering why she felt suddenly rather irritable. Nerves, she thought. We're all living on our nerves. She glanced at her watch, seven fifteen, then, looking up, saw the tall, compelling figure of Martin Ferris checking in for duty.

A few minutes later, the raid began.

Inside the blacked-out church, all the volunteers had hurried to finish readying the place. There were a few camp beds and mattresses and a pile of donated blankets and rugs. The WVS women got the urn going next door in the school, and wheeled the rickety trolley through with its cups and bowls of sugar lumps. Edie had found herself in the company of Miss Hansome once more (though to her relief there was no appearance by Mrs Lordly), and two other kindly women, a Mrs Duke and Mrs Carruthers, both in their mid-forties. Mrs Duke, from Harborne, was very small and round, like a bun, and Mrs Carruthers was very homely in a tweed skirt, with cropped brown hair. She had driven her husband's motor car in from Bartley Green without asking him and was now in a state of great agitation in case it got hit.

'Ronald will never forgive me,' she complained. 'I really should have come on the bus . . .' She'd brought a bag of knitting 'in case it's a quiet night'.

It wasn't going to be a quiet night.

As things began to hot up, Edie found herself, in a brief moment of quiet, beside Miss Hansome and the tea trolley, in one of the side aisles. She liked Miss Hansome, Edie decided. She had gradually found out what a hard life the woman had had – a genteel beginning with both parents dying early, struggling on alone, never really wanted by anyone. Away from Mrs Lordly she was less befuddled by nerves, and it was easier to see her sweet, vulnerable nature.

'Here they come,' Edie murmured.

Miss Hansome nodded. 'You know,' she whispered a moment later. 'I went to the service for Mr Chamberlain. It was most affecting.'

'Did you?' Edie nodded encouragingly.

'He was a good man,' Miss Hansome wiped her pink-tipped nose with her hanky. 'Whatever they say about him now.'

She expanded into detail about Neville Chamberlain's memorial service, which had been at St Martin's Church in the Bull Ring. Edie tried to keep her mind on what the woman was telling her, but within seconds there came a massive bang from outside and the floor snatched so hard they both almost fell over. Miss Hansome screamed and gripped Edie's hand as bits fell from the ceiling and the lights swayed.

Mrs Carruthers gave a yelp of terror. 'Oh my stars, the car!'

It had begun.

By eight o'clock the first trickle of the shocked and homeless began to arrive and turned into a heavy flow, usually guided to the centre by the local ARP wardens, who then plunged back into the inferno outside. Families arrived, dazed and covered in dust, clinging to anything they had been able to salvage, needing tea and kindness and wanting nothing more than to huddle together and wait for it all to end outside so that they could venture back and see what remained of their houses. Some were distraught, knowing that members of their family were missing. The volunteers handed out blankets and assigned spaces in the church, until so many people came that they had to leave them to fight it out among themselves. And fight sometimes they did, over blankets and sleeping spaces, the right to a camp bed. Mostly, though, people tried to pull together and be considerate, especially to mothers with little ones in their care.

Edie and the others handed out cup after cup of tea and arrowroot biscuits, trying to listen to confused accounts stammered out to them by the shocked bomb victims, over the sound of screaming babies and grizzling children. They were a very mixed bag of folk – the roads within walking distance of the church included some of the more respectable, villa-lined streets of Edgbaston and some of the poorest swathes of jerry-built back-to-back housing, squeezed in round the factories and workshops. Edie handed a cup of tea to one lady who thanked her tremulously with well-spoken vowels. She was wearing a dark coat with an astrakhan collar and had a dashing feather in her hat. The next woman in line had a baby in her arms and two other young ones at her side. Her clothes were full of holes and she opened her mouth to reveal a sprinkling of rotten teeth. The smell of the family preceded them in the queue.

'Give us some milk for the babbies, will yer?' the mother demanded brusquely. 'Them's 'ad nowt tonight.'

Edie handed the older children a cup of milk and some biscuits and their eyes widened. They grabbed the food and crammed it into their mouths. The woman moved dully away. Behind her came a stooped, silent old lady in black with a deeply lined face and such gnarled, stiff hands she could barely grasp her cup of tea.

By nine o'clock the raid was still in full swing, spreading a ring of fire round the city.

At intervals there was an attack on the area round the church and the building shook. Everyone cowered, and there'd be a fresh round of crying from the children who had not surrendered to exhaustion. Only the very little ones were able to sleep. Mrs Carruthers kept saying, 'Oh dear,' in a tragic way. Everyone else tried to keep their spirits up by huddling together, making jokes if they were up to it, and sing-songs kept breaking out. Edie was grateful that she was kept too busy for fear.

They'd boiled up yet another urn full of water at about eleven o'clock, and a small group had started singing, when there was a cry from along the church.

'Fire! We can smell smoke. There's a fire down here!'

The ragged rendition of 'South of the Border' from the front left aisle fizzled out immediately. One of the male volunteers rushed to the vestry to investigate.

'Get the bucket!' he yelled back along the side aisle. 'There's an incendiary come through the roof in 'ere!'

'Oh dear,' Mrs Carruthers murmured. 'Ronald'll never forgive me if they ruin the car.'

'Oh, sod Ronald!' Edie snapped, running for the buckets. 'Get the flaming stirrup pump, will you!'

Moments later they were all busy dousing the fire with a mixture of sand and water. It had not taken hold very far, but had begun to lick at the hems of the vestments that were hanging in the vestry. It was soon dealt with.

'Oh, thank heavens,' Mrs Duke said. 'Oh – I could do with something a bit stronger than this tea, I can tell you!'

Edie went, contrite, to Mrs Carruthers. 'I'm terribly sorry, Mrs Carruthers, for what I said.'

'No ... no dear, you're quite right,' the woman said. 'It's really too ridiculous ... It's just that, well – you don't know Ronald.'

Edie went for a wander round between the pews. She came upon the woman whose children had wanted milk, sitting impassively on a mattress at the entrance to the Lady chapel. The filthy, unwashed stench of them hung round like an aura and the boys were constantly scratching their heads.

'Yer gorrany more o' them biscuits?' the oldest boy piped up. 'Gorra piece we can 'ave?'

His mother nudged him hard with her elbow and brandished her fist. 'Shurrup will yer or yer'll get this down yer 'odge!'

'I might be able to find another couple of biscuits,' Edie said. 'I'm not sure if there's any left.'

The woman didn't react to this information. Edie walked on. A woman sat with a baby in her lap, quietly weeping. In a dark little space to one side she saw the old lady in black bombazine with the wizened face, a string of rosary beads in her hand. Her eyes were closed and her lips moved incessantly. When there came another explosion from outside, she didn't even twitch.

Edie picked her way back through all the bodies to see if she could find any more for the little boys to eat. The night felt as if it was going to go on for ever.

*

They almost ran the ARP Warden over. He loomed, alarmingly close to the windscreen, ghoulish under his tin hat in front of the flaming night, and the driver jammed the brakes on.

'Christ—' Martin's driver jumped out indignantly. 'We're supposed to be picking up casualties, not running them over with the bloody ambulance! What the hell're you playing at?'

'Take 'er will you?' He had a small child in his arms. 'We found her in one of the front gardens, cradle and all. Direct hit on the house. God alone knows how she got out there. I've got to go back . . .' And he was gone.

'Here, take her.' Martin suddenly found himself with a small, plump child in his lap and they drove on. In the dim light he could just make out traces of tears, like slug-trails, down her cheeks, and a bit of a snotty nose, but she was not crying now. Two dark eyes stared unwaveringly into Martin's face.

'Hello,' he said. 'Well, that's very odd. I wonder what happened.'

'Blast, I expect.' The driver stared grimly out through the windscreen, trying to see his way. 'Does the oddest damn things. She's very lucky.'

Not that lucky, Martin thought. Not if there's no one else left for her.

As if reading his thoughts, the driver said, 'I wouldn't fancy the chances of anyone else in the house. Look.' He glanced round for a second. 'We can't keep her with us. There's a rest centre up here, in that church, St Matthew's. They'll look after her in there.' Grimly, he added, 'If it's still standing.'

*

Edie noticed the tall man come hurrying into the church. The first person he saw was Miss Hansome.

'Can you take her?' he held the child out. 'If anyone comes looking, she was found in the road, just a few streets away. Seems fine though. I don't think we need to take her to hospital. But we need to get going.'

'Oh!' Miss Hansome dithered, holding her arms out uncertainly.

'Course we can,' Edie said. 'Shall I take her, Miss Hansome?' The man bundled the child's chubby form into her arms, called, 'Many thanks!' and ran out again.

'Isn't she pretty?' Edie said. 'Hello, little one. Oh aren't you lovely? He did say it's a girl, didn't he?'

'I think so.' Miss Hansome's face softened. 'She is really very bonny.'

Edie pressed her cheek against the baby's rounded one for a second. Oh, how lovely she felt! 'Aren't you filthy though!' She realized the child was coated in dust, her hair thick with it. 'You've had a lucky escape, beautiful, where's your mom then? Shall we have a little peep and see if you're a lad or a lass, eh?' She found a space at the end of a pew and pulled back the little one's nightclothes. They were of good quality, and seemed dry, though the dust seemed to have made its way into every fold. The child was obviously well cared for. Edie peeped inside until she'd seen all she needed to know.

'Aha, so you're a little lad then, are you?' As she picked him up, the dark brows drew together in anxiety for a second, then he let out a loud chortle. 'Oh, listen to that!' Edie laughed. 'Not much wrong with you, is there?'

The other women were all very taken with him as well and he got passed round and loved and they fed him milk from a spoon.

'He must be about a year, wouldn't you say?' Mrs Duke asked as she held him, jiggling him up and down.

'About that,' Mrs Carruthers agreed. 'Certainly not less. I wonder what's become of his family.'

'And what his name is,' Miss Hansome said.

'What's your name?' Edie went up and stroked her finger down his warm, plump cheek. He lurched in Mrs Duke's embrace and held out his arms.

'Oh!' Miss Hansome tittered. 'He's taken a liking to you, Edie!'

'Here, you'd better take him or we'll never get anything done. How about you looking after him for a bit and the rest of us getting back to work?'

Edie couldn't have agreed more eagerly. For the next few hours she found herself in charge of the little boy. She was so taken up with him that she became oblivious to the danger outside. She walked up and down in the fetid atmosphere of the church, stepping over legs and belongings. The feel of the warm, plump baby was so reassuring to her.

He was playful at first, pulling at strands of her hair. Then he became fractious and she walked and rocked until her arms ached with the weight of him. At last he fell asleep and she was able to sit down wearily at the end of a pew with him cuddled on her lap. She looked down at his long dark lashes, leaned down and kissed his cheek. How lovely it was to cradle this sweet child in her arms! She felt so happy and complete having someone to hold and love. She wouldn't think about what was going to happen in the morning. A great wave of tiredness came over her and, with the boy held close to her, she dozed, waking when there was a loud noise or the little boy squirmed, but soon falling asleep again. The first thing she heard which really roused her was the 'All Clear', its sombre, unbroken sound wailing through the destruction outside. It was four thirty in the morning.

'Well, sweetheart,' she whispered, stroking the sleeping infant's head. 'It's over for another night. And we're still here.'

As the dawn broke, smoke from still-smouldering fires mingled with an early morning mist.

Some of the occupants of St Matthew's took to the streets, shivering in the freezing morning, to revisit the ruins of their houses.

'We'll have to find somewhere for that little one to go,' Mrs Duke said to Edie as she got up, still holding the sleeping boy. 'You've done a good job looking after him, I'll say that. He'll be hungry again when he wakes, though, and he's had a shock. He needs a safe place to go. I can't manage to have him myself, I'm afraid.'

Edie needed to go home. She had to be at work in a couple of hours. The raid had gone on so long! The little boy was weighing down her arms, his body a warm, slightly damp bundle against her. She must hand him over and get on her way. But hand him over to who? Part of their job was to find refuge for children after the bombing. And the thought of him being taken away from her now filled her with dismay.

'I could. I mean, my family could look after him for a while, I'm sure,' she heard herself saying.

'Could they really? That'd be marvellous,' Mrs Duke replied eagerly. Another problem solved. 'Well, good for you. I'm sure a place can be found for him in a few days if no one comes to ask for him. In the meantime, it'd be a godsend if you could.'

'I can give you a run home,' Mrs Carruthers said. 'Goodness knows what buses will be running today – and you can't walk all that way with him.'

So Edie found herself stepping out into the cold November morning with the boy wrapped in an extra blanket. 'Heavens,' Mrs Carruthers breathed, horrified at the destruction and ruin all round them. 'What a mess! Dear Lord, look what they've done. It's terrible!'

For a moment they just stood and stared at the devastation all round them. A warehouse along the road, whose bulky outline had dominated the skyline, was now a smoking shell and many other buildings were scarred and smashed. A bus lay on its side, slewed across the road. Many scattered fires were still burning. Firemen were still trying to put out the flames and dampen down smouldering buildings. The street was awash with water.

Edie was to be driven in Mr and Mrs Carruthers' motor car, which was mercifully still in one piece by the kerb. She felt guiltily grateful towards poor Ronald Carruthers after all. They set off on a slow, careful drive along the pot-holed road, seeing families moving, stunned, along the streets, pushing prams, carts loaded with salvaged possessions. Mrs Carruthers swerved to avoid chunks of debris. The further they got away from town the easier it was to make progress.

'You say you live off Oak Tree Lane?' Mrs Carruthers said.

Edie nodded. The child, who was rather damp by now, was starting to stir in her arms and she was relieved at the thought of being able to put him down.

As they turned out of Oak Tree Lane, Edie gasped in horror.

'Oh my!' Mrs Carruthers exclaimed.

In front of them was a terrible sight. Kitty Road, off

which ran Charlotte and the other roads had been hit. There was a huge gash through the middle of the houses, jutting timbers, piles of rubble, bricks strewn everywhere. Parked in the road was a Cadbury's Cocoa van, round which stood a stunned gathering of people drinking cups of warm chocolate. Edie felt tears of shock come to her eyes. It had hit so close to home! So many familiar things were being smashed and destroyed.

'I'm so sorry, dear,' Mrs Carruthers said. 'Thank goodness your street looks all right.'

'Yes,' Edie looked anxiously round. Charlotte Road was intact.

She thanked Mrs Carruthers for the lift, and, hoisting the boy better into her arms, went to number twenty-seven. She tapped the back door and Nellie Marshall answered, face taut and grey with exhaustion, her coat still on.

'Mom – are you all all right?'

'All right as we'll ever be,' she complained. 'Frozen to the marrow. We've only just crawled out of the bleedin' Anderson. What a night . . .' Edie heard Florrie in the background, dealing with the boys. 'That shelter wasn't built to hold this many. Florrie – get that kettle on. What did yer want, anyway?'

She took in suddenly what it was Edie had on her arms.

'Whose is that babby?'

'I don't know.' Edie's heart sank. Why on earth had she brought him here? She'd fallen into some delusion that she'd be welcome! But she explained how she came to be in charge of the child.

'There was nowhere for him to go and so I said – I mean he's only little and I thought maybe he could stay here – just for today – until they find somewhere else.'

'Stay 'ere?' Nellie's face hardened. 'What, with me, while you go swanning off to work? You've got another think coming if you imagine I'm going to take in some brat I've never seen before! I've already got more on my plate than I deserve with Florrie and her two with their muck and mess. Oh no, I'm not having this. You can stay for a cuppa tea and then you get it out of here. You must think I'm running a cowing charity home, that you must!'

Sixteen

For a moment Edie stared at her mother, unable to believe what she had heard. Hurt and exhausted, she felt tears welling in her eyes.

'I don't *want* your cup of tea. I don't want anything from you ever again!'

She marched furiously back up the road, almost oblivious to the numb crowds in Kitty Road, trying to comfort each other in front of bombed-out houses.

The evil, wicked, heartless bitch, she'd even turn away a helpless little babby! She doesn't know how to love anyone. Why did I have to end up with a mom like that? Tears ran down her face as she turned into Oak Tree Lane and towards the factory. The baby, who was awake now, hungry and cold and seeing her crying, began to wail as well.

'Oh, don't,' Edie sobbed, cuddling him. 'Don't you cry as well. It'll be all right, littl'un – I'll look after you even if my cowing mother won't help. I *will*. Sssh, my lovely . . .'

Her feet slowed as the reality of her situation sunk in. She stopped to think, jiggling the little boy up and down to try and calm him, but passers-by glanced curiously at her, so she walked slowly on again.

Where do I think I'm going? she asked herself frantically. What the hell am I going to do? It's only an hour 'til I have be at work and I can't take him with me!

She'd banked on leaving him at her mom's, at least for today. She'd have to go and hand him in at another of the rest centres for him to be looked after. But she held him tight to her, kissing his dark curls. She couldn't bear the thought of parting from him. It was as if their hours clinging to one another while the bombs fell outside had bonded them too closely together to be separated. She'd skip a day's work if necessary if she could stay longer with him. The feel of him in her arms was the dearest thing she had known in all these long, lonely months. Surely there was someone else she could turn to?

She thought of Ethel Bonner, Ruby's mom. But she wasn't sure Ethel would be able to manage. Then it came to her. Who was the person who had shown her the most kindness lately? She saw Frances Hatton's dark, sympathetic eyes in her mind. She was already close to the Hattons' house. Could she ask her, just for today – on behalf of the WVS?

Janet opened the door in Linden Road in her nightdress, squinting without her glasses on. She looked exhausted, but her face broke into a surprised smile.

'Edie! Come in, come in. Are you all right? What on earth . . .?' In the hall she peered more closely at the tearful little boy.

'Oh, Janet,' Edie gabbled out an explanation over the child's howls. 'I know it's stupid of me, but no one's come to claim him yet and I know we'll have to take him back. Only he needs looking after and I had him with me all night and I couldn't bear to leave him. I said I'd take him and find him somewhere!'

'Gracious, someone's not very happy—'

Edie heard Frances's calm voice on the stairs. She came down wearing a soft crimson wool dressing-gown, hair woven into a loose braid. Edie looked desperately at her.

'I'm ever so sorry,' she began.

'Who's this little one then?'

'Warden handed him in last night,' Janet said. 'Family were bombed out somewhere off the Bristol Road. He needs looking after for the day.'

'I'll come as soon as I've finished work, I promise!' Edie babbled, overwrought. 'I feel terrible coming to you like this. I can look after him, and tonight I'll go and see if his family's come for him, only I didn't know where to go and I know it's an awful bother for you.'

'Oh, I don't suppose he'll be too much bother,' Frances said. 'I'd have thought it's the least I can do. You brave girls have been up all night, in the thick of it. It might make me feel a bit more useful. Let's have a look at you, shall we?'

She took the child in her arms and he stopped crying for a moment, taking in the change of circumstances, then began roaring all over again. Frances laughed.

'I think a good breakfast and a clean-up would help make this fellow a bit happier. D'you know, I've even still got a couple of ancient napkins of Janet's somewhere – I use them as cloths. And we'll go and make him some porridge.'

'Are you sure?' Edie said. But already she was reassured by the confident way Frances took the boy in her arms. She even seemed to be enjoying it.

'Of course I'm sure. It's no trouble. And what about you, Edie? You look as if you could do with a warm cup of tea and some breakfast. Come along and have some with Janet.'

In her tiredness, and in the face of this kindness after her treatment from her own mother, Edie burst into tears.

'Oh, poor old you!' Janet's comforting arms wrapped

round her. 'It's been the most wretched night, hasn't it? Let's go and get the kettle on.'

The day seemed such a long one. Everyone was full of talk as to how bad the night had been: ten hours of fear, misery and destruction. From her workmates, Edie learned some of the companies that had been hit, and the Great Western Arcade in town, the main signal-box at New Street, putting the station out of action. And houses, businesses, workshops all round Birmingham.

At dinnertime she sat with Ruby in the dining-room. They talked about the damage to Kitty Road. A Mrs Malone who they'd known most of their lives had been bombed out.

'Our mom's joined that stage show,' Ruby said, rolling her eyes comically. But Edie could see she was actually pleased and proud. 'It's cheered her up no end. Only trouble now is she's never flaming at home! And when she is she spends half her time putting greasepaint on her face. Says she's got to practise!'

'You ought to go as well,' Edie said. 'You've got a nice voice.'

'Don't be daft.' Ruby blushed. 'You know what, though – that fella, Wilf, in the Machines Construction department – he's asked me to go out dancing with him!'

'Wilf? He's old enough to be your father!'

'I know, but he's all right. And at least I'll get a night out sometime,' Ruby said petulantly.

'But you're a married woman! What would Frank say?'

'Oh, don't be such a prude, Edie.' She was looking quite sulky now. 'Why does Frank need to know? They

155

have all sorts laid on for them on that base. It's only a bit of fun, and God knows we could do with some.'

Edie saw there was no point arguing. She told Ruby about the baby.

Ruby stopped with her spoonful of leek and potato soup half-way to her mouth.

'What, you took him home? To number twenty-seven?'

'To begin with.' Edie's face tightened. 'Got short shrift from her of course. No, Janet's mom's got him. For now, anyroad.'

'Ahh, has she? She's a lovely lady, ain't she? But where's his mom? Dead?'

'I don't know,' Edie said. 'Don't even know where he came from.'

By the late afternoon she felt dizzy with lack of sleep. As soon as the shift ended she tore back to Linden Road without waiting for Ruby, or Janet.

Frances opened the door, finger to her lips.

'Come and see,' she whispered.

She led Edie into the back room, where Marie Falla was knitting by the fire. She was a slender girl, her black hair cut in a bob. She smiled as they came in, nodding towards the fireplace.

'He's been ever so good,' she said.

In the large bottom drawer of a chest, comfortably bedded down, the little boy was sleeping, clean and happily fed, his dark lashes curling above the angelic apple cheeks, mouth gently sucking on his thumb as he slept.

'A thumb-sucker,' Frances smiled.

'He's beautiful, isn't he?' Edie couldn't stop staring at him. She so badly wanted to pick him up and love him, but she knew she mustn't disturb him. 'I'll have to go back and enquire about him tonight, tell the WVS helpers where he is.'

'Yes, of course,' Frances said. 'But there's no need to take him with you at this stage, is there? It's so cold and miserable out there. He's well settled here, and he's been no trouble, Edie, really he hasn't.'

'Thank you ever so much,' Edie said, amazed once again by Frances's kindness. 'I don't know what I'd have done if you hadn't been so good about it.'

'Not at all. Now, come and have a cup of tea while I put some food on. You look absolutely all in, dear. You both had such a night of it. You must go home and try and get some sleep.'

''Til the next air-raid anyway,' Edie said gloomily.

Sipping her hot tea, she looked up at Frances. 'I expect someone'll come looking for him. But if they don't, well, I must look after him. I just must.'

'I know.' Frances looked up from slicing parsnips the other side of the table. 'He's lovely. And you lost your own tiny one. I do understand, dear, how you must feel.' Seeing Edie's eyes fill, she went on, 'Let's just wait and see. But I've been thinking today. I'm sure we could all manage something between us. We all have to do our bit at the moment in whatever way we can. I'm sure I could help look after him until things are sorted out.'

'Oh!' Edie smiled in wonder. 'Thank you. You're so, so kind, Mrs Hatton!'

Seventeen

'You sound blooming cheerful this morning, Ginger,' one
of the other girls observed, as she and Edie walked in for
the morning shift. The various blocks of the works,
swathed in camouflage, loomed around them in the grey
morning. 'Can't say I'm ever up to singing at this time of
day.'

Edie looked round. 'Singing? I never was!'

'Oh yes, you were! Humming, anyhow.'

'Was I? I never even knew I was doing it!'

'Well, someone's put a smile on your face, haven't
they?' the girl said cheekily, and one of the others joined
in as they went in to collect their overalls.

'Go on, tell us, Ginger! Who is 'e? Bit of a Christmas
cracker then?'

Enjoying herself, Edie raised her eyebrows and gave
them an enigmatic smile.

'What you don't know can't hurt you, can it?'

The others 'ooohed' in response.

'Daft pair,' Edie laughed and went to her workroom
to begin the day.

But it was true, there was a song in her heart. It was
two days before Christmas and this month had been the
happiest she could remember in a very long time. Today
she felt especially fresh after a good night's sleep unbroken by the air-raid sirens, but she had been up very
early when David woke, giving him his morning feed and

changing and dressing him. David was her name for him ('He just *looks* like a David,' she told Frances and Janet.) She thought it a nice, solid name, and right for him.

She sat in the kitchen drinking a cup of tea and cuddling him on her lap until he wriggled to be let down to toddle round the room, slipping on the lino in his little wool socks. Once or twice he sat down on his bottom with a bang, screwed up his face in pained surprise, then scrambled up and was off again. The very sight of him filled her with joy and tenderness and she could hardly wait until the end of the shift each day to get back to him and care for him. Over these very few weeks he had become the centre of her life.

In her happiness she pushed to the back of her mind the knowledge that he wasn't really hers. He *felt* like her own, as if he had been a special gift brought to her to guard and cherish. She had been very jumpy in the first fortnight when he was with them. Every knock at the door set her heart pounding: was it someone who had come to find her little boy and take him away? Someone who had more right to him than she did? Such thoughts especially haunted her when she lay down to sleep at night. Who was she to deserve the care of such a beautiful child? What if his mother was alive, perhaps injured, in a hospital somewhere? Poor, heartbroken woman, to have lost her little boy! But no, Edie told herself. She had enquired repeatedly and left her address with the WVS and for the ARP warden in case anyone came to ask about 'David'. But so far, no one had come. He must be an orphan and she was the one to save him. The thought that someone might still come and claim him was almost too painful to think about.

In any case, most of the day was too busy for her to dwell on these thoughts. The other element of her happiness was her inclusion in the Hatton household. After a week of her rushing back and forth with him to and from Stirchley every day, leaving him at the Hattons in the daytime, Frances suggested that Edie rent the fourth bedroom in their house and share it with David. At first she had been nervous of the idea, convinced she would be imposing on them, but Frances and Janet had gone out of their way to make her feel welcome, and soon, delighted, she agreed.

She adored living there, in the neat house, with its cosy kitchen where there was space for a table to sit round for breakfast. In the front parlour was the more formal, though pretty furniture: chintz-covered chairs round the hearth and the piano, which Frances and Janet occasionally played. There were dog-eared hymnbooks from when Frances had been a Sunday school teacher years ago, Mozart sonatas and 'Für Elise'. But best of all Edie liked the snug back room with its cosy old chairs, colourful crocheted blankets draped over them to hide the bald patches. There were bookshelves and a wireless on the side table, and always newspapers and books and Frances's bag of knitting. Edie came home every day with a sense of excitement at the thought of being so comfortable, so kindly treated and in such good company. Often after work she and Janet knelt on the Turkey rug by the fire making toast, warming a dish of butter on the hearth, and eating it with cups of tea and chatting unstoppably while David played on the floor. She'd never sat and talked so much in her life. Marie Falla was pleasant and easygoing and had found a factory job, so she was also working long hours, but when she came home she'd often come and join in.

As well as her fondness for Janet, Edie revelled in being close to Frances, for whom she felt something almost akin to worship. She would have done almost anything for her. Frances also encouraged her drawing and painting, and Edie had begun sketching her portrait, and was reasonably pleased with it, although she was really stronger at nature paintings. She also made herself as useful as she could, feeling that although she was paying rent she owed Frances Hatton far more than money and wanted to make things easier for her. Soon Frances said she didn't know what she'd do without her in the kitchen.

'Janet's never been very handy like you are,' she confided one evening when Edie had prepared the vegetables for dinner. 'You've done those in record time – and with this little chap pulling at your legs all the time. You're into everything, young man, aren't you?' She bent down to stroke David's curls, and straightening up again, said, 'I do want you to know, Edie, what a ray of sunshine he is for me in the house. I know you feel we're doing you a favour, but you are doing us one as well. I don't see much of my grandchildren. Marian, Robert's wife, isn't very family-minded. Having David about lifts one out of all the gloom of these days. And it's very nice to have your company as well, dear.'

Edie smiled, delighted, and thanked Frances yet again.

'I love living here,' she said. 'You feel like family much more than my own do.'

This was the absolute truth, though there were a number of unfamiliar things to adjust to. She loved the calm civility of the household, the kindness shown to everyone who came through the door. And quite a number of people *did* come through the door, many of whom were members of the Society of Friends. They were always very polite and pleasant, but also rather startling. She had still not puzzled out why so many Quakers felt it necessary to dress as if they were about to go on an extended hike over the Cairngorms. There was a Miss Cave who came from time to time who always wore walking boots and a woolly hat, even when invited for tea. And they were so intense and interested in everything that was going on, as if it was all their own personal responsibilty. Never in her life had she met people who talked like that, about their charitable works, as if they thought they might make any difference to the way things were. So far as she had always understood it, things were as they were and that was that. And she was touched by their concern for each other: there had been sad news over the past weeks. Two local families of Friends had been bombed out. In one case no one survived, but in the other every possible help was given by everyone and Edie saw how kind they all were. She was very nervous in their presence to begin with, but as everyone was so nice to her she soon learned to relax. Even with the idea that they were Conscientious Objectors who would rather go to prison or labour on the land than go to war. What her own mother would have to say about that!

One of Edie's favourite times came in the evening, on the days neither she nor Janet were out with the volunteer services. Frances always made sure the accumulator was topped up and they would shut out the dark, cold nights behind the blackout curtains, and gather round the fire-place with cups of tea and the wireless on for classical concerts and shows, Tommy Handley and 'Hi Gang!'

Frances and Janet taught Edie how to play whist and canasta, as her family had never played cards at home, and Marie joined in enthusiastically. Frances usually had knitting on the go, Edie would sit with her sketchpad and they'd would turn the wireless off after the news and sit and talk until bedtime. Marie usually went up first and often Edie and Janet were left downstairs, Frances getting up wearily and saying, 'Now don't stay up too long you two, will you?'

Last night had been one such evening. Janet and Edie had each had a bath, Janet going first and Edie dipping into the same water and the two of them sat curled up in the two big armchairs in their nightdresses making the most of the last heat from the fire. Frances said goodnight soon after ten, smiling at the sight of the two of them drying their hair together, buxom Janet, rosy-cheeked from the hot water, her hair already beginning to corkscrew into curls when only half dry, and Edie with her elfin looks and freckles. She enjoyed the friendship that was blossoming between them. Edie's background was a lot tougher than some of Janet's other friends, Frances thought as she climbed up to bed. She'd seen that triangular scar on the girl's arm and hadn't liked to enquire. Janet had asked though, and Edie said, 'Oh, bit of an accident. When I was small.' Even so, there was something about Edie that made her feel very protective. Sometimes she seemed scarcely more than a child herself, and she was such a sweet girl: she warmed to her more than she ever had Joyce, whom she found a little insipid. She suspected Janet did too, but was too kind to say so.

'Shall I make us a drop of Bournvita?' Janet asked, struggling to tug a comb through her hair.

'I'll do it.' Edie came back in a short time later with two cups of hot chocolate, half milk, half water.

'We'll get a little tree tomorrow,' Janet said. 'Well, Mom'll get it I expect. We can decorate it.'

'Ooh yes!' Edie said, tucking her feet under the hem of her nightdress in the comfortable chair. 'Davey'll love it, won't he?'

'Of course he will.' Janet smiled, seeing the way Edie's face lit up at the mention of him. She had seen Edie transformed over the past month, from a sad, lost waif into a happy, loving young woman. While she rejoiced with her, Janet trembled for her as well. Supposing David were not an orphan. Supposing . . .? She knew Edie was aware of all these fearful possibilities, but they did not often mention them. It was too painful.

Over the past month the two of them had already grown very close. Sometimes Edie felt bad that she didn't see nearly as much of Ruby as she had before, and Ruby had made one or two sharp remarks about it.

'Aren't you my pal any more?'

'Course I am – don't be daft,' Edie told her. 'It's just that now I'm looking after David I've no time. Why don't you come round to Janet's and see us?'

'Can't, can I?' Ruby said crossly. 'What with our mom off tripping the light fantastic all the time. It's just the same as when she was feeling bad nowadays.'

Edie was sorry for her, but it couldn't be helped. If my own child had lived I wouldn't have seen much of her, she reasoned. And she knew Ruby was hoping to have Frank home on leave immediately after Christmas. At least Ruby had a husband. They all had to get through the best they could these days. And Edie knew nothing mattered to her now as much as David did. But Janet, too, was a great source of happiness. She was so energetic and jolly and thought the best of everyone. Well – unless they were men, that was.

She'd been quite taken aback by her new friend's attitude to the opposite sex. When she'd asked her inno-cently soon after she moved in, if she was walking out with anyone, Janet had said, *'No I'm not!'* so emphatically that Edie hadn't dared pursue it any further. She did wonder though whether those un-Janet like tears she and Ruby had witnessed the first day they met her had been caused by a man. After all, Janet was older than her, nearly twenty-six. She must have had some boyfriends by now. And one day, when they were talking in her room, Janet had opened a drawer to fetch out a pair of stockings. Janet's belongings were always in chaos and from amid the jumbled items of underwear in the drawer, a photograph flicked out on to the floor by Edie's feet. She caught a quick glimpse of Janet standing, with windblown hair, on a pier with the sea behind, beside *someone*. The someone was dark-haired and had his arm round Janet's shoulders. Janet picked it up and immediately tore it up, casually dropping it into the waste-paper basket.

'Some silly old thing,' she said laughing. 'I really should have a turn-out.' Edie hadn't liked to ask questions.

'Feels quiet tonight,' Janet said as they sipped their warm drinks. 'Let's hope it lasts.'

The past month had seen more terrible raids, one lasting thirteen hours. Edie and Janet had been at home that night and had spent the night in the Anderson, Edie carrying David and sitting with him in her arms. By morning they were stunned with fear and exhaustion. And on one of the nights of bombing this month, the bridge carrying the canal over Bournville Lane had been hit, so that water poured into D-block at Cadbury's and the basements under the factory. Janet had told her that the wages department was down there and there had been pound notes floating about with the dead cats and pigeons from the Cut.

'Be a nice Christmas present if they leave us alone,' Edie agreed.

Janet, kneeling on the rug by the fire looked at her, head on one side. 'I was wondering, and don't take this the wrong way, but don't you want to spend Christmas with your own family?'

Edie looked down, flushing, fingering the pale blue winceyette nightdress which Janet had given her.

'Would you rather I did?'

'I said don't take it the wrong way!' Janet reached over and squeezed her arm affectionately. For an uncomfortable moment Edie saw her eyeing the scar and she pulled her sleeve down. 'I don't know how many times I've told you, Ma and I love having you here.'

'You're so nice, both of you. I don't deserve you.' Edie stared into the fire. 'But no, I don't want to go to them. I've bought a couple of little things for Rodney and for Florrie's kids but that's all. Florrie's gone back to Coventry now it's quietened down.' Her mom had the room for her now, but she wasn't going back to that chilly welcome. 'I'd much rather stay here, Janet.'

'Good! And Christmas wouldn't feel right without you now. Edie—' Janet hesitated again. 'Your husband, he died around Christmas, didn't he? I realize it must be a sad time for you.'

For the first time, Edie told Janet everything about Jack, about Scottie MacPherson and how Jack's death had come about. Janet shook her head as she listened, her eyes full of sympathy.

'Oh Edie, how tragic. And he sounded so kind-hearted. And then your baby as well!'

'Sometimes I think about how it would have been if they were both alive – Jack and my little boy.' Edie pulled her knees up under her nightdress and stared into the fire. 'Course, Jack'd be away now, like Frank. He'd just joined up. It was the night before he was going off to training camp. Frank was gutted. He was there, you see. I've never seen him like that before. He's a tough sort normally. They were pals at school, he and Jack.'

There was a silence in which they heard rain blowing against the windows and the fire shifted.

'You don't have anyone then?' Edie said.

'I did.' Janet spoke stiffly. 'Well, I mean there've been a number over the years of course. I've been to dances and so on. No one special until the last one.' She broke off.

'Was he the one made you cry?'

'Cry? Oh yes, he made me cry all right,' Janet said harshly. 'You mean that time at the bus stop? I feel so silly now, thinking about it.' She leaned forward. 'Thing is, Mom knows what happened, but we don't say much about it now. You won't breathe a word, will you?'

'Of *course* not.' Edie felt honoured to be confided in.

'He was married, you see.' Seeing Edie's shocked expression she went on hastily. 'I mean I didn't *know*, that was the thing. Not to begin with. He kept stringing me along for quite a time and of course I was mad about him. When I found out I couldn't just let him go like I should have done. Anyway, I did, in the end. Finish it.' She stared sadly into the fire. Edie sensed that she wanted to say more, but she stopped.

'It sounds awful,' she said. 'How could he?'

'I know, and when I look back on it, he was so arrogant about things. So selfish. But I was in love, you see. He was rather handsome and took me out and about. Well, of course he did, he could hardly take me home, could he? He used me and I let it happen, silly little thing. Lied to my mother when I went to meet him, and that's the part I'm least proud of. I don't seem to be a very good judge of men actually. A couple of others didn't treat me especially well. They don't always seem to realize that we have feelings.'

Edie leaned down and put her cup on the floor. 'You'll find someone nice – I'm sure you will.'

'I'm a lot more wary these days I can tell you. I seem to attract married men though. There's one at the depot—' She stopped herself.

Edie waited. 'Go on.'

'Oh, I don't know why I even mentioned him. Except I got sent out with him one night. I thought he had an interesting look at first, but he turned out to be moody and full of himself. And what's more – married.' She shrugged crossly. 'Time's getting on – we'd best get to bed.' She rearranged the cushion in the chair with a bad-tempered punch. 'What annoys me is the way he kept looking at me. I mean why can't men keep their eyes to themselves once they're married? They ought to know how to behave!'

1941

Eighteen

Good Friday (11 April 1941)

They thought it was going to be another quiet night but by nine o'clock the sirens were going. Since December, through the winter of bitter cold and deep snow, there had been a lull in the bombing: no more than a few scattered raids. But now they were back.

In the ambulance depot, Janet and the others looked at each other and there were the usual comments – 'Here we go —' and 'It's going to be one of those nights.'

The ambulances were ready outside. Janet waited with the others. Joyce was there that night, and Janet had seen to her discomfort as she came on duty; so was Martin Ferris. They had coincided on precious few occasions over the past months, and she had never been sent out with him again. Every time they met he was friendly and made a point of speaking to her. They were always part of the group waiting in the depot and she had begun to relax with him more amid the light, bantering conversations, though she found something disconcerting about her encounters with him that she couldn't pin down. He was such a powerful masculine presence, and he did seem to make a point of singling her out, laughing at things she said, attentive in a way which, had he been available, she would have taken for attraction and interest in her. It was the double message she had from him which unsettled her – how dare he behave like this? Now, though, she accepted that this was just how he was. She kept every conversation chatty and impersonal, and because he was bright, interested in life and dedicated to his work, she found she enjoyed his company. He arrived rather late that night, not long before the raid began.

'Evening Janet, Joyce.' He sat down close to them, laying his hat on the table.

'Hello stranger!' Joyce said chirpily. 'We haven't seen you in a long time.'

'We don't seem to have coincided. Actually I've had to cut down my hours – exams are looming.' He did look exhausted, dark rings under his eyes. He rubbed his hands over his face and Janet saw that his right index finger was badly bruised under the nail.

'That looks painful,' she said.

Martin looked down at his hands. 'An example of my joinery skills.' He gave a rueful smile. 'I'm left-handed: cack-handed more like.'

Joyce gave one of her purring laughs. 'What were you trying to do?'

'Oh, just hang up a picture. Nothing too complicated! Can I get either of you a cup of tea?'

Janet said she'd like one and when he came back they chatted about his exams.

'I'm living and breathing *Gray's Anatomy* at the moment,' he said wearily. 'Even dreaming about it some-times – bones, joints.'

'The thigh bone's connected to the hip bone,' Joyce sang.

Martin gave a faint smile, eyes flickering towards Janet for a second. 'Precisely.'

Joyce was in a chatty mood and kept an inconsequential conversation flowing. They weren't really expecting a raid. But when the time came, Janet found herself detailed to go with Martin to an incident in Small Heath.

They drove off into the threatening, lit-up night. Janet tried to close her mind to the noise outside. Martin, who was driving, glanced at her in the darkness of the cab.

'If you could go anywhere you liked now, somewhere really nice, where would you go?'

'Well,' she laughed, grateful for his attempts to distract her. 'If there was no war on, you mean?'

'Oh yes. Ideal circumstances only permitted!'

'France, I think.' She talked in short bursts, shouting above the engine. 'The south of France. Not that I've ever been! I went to Paris once, when I was sixteen. But I hear the south is very beautiful. I'd like somewhere warm and lovely to look at.'

'Sounds perfect,' Martin looked round again briefly for a moment and she caught a glimpse of a smile.

'Where would you go?'

While he paused, considering, there came a huge explosion from the distance.

'My God,' Janet's voice was shrill. For a moment she was overtaken by panic. 'Look, the whole place is going up!'

'Don't think about it.'

Martin's voice came calmly out of the shadows. She could just see his profile under the tin hat, the prominent, almost beak-like nose and full lips. The sight of him moved her and she pushed the feelings away. *You're so damn susceptible*, she scolded herself.

'Anyway,' he was saying, 'I think I'd go to Greece. Back in our ideal world where it doesn't have German troops crawling all over it. Sunshine, lots of history, warm blue seas.'

Janet smiled gratefully, steadied by him. Her nerves uncoiled a fraction, though her stomach felt horrible, acidic. 'I can't think of anything nicer! Lying in the sun –

no air-raid sirens going off – sleeping as long as you like . . .'

'After the war,' Martin said. 'One day . . .'

They skirted the burning centre of the town, swerving round debris and rubble, turning back where a road was blocked by collapsed buildings. They carried casualties from Small Heath. For the next couple of hours there was little conversation except for sharp exchanges and commands, and their attempts to soothe and reassure the injured. Once again Janet was impressed by Martin's calm, capable manner. She felt she could rely on him completely.

On the second trip out they tried to drive through the centre of town but the fire brigade flagged them down. No hope of getting through there, they said. New Street was a mass of melting tar from the flames and there was so little water they were having to siphon it out of earlier bomb craters. There was a chaos of explosions and flame, the roads full of rubble, the air thick with smoke and dust. Familiar landmarks were gone, so that in places it was hard to recognize where they were, flames leaping from within the shells of remaining buildings and the firemen struggling on with hoses in the hellish light. As ever the businesses and residents of the central wards of the city were having the worst time of it.

They were called out again to a central location. By now Janet was so charged up with the activity she was beyond feeling exhaustion. It felt as if the night had been going on for ever, that this was all they would ever do now, keep turning out into the night filled with sound and fire and never sleep. She could feel her face covered with a layer of sweat and thick dust and she took off her specs to give them a quick wipe. Climbing into the van outside the depot, she banged her head, nearly knocking her hat off on the door frame.

'Damn!' Her eyes were watering.

'You all right?' Martin asked, as they set off again.

'Yes,' she said brusquely. 'Of course.'

'I'd say we're a good team.'

'Yes,' she agreed.

'I just hope we've got enough juice in the tank for this jaunt. We might have to resort to the petrol can in the back.'

The call-out was to a residential street, a crammed block of back-to-back houses abutting a factory, where the bottom end of the row had received a direct hit. The impact had brought down the back wall of the works and the far end of the street was a huge heap of rubble. Martin turned the ambulance so they were ready to load up and depart again as soon as possible and the two of them leapt out. Janet saw a stunned huddle of people from nearby houses standing in the road, a woman crying, wrapped in a ragged sheet. Somewhere, a dog was barking frantically. Two bodies had been laid on the street.

'Too late for them!' someone shouted through the confusion as Janet shone her torch on them. They were an elderly man and a girl of about sixteen, faces red with brick dust, nostrils clogged with it.

'Over there!' The warden shouted. 'Never mind them, get Mrs Tennant!' People were round the bombed houses, calling out, trying to pull away the timbers and bricks.

Janet ran back to help Martin pull the stretchers out of the ambulance.

'The warden's got her. She's down there,' Martin pointed. The warden, a woman in her forties, was bending over a body which lay prone in the road.

'This the only one?' Martin asked her as they panted up with the stretcher.

'So far. God knows,' she said desperately. 'It's all such a mess. Can't hear a thing. I wish they'd get back – there'll be more injuries at this rate.'

'You take her feet,' Martin said. Janet lifted the woman's heavy, sagging body. She was half-conscious, moaning with pain.

As they staggered to the ambulance with the stretcher between them, someone shouted, 'There's someone under 'ere – shurrup all of yer!'

The chances of hearing anything with the raid still going on were very slim. As she and Martin turned from putting the woman in the ambulance, Janet felt a sense of hopelessness sweep through her. How many people might there be alive under the rubble of those houses? They needed a heavy clearance team and there was no knowing how long that would take tonight.

The residents of the street evidently felt exactly the same and despite the ARP warden's pleas that they wait for help, had set to, forming a chain to lift the lumps of brick and wood away so far as they could.

'We can't wait here,' Martin said. There were more planes approaching. He and Janet were standing together at the back of the ambulance. 'There're a couple of women over there with bad cuts – we can . . .'

He never finished the sentence. They had just begun to move towards the casualties when Janet felt herself lifted up in a great rush, a whoosh of air hoisting her above the ground like a piece of litter. Abruptly the force of it ceased to hold her up and she was dashed down into a hard sea of rubble. Blackness was the last thing she knew.

*

It was still black when she came to. She had no idea of time, or where she was. The ground was rocking and she tried to put her hands down each side of her, but pain stabbed like a blade through her left shoulder. With her right hand she felt around her. Something hard, the width of her forearm. Beyond, something – someone. She couldn't remember anything except setting out that evening in a ... That was it! She was on a stretcher in an ambulance.

'Martin?' she tried to say, turning her head to her right where someone was lying beside her. Her voice came out as a croak. Her mouth was horribly dry, coated with dust.

She tried again and managed to say his name a little louder.

'Who's that?' she heard. It was a man's voice, sounding as cracked as her own.

'It's ... Janet ... Hatton. I'm Janet.' Perhaps it wasn't Martin. It could be anyone at all.

'Janet.' He repeated it, wonderingly, as if to be quite sure. 'Janet. Janet.'

'Is that you, Martin?'

'Yes. Are you all right?' She felt him moving, and suddenly sensed he had leaned up to try to look over at her, but it was completely dark.

'I don't know.' She found all sorts of things pouring out of her mouth. 'I don't quite know who I am. I don't think Mummy would be very pleased. She's always been very forgiving though. You'd be amazed what's she's like – even over the most terrible things ... I ought to introduce you one day ...' For some reason she started giggling.

'Sssh,' Martin said. 'It's all right. We're going to hospital.' She felt his hand reach out in the dark to reassure her. Inadvertently he laid it on her right breast, and hastily moved it down. 'Don't worry, dear one,' she thought she heard him say. 'Are you in pain?'

'Yes,' she agreed. 'Pain.' As if it was a general condition that she couldn't pin down. 'And cold – my hands ... What about you? How is your little girl? Is she safe? Is she all right?'

'Janet, sssh. I haven't got a little girl. I'm a student, remember? Just be calm. We'll be there soon.'

'Poor Martin,' she said, thinking, how confused he is. He can't even remember his family! A muzziness filled her head and she felt herself sliding away into sleep. As she did so she felt his hand close around her cold one, and she gripped hold of him. They lay in the shuddering darkness, hand in hand.

Nineteen

When, by the morning, Janet hadn't come home, Frances was white with worry. Edie was reluctantly on the point of leaving for work when there was a knock at the door, and Frances flew to open it. Seeing Joyce on the step, Frances's hand went to her mouth with an anguished gasp.

'No, it's all right, Mrs Hatton.' Joyce looked like a ghost, clothes thick with dust. 'Janet's been in a bit of an accident, but she's going to be perfectly all right. I came to tell you because I knew how worried you'd be. They've taken her into Selly Oak Hospital.'

'Oh . . .' Frances steadied herself against the doorframe.

'What happened?' Edie asked.

'I understand it was a landmine – went off streets away from where they were, and they were caught in the blast. But they'll both recover.'

'They?'

'She was with Martin Ferris, another of the volunteers.'

'Thank you ever so much for coming,' Edie said. She saw Frances's face had turned a sickly colour and she went and took her arm. 'Come on,' she said gently. 'Come and sit down.'

'Here, Edie!'

Edie felt her arm grasped tightly as she went down for

her tea break that morning and turned to find Ruby, looking fit to burst with excitement. Once they were settled with their cups of tea, Ruby leaned forward and hissed across the table, 'I've seen the doctor, yesterday evening. And I'm expecting – I'm going to have Frank's babby!'

Edie forced her exhausted features into a smile. 'Oh Ruby, that's lovely news. We'll both have kiddies close in age, won't we? I'm ever so pleased for you!' She hugged her, but a moment later she had to suppress a yawn. Ruby sat back with her arms folded, looking very put out.

'Well, you don't *look* very pleased.' She folded her arms sulkily. '*I'm* happy about it, even if you aren't.'

'Oh, of *course* I'm happy, Cocoa. I'm ever so pleased for you!' she apologized. 'I'm just so tired after sitting in that shelter all night. You awright – not sick or anything?'

'No, I feel all right. So far. Our mom's over the moon.'

'I bet. That's lovely.'

There was a silence. Edie felt a bit sad. There was a bit of distance between herself and Ruby nowadays. She'd become so caught up with the Hattons, with Davey.

'I'm sorry if I'm not very lively today,' she said. 'Only I'm so worried about Janet. She didn't come home last night and she's in the hospital – got caught up in an explosion. I don't know how she is yet. Her mom was in a state this morning and what with the raid last night we've had no sleep . . .'

'Oh,' Ruby said flatly. 'Is she going to be all right?'

'I don't know. We hope so. Her mate Joyce came over and told us this morning, but I don't know exactly what's happened to her yet.'

'I'm sorry to hear that. So I s'pose you'll be going

over there tonight. I was hoping you might come over to ours later – bring David to see our mom. She's going to be in tonight for once.'

'I'm sorry, Ruby – I can't, not tonight,' Edie said distractedly. 'I'll try to get over another time, but I'll be going to the hospital. It's not easy, what with Davey's bedtime. You can't just do what you like when you have a babby, Ruby, that's the thing.'

'No—' Ruby pushed her chair back and stood up. 'Well, you've made that very clear. I don't need a lecture on the subject.'

Ruby went back to work feeling hurt and out of sorts. She'd hugged her news to herself since last night, bursting to tell Edie and see her face. Edie had always been her admirer when they were younger, the one who envied her lively family, who wanted to be like her. If she'd had something to tell Edie, she'd always been able to command her rapt attention.

Now all she's interested in is darling Janet, and that child. It's not as if he's hers! Ruby thought, furiously slamming down another mask. Someone'll come and take him off her sooner or later and then where will she be?

At least she had a husband and was having a baby of her own. She couldn't wait to tell Frank. Things had been going against her lately. Although she was really happy her mom was feeling so much better, Ethel was out gadding about so much now with the 'Lucky Dip Players', as they called themselves, that she was hardly in, so Ruby had almost as much to do as she had had when her mom was ill. And Frank's last leave had been postponed so it was in February, and nowhere near Christmas after all. Then when he came he seemed tired and distracted, and frustrated that they had nowhere of their own to live.

They'd fallen out several times. Still, she thought, he's due home again in a couple of weeks, and now I've got summat to tell him that'll put a smile on his face.

'There's someone to see you,' the Sister said, appearing at the foot of Janet's bed. 'I shouldn't really allow this, but he's very anxious about you.' She beckoned along the ward. 'Be quick now, please. Just a few minutes.'

With her blurred eyesight, Janet saw a tall figure approaching the bed, a dressing-gown over his pyjamas. She tried to sit herself up to put her specs on, but the pain that shot across her collarbone and left shoulder made her cry out. Tears came to her eyes.

'Martin! Oh – ouch!'

'You don't learn, do you? How are you?'

'Groggy. Can you pass me my specs, please?'

Smiling, he leaned over and handed them to her. His right arm was in a sling, there was a bandage round his head, covering one eye, and cuts all over his face. He sat on the bed, looking warily round.

'I'll be in trouble for this, but never mind. Once I'm fully qualified I'll be able to get away with all sorts of things! Anyway, chap along the ward lent me this very nice dressing-gown so I thought I might look respectable enough to come.' He looked at her seriously. 'Are you all right?'

'I think so. They say I've broken my collarbone.' She winced ruefully. 'It's given me renewed respect for every other person who's ever broken their collarbone.' Martin grinned. 'But nothing serious I don't think. What about you?' She looked properly at him. 'Oh, Martin, your arm, is it broken? What about your exams?'

He waved the unplastered left arm. 'Left-handed – remember?'

'But your eye! Oh Lord, it isn't – you haven't . . .?'

'No, I haven't lost my eye. I'd be in a worse state than this if I had, I can assure you. But it is scratched a bit, apparently. I must have got some rubbish in there. Otherwise, like you, by the looks of it – cuts and bruises. I feel as if I've done a few rounds in the boxing ring.'

'Yes, me too. Is mine very bad? I haven't seen myself.'

'I've seen you looking prettier. But they're not deep.'

Janet explored her face with her fingers. 'What on earth happened? The last thing I remember is putting that lady in the ambulance. And the next thing was . . .' She remembered his voice, in the darkness of the ambulance. *Don't worry, dear one* . . . She found herself blushing. Did he remember? Probably not, she told herself. He must have been confused, in shock.

'It was a mine, apparently. Remember the factory at the end of the street? It was over in that direction – quite a way away. We were caught up in the blast.'

'Well, what about all those people from the houses?'

'A couple of them are in here – the ones by the ambulance with us. Evidently the others weren't affected like we were. I mean it picked us up and flung us down again – but left most of them untouched.'

'How extraordinary!'

'Blast can do very strange things. I think it must have been that high wall at the front of the factory. Jolly good job it was intact. There were a lot killed in the streets behind, of course.'

'Goodness,' Janet said thoughtfully. She could hardly take in how close they had been to losing their lives.

There was a silence. Martin crossed one leg over the

other and they both smiled, the moment suddenly awkward.

'Look, I just wanted to clear something up,' he said, clearly embarrassed. 'In the ambulance, you said something about my daughter. You seemed to think I had a child. I don't know if you remember? You were in shock.'

She did remember. She also remembered the feel of her hand in his large, reassuring one.

'You've three children, haven't you? You said the two boys'd been evacuated.'

'When did I say that?' he asked, bewildered.

'Oh, I don't know, ages ago.' She'd never asked him about his marriage, she realized. Somehow she'd never wanted to hear about it.

Martin shook his head, a smile on his lips. 'I really don't know how you got hold of that idea. The boys of the family I'm lodging with have been evacuated, it's true. And the mother's gone to join them now, with the baby – down in Devon. I mean, here am I, studying hard, living like a monk – unfortunately.' He grinned, his one eye full of mischief.

It was her turn to look embarrassed. 'Oh dear. I really have got the wrong end of the stick, haven't I?'

They laughed, which made her groan with pain. Then there was silence and she looked up to see him studying her face.

'And what about you?'

'No,' she said.

'No?'

'No, I'm not married. Not even thinking about it.'

She cursed herself. That had come out wrong. It sounded so offputting!

Martin smiled politely. 'Well, now we've got that sorted out.'

Soon after, he got up. 'Well, I'd better keep in Sister's good books. She might let me come again!' He stood looking down at her and with sudden, professional detachment said, 'You shouldn't take too long to mend. Look after yourself.'

Watching his long figure in the checked dressing-gown as he disappeared along the ward she felt she'd made a right mess of things. She found herself aching for him to come back.

Twenty

'What's up?'

Edie went into the back room in Linden Road, David trotting along beside her as usual, to find Janet staring pensively out of the window, a sheet of paper on the table in front of her, her specs in her right hand, dangling from between finger and thumb. It was nearly two months since her accident, and the bone was nearly healed, though she still wore her left arm in a light sling. The window was open and a bird was singing outside. Edie could see Frances bending over the beds in the garden in a flowing, smock-like garment she had made from an old curtain. 'My grubbing about outfit,' she called it.

Janet turned, putting her specs back on, and held out her good arm for Davey, who ran towards her with a gurgling laugh.

'Hello, darling!' She looked at Edie over his head. 'Why should anything be up?'

Edie smiled knowingly, head on one side and came to sit opposite her. 'I think I know you well enough by now.'

The colour rose in Janet's cheeks. She helped Davey up on to her lap and he reached up to play with the beads round her neck. 'Don't pull those too hard, will you, sweetie? I'm just trying to write a note to wish Martin Ferris luck in his exams. You'd think that was pretty

186

straightforward, wouldn't you? Only I seem to have dried up after "Dear Martin".'

Edie tutted, leaning her chin on her hands. 'I don't know. I just don't understand the pair of you.'

During the week Janet was in hospital Edie and Frances had both met Martin Ferris. Edie was thrilled when she recognized him as the ambulance man who had brought David into St Matthew's that night. For her he had a magic about him for that reason alone. Frances was also charmed by him. Edie could see how nice he was, but found him a bit intimidating. He was very well-spoken and had been kind and polite to her, but she had been rather overwhelmed by his height and striking presence.

One thing she had seen immediately, though, was Martin's special interest in and tenderness towards Janet. To Edie it was obvious that his polite solicitude for her was only the outer shell covering much deeper emotions. After all, why was he there every moment he was allowed to be?

She was touched by the sight of them both when she visited the hospital one evening. Janet was propped on the pillows with her arm strapped up and the cuts on her face beginning to heal, and Martin sat beside her in his navy pyjamas, his face equally scarred, with that dressing on his eye and nursing his own injured arm. They were talking, rather seriously. Then Edie saw Janet's round face break into a grin over something he'd said. She was obviously in love, Edie could see. Yet here they were, two months later, still tiptoeing around each other. In fact Janet had barely seen Martin because he was 'swotting' so hard, and she had insisted on going back to work, even though she could only type with one hand.

'What's he going to do when he's finished?' Edie asked.

'Join up. Army medic, I think.' Janet said bleakly. She winced. Davey had his hands in her curls and was tugging, chuckling away as he did so. 'Ouch, you little brute! Pick on someone your own size!'

Edie smiled adoringly at his mischievous expression. 'Are you bullying Auntie Janet, you little rascal? Come on, down you get. We'll find something else for those busy fingers.' She lifted him down and emptied a little box of wooden bricks on to the floor for him. Returning to the matter in hand, she demanded, 'And you're just going to let him go off, even though you've got a flame alight for him fit to burn the house down?'

'I haven't!' Janet laughed. 'Well – maybe a bit.'

'A bit?' Edie looked sceptical.

'But I really don't know about him. Sometimes I think he feels something for me. In fact I feel sure of it. Then just when I think we're getting close he goes into reverse and we're back to square one again! I'm not really sure if he likes me at all or just regards me with a sort of kind pity, like one of his patients – and I can't exactly ask him, can I?'

Frances came in through the back with a few strands of parsley.

'Ask who what?'

'Nothing,' Janet said hastily. Edie gave Frances a wink and she responded with an *Oh, I see* lift to her eyebrows. Holding up the parsley, she said, 'These'll go nicely with the fish.'

Janet stood up. 'At the rate things are going, parsley'll be the only thing left to eat. That and green potatoes.'

'I've just planted lettuces and beans, dear,' Frances said. 'Do try to be more optimistic.'

*

The food shortages were indeed biting hard. There were queues for almost anything not on ration and the meat ration was down to one and tuppence a week. Over the summer, however, food began to arrive via the convoys crossing the Atlantic and they started to see new things in the shops from America: dried egg, canned beans and evaporated milk. For the time being the raids on Birmingham had decreased so that they were all able to get more sleep, but the nightly bulletins from the wireless were grim. In May the Germans sank the battlecruiser *Hood*. In June they invaded Russia. It seemed to be all bad news.

For Edie, the news hit home less hard than for many other people. She had no husband in the services to worry about: she was insulated by her happiness in living with the Hattons. And she had centred her whole life on David. My son, as she dared to call him now. Even so, there nudged in the back of her mind the terrible questions: was there someone out there who he belonged to? A father in the services, aunts, uncles, who now perhaps believed him to be dead? She forced such thoughts aside. She had tried to find out, hadn't she? And wasn't he well and happy here with her, his new mother? She knew that if she was really to call him her own she should apply to adopt him, but somehow she could never bring herself to begin the process. She was afraid to take the first steps, did not want to draw the attention of anyone in authority to the fact that he was with her, as if by disturbing their life, its safety might disintegrate. All she wanted was to live quietly with him beside her. She loved him passionately, obsessively – he was her life now. It was unthinkable that anyone should take him away from her.

*

Ruby was having a more difficult time. After her first flush of excitement when she'd known she was expecting, the reality of how life was going to be when she had a child, on top of everything else, began to hit home. She couldn't look to her mom to help care for him. Ethel, or 'Mimi', was out most of the time, and when she was in she was usually asleep recovering from a show. Unlike most people who were feeling tired and dragged down by the day-to-day struggle of raids and shortages, Ethel was blooming, losing weight, getting herself dolled up.

The worst of it, though, was what had happened the last time Frank came home on leave. He usually had leave from Bomber Command every six weeks. Of course they had nowhere of their own to live, which put a strain on things for a start. Frank would arrive home, all smart with his cropped hair and airforce blue, and they were shuttling between his mom and dad's house and Ruby's. Mostly they stayed at Ruby's, as Ethel was so often out. This last time, he'd arrived soon after Ruby got in from work and was cooking tea. Hearing him tap the door, she ran to greet him.

'Frank!' She flung her arms round him enthusiastically and he cuddled her back. 'When did you get here?'

'Oh, earlier on. Been round to our mom's. Here—' She had been about to go inside but he pulled her out into the little yard at the back. 'Come on – give us a cuddle. We won't have a chance in there.' He nodded towards the back room from where the boys could be heard yelling in high spirits, and pulled the back door shut behind them.

'I'll 'ave to be quick, I've got the pan on!' They clasped each other tightly and his lips immediately fastened on hers. In a moment his hand was working its way up her plump thigh, rucking up her skirt.

'Ooh, impatient aren't you?' she giggled.

'Don't yer want me then?' He squeezed her breast.

'Course I do. But not now. Oi, stop that! The boys might come out 'ere!'

She heard him tut with annoyance as she pulled away and opened the door to go in.

'Never mind,' she whispered. 'Soon be bedtime. And I've got a surprise for yer.'

'What?' he asked, rather grumpily.

'You'll see. Wait 'til later.'

Her brothers looked round, rather awe-inspired by the sight of Frank in his uniform sitting at the table with them. The younger ones' eyes followed his every move as he took off his jacket with a muscular shrug and hung it over the back of the chair. And he was not very friendly towards them. He seemed edgy and morose and Ruby noticed how dismissive he was of George. To a man in Bomber Command, the blokes in reserved occupations were having a cushy time of it. Ruby felt tense with them all there. If only they had a place of their own and a bit of privacy! But I'll cheer him up, she thought, when we can get upstairs on our own.

They at least had the bedroom to themselves, as Ethel was out. The Lucky Dips were doing a show for the night shift at the Austin works. But having the boys next door through the thin wall made it impossible to relax together. Ruby undressed quickly, feeling suddenly shy as Frank seemed so tense and distant from her. She slipped on her nightdress and got into bed. The springs creaked horribly and Frank tutted angrily. Ruby lay with her dark hair spread over the pillow and watched him undress in the candlelight. His body was lean and muscular, skin gleaming in the shadowy light. She felt excitement rise in her as she watched him. What a figure of a man!

191

'Come on,' she patted the bed. 'In 'ere, gorgeous.'

Without a word he came and looked down at her for a moment, his face expressionless. Then he climbed in. The springs shrieked.

'Jesus Christ!' he muttered furiously. 'What a home-coming.'

'Never mind, it don't matter.' Ruby stroked his chest, trying to relax him. 'Come on, we'll make you feel better.'

Their lovemaking didn't take long. Once they'd dispensed with the last of their clothes, Frank had barely touched her before he was pushing Ruby on to her back and thrusting into her with sharp, aggressive movements until he climaxed with a groan, head flung back, arms braced rigid. She wanted to tell him to be careful. What if he hurt the baby? But she might as well not have been there. He climbed off and lay on his back, reaching for cigarettes and lighting up. He smoked in silence. There wasn't room for Ruby to lie on her back as well, so she lay squashed on her side, watching him. A lump came into her throat. She was so lonely, coping on her own all the time, even though she tried to make the best of it. Her mom was no help: Edie did her best to be a pal, but she was so thick with Janet now. Frank was the one who was supposed to make it all right. He was her husband, after all! Why didn't he take her in his arms and say he loved her? How could she tell him they were going to have a baby when he was like this?

'Frank?' She kept her voice soft and even, though she felt so sad, the beginnings of her own desire burning unsatisfied between her legs.

He turned his head a little. 'What?'

'I've summat to tell yer. A surprise.'

'Yeah, you said. What?' He didn't sound very interested.

'Frank!' It came out almost as a wail. 'Look at me, won't yer? Give me a cuddle, eh?'

He stubbed out the last of his cigarette and turned over, putting his arms round her. She snuggled against him, reassured.

'Guess what?' she said into his chest. 'I've been dying to tell you, only I wanted you to be here. I found out, last week – I'm expecting, Frank. We're going to have a little babby of our own!'

There was no reaction for a moment. Then he moved over on to his back again and gave a long sigh. Ruby was cut to the heart.

'Well, say summat. Aren't you pleased?'

Frank pushed back the covers and sat on the edge of the bed. He lit another cigarette and breathed out the first lungful of smoke. 'When?'

'November, the doctor said.'

There was silence, then again she heard him say, '*Christ.*'

'Frank!' Ruby couldn't hold back her tears any longer. She sat up and touched his back. Why didn't he take her in his arms and tell her how pleased he was? Why was he being so cold and cruel? 'I thought you'd be happy, us starting a family. It's your little babby, Frank, maybe a son for yer! Oh tell me you love me and you're pleased?'

He got up with a wild movement and went to the window, pushing back the curtains and forcing the sash up, Ruby almost thought he was going to jump out.

'Frank!'

'I never bargained for all this.' He turned round, abruptly. 'I mean when we got married I wasn't thinking straight. I never thought how it'd be. Coming back 'ere, nowhere to call our own, no freedom. And then a screaming kid on the way. I can't do this, Rube. I feel trapped. I can't breathe.'

Ignoring her sobs, he snatched up his clothes and hastily put them on.

'I'm going to our mom's. I can't even 'ave a bed to meself in 'ere.'

'Oh Frank, don't leave me.' She got up to try and stop him.

'*Don't.*' He pulled away from her. 'Look, Rube, I'll see yer around. Give me a chance for it to sink in, all right?'

And he was gone, down the stairs. She heard the back door bang shut, his footsteps along the street. Ruby lay in bed with her arms wrapped round herself for comfort, sobbing wretchedly.

Mrs Gilpin let Frank in, her hair up in pins.

'What're yer doing back 'ere, son?' she asked quietly, seeming to guess the answer already.

'There ain't no space over there. I've come 'ome for a good night's sleep.'

She didn't get any more out of him, and looking knowingly at him she went back to bed.

Frank lay in his room, smoking one Woodbine after another. Jesus, what a mess! Here he was, his first months away from home in the forces, first taste of life's possibilities, even in one of the most dangerous jobs in the world, he reckoned. And here he was saddled with a wife and a babby on the way. What had possessed him to get married?

He knew what it was in his heart. Marriage was where you got what you needed without having to go looking, wasn't it? And Ruby had offered it, with her ripe body and those 'come hither' eyes, and wouldn't give it him unless they were married, but it wasn't marriage he really wanted. Not all that daily grind and blarting brats. Especially now. Every mission he flew might be his last. His mind drifted inevitably to Monnie, one of the young WAAFs at the base, fresh from Lancashire. What had happened when he was teaching Monnie to drive that truck. Monnie was offering what he needed all right, plenty of it. And so far as he could see, he could have that without bothering with marriage at all.

Twenty-One

By the summer of 1941, war had become a way of life. As well as the rationing coupons and queues for food outside the shops, now clothing was on the ration as well. At work, the chocolate still produced at the factory was scaled right down, and powdered milk used to replace the gallons of milk which used to pour into the factory every day.

Edie, Ruby and Janet were all working long hours, and Edie and Janet were still volunteers. Edie helped out with clothing distribution for the WVS once a week now, leaving Davey safely with Frances. There was not a lot of free time, but as the weeks went by the three of them found themselves more and more in each other's company.

One sultry evening, Janet answered a knock at the door in Linden Road, to find Ruby on the step.

'Oh, hello!' Edie, in the back room, heard the surprise in Janet's voice. 'Come in.' Ruby came through to where Edie was cuddling Davey, giving him a last drink of milk before bed.

''Ello Rube! What're you doing here? Is your mom at home tonight then?'

Ruby nodded gloomily. 'And George.' Ruby sank down on a chair beside the table. She was five months pregnant, now, the little bump well visible through her pink frock, and she felt very tired by the end of each day.

'We're s'posed to be rehearsing for the play tonight. I've let them down, but I'm just not in the mood. I hope you don't mind me turning up.'

Edie was puzzled. Ruby loved the Drama Club, and usually she'd do anything to avoid missing a rehearsal.

'You're welcome any time, you know that,' Janet said. 'Can I get you a cup of tea?'

'Oh, I'd love one,' Ruby said.

Janet smiled at Edie as she went into the kitchen. She was pleased Ruby had come round. Numerous times they'd talked about Ruby being a bit jealous of their friendship, and Janet didn't like to feel she'd come between two old friends, even if she did find Ruby prickly towards her.

'Where's her mom?' Ruby whispered to Edie.

'Frances? Oh, upstairs, having a bath I think. What's up, Rube? You all right?'

To her astonishment, Ruby burst into tears. Janet heard her and came back in and Edie laid the sleepy David down in the armchair. They drew up seats either side of Ruby and tried to comfort her.

'This isn't like you, Rube!' Edie put her arm round Ruby's shaking shoulders. 'Oh, it must all be so hard for you. Are you missing Frank?'

Frank had been back the week before for another few days' leave. So far as Edie knew, both this visit and the one before had gone off well. Ruby hadn't felt able to tell them the truth, but now she couldn't hold back any longer. She shook her head, crying miserably.

'Frank's not happy about the babby,' Ruby sobbed. 'When I told him last time he came home, he went all funny with me and moved out to his mom's. I thought it was just the shock of it – you know, getting used to it. And he came back the next day and was all right. Tried

197

to make the best of it. But when he come back this time he was so cold and cross with me. And I think he's got someone else. I mean he called me "Mon" by mistake and I shouted at him, "Who's this Mon?" and he just laughed it off and said I was getting upset over nothing and 'e'd said "Mom". But 'e 'adn't.' She stopped to blow her nose, saying wretchedly through her hanky, 'I mean, why would he say that?'

'Oh Ruby!' Edie wanted to tell Ruby she was imagining things, that Frank would never do such a thing, that her imagination was running riot because she was alone and expecting a baby. But she had a horrible misgiving that Frank was perfectly capable of behaving like that, and all the more so now, with the strain all those blokes were going through in Bomber Command, far away from home.

'I don't know what I'm going to do,' Ruby cried. 'I mean even if Frank was happy about it, he's still not here. How am I going to manage when the babby arrives? Our mom's no good and there's no one else. Me auntie's too far away to help and she wouldn't want to anyhow. I'll have to give up my job – I'll lose my wages, and the factory's the only place I get out to and see anyone. I think I'll go mad at home on my own!'

'You don't have to give up work, do you?' Janet said. She took Ruby's hand and squeezed it. 'If you could find someone to look after your baby?'

Ruby shook her head. 'I don't know. I can't think straight. Last week was so hard with Frank and I can't get anything sorted out in my mind. I just feel all mithered.'

'Look.' Janet stood up. 'You just try and calm down. The kettle'll have boiled. I'll make us a nice cup of tea and we'll all try and put our heads together. You shouldn't be having to worry about all this on your own.'

By the time the tea was brewed, Frances had emerged from upstairs in her dressing-gown, combing out her wet hair. She looked a little taken aback to find a visitor in the house, but seeing Ruby's tear-stained face she immediately looked concerned. Edie was, once again, filled with gratitude for her kind nature. They drank Frances's favourite Mazawattee tea, nibbled a biscuit and talked about Ruby's dilemma.

Ruby explained about her mom's job with ENSA, and the irregular hours she kept. 'To be honest with yer, Mrs Hatton, she isn't that reliable when she's around, bless her. She's worse than the lads in some ways.'

Frances smiled faintly at Ruby's assessment of her mother.

'Well,' she began slowly, 'what I can suggest is this. Once your baby's born and old enough to be left with someone – when it'll take a bottle and so on – if you're agreeable, you could bring it to me. I'm already looking after Davey here. I know how to look after small children. That's at least something I can do while we're in this terrible state of war. I'm doing precious little else.'

Janet beamed at Frances, then jumped up and kissed her. 'That's a marvellous idea! Do you really think you could cope?'

'I think so,' Frances said with dignity. 'I'm not quite in my dotage yet, dear. And there are you two, and Marie about – well, occasionally!' She rolled her eyes. Marie Falla was courting and barely ever seemed to appear for more than bed and breakfast these days.

'Oh, Mrs Hatton!' Edie said excitedly. 'Isn't that a wonderful offer, Ruby?'

Ruby looked amazed, as if what Frances had said wasn't sinking in.

'D'you mean it? Would you really? Oh, that would just solve all my problems! Well, some of them, anyhow.' She wiped her eyes. 'It's a lot for you, though,' she added doubtfully. 'What with all the hours we're doing.'

'Well, I'm already getting back into the swing of it with David,' Frances said, pulling back her magnificent hair and knotting it loosely at the back of her neck. 'I'm sure I'll be able to manage – it'll help keep me young. And a couple of my friends from Meeting are looking after grandchildren. We can join forces and help each other.'

Ruby was full of thanks and renewed hopefulness as she drank her tea, and already she and Janet were more at ease with each other.

'When Frank sees the babby, he'll feel differently, I expect,' she said, suddenly full of optimism.

Well, Edie thought, we'll see, won't we? I hope so for your sake, girl. But she glowed with happiness herself as she looked round the room at her friends, and at her boy with his long lashes and curling hair fast asleep on the seat of the armchair.

Martin called round at the house at last. Edie saw Janet's startled look when her mother came in and announced who was at the door. She quickly recovered herself.

'Well, ask him in then, Mother!' She stood up, smoothing her clothes, taking a quick glance in the mirror over the fireplace. Edie watched, pleased for her. Perhaps Martin had called to ask her out. Maybe at last they'd talk to each other properly.

A moment later Martin, hat in hand, was being shown

into the parlour and Frances was offering tea. 'I'll just find Janet,' she said. To Edie's amazement she heard him reply, 'I do hope you'll join us, and Edie if she's here. It'd be nice to see you all.'

Janet and Edie exchanged glances. Edie thought Janet must be disappointed and she flushed slightly, but they both went into the front. Martin was quite casually dressed, no tie, a light jacket over his flannel trousers. As he stood up to greet them, Edie saw his gaze fasten immediately on Janet.

'We haven't seen you for a long time,' she said, with calm formality.

'I know,' he said. 'I'm sorry.' They all sat down. 'I've been completely embroiled in final examinations. Burning the midnight oil night after night. There's so much to retain, you feel your head's going to explode. But it's over now, finally. I've been home for the last week.' He talked about his visit to his parents in Staffordshire as Edie helped Frances bring the tea in.

'Anyway, they've rushed all the marking through and the good news is, I've passed!'

'Oh, marvellous!' Janet said, delighted for him. Already she was beginning to come alive in his presence. The others added their congratulations as well. 'So you're a doctor now?'

'I am.' Martin grinned. He sat forward, stirring his tea, looking very large and muscular. 'At least, so they tell me. Bit of an awesome thought really. But the thing is, soon as I qualified, I received my call-up papers. Medical Corps. RAMC. I leave for basic training on Friday.'

It was Wednesday night. Edie saw the barely concealed expression of dismay on Janet's face.

'So,' she managed to ask composedly, 'do you know where you're going?'

'Somewhere near Leeds. Square-bashing and all that sort of thing. I don't quite know why medics need that but I suppose it's meant to instil discipline!' He laughed. 'Cuts us all from the same cloth, I suppose.'

As they drank their tea he didn't seem to want to dwell on his news.

'Where's little David? Asleep?'

Edie smiled. 'Out like a light.'

'I'm sorry to have missed him. I suppose I feel a slightly paternal interest in him after having him handed over to me like that. No news of his background so far?'

Edie shook her head. Such questions filled her with dread. She wanted to forget that David had any other 'background' than with her.

'And he's in good health then?'

'Oh yes,' she enthused. 'He's bonny, isn't he?' Frances and Janet nodded.

Martin smiled at Edie's evident besottedness. 'He's been much luckier than some.'

They spent a pleasant evening catching up on news of aquaintances. They told him about Ruby and about a picnic Cadbury's had arranged for the day out in a pretty Worcestershire village. Edie had loved watching Davey's face as he caught his first sight of cows, and a bull. But all the time they were talking, Edie was thinking, doesn't he want to be with Janet on her own? Janet was behaving in a very breezy manner, as if he was like any other friend whose company she enjoyed. Edie was baffled by the pair of them.

Eventually Martin got up. 'I must let you people get to bed. It's been lovely to see you all.'

'Janet, you show Martin out, will you?' Frances said.

Martin shouldered his coat on in the hall. Janet, going to open the front door, could feel her heart beating madly and hoped he couldn't tell. You are *not*, she chastised herself, going to make a fool of yourself. Not again. Close to him, in the confined space, she felt weak-kneed and as if all the hairs on her skin were standing upright. But she had no excuse for delaying him.

'Just a second.' He laid his hand over hers to prevent her undoing the latch. She looked up at him, seeing his strong-featured face so close to hers, looking into her eyes.

'I wondered if I might write to you, while I'm away? I'd love to hear from you, of course. It would mean a lot to me.'

'Write?' She almost laughed. *Write to me?* I want you to take me in your arms and kiss me. I want, I want . . . She smiled. 'Yes of course, Martin. I'd love it if we could keep in touch. Drop me a line, won't you, and let me know where to write to?'

She opened the door. He leant down and kissed her on the cheek. Stepping outside, he put his hat on and turned to wave.

'Good luck!' she called.

'Bye!' His voice was soft. And then he was gone.

Janet put her hand over her cheek where she could still feel the touch of his lips, tears welling in her eyes.

Twenty-Two

Ruby's daughter was born on 10 November at Selly Oak Hospital. As soon as Edie and Janet heard the news they went in to see her.

They found Ruby sitting up in bed in a frilly bedjacket, hair brushed and hanging loose, lipstick and mascara on. Edie kissed her and hugged her close.

'Hello Cocoa!' she said fondly. 'Congratulations! Are you all right?'

'I'll live.' Ruby gave a wry grin, shifting herself up on the pillows. 'My God—' She rolled her eyes. 'Never again though. I can tell yer that. It's like being put through the mincer!'

'You look very well on it,' Janet said, handing over her little posy of winter greenery and flowers. 'We brought you these from the garden to brighten the place up a bit.'

'Oh I don't know if I'll be allowed those,' Ruby said. 'The matron's a right tartar. She's already had a go at me about my warpaint. And I'm *dying* for a fag.'

They stayed for a while, hearing all about the birth and Ruby's new little girl who'd weighed seven pounds ten ounces and was feeding like trooper.

'She's definitely a Bonner with an appetite like that on her,' Ruby laughed.

'What're you calling her?' Janet asked.

'She's going to be called Marleen Bette. After Marlene Dietrich, only I'd thought we'd say it the English way.'

'And Bette Davis?' Janet asked.

'Yes,' Ruby grinned. 'How did you guess?'

'Have you asked Frank?' Edie asked.

'No I bloomin' ain't.' Her face hardened into defiance. 'He'll just have to like it, that's all.'

They didn't stay long. Ruby recounted to them a few funny stories about people on the ward and Edie told her odd bits of chat from work. Then the nurses started to bring the babies to be fed and they caught a glimpse of young Marleen Bette as she was carried squawking to her mother.

'Oh Ruby, she's lovely!' Edie cried, seeing the baby's crumpled face. She felt her whole being contract with longing. Thank God she had David to fill her life now! How could she have stood seeing this little one without terrible bitter feelings if he had not come into her life?

'She looks beautiful and healthy,' Janet said. 'Well done again, Ruby.'

Edie was startled to hear the tearful edge to Janet's voice.

As they were leaving, and Ruby saw Edie and Janet disappear with a final wave along the ward, she latched Marleen on to feed. Sharp pains shot through her nipples and belly as the baby began to suck. My God, she cursed, this is a mug's game. Why does it have to hurt so much? Through the tears in her eyes she watched the others disappear, Edie's petite figure followed by Janet's egg-timer one, through the doors.

Well done, Ruby, she thought bitterly. Looking down at her baby – *my baby*, she kept having to remind herself, she tried to summon more positive emotion in her. Had she really given birth to the child? The birth now seemed like a long and painful dream and she'd hardly seen Marleen since except to feed her. I *do* love her, she told herself. Except she hurts me. The child's nagging mouth on her breast oppressed her. Someone else to look after, day after day. Work and washing and feeding and never a moment to herself, years stretching ahead. Edie was the lucky one, she found herself thinking, losing her babby like that. Oh what a wicked thought! How could I even think it? But if only Frank was here to look after us!

Lately, Frank seemed like a different person whom she barely knew, with his stubbly hair and tense, terse manner. When he was home they spent some of the time together, made love sometimes. Only it didn't feel like love: she felt used, dirty almost, and was relieved when his selfish thrusting was over.

The larger she grew with the baby the more enraged he seemed by the sight of her, and numerous times he'd left her weeping in her house when he'd taken off to his mom's again, leaving her rejected and lonely.

In the end Ruby voiced her suspicions. 'You're going with another woman, aren't you?' she screamed at him one night. Frank denied it, told her not to be so 'cowing stupid', but things were never easy between them.

He had said though that his tour of duty would be over this year. The Bomber squadrons flew thirty 'ops', as he called it. These only counted as completed when they had attacked the right targets. Then he'd be rested and given another job for a few months. Things would be better then. Ruby did not really understand the full nature of the work but she knew he was living on his nerves on that airbase, doing such dangerous flights. It wasn't natural.

Ruby stared down at her daughter, trying to get to know her, to feel part of her. At least she'd had a girl and she could dress her in some pretty things when she was a bit older.

'Marleen,' she whispered. 'However're we going to get by?'

Maybe, she thought desperately, when the tour was over and Frank wasn't under such strain they could start again. Maybe it wasn't too late? She had to believe that, or she'd go mad.

Edie's hard-won happiness was all the more precious to her when set against the gloom all around. On 7 December the Japanese attacked Pearl Harbor, bringing America into the war. There was grim news coming from so many quarters of the world. But in her own life things seemed to get better all the time.

David was growing and thriving. They had got into a routine. Frances seemed content and went to the welfare every week for Edie to collect his cod liver oil and orange juice. She looked after him very well in the day and Edie came and took over every moment she could. Now Ruby had her little Marleen they saw a lot more of her as well. The week before Christmas, Ruby's mom, 'Mimi', and the Lucky Dip Variety Players had come to Cadbury's for a lunchtime performance and Ruby had popped in with them for a visit. They sat in the dining-room as the troupe ran through their songs, sketches and corny jokes. When Mimi got up, caked in lashings of eye make-up and wearing a marvellous aquamarine costume which was a joyous contrast to 'utility' clothing, Edie, Ruby and Janet led the cheering.

'I'm going to start with a medley of Sunshine Songs to brighten you all up!' she called out to the audience, and they all applauded and whistled enthusiastically. Edie was impressed at the way Mimi belted out her songs, throwing in a few gentle dance steps to the accompaniment of the piano, holding out her full skirt: 'On the Sunny Side of the Street', 'You Are My Sunshine' and 'The Sun Has Got His Hat On'. Everyone was soon clapping along.

'She's marvellous!' Janet said to Ruby, who blushed with reluctant pleasure. Edie could see Ruby warming more and more to Janet and this also made her happy. There was only one person she wanted to see happier now and that was Janet herself. Janet, who was so kind to everyone else. Martin had written to her from Leeds and he was now with his parents in Staffordshire. Edie was convinced he felt more for Janet than he was letting on, so what was the matter with him? Why didn't he tell her before some other terrible thing happened in this war and it was too late?

Over the past couple of months Martin had done his basic training at the RAMC depot in Leeds and then been moved to Oxford, from where he told Janet he was being given instruction in tropical medicine. He wrote to her regularly, every week, telling her all sorts of everyday details about his training and the two different cities to which he'd been sent. Of his heart he said very little, except that he missed her company. At first Janet was disappointed. She saw such warmth in his eyes when he looked at her – surely he felt *something* for her? And yet he wrote to her like an old friend, a *chum*, she sometimes thought, when she had wondered whether, on paper, he might say more to her that he couldn't say face to face. At first his letters sent her into a state of frustrated longing every time they arrived. I love you, she raged to him in her head. Don't you love me? If so, why don't you say so?

Occasionally she wept, missing him, wanting to know

how he really felt. But she knew she mustn't say anything first, oh no, definitely not! She'd done far too much making a fool of herself in her life already. And after a few weeks she forced herself to be calmer and more accepting. Martin obviously regarded her as a friend and nothing more. In any case, he'd soon be posted abroad somewhere and she might never see him again, so she should stop mooning over him and accept things as they were. But her heart ached at the thought.

She had a letter wishing her and her family a happy Christmas and saying he was coming to Birmingham just before the New Year, and might he please call and see her? As she read the letter the corners of her lips curved up in pleasure. She looked up to find Edie watching her.

'Martin?' Edie asked, smiling.

Janet nodded, pressing the letter to her heart without realizing what she was doing. 'He's coming – next week!'

Edie shook her head in mock despair.

The night he came, they heard his motorcycle before he ever knocked the door. It was already eight o'clock at night.

'Mother, will you answer it, or you, Edie?' Janet said, all flustered. 'I don't want him to think I've been camping on the doormat!'

'I'll go,' Edie opened the door into the cold darkness to find Martin looming on the step, collar up, his face wrapped in his scarf except for his eyes and nose, and his helmet under one arm.

'Oh my word!' Edie exclaimed. 'It's a good job we was expecting you or you'd've scared the life out of me in that get-up! Come on in, quick – you must be frozen.'

'Hello, Edie,' there was laughter in his muffled voice. 'Brrr – it's perishing out there.' As she closed the door he unwound the scarf from his head. His large nose was pink with cold but he looked very fit and, in his khaki uniform, even bigger than she remembered. He leaned down and kissed her on the cheek.

'Nice to see you.'

Janet stood up as he came in, cheeks red. Although she'd tried to fasten her hair back securely, tendrils of it were escaping as ever and hanging in little coils round her cheeks. For a moment her legs wouldn't seem to do what she wanted them to, but she forced them to move.

'Martin!' Her voice sounded over-jolly and she held out her hand. Martin took it, but pulled her closer and kissed her cheek as he had done Edie's.

'Hello, Janet – how are you?' He looked intently into her eyes and she felt her blushes deepen. For goodness sake, stop being so dippy! she roared at herself in her head. He's probaby just come on a courtesy call.

'Very well,' she told him. 'And you look terrific! Army life must suit you.'

Martin laughed and greeted Frances, who shook his hand and added, 'She's missed you, you know.'

'Shall I make us some tea?' Edie said. 'It might be rather weak, I'm afraid.'

As they sipped their tea Martin regaled them with tales of army life, some of which Janet had heard in his letters. Frances asked if he knew where he was going next and he said no, but he was due to go in a couple of days. The destination was a secret. He asked them all about themselves and Edie took him up to have a peep at Davey, who was asleep.

'My goodness, how he's grown!' Martin whispered. 'You're obviously doing a fine job with him.'

Edie smiled, full of pride. When they went back downstairs Frances said, 'Edie, why don't we go up for the night and leave Janet and Martin to talk for a while?'

Janet felt as if her heart was going to clamber out of her chest. She was grateful to her mother, knew what she was trying to do, but how embarrassing! Suppose Martin had nothing whatever to say to her and was now being forced into her company! He hadn't even sat down again, as if he was impatient to be off, and was saying, 'Oh, there's no need for that. I don't want to chase you out of your own sitting-room.' Janet looked into the fire, almost unable to control her disappointment. But then she heard him go on, 'But I did wonder, I know it's very dark out there and cold, but Janet, would you fancy a little walk?'

She looked round, beginning to smile. 'Now?'

'Yes. I know it's not much of an invitation, but it may be some time before I see you again.'

Outside, well wrapped up, they stepped cautiously over the icy ground. It was a cloudy night, raw and still, and hard to see far ahead.

'Here, be careful,' Martin said, taking her arm. They walked slowly down the hill towards Bournville Green, helping to hold each other upright. Janet felt the strangeness of this sudden physical closeness when mentally they still seemed a long way apart.

'Perhaps this was a bad idea,' Martin suggested as they slithered along by the light of his little torch.

'No!' Janet felt she'd protested too abruptly. 'No, it wasn't. It's just rather bad underfoot, isn't it?'

There was a brief silence, then he said. 'Is everything all right? Your mother looks well, and Edie. She's making a very fine job of looking after David.'

'Yes, Mother's fine. Really very purposeful actually. And Edie's happy I think. Certainly happier than she was. In a way I worry for her . . .'

'Why's that?'

'Well.' Janet realized she hadn't put this thought into

words before. 'Her own family situation isn't very happy, you know. D'you know, she only popped in to give her brother a little present on Christmas Day and her mother was so unpleasant. And what with losing her husband and her own child she's had a very rough time of it. Now she's got David she's completely wrapped up in him. Besotted really. I just worry that if anything was to happen. I mean, that night, when you took him in from the warden, he said there was no one else didn't he?'

'All I remember, in the confusion of it all, is that he said there'd been a direct hit. I'm not sure exactly where, and I've no idea how David came to be outside. But the warden knew where we were taking him and really, if no one's come forward by now, it's very unlikely.'

'I know. I just worry for her sometimes. It's funny – I didn't even know her before the war, and now our lives have become so mixed up in each other's. And Ruby's – she lives under a lot of strain really, you know.'

As she talked about her concern over Ruby and Frank, they reached Bournville Green, the pretty, open space between the Day Continuation School and the shops and Cadbury factory on the other. In the middle of the green stood a round building called the Rest House, with an overhanging roof round it under which were benches. They went and sat down, facing back towards the Friends' Meeting House.

'So what about Janet?' Martin said gently. 'Who's going to look after you?'

The bitter thought stole through her mind, *well not you, obviously, since you're not going to be here.*

'Oh, Mother and I get on all right, you know.'

She could feel him looking at her in the darkness. She felt vulnerable, suddenly petulant. Was he playing with her?

'Don't you have room for anyone else in your heart?'

'Yes.' She looked away, across the Green. 'But I don't seem to notice an orderly queue forming at the front door.'

Martin gave a low chuckle. 'Have you any idea,' he said, 'how completely terrifying you are?'

Terrifying? Her? Bumbling, funny old Janet? It was so preposterous that she burst out laughing.

'What on earth are you talking about?'

'Well...' Her breath caught as she felt him gently removing her hat, his bare hand stroking the right side of her face, her hair. 'Ever since I've known you you seem to have had a big sign pinned across your chest saying, "Trespassers will be prosecuted".'

'Have I?' She felt rather injured by this accusation. Was it her fault he had been so reserved? Hadn't she put on a suit of armour after Alec, determined not to make a fool of herself or let her feelings show again? 'I'm sorry,' she said abjectly. 'It's just – I'm not all that good at this, that's all.'

He stopped stroking her face and took her hand. 'If I wasn't being posted, goodness knows whether I'd've found the courage even by now.' His voice came to her, half teasing, half serious. 'Thing is, I didn't want to rush anything or push you – especially after the night that mine went up. We were both in shock. But also, I've seen my own sister, Mary, rush into things when it was quite wrong. Her marriage has been a disaster and it's made me very cautious of mucking up anyone's life like that.' His voice came out in nervous bursts. 'But the thing is I am going away and I've no idea for how long. I couldn't bear to go without telling you how much you've come to mean to me – what I feel for you, and I wondered whether there was any chance of you feeling the same?'

213

'Oh Martin.' There were tears of relief in Janet's voice, although she was so happy. 'All this time I thought you didn't really think much of me, and I love you so much I don't know what to do with myself sometimes! Oh dear, and I'm saying too much again – I told you I'm hopeless – a lost cause.'

'No,' he laughed, 'not hopeless. You're so lovely my dear one—' He drew her into his arms and held her close, laughing with happiness. 'D'you know, I couldn't stop looking at you from the very first night I saw you. There's something so captivating about you.'

'But you were married then,' she teased, 'so far as I knew.'

'Ah, yes, well!' He kissed the top of her head. 'I do love you. God, I do.'

'And I love you.' She snuggled into his greatcoat, her arms round his waist, and looked up at him, just able to make out the shape of his face in the darkness. She felt somehow as if she'd known him always. 'Oh Martin, I'm so happy.'

'My lovely one.' His large hand caressed her head. She reached up and found his lips searching urgently for hers.

1943–5

Twenty-Three

September 1943

'Oh dear,' Frances sighed, looking at the little blonde child curled in the armchair. 'She's dead to the world now – I can't make her stay awake any longer.' She eased herself out of her chair and went to lay a shawl over Marleen's sleeping form. 'And no wonder,' she whispered. 'It's gone nine.'

'We might as well just put her to bed,' Janet said, looking up from a skein of knitting. 'Honestly, Ruby really is the end.'

'I'm ever so sorry,' Edie said, kneeling down beside Marleen. She felt very tense and guilty. Frances had been so generous in looking after Marleen and now Ruby was letting them all down.

'Don't be silly—' Frances touched her shoulder as she passed. 'It's not your fault, dear. Look – we can settle her in with Davey upstairs. You wouldn't mind, would you, Edie? There's no point in Ruby waking her and going home just to bring her back first thing. I'll go and sort the bed out.'

'Honestly, I could throttle Ruby!' Edie hissed to Janet across Marleen's head. 'Putting your mom out like this. What the hell's she playing at?'

'I think we know what she's playing at.' Janet pushed her needles into the ball of navy wool and laid it aside. 'And, in some ways, the way her marriage has gone you can hardly blame her.'

217

'Oh yes, you can blame her!' Edie fumed. She felt so obliged to Frances after all the help she had received. She couldn't bear the way Ruby was taking advantage of the situation. 'I know Frank's never been much of a husband to her but little Marleen's not even two years old – she should be the one she puts first and she doesn't seem to give her a thought, gadding off here there and everywhere. No wonder the child's such a little madam. I think it's terrible – and we've given Ruby the benefit of the doubt enough times. She's taking advantage of your mom's kindness and I can't see it go on any more.'

'Mum is looking a bit tired,' Janet conceded.

'Of course she is. Wouldn't anyone be after a day with Marleen and her tantrums? I mean it's enough having Davey but at least he's a bit more easygoing.' She stood up. 'I'm going to take her up, so at least Frances doesn't have to do that as well.'

It was ten o'clock when Ruby finally arrived and Marleen was tucked up at the foot of Davey's mattress. Frances opened the door to her and Ruby came in, flushed and cheerful as if there was nothing at all abnormal about rolling up at this time of night.

''Allo Mrs Hatton – sorry I'm a bit late, only I got held up.'

Edie stood watching, furious, arms folded.

Frances said, 'Come in, Ruby,' in her measured way. 'I'll go and see if she's stirring, but I expect she's fast asleep.'

As Frances climbed the stairs, Edie seized Ruby's wrist and pulled her into the front room.

'Eh Ede, go easy!'

'Where the hell've you been?' Edie demanded. 'D'you know what time it is? You come swanning in, your breath stinks like a distillery and your daughter – remember her? Marleen? – has cried herself to sleep. Poor Frances is exhausted. It's not fair on her – you're taking advantage, Ruby, and it's got to stop.'

'I know, I know . . . I'm sorry . . .' she said, still too tipsy and on cloud nine to sound sincere.

Edie exploded. 'You're not sorry at all! Have you any idea how selfish you're being?'

'I *am* sorry,' Ruby sat down on the piano stool, her back to Edie. 'Of course I am. But when do I ever get a bit of time for myself, week after week?' She was swinging her legs, and it aggravated Edie even more, glimpses of those legs 'tanned' with gravy browning, the line up the back pencilled in to look like stockings. Ruby was up to all the tricks!

'Well, you manage to find time to doll yourself up all right,' Edie snapped. 'Which is more than I ever do!'

'Oh for goodness sake! Just 'cause you don't ever want any fun.' Ruby knew she was in the wrong but she damn well wasn't giving in. 'All you can think about is flaming kids. You're turning into a real boring cow, you are!'

Absolutely livid, Edie marched over and brought her face close to Ruby's. 'Well it's a good job someone is,' she hissed at her. ''Cause you obviously don't give a damn. And it's Mrs Hatton you need to apologize to, not me. Otherwise you might be back to looking after Marleen by yourself!'

Ruby was sobered a little by this threat. Eyes wide, she said, 'The thing is, Ede – I know I was late tonight – it was really bad, and it won't happen again. Only I met this bloke.' Edie's eyes rolled ceilingwards. Ruby grabbed her arm. 'Oh Edie, 'e's lovely! He's an American, and I just lost track of the time.' She dimpled winningly at her.

'Marleen's OK, isn't she? I mean if I hadn't known she was in good hands I'd never've ... Only I get so lonely, Edie, and Wally's not like anyone I've ever met before.'

They heard Frances in the hall and Ruby went out to her.

'Mrs Hatton, I'm ever so sorry. I know I've let you down – and Marleen, and you're looking after her so well.'

'Well, never mind that,' Frances smiled wearily. More sharply, she added. 'But she really does need you to be reliable, Ruby.'

'I know.' Ruby looked despondent for a moment. She hung her head. 'I know I ain't much of a mother. And it's not easy with Mom off touring round at the moment.'

'If you want a late night out, we could arrange it from time to time,' Frances said. Edie watched her, stunned by her generosity and tolerance. She felt like giving Ruby a slap for being so irresponsible! 'Then if Marleen's staying the night, we can get her settled into bed at the proper time.'

'Oh no – I shouldn't,' Ruby said. 'I mean, it's too much for you – you've had her all day.'

'Didn't seem to worry you earlier,' Edie murmured.

'Now,' Frances said firmly. 'It's late. Leave her here for tonight and think about what I've said.'

'Oh I will,' Ruby said. 'You're so kind, Mrs Hatton. I'll try and do better – I really will.'

Ruby walked home to Glover Road. There was a whiff off woodsmoke in the air and the chilly night cooled her flushed cheeks. She felt a little ashamed of herself – after all, Frances Hatton had really been very kind to her.

But the way they were all staring at me like that when

I went in! Edie looking like the wrath of God! She let out a giggle. Anyone would think I was the Scarlet Woman or something! I mean I'd only been out for a quick drink. What harm's that to anyone? Staying in with a babby night after night's enough to drive anyone round the bend.

Ruby had found the first four months of staying at home after Marleen's birth quite enough, and as soon as she could get her to take some formula from a bottle she went back to work. Frank had come home when Marleen was a month old. Ruby saw how little interest he took in her. Maybe, she'd thought, if I can get back to normal, and Frank and I can have some time alone together, give him more attention, things'll be all right again. After all, it was from the time I was pregnant that everything went wrong, wasn't it? He didn't like me when I was carrying and I wasn't giving him what he needed. Next time he comes I'll see if she can stay with Frances. Frank had just finished his tour of operations and was not being sent on bombing raids. He would be more relaxed. They could start again.

But the next time Frank came home on leave he brought two pals with him, Australians who'd been posted to the base and were keen to see a bit more of the country. One of them stayed with Frank at his mom's: he asked Ruby if the other could stay with her. So instead of her own husband staying in her house, Ruby found herself with a stocky Australian bunked up in George's old room. George and Dorrie had been married soon after Marleen was born and were living in Bournbrook with Dorrie's mom.

It came home to Ruby fully, then, that her marriage really was over. When she managed to get Frank on his own, though, she could never get him to talk about it, as if he couldn't face the fact that he'd ever been married at all. Ruby felt very hurt and foolish. I'll show him, she thought. He's been no husband to me anyhow. Why do I need him?

So she'd taken to going out on the town as often as she could, occasionally with George and Dorrie, though they were so *staid*, like a middle-aged couple, or with Jessie Baker from number ten who was back living with her mom while her husband was away. Ethel was barely ever at home now, but Alf was eleven and he, Perce and Billy were old enough to look out for each other. At least she could get out and have a drink to cheer herself up!

She'd never let it get as late as this before. But that's because I hadn't met Wally before, she thought, hugging herself as she walked down Oak Tree Lane.

She and Jessie had been sitting in a tavern on the Bristol Road. Sometimes the older men in the pub stared at them, seeing the place as their territory, but Ruby would just outstare them or give them a wink. I like to get out of an evening as well, her look said. And where else am I s'posed to go?

'Can I get you something to drink, ma'am?' The soft, very polite voice came from somewhere above her. The fingers of his huge hand rested on the table and Ruby looked up to see what seemed like a giant standing over her. He was broad and stocky, with a squarish face and clear blue eyes.

'Ooh – I'll have a rum and black please!'

He frowned. 'You might have to explain that?'

Ruby laughed and told him what she'd like.

'And your friend?'

Jessie said she'd have a ginger wine and gave Ruby a wink as the man went to the bar, pulling out his wallet.

'Looks like you're in there, Ruby. Shall I make myself scarce?'

'Well – we'll see,' Ruby grinned. 'Have your drink first, anyway.' Ruby was grateful to Jessie. She was the one person who didn't behave disapprovingly to her about going out and having a laugh.

'Frank's treated you disgracefully, I think,' Jessie said to her sometimes. 'Deserting you and leaving you to bring up his child. You deserve some fun – and with this war going on none of us knows how long we've got, do we?'

Ruby flicked her hair back over her shoulders, smoothed her skirt and arranged a welcoming smile on her face for when the young GI came over carrying their glasses. Ruby pulled out a chair for him and he swung down on to it with muscular ease.

'Well – nice to meet you ladies.' He held his hand out. 'I'm Walter Sorenson – folks usually call me Wally.'

Ruby put her hand into his enormous palm. It was leathery and warm.

'Ruby Gilpin,' she said, glad she'd taken off her wedding ring.

'Well, hi there, Ruby.'

Jessie introduced herself, but Ruby wondered if she imagined that he quickly switched his attention back to her. She felt attractive tonight. True, she was in her old red dress (though he didn't know it was old, did he?). But her hair was clean and felt soft and glossy, pinned in a roll at the front and hanging loose, Veronica Lake style, and she'd made herself up, a touch of rouge and lipstick. She felt Wally's eyes lingering on her ample figure.

Wally offered round a packet of Lucky Strike and the three of them lit up and sat in the clouds of smoke chatting amiably. Wally told them about his family in

223

Fairmont, Minnesota – one sister left behind with his parents who ran a store – and a brother who was also in the forces in England.

'But he's down in the south somewhere – in Corn–wall?'

'Yes.' Ruby laughed at the way he pronounced it. 'Cornwall – that's right.'

Soon after she'd finished her drink Jessie winked at Ruby and said, 'Well – better be off. See you, Rube! Nice to meet you, Wally.'

''Bye, Jess!' Ruby gave her a wide smile. What a pal! No doubt Edie would have stayed to make sure she didn't get up to anything, she was so flaming strait-laced these days.

'Your friend in a hurry?' Wally asked.

'Oh – she doesn't like to stop late,' Ruby told him. 'Her husband's in the RAF and she feels a bit bad if she goes out and about too much.'

'So what about you, Ruby? You have a husband?'

'No – I don't.' Ruby crossed her fingers under the table. God forgive me! she thought. But you couldn't call Frank a husband these days, could you? After all, he never even made a pretence of coming to see her any more. She was as good as telling the truth. 'And you?' She felt herself being flirtatious. 'Is there a nice girl back in Fairmont, Minnesota?'

Wally's shoulders shook with laughter. 'Plenty of nice girls – oh yes,' he said. 'But I don't have a special sweetheart, if that's what you mean. Come to think of it, I haven't met *any* girl as lovely as you, Ruby.'

She loved the way he kept saying her name like that, looking straight into her eyes. It was very warming, like a verbal caress, and she felt herself blossom under his attention. They chatted on for quite a time, Wally laughing in

224

his relaxed way at things she said. He really seemed to listen to her as well, she thought, not like Frank. And he was very intrigued to hear that Ruby's mom was 'on the stage'. Ruby dressed the situation up a little. She didn't want to admit that Mimi had been dragged out of retirement in quite the way she had.

They had a couple more drinks and stood up to go. Ruby felt herself swaying slightly and Wally took her arm in a gentlemanly fashion. She felt excitement rising in her. Would he put those big strong arms round her, now they were out in the darkness? She wanted him to. She liked him, desired him. But she didn't want him to think she was fast. He seemed full of homespun courtesy. She'd better hold back, wait and see.

'Thanks ever so much for the drinks,' she said when they stopped on the corner of the street.

'You're more than welcome. I enjoyed the company.' He seemed reluctant to release her, and turned to look at her, holding the top of her arm firmly. 'Say, I'll be around for a while, Ruby. I'd like to see you again if that's all right with you?'

'Yes. Oh yes – I'd like that.' She ticked herself off for sounding too eager. In the last threads of evening light she could see him looking down at her and she met his gaze, raising her face to his. 'Wally?'

'Yes?'

She didn't say anything more, just gazed at him, her lips parted.

'We-e-ell,' he said, caressingly, the strong arms drawing her to him at last. They were standing by someone's garden wall, topped by a small hedge.

'You're quite a girl, aren't you?' She felt his hand stroking her back and he let out a soft, admiring whistle, his hands moving down, pulling her in closer.

Twenty-Four

Janet hurried through Bournville along the dark road, her nose and cheeks stinging in the cold air.

Will there be anything today? Will there . . .?

The question burned in her mind every day, amid the clack of typewriters while she was at work. She let herself into the house and went straight to the hall table. Nothing. She hung up her hat and coat. Maybe her mother had put it somewhere else . . .

She could hear Marleen's screams from the kitchen and went through to find Frances reaching over the table, trying to stop the little girl slapping her hands furiously in a spreading pool of milk. Davey was watching, wide-eyed, from the other side of the table, one arm shielding the drawing he had in front of him from the advancing milk. Janet rushed for a cloth while Frances airlifted the furious child from her seat.

'Oh dear, like that is it?'

'Not really, only just the last few minutes.' Frances raised a finger at Marleen, who looked as if she was thinking of running off. 'No, madam – no moving yet. She's getting tired, that's all.'

'Ruby'll be along soon, I expect.'

'Oh I'm sure she will.' Ruby had been turning up as regularly as clockwork over the past few weeks.

Ignoring the child's grating screams, Frances said, 'Tea's ready – Edie'll be in in a minute as well.'

Janet wondered how on earth her mother could remain so calm with all this ghastly racket going on. It would drive her round the twist. And she did look very tired. But Frances assured her that despite it being demanding, she was enjoying looking after the children.

'Keeps me young,' she kept saying. 'And what else can I do for the war effort except for knitting socks for sailors?'

At last, trying not to sound too desperate, Janet asked, 'Was there any post today?'

Frances wrung out the cloth over the sink. 'No, darling – I'm sorry.'

Janet leaned over and ruffled David's hair. He was busy colouring in a picture with a thick red crayon. 'That's very good, Davey! They'll be pleased with you when you get to school.'

'The post from overseas is terrible at the moment.' Frances hadn't missed the tear-thickened tone of Janet's voice. 'Everyone's saying so, love. Try not to read the worst into it. Martin's a good chap and I'm sure he's doing his best.'

'I know,' Janet wiped her eyes but more tears came. She was feeling very low today. 'But it's been so long and he feels so far away. I mean if I even knew where he was it'd be easier. I could picture him there . . . Oh I'm sorry, Davey. It's all right, don't you worry.' She kissed the top of the little boy's head as he looked up anxiously, hearing the upset in her voice. 'Look – I'll just go up and pull myself together. I don't know why, but I really had a feeling I might hear from him today.'

She went up to her room and lay on the bed, giving in to a short, sharp weep to release her feelings. Bunching up the eiderdown, she hugged it close.

'Oh Martin – where are you, my love?' she whispered.

'Why don't you write? Just let me know you're all right and you still love me – please.'

The last letter had come five weeks ago. Martin had held her in his arms in the dying days of 1941 and told her he loved her, loved her so much. They had walked half the night in the freezing darkness, talking, touching, kissing. And she knew then that she had found the love of her life. She ached with longing for him when he'd gone, sailing off into the first days of 1942. All she knew was that he was with SEAC – South East Asia Command. No post was sent from the ship until they reached their destination, wherever it was, and the voyage had taken about two months. She worried herself sick in that time, constantly on edge for news of sinking vessels. When his first letter came she wept with relief. He was safe! But the letters were so heavily censored – even mention of the weather was barred – that their contents seemed flat and impersonal. Martin could not breathe any colour and atmosphere into them for fear of giving away his whereabouts and he expressed his frustation about this. What she fed on were his words of love and how much she meant to him, how he longed to be with her again.

Those first weeks she'd been happy just knowing they loved each other. But by now almost two years had passed since they had parted and she had to work hard to keep the image of him and his love alive. She struggled to see his face in her mind. Who was he, really, that stranger who left her all those months ago? Was he real? How could she love someone whom she could barely remember? Why could love never be straightforward in her life? She had lost Alec, the baby, and now Martin had been snatched from her as soon as she had found him.

She had started knitting a big navy blue sweater for Martin, each stitch an act of love. She imagined him wearing it across his broad shoulders. It felt like a physical link with him.

She lay trying to recall the feel of his lips on hers, that overwhelming look of love in his eyes.

'I love you,' she told the image. 'I do. I'm waiting for you, Martin darling. Only please write and tell me you love me. If it wasn't for this wretched war, we'd be together – maybe even married by now.'

She heard the front door open and Edie and Ruby came in together. Janet lay listening to the assorted sounds of the two of them and the children. Once Ruby had gone, she heard Edie coming upstairs, and sat up, wiping her eyes.

'Janet?' Edie's voice came through the gloom. 'Are you in there?'

'Yes.' She tried to sound normal. It was only then she realized she'd been lying in the dark.

'Goodness, I can't see a thing!' Edie groped her way across the room and Janet felt her sit on the bed. 'Frances said you were upset. Nothing from Martin again?'

Janet tried to speak but only a sob escaped.

'Oh Janet – oh dear!' Edie's arms were round her immediately, letting her cry it out. She knew how Janet was suffering, week after week. 'You poor thing . . . I wish I could *make* a letter come for you!'

'Oh – I'm just being silly. But it all wells up sometimes. Sometimes I think I dreamt him.'

'Well, you *didn't*,' Edie said fiercely. She stroked Janet's back. 'He really loves you. And you're so brave about it. I wouldn't be, I know.'

'Oh, you would,' Janet said, thinking how many times

she'd admired Edie's quiet strength, her devotion to people she loved. 'I'm sure you would.'

On Sunday, as the day was bright and calm, Edie took Davey for a walk to the park while Frances and Janet were still out at the Friends' Meeting House. Sometimes they went along as well, and Edie enjoyed the serene silence of the hour, but she had not made any commitment to go all the time and today she felt like getting out in the fresh air. She was always pleased to get some time to herself with Davey, to walk through the park to the boating lake. It was nice not having Marleen around, screaming and carrying on every time something didn't go her way. They walked down past the Bournville School with its carillon in the tower.

'Will the bells ring?' Davey's serious face turned up towards her.

'Not now – it's not the right time.' Edie smiled down at him. He had grown into a beautiful child, pink-cheeked, with long-lashed brown eyes and dark curls. She had cut his hair yesterday though and he suddenly looked older. A proper little man, she thought.

'How *many* bells are there?'

'Well now – d'you remember, Frances told us this?' Davey was always asking earnestly, how *many*, how *much* of everything. 'They built it again, in 1934, and added some more bells. There are forty-eight now.'

Davey's brow wrinkled. 'How many were there before?'

'Oh dear – I can't remember exactly. We'll have to ask Auntie Frances again. But I do remember she told us that the biggest bell weighs three tons!'

'Is that very heavy?'

'Yes – ever so heavy.'

'*How* heavy?'

Edie tutted. She sometimes felt that although Davey was not even four, he was already in some way beyond her.

'Very, very heavy, sweetheart. Not even a big strong man could lift it. Come on – let's go down to the water.'

His favourite pastime of the moment was throwing pebbles into the little brook which ran through the park, and he was soon trotting up and down, pink knees visible between short trousers and socks, absorbed in picking up every stone he could find and earnestly watching the splash it made. Edie stood watching, hugging her old black coat round her, enjoying the winter sun on her face, loving the sight of 'her' boy playing. She felt suddenly lighthearted. The sirens very seldom went now and the fear and pressure of the Blitz had receded. She had been moved to several different jobs at work over the past months, filling anti-aircraft rockets in the Nissen huts which sprung up on the bank of the canal, then assembling parts for Spitfires. Now she was back on respirators. There was still chocolate being produced – Ration Chocolate, Blended Chocolate made with powdered milk for the nation's chocolate ration – 3 ounces a week.

For many, the war meant separation, worry, and the daily inconvenience of shortages. Edie suffered on Janet's behalf, knowing the awful waiting to hear from Martin, but for herself she counted these years, almost guiltily, as the happiest of her life. She felt cocooned living with the Hattons, cared for and happy with Davey. She had no husband or sweetheart to worry about and didn't miss married life. She enjoyed the hours of companionship with Janet, Frances and Ruby and felt she was living in a happy dream, with the camaraderie of work and the cosy domesticity of home. For the last two summers the Lord Mayor had begun, through Cadbury's, a 'Stay at Home Holidays Scheme' at Rowheath Garden Club and Lido. All they had to do was climb aboard the number 36 tram and walk out into the green of the Rowheath Club, where they could swim in the pool, picnic, join in folk dances and listen to the band. The football pitches had been dug up for allotments, but there was still plenty of space for people to enjoy themselves. Edie had spent many a happy weekend afternoon and summer evening at Rowheath with Davey and Marleen, taking packets of sandwiches and cake to keep them going. It had been heaven.

'Come on, let's walk on a bit,' she called to Davey.

'One more!' He threw overarm, hurling a stone down into the water with all his strength, then trotted after her, cheeks glowing.

'Whose birthday is it this week?' she asked, taking his hand.

'Mine?' As far as he knew, his birthday was 19 November.

'Yes – put your mitts on, your hands're cold.'

'And I'll be four!'

'You're getting big.'

'*How* big am I, 'zackly?'

'Oh Davey!' she laughed, exasperated, laying a hand on his head. 'You're *that* big – that's how big!'

Janet came into the hall when they got back.

'Someone called to see you while you were out.'

'Who?' Edie was unbuttoning Davey's coat.

'I don't know. She wouldn't say.'

Something in Janet's tone made Edie straighten up, her pulse quickening.

'Well, what did she want?'

Janet wore a slight frown. 'She just came to the door and said was this where Edie Weale was living. I asked if she wanted to wait and she said no, she'll come back but she needs to see you. She wouldn't give her name.'

Edie felt as if her veins were full of ice water. She sank down on to the chair in the hall.

'What did she look like?'

'Pale face, dark hair.' Janet shrugged. 'Rather serious-looking.'

'Oh—' Edie's hand went to her throat. Seeing Davey looking up at her she urged him towards the kitchen. 'Go on, bab, go and see Frances.'

Janet understood immediately. This was what Edie dreaded most, year after year, in an unspoken corner of her mind. That someone was out there who belonged to Davey – that one day they would find her, come to claim him as their own. She put her hand on Edie's shoulder.

'Look – it's probably nothing important.'

'Dark-haired, you said?' The colour had drained from Edie's face. 'Dark, like him. Oh God, Janet, it could be his mother . . .'

'Yes, Edie – but then it could be absolutely anyone. Come on – lunch is ready. I'm sure it's nothing to worry about. You mustn't fear the worst just because someone calls at the house.'

The last thing Edie felt like was eating, but she did her best to appreciate the ration of meat that Frances had managed to get hold of for the weekend. They didn't talk about what was on her mind, not in front of Davey, and Edie tried to concentrate on Frances's news about their Quaker friends. All the time her mind multiplied its fears. It had to come – she had had too much happiness while other people were suffering. She had taken a child that wasn't hers and now they were coming to take him away. How could she have thought life would carry on in this tranquil way? She heard her mother's mocking voice in her head. 'Nothing comes without a price, wench – and don't you forget it.' After the meal she washed up, her hands shaking, ears straining constantly for that knock at the door.

She was playing on the floor with Davey, building towers and forts out of wooden blocks, when the knocker rapped abruptly, three times. Eveyone looked at one another for a second. Edie got up, legs shaking.

'I'll go.'

She tried to see if she could make out the caller through the distorted glass light in the door, but she could only see the top of a green felt hat. Bracing herself, she pulled the door open.

For a second she was so primed to see a stranger that she didn't recognize her. Then she almost burst into tears of relief.

'Florrie! What in heaven's name're you doing here? Was it you called earlier?'

Florrie nodded. She seemed wary of the house. 'They said you was out.'

'Why didn't you give your name? I couldn't think who could be calling. You coming in?'

'Oh no, I don't think so.' Florrie pulled at her coat cuffs in an agitated way. 'Thing is, Edie, I come up last night with the kids to see our mom. And I've found her in a right state.'

'State? What about?'

'Not like that. She's bad, Edie. There's summat bad the matter with 'er. Course she hadn't let on, she ain't said nothing to you . . .?'

'I've not been in months,' Edie said stiffly. 'I don't get

234

any sort of welcome when I do, so why bother? Rodney's been up here, and I've seen our dad a couple of times . . .'

Florrie wasn't listening. 'I got it out of 'er in the end. The doctor says she's got some kind of growth inside 'er. She looks bad, Edie, thin as a rake, except her belly's all out as if she's nine months gone. She won't hear about it though. Just keeps saying not to make a fuss. Only I can't keep coming up all the way from Coventry. You'll 'ave to go over and give her a hand.'

Edie agreed that she'd call in, and after hearing briefly about her sister's family, watched her skinny figure hurry off down the road. She had to get the kids on the train to Coventry. Edie caught herself letting out a tremulous sigh of relief. Although it was bad news, she knew that it wasn't the worst, the news she truly dreaded. That could only ever be something connected with Davey.

Twenty-Five

Rodney let her in. As soon as she stepped into the Charlotte Road house Edie knew things had changed. No one was in the back room and it was so quiet, even for the middle of a Sunday afternoon, that she found herself whispering, 'Where is everyone?'

Rodney nodded towards the front room.

'Our dad made up a fire in there today.'

'Why didn't you tell me Mom was poorly?'

Rodney shrugged gracelessly. ''Er never said. It were only when Florrie came . . .'

Edie had waited until she was sure Florrie would have left for Coventry before going over. She could do without her sister's bossing. She crept to the front room. It was very warm and there was an odd, sickly smell. Her father was asleep in the chair, his braces loosened, head back and mouth ajar, breathing loudly. Something about the sight of him troubled her and it took her a moment to pin it down. He hadn't shaved! Dennis Marshall, gentleman barber, had a growth of stubble on his chin! Tiptoeing round to look at her mother, Edie stifled a gasp. Nellie never, ever succumbed to sleeping in the daytime, even on Sunday. That in itself was startling enough, as was the fact they were sitting in the front room and even more, the incongrous sense of companionship which seemed to have arisen between her parents as they snoozed here together – something they never achieved

236

when they were awake. But most shocking was her mother's wasted appearance, her face sallow against the hard blue of her dress, the hair faded so there was barely a trace of ginger left. Her body looked shrunken suddenly, as if it had collapsed in on itself, and her wrists were stick-thin. The veins stood out on her wasted hand resting on the arm of the chair. Most disturbing of all was her prominent pot-belly, just as Florrie had described, as if Nellie was well advanced in pregnancy. For a crazed second Edie wondered if she *was* – was that it? – before telling herself not to be so stupid. Her mom was well past childbearing age.

She shoved Rodney back into the other room and pushed the door shut.

'How's long's she been like that?'

Rodney shrugged. 'Few weeks I s'pose. It sort of crept up, and one day 'er suddenly couldn't never seem to get about. What's up with 'er, Ede? She ain't said nothing to me.'

'She will if she catches you saying "ain't" like that,' Edie snapped. 'Look – get the kettle on and I'll make 'em a cup of tea. I need time to think.'

When she carried the tea through her father stirred, gave a startled snort and stared at her blearily.

'Edie? I thought Florrie was 'ere . . .?'

She handed him a cup of tea. 'Thought I'd call in. Florrie said our mom was poorly.' They looked across at Nellie, who was moving her head restlessly, eyes still closed. 'What's up with her, Dad? Florrie said summat about a growth.'

Dennis Marshall stirred his tea and wouldn't meet her eyes. 'Ar well . . . They did say summat like that . . .'Er's a bit under the weather like, you know.'

'*Under the weather?* Dad, she looks terrible!'

'She ain't been too well,' he admitted. 'But she don't make a fuss. You know yer mother.'

Tutting furiously, Edie went to her mother. 'Mom?' She found herself speaking softly, as if to a child. 'Here's a cuppa tea for yer. You going to wake up and have it?'

'Ooh—' Nellie's eyes opened, struggled to focus for a second, then fixed Edie with her cold blue stare. 'I must've dozed off for a minute. What're you doing 'ere?'

It would be no good asking any direct questions straight away, Edie saw. 'Just thought I'd pop in. 'Ere, Rodney – your tea.' Edie drew up a stool and sat between her parents, facing the fire.

'Not brought that lad with yer then?' David was always 'the boy' or 'that lad' now he was older. Nellie would never acknowledge him as Edie's son.

'No. We went to the park this morning and he's having a nap at home.' There was a silence. 'It's his birthday in a couple of days. He'll be four – hard to believe, isn't it?'

They talked fitfully about day-to-day things, Florrie's kids, neighbours. Edie kept watching her mother when she wasn't looking and twice she saw her whole face twist, contorted with pain. She pressed her hand against her belly as if to ease it and her face turned even paler. It was terrible to see. But it was only after some time Edie felt she could say anything.

'You're not looking very well, Mom.'

Her father stared into the fire. Edie was horrified to hear her mother let out a hard, bitter laugh, which ended in a gasp of pain, her hand pushing once more against her belly. 'Ah well, fancy *you* noticing,' she said spitefully. 'It's taken you long enough to get here.'

Edie swallowed the retort that if she'd ever found a

welcome here she would have come more often. 'What do they say it is?'

Nellie was easing herself forward, trying urgently to get out of her chair. Edie instinctively went to help her, but her mother's bony hand pushed her away.

'Oh stop mithering. I need to go out the back . . .'

Walking half bent over, holding on to the wall, she felt her way towards the outside toilet.

'Dad! Why didn't you come and tell me?' Edie demanded.

'Look, wench, don't keep on.' He stood up, leaving his teacup on the hearth, and went out through to the back.

'Why's he being like that? She can't help being bad, can she? What's going on, Rodney?'

'*I* dunno, do I?' Rodney said mulishly. ''E don't want to talk about it.'

'Oh, for goodness sake – you're all as bad as each other!' Edie furiously cleared away the cups. 'It's not just going to go away because you pretend nothing's the matter!'

She waited until her mother came groping her way back to her chair, clearly exhausted. Resting for a moment, leaning on the wall, she snarled, 'That's right, take a good look.'

'Mom . . .'

'Oh leave me alone . . .' She sank back into the chair and closed her eyes.

Edie stood hovering over her for a moment, torn between pity and anger. What was the point in ever trying to be a daughter to her? Going through to the back, she found her father sitting by the range, the newspaper in front of his face like a guard.

'Dad – look, I've got to go. But I'll come in and give her a hand all I can. When she'll let me, anyhow . . .'

'Awright,' he said. 'Good of yer, wench.' He didn't put the paper down.

The next Saturday morning, Edie was preparing a tea party for David's birthday. He had turned four two days before and Edie had been saving for months to buy him a little tricycle with red mudguards and rubber grips on the handlebars. David squeaked with astonished delight when he first saw it. She kept catching glimpses of him now, well wrapped up in his coat and balaclava, riding the trike up and down the back garden path.

With a saving of her butter rations and powdered egg she had baked a Victoria sponge – of sorts, anyway, and managed a thin layer of jam in the middle. She trickled some glacé icing over the top and piped a pale blue '4' across it. Frances had found enough birthday candles and the cake stood proudly on the kitchen table under a mesh, waiting for the children to arrive in the afternoon.

Edie stood humming to herself, slicing bread as thinly as she could for the sandwiches. Lately she'd been listening to 'Kitchen Front' on the wireless and had become preoccupied with feeding her boy the very best food she could.

'Dr Hill says brown bread is best,' she'd told Frances. 'I think I'll try and give him more of that.'

'Well, it'll be better for all of us,' Frances said. 'I'll buy half and half – how about that?'

So she cut some neat brown sandwiches with fish paste and some white ones with jam, and they'd baked a few cheese straws. There weren't to be very many guests – David and a handful of neighbourhood children and of course, Marleen.

'Well it all looks lovely,' Frances said when she saw

240

the little spread. 'You've done a marvellous job. We can have a bite of lunch when Janet gets back from the shops. And are you planning to call in to your mother's before everything gets started?'

'If there's time.' Edie sighed.

'You can only do your best,' Frances tried to reassure her.

'Oh well – where's that ever got me?' Edie retorted, vigorously wiping the crumbs off the side. 'Sorry, Frances. I know you're right. Only when I go and try to help she's so nasty and ungrateful. I mean I know I didn't go home for a long while, but that was because she never seemed to want me when I did. I suppose I *want* her to need me there. I can't imagine not wanting to see Davey if he came to see me! Sometimes I think she's a wicked woman, I really do.'

Frances listened, troubled by the hurt she saw in Edie's expression, the bitterness in her voice. She'd never met Nellie Marshall and was disturbed by the harsh feelings she brought out in Edie, who was normally so sweet-natured. She wondered again about that scar on Edie's arm which she was always at such pains to keep hidden.

'Perhaps she just doesn't know how to say she likes you going,' she suggested.

'Huh,' Edie wrung the cloth tight over the sink. 'She doesn't know how to like *anything*.'

There came a sudden hard knocking at the front door and Frances hurried to answer. 'Gracious me – sounds as if they're trying to batter it down.' Then Edie heard a distraught voice, and sobbing coming along the hall and Ruby's tear-stained face appeared.

'Ruby? What's happened? Where's Marleen?'

Ruby sank down on a kitchen chair, still in her coat. 'It's not Marleen. Perce has got her. Oh Edie, it's Frank!'

For a split second Edie couldn't think who Frank was. The only person Ruby talked about these days was Wally, her American. It was Wally this and Wally that all the time.

'I've just heard and I had to tell someone. They say he was shot down and he's missing – but that means he's been killed, I know it does!'

'But Ruby, he wasn't flying any more.' Edie put her arms round her old friend's shoulders. 'It must be a mistake.'

'It's not a mistake.' Ruby managed to calm herself down enough to explain. 'I had a letter from his squadron-leader. Frank volunteered to go out on a raid. He'd done it before, the man said – even when he didn't have to. Some of the other blokes from his old crew were still going out, and he wanted to go with them. They said he was very brave and heroic to do it . . .' She started crying again. 'Oh, I know we didn't have much of a marriage, but he still was my husband. He's too young to die!'

Ruby put her hands over her face and sobbed while Edie and Frances tried to comfort her. After a sharp weep she recovered remarkably quickly.

'Imagine if I didn't have Wally,' she said, dabbing her face. 'I don't know how I'd be able to carry on.'

They managed to persuade her to go home and get Marleen ready to bring to the party. It would give her something else to think about. By three o'clock all the little guests had arrived. Ruby was all dolled up in a beautiful emerald-green dress which shimmered over her broad hips. ('She didn't get that with her coupons!' Janet whispered to Edie, who grinned back.)

'Eh Rube, where d'you get those nylons from?' Edie ribbed her.

Ruby hoiked up her skirt and made a cheeky curtsey. 'Wouldn't you like to know!'

Marleen, whose birthday had been the week before, was in a frilly little frock made of yellow and white gingham which looked very sweet with her blonde hair. Ruby seemed to have recovered enough to beam proudly at the sight of her daughter waddling about in her tiny shoes.

They had just enough children to manage a few games in the front room: blind man's buff, musical statues – Frances playing nursery rhymes on the piano – and an attempt at musical chairs which made Marleen roar with fury because she was too young to keep up and they had to abandon the attempt. Edie had done a 'pin the tail on the donkey' for them.

'Not my best drawing ever!' she laughed, looking at the donkey's too-long ears and squiffy shape.

The sandwiches, jelly and biscuits were all devoured, the tablecloth emblazoned with crumbs and runaway blobs of jelly. Then Edie carried the cake in with the candles lit. Davey's expression as she laid it proudly on the table brought tears to her eyes.

'Is that for *me*?' he said in rapt wonder.

'Of course – you're the birthday boy,' she said, kissing him.

'But is it *all* for me?' The adults laughed.

'You might like to share it with your friends,' Janet told him. 'Or you're going to be a poorly boy later on!'

They sang 'Happy Birthday' and cut the cake, and then Ruby started saying she had to go.

'Thing is, Edie,' she whispered. 'I said I'd meet Wally. So I'm sorry to rush off.'

So that was why Ruby had got all dressed up, Edie

thought. She was a bit hurt at her leaving Davey's party before it was really over, but she smiled. 'Off you go then. Mustn't keep him waiting.'

Ruby said goodbye to Frances, obviously hoping Frances would offer to keep Marleen for the evening. Frances responded warmly, but made no such offer. Marleen bawled inconsolably at being removed from the party before everyone else and had to be carried out kicking and flailing. Frances shook her head and gave a wry smile as the frenzied howling was muffled abruptly when the front door closed.

'She really is the end.'

Twenty-Six

February 1944

'Why don't we go into town? Have a mooch round the shops?'

Janet looked up, suddenly realizing Edie was speaking to her. She'd been staring out at the garden, miles away.

'I know there's not much to look at – but it'll take your mind off it,' Edie said.

Frances looked up encouragingly from her knitting. 'Good idea, Edie. You could both do with an afternoon out.'

Janet knew her mother was worried about them both. Edie was wearing herself to a wafer trying to help her mother after work. Not that she seemed to appreciate it, from what Janet could gather. She didn't feel like a trip into town, but Edie was right – she could do with something to distract her from the worry that nagged constantly at her. And it made a change from sitting indoors. She yawned and stretched. 'All right. Sounds like a nice idea.' The two of them went to get their coats and get David ready.

All that week, Janet's spirits had been at rock bottom. She hadn't heard from Martin in months. It was impossible to know whether this was the fault of the erratic postal service, or his work keeping him too busy, or – the thoughts she tried desperately to banish – that something awful had happened to him or that his love had grown cold. The affectionate words at the end of his last letter back in November had long lost their impact and though she read and re-read the letter until it was tearing along the folds, it almost felt now as if it was from a stranger, not from the man she loved. But she kept telling herself it was the same for so many people, that she had to keep faith and one day she would see him again.

They caught the bus to town, and took Davey into Lewis's toy department.

'Oh look!' Edie cried, spotting a little wooden train that you could pull along the floor. 'Isn't that lovely! Oh – I can just about afford that – d'you think I should?'

'Definitely,' Janet smiled, watching Edie tenderly. She's just as excited as he is! she thought. The painful memory came to her of coming into this same store that winter after she had miscarried. She had never felt much regret about it at the time – there had been too much relief at being saved from a hopeless situation. But occasionally, seeing Edie with David, she couldn't help wondering, with a sense of loss, who that child might have been. Would she have felt the same besotted love that Edie did? Edie had been opening up more and more lately about her home life when she was growing up. Janet was appalled at the few things she had told them. One Christmas night, when she was nine, because of something naughty she'd done, Nellie had locked her out of the house for the night and she'd been forced to sleep in the freezing brewhouse. Janet felt herself tense with rage when she heard things about Nellie. Edie had at last told her why she had that burn mark on her arm. The woman sounded like a lunatic! No wonder Edie clung so passionately to David. With all she'd been through she deserved all the love and help they could give her.

'Look, Davey!' Edie was saying, her eyes shining as

she showed him the little locomotive with its painted red wheels. 'Oh, we'll have some fun with this, won't we?'

David held out his arms for it, jumping with excitement.

'He loves machines, doesn't he?' Janet said. 'We'll have to find you a proper train set when you're a bit older. In fact – oh, Edie, I've just thought, Mum's probably got Robert's old set packed away somewhere. She never gets rid of anything! That would be perfect.'

'D'you hear that, Davey?' Edie guided him over to where they could pay. 'Auntie Frances might have a whole set of choo-choo trains for you. You don't think she'd mind?' she added anxiously. Still, in her heart, she could never quite believe the extent of the Hattons' kindness to her. Even the smallest things seemed incredible.

'Don't be silly – she'd love it. In fact I'm surprised she hasn't suggested it herself.'

They wandered round the town centre and the Bull Ring and it was getting dark when they headed for the bus stop. They were walking through the bustle of Corporation Street when Janet's shoulder was jostled hard by a passer-by.

'So sorry—' He turned to apologize, and she found herself looking up into a handsome face, with black hair and boyish blue eyes. Familiar eyes: the eyes of Alec Storey. She felt a lurch of emotion, like a reflex. Both of them stopped, uncertain how to react.

'Well,' he said after a moment. 'How are you?'

'Oh, very well!' Janet could hear a forced jollity in her voice. 'This is my friend Edith – she and her little boy are living with us for the time being.'

Edie sensed who the man was. 'I'll take Davey on

247

home,' she said. 'Give you two a chance to catch up – if you want to?'

Janet knew she ought just to turn and go. Alec was part of a painful past, and should remain so. But suddenly seeing him like this . . . It would be nice just to have a talk.

'Are you,' she looked around, 'here with the family?'

'No – not today.' He seemed bashful talking in front of Edie. As he well ought to be, Janet thought. 'I've time for a drink if you have.'

Janet felt Edie watching them. 'All right,' she said, evenly. 'Tell Mother . . .' She couldn't think what excuse to give.

'I'll just say you're on your way,' Edie said. 'Come on, Davey, let's go.'

'So, what d'you fancy – tea or something stronger?' Alec asked, a little too jovially.

'Tea would suit me very well. Lewis's tea room?'

The street was crowded enough to make conversation difficult. Once they were seated at a table with tea on the way, Janet felt Alec examining her, sitting back in his chair with an appraising expression. She felt uncomfortable, as if he was looking for blemishes, or to see how much she had aged. He seemed older himself, in fact, since she had last seen him. His sleek hair was thinning on top. But he still had the little moustache, and his eyes were as large and persuasive as ever. It seemed such a short time, suddenly, since she last spent time with him. Last time, when she was carrying his child . . .

'You look marvellous,' he said softly. Already his tone was seductive.

'Thank you.' She brushed a strand of hair from her face, feeling as if he were undressing her with his eyes, and cursed herself for blushing.

She asked after his family and he said they also had a daughter now, and that everyone was in good health.

'A daughter?' she found herself saying. 'How nice.' Yes, how nice, the perfect, tidy family. No complications. It had been her decision not to tell him about the baby, yet now she felt livid, boiling inside that he did not know of the consequences of his infidelity. She wanted to tell him, to rub his nose in it – yet she would not, would never let him know that she had been made that vulnerable by him.

'How's your mother?' The old note of mockery in his voice. Knowing, superior. 'Old girl still bearing up, is she?'

Worth twenty of you, certainly. 'Actually, she's really splendid. The war's made her come into her own. She's taken in refugees – we've a girl called Marie from Guernsey living with us, though she's leaving us to marry in the summer. And now Edie and her son – and Mummy looks after another child as well. She's been a brick about it all. I'm full of admiration for her. After all—' she knew there was a barbed tone to her voice. 'Those of us who aren't doing the real fighting have to do our bit.'

'*Touché*,' Alec said. For a second he even managed to appear vulnerable himself. 'You needn't think I need reminding that I'm having a soft war.'

The pot of weak tea arrived and there was a pause as cups and jugs were arranged on the table. As soon as they were alone he leaned forward and held out his hand for her to put hers in, as she once would have done. Janet ignored him and busied herself stirring the contents of the teapot.

'I can't tell you how much I've missed you.' He managed to catch her hand and she could no longer resist. She looked into his eyes and saw them narrow with desire in the way she remembered. The way that always weakened her resolve. That power he had. She felt herself stir in response. 'Remember that day at the beach?' he murmured. *The day I conceived the child*, she thought. 'Oh God, Janet – the number of times I've longed for you . . .'

For a moment she was sucked in, almost hypnotized by him. If they had not been in a public place he might have drawn closer, kissed her and caught her at a weak moment. But she forced herself to her senses. Not this again! He was a user and she'd allowed herself to be used. But not any more! She was worth more than that – and she had Martin, her dear, loving Martin. She pulled her hand firmly away.

'Alec – don't. This is ridiculous. You can't just waltz back into my life like this. And besides—' She laid her hands in her lap and sat back. 'I'm engaged.'

Alec smiled regretfully, as if she had complained of suffering a headache. He offered her a cigarette. She refused it. Lighting up his own, he blew smoke towards the ceiling. 'And where is he at this moment?'

'I don't know.' She looked down into her cup. 'Out east somewhere.'

'Well – I hope he comes back to you. Things over there are looking pretty grim. I don't envy any of those chaps over there facing the Japs, I can tell you.'

'He's a doctor.'

'Even so.' He put his head on one side. 'Look, Janet – I know you're a straightforward sort of girl, strong morals and so on. But the war's a long haul – it changes everything. I mean we're in it for the duration and none of us knows how long that is. All the rest of our youth could disappear before it's over – and for what? When your fiancé comes back – assuming he does – then of course you'll marry and do the right thing. But until then . . .' Once more he was leaning towards her. 'I'd love to see you again, Janet. I've never met anyone like you – you're so sultry, so exciting . . .'

Once more she felt she was being undressed by his very words. Lured. And the temptation was strong. To have more in life than the factory and the chores of home in the dark nights, of waiting week after week aching for a letter. There was truth in what he said – they didn't know when it would end, or if things would ever be normal again. For a moment all she wanted was the feel of a man's arms round her, his desire for her, and hang everything else.

'Alec—' She sat back. 'Can we change the subject? Please?'

He laughed, seeing how much he had unsettled her, knowing his power over her.

'All right. We'll talk about our war work, and the weather and grumble about ration coupons and everything being grey – like everyone else. But remember – underneath we have so much more than that. We always had.' For a moment he was whispering. 'We used to have a wonderful time together. Chemistry they call it, don't they? You know we did. And we still could, you know. You only have to say the word.'

A few days later, Ruby was on the line in the wrapping department at Cadbury's. She kept looking up at the clock. The afternoon couldn't go fast enough so far as she was concerned. As the blue and red wrappers of the tuppenny Ration Chocolate Bars flashed past her, all she could think about was Wally. He'd be in Birmingham tonight.

Things had progressed with Wally, Oh yes they certainly had. And she didn't have to lie to him any more!

He'd been so good when she'd owned up about her widowhood, and about Marleen. She felt a strange tingle every time she thought of it, of fate working on her side for once. She had told a lie and then it came true! It meant she and Wally were meant to be together. He was the one, and she wasn't going to let him go. A smile crept across her face as she counted the little bars of chocolate into their boxes.

'Ooh, I wonder who she can be thinking of!' one of her friends called across. 'You don't half wear your heart on your sleeve, Ruby!'

'So would you if you had a fella like mine!' Ruby retorted. 'And I'm going dancing with him tonight!'

Six hours to go. It seemed an eternity. Never mind, she told herself, come eight o'clock you'll be in his arms!

She had bought the emerald satin dress she had worn to Davey's party from a lady who had put a little sign up in a shop window on the Bristol Road. When Ruby called on her to see it, it was as if it had been made for her. The vivid green fulfilled her longing for colour in these drab times. It came right down to her mid-calf, not like the skimpy wartime hemlines, and was rather tight, the shimmery green hugging her curves like a second skin, the low-cut neck showing more than a hint of cleavage, and the skirt, though not as full as Ruby would have liked, swinging from her broad hips as she moved. Under it she wore a precious pair of the nylons Wally had brought for her – no more eye-pencilling a line up the back of her legs! – and her feet nestled in her one pair of smart navy court shoes. All in all she felt very silky and seductive.

'My!' Wally whistled admiringly the first time he saw

it, and though she had worn it a number of times, when they met at the dance hall that night he greeted her appreciatively, almost as if he'd never seen it before. Taking her arm he spoke over the loud music of the band: 'You look *swell*. May I have the first dance, ma'am?'

Ruby laughed, delighted by his quaintness and the sight of his strong, uniform-clad body. Scarlet lips close to his ear, she murmured, 'You can have all of 'em,' and he swung her on to the dance floor. It was Wally who had persuaded her that she should dance more.

'Clumsy?' he contradicted when she tried to protest against it. 'Oh no. You should just try it with me. You can dance – I know you can.'

And with Wally's arms round her guiding her she found she could, and revelled in it. She drew the line at jitterbugging – 'I'm too hefty – I'd break your back doing that!' – but found her rhythm to all the favourite swing music, jiving and twirling to Glenn Miller and Duke Ellington, Wally holding her close through the slow numbers. Their favourite song was 'Moonlight Serenade'. Along with all the others out to have a good time and brighten up the bleak wartime days, she felt that an evening of dancing could cheer the whole week. And with Wally, she could almost fly! They danced number after number, occasionally sitting out for a drink to get their breath back, faces glowing, laughing and chatting. For the first time Ruby found she didn't need to be in a group, as she had when they were younger and used to go out with Frank, Jack and the other lads. She was happy just being with Wally. When a slow number came on, Wally held her close, staring straight into her eyes until she was weak with desire for him.

'Let's go soon,' she whispered. 'Where we can be on our own.'

Wally closed his eyes for a second. 'You're my girl,' he said, in that drawling accent which she loved. 'My lovely Ruby, my jewel.'

The only place to go, in the winter cold, was Glover Road. They sat wrapped round each other on the bus, snatching kisses in the murky light. When Ruby let them into the house, to her relief the place was quiet. The boys were in bed.

They were kissing before they'd even taken their coats off. One of the things that excited Ruby about Wally was the way he was such a gentleman when they were out, yet his kisses were urgent and uninhibited. He pressed her forcefully against the wall in the darkness, his hands sliding up under the green silky skirt.

'Wait—' Ruby took hold of his arms. 'I'll go up and see if Perce's put Marleen in my room . . . I can move her out . . .'

But his hands continued to caress the back of her thighs. 'Why not here?' he murmured. 'Here and now, baby . . .'

'But what if they come down?'

'Why would they? Why don't you just light a little candle so I can see you?'

Once she had done so, hands fumbling for the matches, he removed her coat, then his own, and began to unfasten her dress, peeling it down over her breasts, kissing, stroking her until she could make no more common-sense suggestions about going upstairs. She felt her dress slither down over her hips to the floor.

'Come here—' He led her to the chair and knelt in front of her, continuing to undress her, sliding her stockings down to her ankles as they kissed.

In moments he was reaching for his jacket, fumbling in the pocket.

'Damn!' he shook it.

'What's up?' She was sitting naked, hair a dark cascade down her shoulders. But she knew what he was looking for. French letters, US army issue, which he always carried.

'They're not there!'

'Try the other pocket,' she suggested impatiently. She wanted him so badly!

'No – nothing. Oh goddam!' He flung the jacket down.

They couldn't stop now, Ruby thought, they just couldn't. She pulled him close, reaching down to caress him, inflaming him further until he groaned helplessly.

'Come on,' she whispered, clinging to him. 'It'll be all right just this once.'

The first thing she was aware of the next morning was the feel of Marleen's pudgy hands moving across her face, trying to prise open her eyelids. She slept in a little bed beside Ruby's now, which she could climb out of by herself.

'Oh Marleen!' Ruby groaned. 'Gerroff, will yer? What time is it?' In the blacked-out room it still felt like the middle of the night.

'Get in,' Marleen insisted.

'All right then.' Ruby budged up and Marleen cuddled in with her. 'But I'll have to get up soon.'

Last night came back to her now, a delicious memory, and she smiled, snuggled in the warmth of bed. She could recall intensely the feel of his body, the urgent desire on his face as they clung to one another in the candlelight. He had wanted to lift her up, make love to her carrying her around with her legs round his waist.

'Don't be daft!' she giggled. 'I'll break your back!'

So he'd flung himself down into the chair instead and patted his lap.

'Here – come *on*!'

She relived it all, trying to block out Marleen's chatter. What an evening, what a fella ... Then it struck her like being doused with a bucket of water. Her heart began pounding. They hadn't, they couldn't have done! God in heaven, she'd let him make love to her with no protection – positively encouraged him, in fact! How could she have done anything so insane – what if she caught for another babby? The very thought brought her out in a cold sweat. One time around was quite enough, thank you very much. She tried to calm herself. It had taken her quite a time to catch with Marleen, hadn't it? It didn't happen doing it just the once. They just mustn't do it again. And Wally was a good man. Solid and true. He'd stand by her if anything happened. He'd been so good about Marleen. Once again she pictured him, the sweet way he'd kissed her goodnight before he left for the barracks. She found herself full of a tender, unfamiliar emotion.

I do believe I love you, Wally Sorenson, she thought, somehow surprised. Really and truly love you.

Twenty-Seven

'Yer better come, Edie. Our mom's come over all queer and I can't get 'er to talk to me!'

It was late and Edie had answered the door to find Rodney's gawky figure panting outside.

'What – you mean . . .?' Edie had only left Charlotte Road two hours ago, but her mother had been tucked safely up in bed, though she was looking very poorly. Edie grabbed her coat. 'Is she still breathing, Rodney?'

'I think so . . .' His distressed face looked younger than his fourteen years.

'Would you like me to come with you?' Janet asked.

'No . . .' Edie said. She couldn't bear Janet to see her mother, however grateful she was for her sympathy. 'Thanks, Janet – there's not much to be done I don't think.'

On the way she quizzed Rodney as they hurried along through the dark.

'So what happened? And where's our dad?'

'Nothing happened, 'er just slipped away – I don't mean passed away, but it was like 'er falling asleep, 'cept I couldn't wake 'er.' Rodney tried to explain in his gruff, adolescent voice. 'Our dad's out. I dunno where. Down the Steps, I s'pose.'

Edie cursed. 'Just like 'im to be getting tanked up down the pub when 'is wife's dying. So no one's with 'er?'

'No, I thought I'd better come for yer.'

'You did right, Rodney.' Edie reached out to squeeze his arm for a second. 'You shouldn't've been alone with 'er in the first place.'

They walked into the silent house and climbed the stairs. Full of dread, Edie crept into the front bedroom where her parents slept. Her mother lay in the double bed, nearest the door, under the bleak light of the gas mantle, the bedclothes pulled up close under her chin. Edie guessed that Rodney must have done that. Only her face was visible and her right hand, protruding clawlike from the edge of the sheet. A severe frown tugged at her eyebrows.

Edie leaned over her, hearing her tiny, shallow breaths. A pungent, sickly smell hung round her. Should she send Rodney for the doctor, she wondered. But no – he'd long said there was nothing more to be done for Nellie.

'Rodney – go and get the kettle on, bab. It might be a long night and we'll need summat to keep us going.'

He clattered off down the stairs and Edie, glad still to be wearing her coat, drew it round her and sat on the chair by the bed. She looked round the room. Though her mom and dad had slept here all her life, she had seldom been in there. They had certainly not been children who cosied up with their parents in bed. The room felt unfamiliar, and somehow alien. The floor was covered in brown lino and the walls with faded paper patterned with scrolling ivy leaves. Apart from the bed there was a painted chest of drawers, a dark cupboard, a chair either side of the bed. On the wall to the left of the door hung the only picture. Edie peered at it. She had never seen it before. It showed a rosy-cheeked woman with a group of children in old-fashioned bonnets and pinafores, picnicking near a stream in a meadow, with trees behind.

The sight of it filled her with bitterness. Isn't that just typical of Mom, she thought, to have such a downright lie hanging on her bedroom wall! When did we ever go for a nice outing with her? Or feel anything of the comfort of a mother? She looked down at the woman lying beside her and tried to summon up at least sorrow or pity if she could not manage love. She could find pity for her wasted state, but she could feel no sympathy for the past, for all the coldness and *contempt* – yes, that was it – that she had shown them. As if her lip curled with loathing at the sight of them all. Instinctively, Edie fingered the scar through her blouse.

'You didn't know what being a mother should be, did you, Mom?' she whispered. 'Why were you so hard and cruel? Couldn't you have been kinder to us? We wanted to love you – we did . . . We wanted it so much . . . Ruby's mom was more of a mother to me than you ever were.'

Tears slid down her cheeks and her throat ached. Poor little things we were really, she thought. She thought about Davey, what she felt for him, how much she hungered for his love, and her mother seemed more of a terrible puzzle to her than ever.

Rodney came back up with a cup of tea and they sat drinking together.

'I'm glad yer 'ere, sis,' he said.

'Course I'm here.' She tried to smile back at him. 'This is a lovely cup of tea – just what was needed.'

'Is our mom going to wake up again?'

Gently, she said, 'I dunno, bab. I don't think so.'

Rodney nodded, eyes fixed fearfully on his mother's face.

They were just draining the dregs when they heard the front door close with a slam which made the windows rattle. Edie's and Rodney's eyes met.

Edie got up and Rodney followed her downstairs. They found Dennis Marshall leaning over the dying fire in the back room, poker in hand.

'Who let the cowing fire out?'

'Dad?'

He straightened up laboriously and faced her, swaying a little. His face was red and shiny, eyes bloodshot. She could smell the pub on him, smoke and ale.

'Edie? What're you doing 'ere?'

She just managed to stop herself demanding why *he* hadn't been here, leaving his wife in that state. She could feel Rodney watching from across the room.

'It's Mom. She's sinking. Yer'd best go up and see her.'

'What're yer saying, wench?'

'Rodney came to get me. Said she's slipping away. He was here on his own with her.'

His alcohol-befuddled mind struggled to take in the situation. 'Slipping away? Nellie? But she were all right earlier on.'

'All right?' Edie's temper began to get the better of her. 'Mom hasn't been awright in months, as well you know!'

'Don't you start giving me lip, wench—'

'Just go up, Dad, will yer?' she said, sternly.

As their father groped his way up the stairs, Rodney came over to her, his face anxious.

'Are you staying for a bit, sis?'

'Course I am. Don't know that she'll last the night. I'll sit up with her.'

He looked down at the floor.

'It's all right. You don't have to if you don't want. It's nearly midnight as it is. You go up to bed.' She leaned forward and kissed his cheek and he didn't push her off.

'Wake me if . . .'

'I will. Go on – off you go.'

She refilled the kettle, put it on the gas and stood in the scullery waiting, hearing her father and brother moving about upstairs. The waste bucket by the sink stank and she took it outside. She tried not to think about the long, desolate night ahead. She had to be up for work in the morning. Why am I here anyway? she found herself asking. What was it that bound her to the sick woman in the bed upstairs? Not affection, barely even respect. Duty, she thought. Blood ties. No choice – it was what you had to do.

When the kettle boiled she took her father a cup of tea to help sober him up and found him sitting on the chair she had occupied earlier, leaning forwards, elbows resting on his thighs. His clothes were tidy, hair cropped short in almost military fashion as ever. Oh yes, he always took pride in himself, she thought. The hair was almost white now. He was turning into an old man: so familiar, yet somehow a complete stranger to her. When had he ever been around to stand up for her when her mother started on her?

'Here—' She held out the cup and saucer.

'Ta.' He took it without even looking at her and she went and sat on the chair on the other side of the bed. He slurped the tea noisily. Nellie had not moved her position, but her breathing seemed a fraction louder.

Edie didn't know how long they sat there in silence. She heard Rodney's door close. Her father finished the tea and put the cup and saucer down on the floor, belching as he did so.

They sat watching Nellie's face. Edie felt herself starting to breathe in time with her. There was no other sound except their breathing, or one of them easing into a new position on their chair. Edie felt she was in a trance, caught up in the rhythm of inhaling, exhaling, barely knowing if she was awake or dreaming, yet she knew really that she was not asleep. Time seemed to drift. After a while she had no idea how long she had been sitting there. The road was completely quiet outside as the small hours of the night ticked past. It felt as if they were the only people alive. Nellie was peaceful. Her breathing quietened again as if she could barely even raise the strength to do it, so shallow it did not disturb the bedclothes.

'Nellie? Nell – can you hear me?' He spoke quietly, but his voice still sounded raspingly loud after the silence. Edie wondered what had suddenly driven him to speak. 'Nellie?' But there was no reply, not even the flicker of an eyelid.

He reached under the covers, apparently in a panic and took hold of her wrist, feeling for a pulse.

'Thought she'd gone there, for a minute.'

Dennis examined his wife's face again for some time, then began slowly to shake his head.

''Er was pretty as a picture once, yer know.'

To her astonishment, horror even, she saw his shoulders begin to shake. He put his head in his hands and sobbed. Edie sat paralysed, staring at him. Tears ran out between his fingers. She had no idea how to comfort him, couldn't bear this sentiment.

He lowered his hands, taking a great shuddering breath. 'You should've seen 'er. Fresh and pretty ... A picture she was.' He wiped his face with the backs of his hands, leaving his cheeks shining wet.

'You've no idea about 'er, 'ave yer?' He was aggressive suddenly. 'No bloody idea.'

Edie stared at him. What was he saying?

'D'you know what yer mother was when I met her?

Do yer? She was a hoower – a common hoower on a street corner.'

Edie leapt up, blazing at him, at the wicked absurdity of his words. Nellie, pillar of respectability!

'How can you say that? Your wife's lying in front of you and you're sitting there making up yer filthy lies about her! God knows, she wasn't a loving mom, but what kind of man are you, saying that?'

She expected him to jump up as well, shout back, but he sat shaking his head.

'Sit down, wench. T'ain't like you think. You think I never loved her. That it was always like this . . .' Edie sank down into her chair, eyes fixed on his face.

'When I married 'er she closed the door on the past – all of it, family, the lot. You've aunts and uncles yer know, somewhere in Brum, five of 'em if they're all still alive. I used to say to her in them early days, "Nellie, why don't you go and look up yer sisters? Let 'em know how you're getting on. You could help 'em." But 'er never would. She'd say, "They'll've had to fend for themselves by now. No use me going stirring things up."' He paused. 'I don't think 'er could bear it – if they were suffering, like, she didn't want to see it. Thought it was her fault. She just put it right out of 'er mind.'

Edie sat very still, drawn in to what he was telling her. Her chest felt tight.

'Why would it be her fault?'

'Well, Nellie was the one left to fend for 'em. 'Er was the second eldest of the O'Riordans – after a brother. Born 1894, Nell was, and five more followed – them that survived, anyroad. They lived over Bordesley way – but her father was from Ireland before that. Sligo. 'E come over on the boat.' He paused, scratching his head.

'The mom died after the youngest was born. Well –

they was already poor as roaches and the dad were left with seven kids. Nellie never went to school after nine years old – she had to be a mother to 'em all. Then when 'er was sixteen the dad was killed, crushed by a wall falling in on him. Well, Nellie's brother was out at work. Next thing, 'e took sick died an' all and it was just Nell. She took in carding and anything she could at home to stay and look after the five little 'uns, but it wasn't enough to make ends meet. Nellie was desperate. That was when . . .' A sob caught in his throat.

Both of them looked at Nellie, lying between them. Edie was numb with astonishment. This woman her father was talking about was like someone else. She couldn't take it in! Her mother had no living family, that was the version she had grown up with. No one in the world. No family, no past . . .

'I first saw her in a pub in Bradford Street. It weren't an Irish pub. I'd met up with a pal for a drink and she came in with a fella. I mean I didn't know then what 'er was. She weren't – you know – all dressed up like a . . . She hadn't the money for finery. Her looks were enough. Hair all up, bright as a copper kettle, those eyes flashing, and her face was fresh as a milkmaid's . . .' He choked, wiping more tears from his eyes, then continued talking in short bursts.

'I was older, of course – Nell were only a kid. I'd been working with my father for years by then, was almost set to take over . . . Anyroad—' He made a wiping motion with his hands, as if ironing out all that came in between. 'We were wed. Nellie was eighteen when we tied the knot and I was twenty-five. I daint know everything straight away . . . I mean she made up to me – saw I had a steady job, prospects.' With bitter sadness, he added, 'That was what Nellie wanted. Safety. Prospects. I only wanted her.

'Things came out of course. Er'd had a ... well of course I knew 'er was no vestal virgin, but er'd caught for a babby and, well, she had it done away with ... And there was her family – she wouldn't have it. Nor the Catholic Church. Wouldn't go back there. There was no one in the church except my side, on our wedding day ... Florrie came along the year after and Nellie seemed contented enough with her. Then I was away of course, the years of the Great War.' He stopped, apparently wondering, trying to make sense of it. 'I s'pose she 'oped I wouldn't come back.'

Edie made herself look at his face, the misery etched in it. She clenched her fists. He wanted her to feel sorry for him, was working on her pity. And she did feel more sorry than she could ever have imagined, picturing the proud, handsome young man who had been her father, madly in love with a woman who couldn't love him back. Their marriage seemed to open up in front of her like a long road growing bleaker and sadder by the year.

'Course, Florrie was a grown-up child when I came home, already at school. Nellie had found it easier than most – one child when she'd had to look after five before. 'Er was happy enough on her own, I think, in lodgings where no one knew anything about her. We moved in here then – and you come along, and Rodney after. All she wanted – a house, a nice road. Oh, she was so proud that we lived in a road not a street!' A slight smile reached his lips for an instant. 'Well – for a time. Nothing was ever good enough for long. And 'er never wanted me after that. Hardly ever. Not as a husband.'

There was a long silence.

Edie spoke eventually. 'I wish she'd've said.'

He spat out a bitter laugh. 'Said? Oh – she'd never've told yer. Rather've had her tongue cut out.' He stared at her wasted features. 'Poor old Nellie. We brought out the worst in each other, that we did. If things'd been different . . . I dunno.' He stood up. 'I'll 'ave to go down for a tick. All that tea . . .'

All that ale more like, Edie thought as he went to the door.

Edie sat on, trying to digest all she'd heard. She felt immensely sad and weary. And very uneasy. Had her mother heard all of that? Had he taken some pleasure in revealing her past when she was not in a position to stop him? In the quiet, Nellie stirred suddenly, gave a sharp sigh.

'Mom?' Edie stood over her immediately. 'Mom, you all right?'

There was no reply. Edie saw that her mother's face had changed. The frown was gone and her features smoothed and relaxed as if massaged by gentle fingers. Edie did not need to check her breathing to be sure.

When her father came clumping back up the stairs and into the room she was holding her mother's hand. Gently, she said, 'She's gone.'

Twenty-Eight

A week after Nellie Marshall's funeral, Janet sat at her desk in the buying department, fingers flying over the keys of her typewriter. The sun shone in from outside, though more weakly, now the afternoon was waning. It had been a bright March day, and on the way to work she and Edie had enjoyed the sight of clusters of crocuses and daffodils in Bournville Lane just beginning to open in the morning sun.

She finished the latest order, rolled the paper from the typewriter and sat back for a moment, flexing her aching fingers. She felt tense, coiled inside as if the slightest thing might make her explode. When she and Alec had parted in Corporation Street that Saturday afternoon he'd said, 'Look Janet – I know this isn't an ideal situation – for either of us. I only wish things could be different. But I have to say, I miss you like mad.' As he said that he reached out and touched her cheek. 'Remember Wednesday night was our night? Well it still could be. I'll go for a drink in the Midland, usual time, if you want to join me. I'll leave it up to you.'

Of course she had not rushed to join him. There had been Edie's troubles over her mother, and she had no intention of ever seeing him again. Of course she didn't. But then the notes started arriving. Not many, or with any regularity. Three had arrived now, slipped through the door, since she met him. Frances saw one of them and

Janet made an excuse for it. Something about the Bournville tennis club, she'd said. Lies, again. They were short notes. 'Meet me – please.' 'I'll be there – Wednesdays, as ever . . .' The latest had come yesterday. 'I'm waiting for you . . .' And she just couldn't seem to get him out of her head, the way he looked at her, eyes full of wistful desire. The disturbing, primitive effect he had on her had not faded completely. He excited her – had done from almost the moment they met. And she needed excitement through all the drabness of the war, single at her age in a house full of children and Martin so very distant. She just wanted a bit of male company. Sometimes life felt so bleak and stifling.

The ridiculous thing is, she railed to herself as she prepared to begin her new piece of work, amid the ringing of telephones and clacking of other typewriters, that I don't even *like* Alec very much. Everything about him is at odds with our morals – he's a philandering husband, a manipulator! Fancy writing those notes when he knows I'm engaged. How *dare* he! I shouldn't want the first thing to do with him. Oh, if only I hadn't run into him again! Oh, I do wish I could talk about this to Edie, but she's so straight and honourable, she'd never even think of doing something like this – and she's got quite enough on her mind.

Edie had kept all that she'd heard from her father to herself for the days after Nellie died. Janet and Frances came to the funeral with her, and after it, when they got home and David was in bed, she broke down and told them all about it. It was a heartbreaking story, Janet thought. How Mrs Marshall must have loathed herself to be so vicious towards her children. Yet it was one of those tragedies caused by circumstances and not really by anyone's fault.

Not like me, she thought. Oh, I must get a grip on myself and not spoil everything for Martin and me – if he's still alive somewhere. If he still loves me at all ... Oh Martin, where are you?

When the day's work ended it was dark. She set off towards home, but found herself walking past the house, and further on, until she reached the main road and caught a bus into Birmingham. Sitting in her seat, thinking nervously of seeing him, she found herself longing to smoke, even though she had broken the habit long ago. But the situation seemed to demand that she carry cigarettes in her bag. It seemed to turn her into someone else.

With a sense of disbelief at herself she walked down New Street, her coat collar up, heels clipping along the pavement. Memories filled her mind, almost like being at the pictures watching a show about herself, of the times she'd been with Alec, the intimate drinks together, drives out to the country, the day at the beach. As she neared the hotel she slowed, daring herself to go on. Outside the big doors she stopped. He would be in there, at a corner table, waiting for her, hat on the seat beside him. When he saw her his eyes would follow every line of her, caressing her ...

Aware that she must look strange and that a doorman might ask her what she wanted if she dithered any longer, she wrenched herself round and forced herself to walk back up the road towards the bus stop, the tension in her beginning to ease. No! She didn't want him. Not all that again. Not even if Martin never came home. Not if Alec was the last man on earth. She must have gone out of her mind going anywhere near him again!

Frances didn't quiz her as to why she was late home. She often was, stopping to finish work. But she did come into the hall, smiling as she heard Janet arrive.

'Darling – at last. Of course you would have to work late today of all days. Look—' From under her silky shawl she brought a letter.

'Oh!' Janet cried. 'Oh – is it . . .? It's from Martin!'

She seized the letter and set off upstairs without taking her coat off. 'Down in a tick!'

Sitting on her bed, she tore it open and read it so fast and hungrily! The letter provided the usual combination of hope and anticlimax. He could tell her so little of his whereabouts, his life. But he was alive and in the letter he included his parents' address in Warwickshire. He didn't say 'just in case' but she knew that was what he meant – it was they, not she, who would be sent any news of him. The letter ended with words of such tenderness that it brought on her tears. 'My own sweet darling,' he called her. Oh, the pleasure of it – and the shame, reading his words of love on a day when she had come so close to being disloyal to him! She held the letter to her breast and lay on the bed, weeping with relief and longing.

Ruby had tried to shut it out of her mind. She'd missed her monthly visitor twice since that night with Wally, the time they'd made love without any precautions. She wouldn't catch for a babby just from the one time, surely! But two days ago she had woken feeling sick. And there were the other signs, the terrible tiredness, the way certain smells made her feel queasy. She lay in bed, while her mind raced doing calculations. It was February when she must have caught. That meant she'd be having it in – she counted on her fingers – November. Almost exactly three years after Marleen! Oh no, it couldn't be. Please, let it be a horrible mistake. Let her just be poorly instead!

She pushed herself up groggily and sat hugging her

rough blanket over her knees, the implications of it all forcing themselves into her mind. It would mean leaving work again, at least for a few months. She'd have to go through the hell of another birth – just the thought of the hospital made her go cold – and all that horrible feeding, and bringing up two children on her own. And what was far, far worse was, she wasn't married! Everyone knew Frank had been killed. Surely she wouldn't be able to carry on working at Cadbury's if they knew that! What if she told Wally? Immediately she thought of that leave with Frank, so hurtful and humilating, when she had first been expecting Marleen. If she told Wally now he might take to his heels just like Frank. A man didn't like that sort of surprise, that was one thing she'd learned the hard way. No – she couldn't tell him. At least if she kept quiet she'd have him for a few months longer, before it became obvious and he left her anyway. A few tears trickled down her cheeks, but she wiped them angrily away. Where was that going to get her? There was no one to dry her tears: she would just have to get on with it, up and out of bed, get the kettle on for a cuppa.

The next day she was due to meet Wally. Once again they'd arranged to go dancing. Although Ruby was tired, she felt better by that time of day and she dressed herself up in her green frock and powdered her face to hide the dark circles under her eyes, adding a touch of her brightest red lipstick. She smiled determinedly at her reflection in the mirror.

'Ready for anything, eh, Rube?'

She was determined to be as happy and loving as possible.

'Here's my gal!' Wally greeted her with his usual enthusiasm, flinging his arms round her and kissing her and Ruby was reassured. He was a good man, Wally was.

She linked her arm with his and smiled up at him as they stepped into the dance hall, with its smell of floor polish, of sweat and cheap perfume.

They danced to the fast swing numbers, the colour coming to their cheeks, twirling round one another. Ruby laughed and joked as if she had no cares in the world, kissing Wally amid the clapping and whooping when the music stopped. At the moment she felt as if all her safety and her future depended on him. And she felt so much for him – she did! When a slow waltz number came on and they were gliding round the floor together, she put her lips close to his ear.

'I love you, Wally.'

He laughed. 'And I love you too, babe.'

'But I *do* love you,' she insisted.

He drew back and looked at her quizzically. 'I know you do. Why so serious tonight?'

'I don't know.' She pulled him close again, not wanting him to look into her eyes. 'Sometimes I think about the future, that's all. With the war on we never know from day to day. Wouldn't you like to settle down and have a family one day, Wally?'

'Sure, course I would. Some day, when all this is over.'

When she hesitated he drew back to look at her again.

'You're not trying to tell me something are you, babe? I mean you're not . . .?'

'No!' she laughed, pulling him close again. 'Don't be daft. I was just thinking, that's all. I wanted to know how you felt.'

'Right now –' He pulled her to the side of the dance floor. 'I feel like a drink. How 'bout you?'

She looked at his broad back as she followed him to

the bar. No, she mustn't tell him. Not now. It would spoil everything.

She confided in Edie, who tried hard to persuade her she should tell Frances and Janet.

'I don't like keeping anything from them,' she said. 'And they're going to have to know sooner or later.'

'No! Not yet. I need time to think what I'm going to do,' Ruby kept saying.

'Well, you should tell Wally,' Edie said. She'd only met him once but she had liked him. He seemed honest and kind. 'He's a nice man. You could get married. He might be pleased, you never know.'

But Ruby was not to be persuaded. ''E is nice. I think 'e's a faithful sort, but I'm frightened to death of telling him. I just can't at the moment, Ede. And what about Cadbury's? What on earth am I going to tell them?'

As the spring wore on, Ruby started wearing a ring to work and calling herself Ruby Sorenson. Lightning romances and hurried weddings were nothing all that unusual these days and apart from receiving congratulations and accusations of being a dark horse, this raised very little comment.

The days became warmer. Trees blossomed. Ruby continued to see Wally whenever he could get away. Several times she came close to telling him, but the pregnancy was barely showing yet and she put it off every time, frightened he would reject her, even though he kept telling her she was his girl and he loved her.

Men are full of flannel, she thought. He's all lovey-dovey now, but that could soon turn on its head when he knows there's a babby coming. Some of the time she was full of fear and anxiety, and at others, when she was with him, she tried to forget and enjoy herself. She wanted everything to be normal.

But she was soon in for a shock. She met Wally for a night out at the end of May. They walked up Bradford Street to Highgate Park, where the air felt a little cleaner among the trees. Strolling along the path with his arm round her shoulders, Wally said, 'Look, sugar, you aren't going to like this, but I don't think I'm going to be able to see you – least not for a while.'

Ruby felt his words sink through her like a heavy stone. Her chest tightened. He had guessed, that was what it was! This was his way of getting rid of her. Oh, why did this always happen?

'And why's that?' Hurt, her voice came out full of aggression.

'Hey – hey, babe.' He stopped and took her in his arms as she fought back tears. 'What's all this? This isn't my idea, I can tell you – it's all beyond my control. You know us Yanks're here for a reason, don't you? Well, things are hotting up – we're confined to barracks after today. Orders – nothing I can do about it.'

'Oh, Wally!' Ruby wailed. She hid her face in his chest, against the tough serge of his uniform. 'I can't stand it. What am I going to do without you?'

'Ruby . . . look at me, Ruby.' His voice was tender and the seriousness in it made her look up at him.

'Wally,' she said, her voice trembling. 'I love you. I do. I'm not just out for a good time.'

'And I love you too, babe. You know that. You're my gal. But I'll be back – when it's all over. You'll love the States – wide open spaces, the big cars, everyone neighbourly. My family'll love you!'

Ruby stared at him, unable to speak for a moment.

'D'you mean ... We could ...? What – you'd marry me?'

Wally released her and suddenly she was looking down at him as he dropped on to one knee in the middle of the park. 'Ruby, my lovely Ruby – will you do me the honour of becoming my wife?'

Tears ran down her cheeks. 'I've been so worried,' she cried. 'I didn't know if you really wanted me and I'm expecting our babby and I didn't know what to do!'

He was on his feet immediately, hands on her shoulders. She saw a muscle twitch in his cheek. 'Oh, my golly.' But his tone was awed, not angry. 'Are you sure?' He looked down at her. 'There's nothing – I can't see anything.'

'I'm only three months gone – a bit more. You can see if you know. Feel.'

She took his hand and laid it on her belly. There was a tiny bulge, hard to detect in her already rounded stomach.

A smile, full of wonder, spread across Wally's face. 'Is there really a Sorenson Junior in there? Well I'll be! Why didn't you tell me, for heaven's sakes, Ruby? I mean how does it look if you're having another baby without a husband? Jeez—' He stepped back, exasperated, and paced up and down. 'If you'd said before we could've gotten married. I mean I won't be free after tonight. Why didn't you tell me?'

'I was frightened you'd leave me.'

'Oh, Ruby.' Once more she was in his arms. 'Whatever happens, even if we aren't married yet, we will be, OK? I want you to be Mrs Sorenson of Fairmont, Minnesota, and we'll settle down in a house close to my folks and raise a family. We'll have, let's see, not too many – three children? How d'you like that?'

Laughing and crying together, Ruby flung her arms

275

round his neck. 'Oh I like it! I love it – and I love you, Wally Sorenson!'

Within a very few days the GIs who had not already been moved south left the Midlands. On 6 June airborne troops preceded the infantry in invading the coast of Normandy. Many of the troops were American, as well as British and Canadians.

Ruby, Edie and Janet went out to the pictures together one evening. Ruby was more at ease with Edie and Janet now that she'd come clean about her pregnancy and told them she and Wally were as good as married. They tried to be positive and hopeful for her. Frances did point out dryly that as good as married wasn't the same thing as *actually* married at all, but she promised Ruby she'd give her any help she could.

There was a long queue outside the cinema. Ever since the news of the Normandy landings the newspapers had sold out in minutes and everyone listened with total attention to the radio news bulletins. The three of them sat in the smoky picture house, watching the newsreels about the invasion, thousands of men running off the landing ships and on to the French beaches. Edie and Janet sat either side of Ruby and tried to comfort her when she started to cry at the sight of it, and they heard other people sobbing.

'D'you think Wally was there?' Edie said as they walked to the bus stop afterwards. The light had not yet died. They all wore cotton frocks, cardigans draped loosely over their shoulders, it was so warm. Janet wore her sunflower-yellow dress, Edie's was mauve with a white collar and Ruby's pale blue, and dotted with big pink roses.

'I don't know.' Ruby had been awed by the Pathé film, really frightened at seeing where Wally might have gone, running from that grey, heaving sea into the gunfire. 'Oh God, I hope he's all right.' It came home to her with great force how much more worried she was for Wally than she ever had been for Frank. She hadn't ever really loved Frank, not like this, with the tender ache she felt inside for Wally. 'I understand more what you've been going through, Janet. You've done nothing but wait, have yer?'

'Sometimes it wells up,' Janet said. 'Especially if there's something in the news. A lot of the time I just feel numb. It's been so long.'

'Had any news lately?' Ruby asked.

Janet shook her head. 'Not since March. Two and a half months. That's normal, I know, but you can't help worrying.'

'Oh,' Ruby said bleakly. March seemed aeons away to her.

Edie listened to the two of them. If anything good was coming out of all this anxiety it was that Janet and Ruby were growing closer through all these struggling days of war, going through some of the same things. Edie squeezed Janet's arm, knowing how she watched the war in the East, the desperate fighting there had been against the Japanese in India and Burma, wondering if that was where Martin was. The towns of Kohima and Imphal had been cut off by the Japanese, and although they had broken through at Kohima, Imphal was still under seige. Janet could hardly bear to think about it. Was he trapped in there? Had he been captured by the Japanese? Or had he been lying dead for weeks without anyone to let her know? In desperation she had written to his parents asking for news, but she had had a worried letter in reply saying they had not heard from Martin either. Of course he might not be in any of these places. He might be safe somewhere in South India. But if so, why had no one heard from him?

'Never mind.' Despite her pain and anxiety, Janet heard herself sounding like her mother. 'All we can do is wait and help each other through whatever happens, isn't it?'

'Us wenches stick together through thick and thin!' Ruby cried, and slipped her arms through Janet's and Edie's. On impulse, she started on a verse of 'Let's swing out, to Victory!' and the others joined in. Singing and laughing, the three of them made their way home, arm in arm.

Twenty-Nine

September 1944

'Hello my beautiful boy!' She took Davey's face in between her hands and kissed him as he sat at the kitchen table, dunking arrowroot biscuits into warm milk. He had a thin, milky moustache. 'So how did you get on?' He looked blankly at her.

Edie smiled. 'First day at school – remember?'

'It was all right,' he said contentedly, biting into a second biscuit.

'Here,' Frances handed Edie a cup of tea and sank down wearily at the table. She was already wearing her slippers for comfort. 'Come and join us for a minute. He's got along very well, haven't you, Davey? We went along to the school and there were other children on the way of course. And I asked him if he wanted me to come in, but everyone else was saying their goodbyes outside – a few tears from some of course. He said no, he'd go in by himself and off he went. Didn't turn a hair.'

Edie had expected Davey to be nervous and tearful on his first morning, but instead he'd been so excited he couldn't wait to get there. He'd had his uniform on even before she left for work. It was Edie, not Davey, who was churned up inside and had a lump in her throat at the thought of letting him go.

Letting Davey out of the cocoon of safety and privacy of home after all these years had disturbed her ghosts. All this time she had kept him close to her, living their quiet life, hoping no one would come looking for him. Her few close friends knew how he had come to her in the Blitz of course, but Edie didn't want to attract attention to it. Frances had suggested a number of times that she adopt him properly to put her mind at rest, but she wouldn't do it. She had even dreaded taking him to the doctor when he had earache, and went to a surgery in Selly Oak where they didn't know her. She was frightened of anyone asking questions. When she went to Davey's school and stood under the headmaster's gaze, she had felt flustered, panic-stricken. She'd have to tell him lies! Supposing he asks for Davey's birth certificate! I'll have to say we've lost it, she thought. I don't even know what day he was really born on. I don't know the first thing about him! But for all that, Davey was *her* boy. She'd looked after him all this time, felt the emotions of a mother. And now she had to send him out into the world with nothing but a satchel and fourpence for his dinner!

'So did you like it?' Edie pressed him. 'Are there some other nice children?'

'Oh yes,' Davey said airily. There was a pause, then he added, 'They don't know much, though.'

Edie and Frances looked at each other and both started laughing.

There had not been a lot to laugh about as the summer months went by. Though the news started to be better, the defeats of the Japanese out east, the Allies marching into the August heat of Paris, still neither Janet nor Ruby had heard from their loved ones. There was every reason to fear the worst. The three women had grown even closer over the past months. Janet, who had parted with

Martin so long ago, was the least able to feel hopeful. What they had heard about the fighting in south-east Asia was appalling. How could Martin have survived? And if he had, then why had she heard nothing? The same desperate thoughts went round and round inside her head. Sometimes she was very low, and Frances, Edie and Ruby did their best to comfort her.

Ruby was convinced that Wally was alive. 'They can't have time for writing letters with all that going on. But I'll hear from him any day – I just feel it. Big strong bloke like him!' She scanned the newsreels, the units of Americans marching into Paris in August, hoping that by lucky chance she might see his face, but so far if he was there, he was at the back of the crowd.

She was blooming now, heavily pregnant with a couple of months left to go, and she seemed incapable of worrying too much about anything.

'Of course, I'll look after the baby when its old enough,' Frances told her. 'Although I do believe this might have to be the last one I take on. I'm getting far too old for it! But Ruby, dear, you do need to think about how you're going to manage things. Especially in view of your mother's news.'

Ethel Bonner, alias Mimi, had come home one evening from an extended ENSA jaunt round the Midlands, hair peroxide blonde, heels clicking up the front steps, and announced, when she was scarcely through the door, that she was to remarry, a man called Lionel who was her pianist with the Lucky Dip Entertainers.

Her children all gathered round, full of questions.

'I'm very happy for you, Mom,' Ruby said when the hubbub had died down. 'But as you can see, I'm in the family way again and I'm not going to be able to look after the boys for yer any more. You've got to come home and be a mom to them. You've left us to fend for ourselves long enough.'

The pregnancy had not been showing enough to be obvious last time Ethel had stopped off at home. It was the first time she'd heard of it.

'*In the family way?*' Ethel seemed to come down to earth with a thud. She sat down abruptly by the range. Ruby noted that she had nice sheer nylons on under the smart suit. 'But yer a widow! Who's the father, Ruby? Who the 'ell've yer been playing about with?'

'I haven't been playing about. He's an American soldier called Wally Sorenson and I love him. He's much better to me than Frank ever was.'

'Oh yes, and where 'is 'e now you've a babby on the way?'

'Fighting in France,' Ruby said proudly.

'Oh ar – and you've heard back from 'im, 'ave yer?'

'Well . . . no. But 'e loves me, Mom, I know 'e does and 'e's asked me to marry him! I s'pect 'e's been too busy, what with the invasion and everything, marching across France . . .'

'Busy spinning the same tale to some French wench by now – that's if 'e's not six foot under,' Ethel said. 'Ruby – how could yer be such a fool?'

'Oh, I wish you'd never come home!' Ruby got up and pulled herself heavily upstairs to her room. She lay on the bed and cried bitter tears. Where was Wally, her lovely strong man? Her husband to be? It was a terrible thing, hearing her mother voice her own fears so brutally.

But after a short time she heard Ethel coming upstairs. She sat on Ruby's bed, a proper mom again suddenly.

'Look, bab – it'll be awright. I'll be at home more now – I'll try to make sure of it. Soon as the war's over this'll all be finished for me anyway, Rube. And Lionel and me want to have a proper marriage, not running here and there, pillar to post.' Ruby felt her mom put her hand on her back and she sobbed even harder.

'What's he like?' Ruby asked eventually.

'He's kind-hearted, Rube, like yer dad was. And 'e plays well, like Sid did. I know 'e's not yer dad, but 'e's a good'un and I hope you'll do your best to make him welcome. He makes me happy.' Ruby had to admit to herself that her mother seemed even more changed. Slimmer, her hair cut nicely and an easy smile. She couldn't begrudge her that. But she had worries of her own and she so much needed her mother's support. She sat up, pressing her hand over her stomach.

'I don't want to go through it all again, Mom. I hated it in the hospital—'

'You don't have to go up the hospital to have it, do yer? I had all of you at 'ome – never went near a hospital. We can call the midwife in. When's it due? Not long, by the look of yer.'

''Bout two weeks. Will you be there, Mom, this time?' Ruby felt like a little girl again, desperate for comfort.

'I'll do my best,' Ethel said. 'It all depends when his majesty decides to put in an appearance, doesn't it?'

Ten days later, Edie was in the cloakroom taking her overall off at the end of the shift when Ruby appeared next to her.

'It's started, Ede.'

'What?' Edie frowned.

Ruby laid her hand on her bump. 'It's coming. I've been on the go all afternoon. It's not too bad yet though – just sort of gripey.'

'Flippin' 'eck – why didn't you go home?'

'Oh, I'll be awright. It'll be a while yet.'

They went out into the stream of workers coming off the shift, into the winter darkness. The pavement was covered in mushy leaves and they caught a whiff of chocolate on the air.

'You all right?' Edie kept asking.

'Course I'm all right,' Ruby said, sounding a lot calmer than Edie felt. 'It won't be along yet.' But after they'd crossed Bournville Green and started up the slight hill, Ruby stopped for a moment, holding on to someone's front wall, breathing heavily.

'Oh my God, Ruby!' Edie was all of a dither. 'You should've gone home hours ago!'

'Will you stop mithering,' Ruby said, recovering herself. 'That's better – another one over.'

'Shall I take your arm? You need to get to the hospital.'

'No I don't. I ain't going. I can't stand the hospital – I'm staying home to have it.'

'Oh.' Edie was taken aback. Ruby hadn't said a word about her plans until now. 'You having Mrs Jessop in?' Mrs Jessop had been bringing babies into the world in the Glover Road neighbourhood for years.

'Maybe. But the person I want to do it really is Mrs Hatton.'

Edie's jaw dropped. '*Frances?*'

'*Me?* But I haven't delivered a baby for more than thirty years!'

Frances's amazement was even more complete than Edie's. 'I don't even know if my registration is in order any more! Oh dear, look, it's getting heavy going, isn't it, dear? We really should get you some proper help.'

Ruby was holding on to a chair in the front room, breathing through the latest contraction. The walk home seemed to have speeded things up.

'Never mind your registration,' she panted. 'You can't forget how to do summat like that, can you?'

'Well no . . . Oh dear, oh goodness . . .'

It was the first time Edie had seen Frances well and truly thrown by something and for a moment she felt cross with Ruby. Frances had done so much for them all, was kindness itself. But she was not young – a strain like this wouldn't do her any good.

Just then Davey and Marleen got wind that something was going on and came running through from the back.

'Hello, pet!' Edie kissed Davey. 'D'you have a nice day at school?'

'What's wrong with Auntie Ruby?' David asked, with a five-year-old's directness as Ruby puffed away over the back of the chair.

'She's got a pain in her tummy,' Edie whispered.

Marleen looked back and forth at all of them, trying to make sense of things.

'Right.' Frances switched into a different gear in front of their eyes. 'Well, if this is the situation we shall have to do our best. Ruby – what about your mother?'

'She's at home,' Ruby managed to say. 'Edie – could you fetch her?'

'Well, yes – if you think . . .' Edie looked at Frances. 'Is she having the babby here?'

'I don't think she has any choice by the look of things,' Frances said briskly, taking Marleen's hand. 'Now, come along Marleen. Your mummy's going to give you a little brother or sister to play with. But you have to come with me and be good for a bit. Edith, could you hurry, please?'

Edie tore down the hill to summon Ethel, and ran

back ahead of her without leaving her any time to ask questions. When she got back to Linden Road, Frances seemed to have recovered her midwife's instincts and was moving energetically round the house, sleeves rolled up and a clean white apron on over her skirt and blouse.

'Now, Edie.' The list of Frances's thoughts spilled out. 'I've taken her up to your room – that seems the best place. I've sent David and Marleen up with some newspapers, but from now on I shall need you to keep the two of them out of the way. Janet can help when she gets in, and there's a fish pie in the oven. I'm looking out old sheets, I still have most of my basic equipment and we shall have to pray for a nice healthy delivery. If anything goes wrong she'll need to get to hospital. Now the kettle's on and a pan to boil. Ruby's mother can help you – oh—' She stopped, half way up the stairs. 'Give her some fish pie if she hasn't had any food . . .'

'Don't worry,' Edie said, following her. 'I'll come and get the kids out of there.'

She was surprised at the sudden speed with which Frances managed the stairs. She followed her rounded figure up to the bedroom, full of respect and fondness for her.

'I'm sorry, we've landed you with yet another thing,' she said.

Frances turned, a smile lighting her face. 'Well – I'm a bit anxious. It's been a long time. But awfully exciting as well . . . I can't help feeling flattered.'

As Edie took the children downstairs, Ethel arrived.

'I'll go and be with her in a minute, when I've got my breath back,' she panted, pulling her coat off. 'Dear, oh dear, our Ruby's given me some shocks in her time. Is she all right? Mrs Hatton's a midwife then?'

'Yes,' Edie answered both questions, still full of wonder as she took in fully the change in Ethel's appearance. 'She'll look after her all right.'

Ethel had had the presence of mind to bring some of Ruby's things and also a few of Marleen's old baby clothes ready for the new arrival. She was in the process of unpacking the bag when Janet appeared.

'Hello.' She looked round in amused bewilderment at the children still up and playing about, Ethel's platinum blonde head bent over the bag of clothes and the general atmosphere of something going on.

'Ruby's having her baby,' Edie said.

'Is she?' Janet said, taking her coat off. 'Oh, marvellous.' It took a moment for the penny to drop. 'What, you mean, *here*?'

Edie pointed towards the ceiling and as she did so a bumping sound and a groan came from upstairs.

'Right,' Ethel braced herself. 'Can you show me the way, Edie?'

Edie took Ethel upstairs. Edie's room had been transformed: newspapers spread out and everything cleared out of the way. Frances stood hurriedly arranging some things on the table and Ruby knelt by the bed, hands clenched on fistfuls of the covers, breath hissing through her teeth. At the height of the pain a strangled cry came from her.

'Well done, dear,' Frances said as she came through it.

'Your Mom's here,' Edie told her. She hesitated and then seeing Ruby gathering herself up to face more pain she said, 'Can we come and be with you when it comes? D'you mind, Ruby?'

'I don't bloody care who's 'ere, I just want it out!' Ruby roared as the contraction seized her again.

Edie looked at Frances, who nodded. 'I think you'll be able to tell when!'

Edie retreated downstairs. She and Janet sorted out

makeshift beds for the children on the floor of the front room, gave them their milk and kept them occupied until they were both sleepy. Marleen dozed off in Janet's arms over a story. Davey was more aware of the strangeness of the evening.

'Why is she making those noises?' he asked Edie. 'Is her tummy hurting?'

'Probably a bit, yes,' Edie agreed. 'Now Davey, if you're a good boy and go to sleep there'll be a new little friend for you to play with in the morning.'

'Who?' he asked, wide-eyed as she settled him beside Marleen.

She kissed him. 'Just you wait and see.'

Edie made tea and took cups up to Frances and Ethel. She and Janet sat in the back room. It was impossible to think about anything other than what was going on upstairs.

'The sound of someone else in pain makes me feel all wobbly,' Edie said.

'Me too. It's enough to put you off childbirth for life!' Janet said. 'Shall I put the wireless on?'

'No!' Edie protested. 'I want to know what's going on!'

'Would you go through it again?'

'Oh yes . . .' Edie hesitated. Hearing Ruby brought so much of it back, the overwhelming experience of childbirth, which had ended so tragically for her. 'But not if I was going to lose him, like last time.'

There was a particularly blood-curdling screech from upstairs. Edie jumped up. 'Oh my God, listen to that, she must be getting close! You coming, Janet?'

'I don't know.' Edie saw her worried expression. 'I don't want to faint and get in the way or anything.'

'Come on – you won't,' Edie laughed. 'You don't want to miss it!'

They ran upstairs and found they were only just in time. Ruby, now clad in a pale pink nightdress, was sitting on the very edge of the bed, with Ethel doing her best to support her.

'Edie, Janet – help hold her up!' Frances commanded.

They pitched in, Ethel and Janet each taking one of Ruby's arms over their shoulder and Edie kneeling behind her and trying to give extra support under her arms. Fortunately it was quick or they would all have collapsed in a heap. Ruby lifted herself half off the bed, leaning heavily on her mother and Janet. Frances knelt in front of her.

'God Almighty, Rube,' Ethel puffed, 'I can't keep going like this for long!'

But Ruby was too busy screaming to hear her.

'That's it!' Edie heard Frances say excitedly. 'The head's coming!'

From then on there was a hubbub of everyone shouting, 'Come on! You can do it!' and Ruby yelling and cursing ripely at the top of her voice, and Edie stood up on the bed in time to see a dark, wet little head, soon followed by a long, slithery body, then they all collapsed panting back on the bed and the baby was screaming frantically in Frances's arms.

'Oh, Ruby dear, very well done!' Frances looked up, beaming. 'You've got another lovely little girl.'

Edie felt as if every emotion she had ever felt was passing through her in that moment and she burst into tears.

In a few moments Ruby was calmly holding her baby. She looked up to see Edie crying stormily, Frances wiping her eyes, and Janet and Ethel both tearful as well, all in a ring round her. She grinned suddenly.

'Oh my God,' she said, 'Look at the state of you lot!'

Thirty

'Well, he's certainly brought a smile to her face.'

Edie sat down next to Ruby, who was discreetly feeding Greta Mae, the new baby, a cardigan draped over her so no one could see anything. Ethel and Lionel had been married that afternoon and were having a knees-up in a little dance hall off the Bristol Road with as many friends and neighbours as they could squeeze in. All the cast of the Lucky Dip Entertainers were there, as well as family and friends. They'd strung up some bunting and streamers, everyone had rallied round to bring plates of food and all the drink they could lay hands on, and the troupe were in fine fettle. There was always someone banging out a tune on the piano in the corner, and as often as not a group of the others singing and dancing along. Even Frances got up and joined in the singing. When Ethel had spotted the piano in the Hattons' house after Greta was born, she asked Frances if she played, and since then there'd been a couple of sing-song sessions at each other's houses. The two had bonded in what at first seemed to their daughters an unlikely friendship.

'They balance each other out somehow,' Janet said to Ruby one day when they were puzzling over it. 'Your mother brings out my mother's light-hearted side.'

'Yes.' Ruby thought about it, head on one side. 'And Mom's got quite a serious side to her, you know, thinks more deeply into things. Frances makes her a bit more sensible!'

Whatever the case, the sharing of Greta's birth had certainly brought them close and they were both standing up by the piano belting out 'As Time Goes By' with full enthusiasm, Frances in a soft blue dress, Ethel resplendent in a skin-tight, shimmering, buttercup-coloured creation and plenty of make-up, her lips red as poppies. Janet was up there with them, and David, standing rapt at the edge of the group, a fascinated smile on his face which made Edie smile too.

Ruby looked over at the happy gathering round the piano. 'Yes, he's awright, Lionel is, he's kind-hearted and good with the boys. I mean I was bound to be suspicious of him at first, wasn't I? No one's going to take the place of our dad, ever.' Lionel was a lean man, rather suave, with a face marked by laughter lines and a smoker's tarry voice. 'I like him, and you just have to look at Mom. They're only doing local shows now. No more touring, so things're a bit easier.'

'Your Mom's dress is gorgeous – where'd she get that?'

'She's had it years,' Ruby said. 'Says she can just squeeze back into it now. Ah – look at your Davey. Never seen anything like it, has 'e?'

Edie smiled fondly, then looked closely at her friend. 'You still look all in though.' Ruby's round face was pale and she looked as if she had not slept properly in a long time. Her expression had a lifeless look. 'You all right, Rube?'

She didn't ask if there was news of Wally. She knew there wasn't. She ached with sorrow for both Ruby and Janet. Ruby looked down and shifted Greta's weight on her arm but Edie could see she was hiding her tears.

'Oh Ruby, I'm ever so sorry for you—' She put her

arm round her shoulders. 'I so wish there was summat I could do for you – both of you. I'd do anything . . .'

'I know.' Ruby blew her nose. 'Look, don't set me off. I want to be happy for Mom today. But I tell you, Edie, I can't stand not knowing what's happened much longer. I don't half miss work. At least it kept my mind off it. I mean if I'm never going to see Wally again I'd rather know now, one way or the other. I can't stand imagining all these terrible things. Janet wrote to Martin's parents didn't she? I thought I might to write to Wally's mom and dad and find out if they've any news.'

'In America? D'you know where they live?'

'Not exactly. But I know the town and their name – they own a shop. It might get there, mightn't it? Only trouble is, I'm frightened to.'

'Why?'

'Oh, I don't know,' Ruby sighed. 'Some days I feel so sure of what Wally was to me, and others I feel I didn't know him at all. I might find out he's married with a family already . . . I'll do it when I feel strong enough.'

Edie got up after a while and had a sing, but most of the evening she stayed close to Ruby and Greta, bringing Ruby drinks and things to eat. The Lucky Dips put on a show, dances and stand-up ('Keep the jokes clean tonight please, folks!' Lionel called out, to everyone's laughter). Frances and Janet came and sat with them, Frances looking happy and invigorated.

'What a marvellous occasion!' she said. 'We haven't been out and enjoyed ourselves for far too long!'

Edie sat Davey on her lap, handed him a spam sandwich and looked up at all the faces round the table. For a moment she felt a pang, the old longing.

'What's the matter, dear?' Frances leaned close to her. 'You're looking a bit glum.'

'Oh – nothing really. I was just thinking about my own family – such as it is. No one here of mine.' She tried to laugh it off. 'Same old story, really.'

'Well—' Frances put her arm round Edie's shoulder. 'I suppose that's the reality of it. But you know – we're your family. I can scarcely remember life before Edie now. I don't know if that helps at all.'

Edie took Frances's hand and squeezed it. 'Oh, it helps.' She smiled into Frances's serene face. 'More than I can ever tell you.'

That winter everyone was tired and worn down by all the years of war, and of living within the tight restrictions of shortages and rationing. From Aunt Maud down in Kent they'd heard about the strain of living under the flying bombs. The news was improving – the Allies reclaiming cities one by one, Brussels, Antwerp, Athens – and the blackout had, in September, been eased to 'dim out', but it seemed to Edie that people were finding it harder to keep going, especially those carrying losses and sadness, or uncertainty about loved ones. Whenever she thought of this she felt lucky. Davey was her world and he was safe and happy at school. His teacher told her that Davey was an extraordinarily bright boy and quick to learn, and she had glowed with pride in him.

In the Hatton household they prepared for Christmas in the usual modest way.

'We must make it nice for the children at least,' Frances said. Edie had begun taking Davey regularly to the Friends' Meeting House now he had started school and he liked to go and join in activities with the other children. Frances was delighted that they went. 'But I don't want him to think of us as being miserable and not celebrating ... We'll put up some decorations. All the children will like that.'

She got the children making paper streamers out of all sorts of scraps of paper, and paper angels and stars. They spent weeks making a nativity scene out of empty cotton reels and scraps of wool and packets and material. Marleen was immensely proud of it. There was a holly bush in the garden from which they cut sprigs each year to decorate the house and on Sunday afternoon Edie and Janet had gone out with Davey to snip them in the crisp afternoon air, and tug tough strands of ivy from the wall, to drape over picture frames and the mirror in the hall.

The next evening, when Edie finished work, it was damp but clear outside. She stopped for a moment as the others hurried past and stood looking back at the factory, Q-block stretching away to her left. The camouflage had been removed now and lights were visible inside, and Edie smiled at the sight of it. It was home to her. The factory had always looked enormous and splendid lit up at night. It was a sign of things getting back to normal.

'Edie!' She turned to see Janet hurrying to catch her up, hair bouncing as she ran, her bag tucked under her arm.

The two of them walked home chatting about their day. As soon as they got home, Marleen appeared. She had a little bow in her fair hair and was wearing a navy pinafore dress. She immediately seized Edie's hand and pulled at it in her usual imperious fashion.

'Come and see. We finished it!'

'The nativity, is it?' Edie laughed. The smile died on her lips as Frances came into the hall. Out of the corner of her eye she saw Janet's hand go to her throat.

'Oh ...' Her breath seemed to have got trapped. 'Oh ...!'

Frances was holding out a flimsy envelope and her expression was very solemn.

Janet reached out for it. Edie could see how much she wanted, and yet did not want to read the letter. White-faced, she took it without a word and went upstairs.

'It came at midday,' Frances said, shakily. 'I've hardly been able to bear not to open it. It's not Martin's handwriting.'

Edie shook her head, sick with dread. Marleen was still pulling at her, chattering.

'Now Marleen, just stop it,' Frances snapped. Edie could see what a state she was in. There were tears in her voice.

'It's all right.' Edie touched her arm. 'I'll go and see the nativity and keep her quiet for a bit. Janet'll need you.'

But as she was following Marleen a scream came from upstairs and they both rushed back into the hall.

Janet appeared at the top of the stairs with the letter in one hand and from the other something large and dark hung down. Her face was quite still, white, like a mask. She started to come downstairs but several steps down her legs gave way and she sank down, clutching the dark thing to her. It dawned on Edie that it was the jumper she had spent so much time knitting for Martin. She saw Janet bring the back of her left hand to her mouth and bite on it as the sobs began to shake her body.

'Oh darling, I'm so sorry . . .' In terrible distress, Frances moved towards her but Janet started shaking her head. She wrenched her hand away from her mouth.

'No . . . You don't understand . . .' She held out the letter. 'Oh my God . . . I can't believe it! He's alive. Martin's alive!'

The letter was on a sheet of thin, lined blue paper, in a

rather cramped, sloping hand. Edie and Frances stood poring over it at the foot of the stairs:

British General Hospital
Calcutta, India
16 October 1944

Dear Miss Hatton,

I am writing this letter on behalf of Dr Martin Ferris as I am a fellow patient here and have recently become well acquainted with him. He is most anxious to let you know that he is alive and thinking of you. From what I gather he has had a dose of some of the worst this region has to offer in the way of illnesses, on top of months of overwork. He is still very weak indeed and has a long way to go in his recovery, but is doing well.

He wants you to know that he will be coming home when he is strong enough to be moved though it is not clear yet when that will be.

He is watching me write this letter and he has just whispered to me, 'Tell her I'll be home for that wedding as soon as I can.'

I hope this letter serves to set your mind at rest.

With kindest regards,

John Latimer (Major)

Both weeping, Frances and Edie went and sat on the stairs on each side of Janet and put their arms round her. When Marleen climbed up to them, her little face stricken at the sight of them, they pulled her into their embrace as well.

*

Janet was like a person reborn. It was only now she saw her with hope again that Edie realized just how miserable she had been over the past months. They had a happy Christmas in the house, but a shadow still hung over everyone.

'If only Ruby could have the same news,' Janet said one evening. 'After all, she's already lost one husband and she'd got so much on her plate with the girls. I hope her letter managed to find Wally's family.'

News was not long in coming. Within weeks after Christmas Ruby received a letter from the USA, in a sloping, looped hand, from an Ed and Louisa Sorenson. She brought it up to Linden Road to show everyone. Edie was surprised at her calmness.

'I knew really,' Ruby said dully. 'I knew Wally was a good man and I know he loved me. If he could have been in touch with me somehow, he would have done.'

> 1071 Haselbach Avenue
> Fairmont, Minnesota
> January 4th, 1945

Dear Ruby,

We received your letter yesterday and although we were so happy to hear from you, in some ways we wanted to delay writing because in replying to you we can only relate bad news.

We received notification last June that our son Walter was killed on Omaha beach on the sixth of that month, the first day of the Normandy operation. Of course we and his sister are grieving for him terribly and we were touched and happy to hear from you. When he wrote us from England he told us about you, Ruby, and how much you meant to him.

297

He had said that he had every intention of making you his wife after the war was over, and nothing would stop him getting back there safely to you in England. We are so sorry this has not turned out to be his future and yours. And of course we had no way of knowing where you were.

We can only offer our warmest condolences and know that you are also grieving for our beloved son.

Ed and I wish you every blessing in your future, Ruby, especially after this terrible war is over.

With our warmest wishes and may God bless you,
Louisa Sorenson

'Oh,' Edie handed the letter back. 'What a lovely kind lady.'

Frances was frowning slightly. 'They sound a very nice couple,' she said sadly. 'But, Ruby, they don't know about Greta, do they? They don't realize they have a grandchild over here?'

'Well, no.' Ruby blushed. 'Thing is, Mrs Hatton, I didn't know what sort of reception I was going to get, did I? Now they've written me such a nice, kind letter I'll write back and tell them. They sound lovely people.' She swallowed, eyes shining with tears. 'Just like Wally.'

Part Two

1954–6

Thirty-One

November 1954

Janet closed the door of the doctor's surgery behind her and went out into the darkness of Vicarage Road, hurrying until she reached the park. She walked hurriedly across the grass, not caring about the mud on her shoes. Beyond the fringe of light from the road she stopped, and allowed the sobs to come, releasing some of her pent-up grief. She had fought grimly against crying in front of the doctor. But now it didn't matter if anyone heard and she was too distraught to care.

Dr Aitchison's final, dismissive words were burned into her mind.

'I'm sorry, Mrs Ferris.' He spoke in a clipped, almost hostile way, as if giving bad news kindly would have cost him too much effort. 'There's nothing more I can do. I think after all this time we'll have to accept the fact that you're infertile. You'll just have to keep busy and find other ways to fill your life.'

But I'm not infertile! she screamed in her head. It was the one thing she could not tell them, any of them. That time with Alec: the miscarriage. She had been pregnant and she lost a baby! Until her marriage she had buried all thoughts of that time. She had never even told Edie about it. Of course, she was ashamed, but it was more than that. It had never seemed entirely real. It was more like a bad dream from which she had woken and the baby was no more. She had closed her mind to the reality of it. But now, oh, the pain of remembering was real now all right.

It was true that some women could never bring a child to term. She knew that from years of living with a doctor and hearing him discuss such things, but with Martin she had never even conceived. She knew *she* was capable of conceiving a child, but no one seemed interested in whether Martin, a fellow doctor, could give her one. The problem was always assumed to lie with her, and it had barely occurred even to her that it might not, until Frances said quietly one day, 'Of course, a man can have problems as well . . .' And things fell into place.

She stood for a long time on the damp grass, barely noticing the cold, until she was calmer. A man walked past near her with his dog and she saw that she must look peculiar standing there alone in the dark.

I must get home and get the supper on, she thought dismally. Although goodness knows what time Martin'll be in to eat it.

For two years after she and Martin were married she had given up her job, taking it for granted that soon she would be busy with a family. When the children she longed for failed to arrive she decided it was no good moping about it at home, filling her time with curtain-making and bits of voluntary work. If she went back to Cadbury's and took her mind off it, she reasoned, the babies would follow. She had been too tense and upset – that was no state in which to create new life. So she had gladly returned to something like her old routine, and the tennis club, happy to be busy, to have company and a sense of purpose. But still she had borne no children.

Reaching home, she lit the oven and put in the crock of steak and kidney casserole she had made the day before. The potatoes could wait 'til later. She sat on the old Indian rug in the sitting-room, twisting sheets of newspaper in her hands to lay in the grate, sighing as she remembered the happy expectation with which she and Martin had moved into the house. She remembered something Edie had said to her recently about the day the war ended and how she'd felt.

'Thing was, I was happy, like everyone else. But suddenly everything felt really bleak and *frightening*. All that time I'd had you and Frances and Davey, all safe together and not much choice about what we did because of the war. And now it was all going to break up and we'd have more freedom and have to start deciding things for ourselves again. I felt terrible that day, even though it was the best day ever.'

As it turned out, Edie's fears had not been realized. Janet knew she had been frightened of someone coming to find Davey, a father in the services perhaps, or an uncle. But months passed, the servicemen trickled home, the prisoners of war, and still no one came, even though her name was recorded with local doctors and the police. Frances had gladly let her stay on as a lodger, especially with Janet marrying. She said it would be like losing two daughters at once if they both went.

Janet hadn't felt the fear then, the flatness. She was caught up in the atmosphere of street parties and rippling strings of Union Jacks and Welcome Home banners across the streets, as she waited for her turn. All she could think of was Martin coming home.

He was given early release from the army in early 1946, on grounds of ill health. Remembering that first sight she had had of him always stirred up the feelings again, the passion, yet the pity of it. It was a grey, freezing day in February when they met on New Street Station. She had not wanted him to come to the house. Not at first. She waited on the platform in the best clothes she had been able to scrape together in those austere times, a straight navy skirt and home-knitted pink twinset, her old camel coat and a handbag over her arm. The train was so late she began to believe he would never come. When she saw him at last, in those split seconds her understanding fought to catch up with the evidence in front of her eyes. It wasn't that she didn't recognize him – his height, his face, were too distinctive for her to mistake him for anyone else. But he was transformed. She saw a gaunt man dressed in civvies which hung several sizes too loose on him, skin stained a sickly yellow, a face old beyond its years. Janet felt her knees go weak at the sight of him, her emotions a mixture of joy, tenderness and also a kind of dread. His sickness had drawn his face in, emphasizing the full mouth, making his nose appear almost like the beak of a bird of prey. He looked temporarily alien, almost grotesque. But his eyes lit with emotion at the sight of her. For a moment they just stood in front of each other without speaking. Then he reached out and touched her cheek. Full of tenderness she held out her arms, the sight of him blurred by her tears. The long, lonely months and years, the shameful thought of Alec, none of that mattered now. It was past. 'Thank you for coming back to me,' she sobbed, as they clung to each other.

Later, he told her, 'I saw so many chaps after they'd had a "Dear John . . ." letter from home. Terrible, when you're out there. I can't describe it. I don't know what I would have done . . . You're what kept me going, my love.'

The early years of their marriage had been spent in adjustment. Martin was very keen to marry as soon as possible and the wedding took place in June 1946. Over the next years he flung himself with almost obsessive enthusiasm into the birth pangs of the new National Health Service. He worked punishingly long hours, even when he was not well himself, and often came home with stories of the people who had come to him with health problems neglected for years.

'It's absolutely incredible what some people have put up with!' he would exclaim. He was passionate about the NHS, about getting help and care to the poorest. He knew his work was worthwhile. But behind all the frenetic activity, Janet knew he was profoundly unsettled. The yellow from the jaundice and mepacrine tablets faded, but his inner turmoil remained. Once he did allow himself some free time, he couldn't sit for long, or relax. Couldn't allow himself just to be. And sometimes his temper flared and he said cruel things about which he was pathetically contrite afterwards. At the beginning she had found a deep, unexpected well of patience within herself. He wouldn't talk in any detail about what they'd experienced during the siege at Imphal, surrounded by the Japanese, barely eating and working in a field hospital day and night in conditions Martin said he could barely begin to describe. In those early years she had not worried so much about the lack of a child, thinking that perhaps Martin would be under par for some time after all his illness. And they needed to spend time together on their own, getting to know one another properly. She was understanding, careful with him. Their lovemaking had been passionate, easily overcoming the initial clumsiness. At times it was very tender. She was deeply moved when he cried in his sleep, tormented by dreams, then half waking, reached out for her, moving his hands hungrily over her as if desperate for warmth and comfort. But there had been times also when he was very distant, closed in on himself, and he did not touch her for days and nights at a time.

'I'm sorry,' he said one day, when they had been married for almost two years. He was standing by the window at the back of the house and she could only see him in silhouette. Things had flared up between them over something trivial – the state the garden was in – when they both knew the row was really about the fact she still wasn't pregnant. He kept saying, 'I'm sorry.' He turned his back on her and stared out. 'I'm trying to settle. Should be through it by now, I know. Civilian life is so different. So small and . . . stifling after all we went through.'

The word 'stifling' cut her deeply. He wasn't happy with her: he found their life petty and stifling!

'I've become hard in a way I don't like. I'm ashamed of it.' He turned to her. 'Please, darling, don't get upset. I hate myself for making you unhappy.'

Tears came to her eyes again as she knelt by the fire, thinking of that day. It was then that she had decided to go to work again. Staying at home alone was too unbearable. To everyone else they seemed settled, Martin developing a fine career as a doctor. It was only to Edie that Janet confided how much they were struggling, and Edie told Ruby some of it.

'Sod's law, isn't it?' Ruby said sympathetically. 'I get pregnant at the drop of a trouserleg with no husband and poor old Janet's having no luck when she could give a child everything it needed. It's not fair. I wish there was something we could do to help.'

It was over the past three years that she had truly begun to despair. Martin seemed more and more distant. She sat trying to think when they had last made love. He was always so tired. She felt at the lowest ebb she could remember. Her marriage seemed to stretch in front of her like a white track across a desert, isolated, unpeopled by anyone she could be really close to. Terrible thoughts came to her sometimes. What if she were to go and find Alec and persuade him to give her a child? Pass it off as Martin's? Or some other man? Someone who could help her ease the lonely ache inside her. She was appalled at herself for thinking this way. And what made it all the worse was that she knew Martin was suffering too, and they just couldn't seem to reach each other.

That night, laying kindling and some small knobs of coal in the grate, she felt so low, so worthless as a woman. She couldn't have children, couldn't seem to make her husband happy. She had always felt sorry for Edie, bless her, but even Edie seemed better off than her now. At least she had David, whom she adored. And she never seemed interested in marriage: there'd been quite a few interested in her over the years, but Edie just brushed them aside. It was only David who mattered. Janet scraped a match viciously along the box and lit the fire. The paper blackened, shrivelled, glowing at the edges, and she watched, trying to reach a place of calm inside. She needed to get the potatoes on, but Martin was bound to be late. He seemed to live on half-burnt dinners. She wasn't a great success at that side of things either, though Martin never complained.

A moment later the front door opened and she jumped violently. Disorientated for a moment, she wondered whether she'd dozed off in front of the fire and it was now nine or ten o'clock. But the clock said only ten to seven.

'Janet?'

He came in, blowing on his hands, his nose pink with cold, coat still on, flapping open. 'Ah good, a fire. It's freezing out.'

'You're home early,' she said cautiously. 'I'm afraid the supper's not quite ready.'

'That's all right – never mind.' He took his coat off, flung it over a chair and stood with his hands on his hips, staring at her for a moment, as if gauging her mood. She wondered if he could tell she had been crying, but he didn't appear to notice. And there was something new in his face.

'Look, Jan. I – I just . . .' He shrugged, a large, helpless gesture. 'I can't go on like this.'

She looked him full in the eyes. Face it. You have to face it, she told herself, taking a deep, desperate breath. 'You mean . . . our marriage?'

'What? *No*, darling!' He swooped down to kneel on the floor beside her. 'No, no, no . . .! Oh God, Janet, it's not you. I mean I know things have been difficult and we can't – I mean let's face it, we're not going to have children.'

Something tightened inside her, as if her very being flinched, even more than when Dr Aitchison had said it. It was the first time he had ever fully acknowledged what had become so cruelly obvious.

'But it's not that. I've come home early to tell you something, or rather, ask you. There's a job I could take, an offer from someone Jonathan knows – in Africa. The Belgian Congo. We could both go – have a new start, wider horizons . . .'

Janet looked up at his face, saw it shining in the firelight. She knew he could see life spreading out, opening up. He was like someone reborn.

'You want me to come with you? Really?'

'*Yes*. Oh my darling, how could you think anything else? Of course! I want you at my side whatever I do!'

Quietly, calmly she said, 'Then we'll go.'

Over the stew and potatoes, Martin told her what he knew about the job, which at that stage was not a great deal, except that he would be in principal charge of a new medical centre in a village called Ibabongo. The village had a mission station, maternity care and a leprosy hospital, but although there were qualified nurses, there was as yet no doctor. He knew his experience in the tropics would count in his favour. 'Although, of course, Africa has a repertoire of diseases all of its very own!' he laughed. 'There'll be a tremendous number of challenges.'

Janet drank in everything he was saying. She would go to the Congo. That she was agreeing to leave everything behind for an entirely new life, taking a risk of immense proportions, was not something she could fully take in. They could worry about what was ahead later. But what was so wonderful about the evening was their sitting talking, laughing together, planning a future, and seeing Martin so excited. Letting something new begin. She began to fold her preoccupation with children away in her mind. It would always be an ache, a deep sadness, but somehow they had to make a new kind of life.

When they got into bed that night, Martin lay on his back and let out a long sigh, as if a great load of tension in him was beginning to melt away. She lay facing him, smiling, and he put his arm round her and looked into her face with a slightly puzzled expression.

'I bet not many people would just say, "OK, let's go to Africa," like that, straight away.'

She looked seriously into his eyes. 'I can't bear to see

you so unhappy. I want us to be happy and I want to be with you. It'll be an adventure.'

Putting her hands each side of his face, she kissed his lips. She saw him close his eyes, felt his hands begin to move over her breasts, and she pressed close to him, hearing his happy sigh of desire.

'I want to see you,' he said. 'I haven't seen you for so long.' She knelt up and he lifted her nightdress over her head, exposing her rounded body, full hips and breasts, hair curling down over her shoulders.

They made love that night in a way that they hadn't in such a long time. As they lay together afterwards, warm and close, Martin kissed her and murmured, 'What a woman you are.'

Thirty-Two

A few days later, Edie experienced another of those moments which threw her so badly off balance that for a few seconds she couldn't think of anything to say.

David waited, across the table from her. Between them lay a dish containing the golden remains of a bread and butter pudding.

'Well, yes, of course you have – somewhere,' she managed, after a moment.

'Where is it?' He watched her in his intense way. 'Can I see it?'

Edie could feel Frances's eyes on her. She took a deep breath. 'The thing is, Davey—'

'Oh, please don't keep calling me that!'

'David. Sorry, love . . .' Edie spoke as lightly as she could. 'Of course I've got your birth certificate somewhere. But what with moving here from Stirchley, and the war, I'm not sure I could lay my hand on it . . .'

Edie felt as if someone had their hand squeezed round her heart. A blush seeped up hot through her cheeks. God in heaven, he must know she was lying! How could anyone mislay their only child's birth certificate? She forced herself to smile.

'I'll have a look through my things, see if I can find it.'

'OK.' David scraped up his last mouthful of pudding and pushed his chair back. 'Thanks, Frances, that was

313

lovely. And I will come and dry up. Just want to get my last bit of maths finished.'

'That's all right,' Frances said. 'Don't rush it. The drying up will wait.'

The two women watched him go. David had grown into what Frances called the 'in between stage', tall and thin, when the body's growth seems to have temporarily outpaced its ability to coordinate itself. His eyes were still large and dark brown, the most attractive feature of his face, which had otherwise long lost its boyish chubbiness for the more chiselled outline of adolescence. He was a lovely-looking boy, Edie thought, and would be a handsome man. He was a rumpled-looking character, never quite tidy, the sleeves of his jumpers seldom properly turned back, shirt often hanging out and shoes scuffed. He was always far too wrapped up in passionate interest in what he was doing or reading to bother with appearance. The door closed and they heard him running upstairs, two at a time.

Edie laid her hand over her heart.

'It shouldn't be such a shock, should it? Him asking me things. I know I've got to tell him some time. It's just the longer I leave it the harder it gets.'

It was a conversation the two women had had many times during David's upbringing. Edie had always said that she would know when it was the right time to tell him, but now it had become a block in her mind. So far as anyone else knew, she was bringing up a boy she'd adopted. People didn't tend to ask how it had come about and soon it was simply taken for granted that she had a son. The thought of David finding out that he was not her child sent her into a most terrible panic. He had begun to grow away from her in so many little ways: his studiousness, the way he had swept effortlessly into the grammar school and was learning French, Latin, German, his interests in engineering and mathematics, clever books he read, the way he didn't want to be babied with the name Davey any more. If she told him the truth, he might be angry, and reject her. Her boy, in whom she'd placed all her hopes and who was the focus of all her love. He was still her little Davey in her mind. What would she do without him?

'I expect his birthday coming up made him think of it,' Frances said, getting stiffly up from the table. Edie immediately got up to help. Frances's beautiful thick hair had turned almost pure white, with only a few streaks of silver in it, and she still wore it pinned up in a soft, attractive style. She was still beautiful, though she walked now with a slight stoop.

'Let me do it,' Edie said. 'You sit down.' Frances reluctantly agreed.

'It just all comes over me sometimes,' Edie said, stacking the plates. 'I know I've been a mother to him, and I love every bone in his body. That should be enough, shouldn't it? I'm the only mother he remembers. But I hardly know the first thing about him. I can't see things he does and say, "Ah well, he's like his grandfather or his uncle . . ." Because he's not part of the bloodline. And here I am telling him it's his fifteenth birthday tomorrow, and I don't know exactly when he was born or how old he is . . .'

Frances watched her face. Though her body was ageing now she was in her seventies, her mind was as lively as ever. She had been a friend, protector and substitute mother for Edie and the two women had long enjoyed a deep trust and comfortable understanding with each another.

'I know it's hard, dear.' She passed Edie a dish across

the table. 'It'll be the hardest thing you've ever done. But the time is coming for him to know the truth, isn't it?'

The first occasion when this happened had shaken Edie up a good deal more, partly because it was the first time and also because of the intimate nature of his question. It was when David was eleven, only a week after he had started at the grammar school.

He came home that night, proud in his new uniform. Frances said he had been unusually quiet. When Edie got in from work she went to find him. Putting her head round the bedroom door, she saw him bent over the table in his bedroom doing his homework.

'Hello, love. Have a nice time at school?'

'Umm.'

'What did you do today?'

'Lessons, of course.' He didn't even look round and there was a savage edge to his tone which was completely unlike him. Edie stood, hurt and uncertain, the edge of the door held against her cheek. She thought about telling him off, but she sensed he had not meant to be rude.

'We'll have a natter when you've finished.' And she went downstairs.

He was almost silent through tea. It was only when he was in bed that she got to the bottom of it. It was always the time he was at his softest. He was the big man in the day when he was with his friends: at night he was still the little boy who wanted a cuddle.

She found him lying with his face turned away from her, curly hair, recently shorn to go to the new school, dark against the white pillowcase.

'Night, night,' she said.

There was no reply.

'Can't you find a kiss for me, Davey? Is summat wrong?'

Eventually he rolled over, frowning and she sat on the bed.

'What is it, love?'

He still couldn't get the words out. He tried to blink away his tears.

'Has someone been nasty to you at school?'

'No – not really nasty,' he managed to say. 'It was just – after rugby . . .'

The story jerked out of him. In the showers, one of the other boys had noticed something about him, something he'd never known about himself, started pointing . . .

'My – you know . . .' He waved his hand over the lower part of his body. 'My *thing* . . . Is different from everybody else's.'

Edie's mind raced. Was Davey different? Blushing at the nature of the conversation, she thought quickly back to any other man's willy she'd ever seen. Not many, when you came down to it. Her father's – never. Rodney, whose napkins she'd often changed and bathed him, and Jack . . .

'They said I'd been circumscribed – or something like that.'

Circumcised! It dawned on her. Yes – of course, he *was*, though she'd never given it much thought before, just taken it that that was the way he was. Weren't lots of men circumcised?

'Then they saw that two of the other boys were the same and one of them, Dan, said it's because he's Jewish. Does that mean I'm Jewish as well?'

Edie felt herself floundering. She was gripped by terrible panic. *I don't know. I don't know who you are or*

317

why they did this to you . . . What should she know about boys being circumcised? Rodney hadn't been done, that was all she was sure about.

'No! No, of course it doesn't!' She tried to laugh, taking his hand. 'You said there was another boy as well – what did he say?'

'He didn't. He didn't seem to know. Why am I? Why were they laughing at me?'

'Well, sometimes the doctors just think it's the right thing, when you're born . . .'

'But did you ask them to do it?'

His gaze seemed to burn into her. She withered inside. Oh heavens, more lies. What could she tell him?

'No, but they thought it was the right thing,' she said firmly. 'It really doesn't matter, love. You're not the only one, are you? Now you mustn't let them upset you. If they say anything, you just say, well, that's the way I am, eh? They'll soon forget about it.'

He was still frowning. 'Circumcised,' he said slowly.

'Look, sweetheart, it's nothing.' She kissed him good-night, babying him. 'You go to bye-byes now. It won't seem so bad in the morning.'

The next evening after work she went home and asked Frances if she could borrow Janet's old boneshaker of a bike to cycle into town. Gripping the handlebars and trying to get used to the wonky brakes, she toiled through the backstreets in the dying evening, the air full of smoke from the chimneys. She reached Highgate, the streets a hotch-potch of terraces and cramped back-to back houses around communal courts. The streets were alive with children playing out before bed and she had to brake hard as a metal hoop, pursued by a young girl, came flying out into the road right in front of her.

'Watch it!' she shouted, screeching to a halt, her heart thudding.

'Watch it yerself, missis!' The girl shouted smartly, disappearing down an entry on the other side.

Another street away and she reached the place where Martin had his surgery. She knew he often worked late, and hoped he'd still be there, though he and Janet lived further out in a little house in King's Heath, a more suburban area. Martin had chosen to go into general practice in a poorer district.

As Edie leaned her bike against the wall of the large terraced house, she saw through the blind that there was a light on in his consulting room at the front. A wizened rose bush splayed against the wall by the front door, and just above it were two plaques displaying the names which shared the practice: Doctors M. A. Ferris and J. R. Weller.

Dr Weller, a pale, but kindly looking man about Martin's age, answered the door and Edie was shown into Martin's room. As she entered he looked up from the shadow behind a pool of light thrown on to the papers in front of him by the desklamp. For a moment as he looked up, she saw in his face an unguarded moment of sadness, of enormous weariness, as if to say, 'What now?' But seeing who she was, he immediately got up, face lightening into a smile.

'Hello there, Edie! This is a nice surprise. Thanks, Jonathan.' The other doctor went out, closing the door, and Martin offered Edie a chair. 'Come and sit down. Let me put the light on so we can at least see each other.'

When he switched on the overhead light Edie saw how

exhausted he still looked. The war, his months of lying close to death, had aged Martin considerably. Though still an imposing-looking man, in both size and appearance, his features were lined and haggard.

Though she was glad to find him still at work, she watched him sink into the chair behind his desk, thinking, why are you still here? Why aren't you at home with Janet, instead of sitting in this bare little room?

He sat forward and tidied a coil of black rubber tubing on his desk. It was attached to a piece of apparatus which took Edie back to the hospital, when she had given birth.

'What's that for?' she pointed. She was nervous and it was something to say.

'This?' He pushed it to one side. 'Oh, that's for measuring blood pressure. It goes by the rather inflated title of a sphygmomanometer.' His lips turned upwards. 'You don't want to have to repeat that after a glass or two.'

'No,' Edie smiled, thinking what a kind face Martin had. It was so sad that a couple like he and Janet should be suffering so.

'Can I help you in any way, or were you just passing?'

'No, I came specially to see you. I hope you don't mind.' She fiddled with the strap of her bag. Martin sat back in his chair, listening. 'I know you're not my doctor, but I wanted to ask you ... It's Davey. He came home from school yesterday and said the other boys'd teased him because one of them saw he'd been ...' She blushed hot all over, suddenly aware of what they were going to have to talk about. 'I mean I don't think my brother Rodney was, in fact I'm sure he wasn't, and Davey must've thought it so odd that I didn't know why he had been ... And I couldn't think what to tell him.'

'Been what?' Martin prompted gently.

'Circumcised.' She spoke staring into her lap. When she looked up, Martin was nodding thoughtfully. 'He asked me if he was Jewish.'

'Well, of course it's possible. Circumcision in general is on the decline these days, among non-Jews at least, but a great many boys used to be done round the turn of the century. I think my father was circumcised, come to think of it. The Victorians got rather keen on it – they seemed to think it was more hygienic, and perhaps that it would stop boys – you know . . . Well, that it would calm them down.'

Edie sensed that even Martin was embarrassed now.

'Seems a horrible thing,' she said, shuddering. 'Brutal when you think of it. But there are still people having it done?'

'Yes, but fewer. More a middle-class preoccupation really. I seldom ever see it round here.'

There was a silence. Edie looked across at Martin, trying to formulate what she wanted to say. She desperately needed a man's point of view. Davey's one question – why am I circumcised? – cut through to the very core of all her worries. There were so many things she was concerned about, on top of the day-to-day problems of bringing up a child, and central to them was that he had no father and was growing up in a house of women. That wasn't so unusual after all the wars, but Edie felt it keenly. Thinking of her own father didn't seem to give her much to go on. And Davey was so different from her, increasingly hard to read. Above all, though, she knew David was starting to ask the biggest question of all: who am I? And it was Martin, who had carried him in that night out of the fire and thunder of the bombing, who might be able to provide her with a clue. The questions swam, half-formed, round her mind, but she could not bring them out. She simply could not bear to ask. Instead, looking into his eyes, she whispered, 'I don't know what to do.'

For a moment he stared back at her and she knew he understood what she was struggling to ask.

'There's very little I can tell you. Really.'

'Oh.' She looked away, at the small wooden cabinet by the wall. Inside were instruments and jars.

Martin pushed his chair back and stood up. 'Edie, Europe is swarming with refugees and displaced children. Davey's one of the luckiest ones. He couldn't have had a happier childhood or a better mother. What more does he need?'

His words brought tears to her eyes. She looked up at him, such a tall, lean figure the other side of the desk. 'I don't know, Martin. That's the problem. But thank you – you've been a help.'

She thanked him again at the door. 'Give my love to Janet.'

'Come and see us soon.' For a second she felt his large hand on her shoulder. 'Look, if you're really determined to dig up more about him it probably won't be difficult. Just ask and I'll give you any help I can. When you're ready.'

Thirty-Three

'*Where?*'

Ruby was the only one who reacted straight away. 'Where the flipping heck's that when it's at home?'

They had gathered to see the New Year in at Janet and Martin's house: Edie, David, Frances and Ruby with Marleen and Greta, settled in, cosy by the hearth, Janet's floral curtains drawn closed against the cold night. Greta and Marleen were kneeling on the rug roasting chestnuts in the fire and being soundly ignored by David, who sat up with the adults, despite Marleen peering hopefully in his direction every few minutes. Janet had passed round drinks of warm, spicy wine and mince pies when they broke the news. Edie was silenced by her astonishment. Surely that couldn't be right? They were talking about moving to the other side of the world!

'The Belgian Congo, on the Equator, north of Bechuanaland,' Martin informed Ruby, laughing at her scandalized expression.

Ruby grimaced. 'Well, I'm none the wiser for that. What d'you want to go there for, wherever-the-hell it is?'

Edie listened as Martin explained their plans. He seemed to laugh so much more freely these days, she noticed. She wondered how Frances was taking the news. She was sitting on the settee, hugging her cardigan round her and staring thoughtfully into the fire. Edie realized that she had already known. She felt hurt for a moment that she had not been told earlier. How long ago had Frances been told?

Janet came over and sat down next to her. Edie looked into her round, sympathetic face. She could see Janet was aware that she was feeling a bit hurt.

'Well,' Edie tried to sounded lighthearted. 'This is quite something. I can't take it in. All I can think of is Katherine Hepburn in *The African Queen*!'

Janet laughed. 'Well – not quite, I hope!' Apologetically, she added. 'We wanted to gather everyone and break the news – and this is the first time we've all been together. But we had to tell Martin's family when we were there for Christmas, so I thought I couldn't go without mentioning it to Mum.' She reached out and squeezed Edie's hand. 'Actually, I couldn't face telling anyone at first. It's made me realize it's real, and it's happening so soon!'

'When?' Edie felt suddenly panicky. They couldn't be leaving yet – she needed time to adjust to the idea!

'March.' She gave a wavering smile. 'Now the New Year's here, that suddenly feels terribly close.'

Edie searched her friend's face, trying to work out what were her real feelings about it.

'D'you really want to go, Jan? What will you do?'

Janet sighed, her fingers fiddling with the pin in her tartan kilt. She gave Edie a wistful smile.

'I do want to. Yes, I think I do.' Edie saw her brace herself to go on. 'It seems certain now that Martin and I are not going to have a family. He desperately needs to branch out and do something new. And I shall ... well, we'll see, won't we? Martin thinks he'll be able to find me plenty of work to do. I shall have to see what's needed when I get there. I have a feeling it'll be all right.' She

324

grinned. 'That's not to say I'm not jolly worried at times though, I can tell you!'

'I bet you are.' Edie was still full of wonder. She could see Janet was quite excited, if apprehensive. For herself, she felt desolate. 'Feels as if everyone's branching out – what with Ruby's American family.'

'What's that?' Ruby called across to her from by the fire. 'Oi – watch it, Greta, you'll have Marleen's eye out with that! Somebody talking about me?'

Making a joke of it, Edie said, 'Well – I seem to be the one to be a homebird!'

'That's a perfectly good thing to be,' Frances assured her. Edie accepted this with a smile, knowing that it was also what Frances had been forced to be, that her stability had allowed everyone else to take wing. She turned her measured gaze on Ruby. 'And when is it you're going?'

'Oh, not until summer I don't think,' Ruby said importantly. 'When the girls're off school.'

There was enormous pride in her voice. She and her daughters were to go and visit the family in America! It was a subject she never tired of. It had taken her some months after the war to work up the courage to write and tell Wally's parents that they had a granddaughter in England, but when she did so, she received a rapturous reply. Neither Wally's brother nor sister were showing signs of getting married and so far they had no grand-children. They knew the pressures everyone was under during those dark times, they said. Of course, had Wally lived he would have come back and married her. He was a good Christian boy: if he said he'd do a thing, he did it. Since they had found out about Greta, Ed and Louisa Sorenson had shown Ruby enormous kindness. Soren-son's store was booming in post-war Fairmont. They had expanded twice, into the buildings flanking them on each side, selling lingerie and garments in one side and garden tools and lawnmowers the other. They had enough ready money to have flown the Atlantic twice now to visit Ruby and Greta. Edie felt that they had been rather startled by Ruby and Ethel and their forthright ways at first, but they were very polite, genteel people, and declared themselves enchanted to learn that Ethel was a singer and once a dancer and they seemed to find Lionel very amusing. Ethel and Lionel had moved out to a new house at Rednal and were able to put the Sorensons up for some of their stay. Louisa showered Marleen and Greta with gifts, especially clothes, and the girls loved showing off their American fashions to the neighbours' kids. Now they were determined that Ruby should take Greta over to see her father's home and said they would pay her fare to visit with the girls.

Edie was relieved and happy that things were turning out so well for Ruby, even though she was still bringing up the girls on her own. It had been so miserable for Ruby, seeing the pictures in the papers at the end of the war of all the GI brides in smiling rows on the decks of ships, bound for the United States and Canada to be reunited with their husbands. How Ruby would have loved that! But for her there had been no husband, no sea voyage, only more struggle and hard work bringing up her daughters alone with rationing dragging on and on.

'We're going to see Nana and Grandad again, aren't we?' she said to Greta, who nodded with enthusiasm.

Edie saw Marleen make a mocking face. She got up and walked across the room as if to fetch something. She was trying to attract David's attention, but to her annoyance he'd sat back and was engrossed in a book. Pert little madam, Edie thought, as Marleen minced past, wiggling her hips in her swinging American skirt. Always after all the attention. She glanced at David's handsome, intent face and smiled to herself. I see my son has good taste. You needn't think he'll show any interest in you, miss. But she could sympathize with Marleen getting fed up with hearing about Greta's exotic grandparents when both sets of her own lived up the road. I suppose she's just trying to keep her end up, she thought.

'Come and sit with me a minute, dear.' Frances beckoned to Marleen, seeing her looking left out. 'D'you fancy a game of rummy? I'm sure Martin and Janet have some cards.'

Marleen nodded rather petulantly, but sat down. Frances was the one person who had full command over her.

They passed the evening happily, eating Christmas cake round the fire, reminiscing and hearing about everyone's plans for the new year ahead. Martin tried to make conversation with David and got as far as, 'What are you reading, David?'

David looked up at him, dazed for a second, as if he was returning to a different and unfamiliar world.

'Oh—' He showed them the cover. 'It's called *Lord of the Flies*. My English master lent it to me. It's extremely good . . .' And then they'd lost him again.

Martin looked at Edie and shrugged and they laughed.

'Never mind,' she said. 'He's quite happy.'

Edie found herself looking round at everyone that evening, Davey and Frances, Ruby and her girls and especially at Janet – dear, kind Janet – and Martin, wanting to slow time down, for them all to stay together as they had done for so long now, their lives entwined both at Cadbury's and at home, sharing all the day-to-day things. But now everything was changing and she could hardly bear to think of Janet and Martin moving so far away. Next year they wouldn't be here at New Year. An urgent thought struck her. *Martin wouldn't be here . . .*

As midnight drew close, Martin handed out glasses of wine and beer to toast the New Year. Edie accepted a tot of red wine. Frances drank lime cordial.

'Is young David allowed beer this once?' Martin asked.

Edie laughed at David's eager expression. 'Go on then – just a bit,' she said.

'When I was a girl, in Bournville,' Frances said, 'the young boys used to go out every New Year and run round the streets, into people's houses and call out "Let the New Year in!" You were supposed to give them a reward for each room that they let the new year into – I believe it was sixpence. That seems to have died out now, doesn't it?'

'It must have got rather expensive!' Martin said.

'Come on everyone—' Janet stood up, eyeing the clock. 'Two minutes!'

They all stood holding up their glasses, ready for the clock to strike its mellow 'bong – bong . . .' Janet jokingly conducted the seconds away with her glass. 'Five, four, three . . . here we go! Happy New Year everyone!'

They all hugged and kissed, wishing each other a happy 1955. Edie embraced Janet tightly and when she released her, both of them had tears in their eyes.

'Oh,' Janet said quietly to her. 'It's going to be so hard, Edie!'

'I know—' Edie hugged her again. 'I don't want you to go. But that's me being selfish. I don't like things changing. But you go and be happy there. Martin looks happier already.'

'He is,' Janet said wistfully. 'And that makes so much difference.'

328

Frances came up and embraced Edie. She smelt sweetly of rosewater. 'Happy New Year to you, dear. Who knows what it may bring?' Edie hugged her back fondly.

She gave the young ones each a kiss, trying not to overdo it with David and embarrass him. Then Martin came up and she was wrapped for a moment in his long arms.

'I hope you'll like it there,' she said.

'Well – I'm hoping so – otherwise I'm dragging poor old Jan across the world for nothing. I know it's asking a lot of her – and all of you. But I think it'll be just the thing.'

'Martin . . .?'

He was waiting, looking down at her with an amused fondness.

'Never mind.' She touched his arm and moved on. 'I'll ask you later.'

He had promised to drive Edie, Frances and Ruby home afterwards and it was quite a squeeze fitting everyone in the old Austin. Frances went in the front and Marleen and Greta had to sit on Ruby's and Edie's laps as they motored through the damp, deserted streets. They dropped Ruby off. She was still living in the Glover Road house. When they got to Linden Road Martin got out and walked round to let Frances out.

'You two go on in,' Edie said to Frances and David. 'I want a word with Martin.' Her heart was pounding suddenly, and she still felt flushed and strange after the wine.

When the door closed behind them she and Martin stood by the car. His features looked heavier in the dim light and she saw he was exhausted.

'What's up?' he said lightly.

'If you're going . . .' She began, then trailed off, looking away down the road. In the silence the carillon began to ring from the tower.

'Half past one,' Martin remarked.

'I need to find out.' Her gaze was fixed steadily on him now. 'Otherwise I'll never do it. I need to find out anything I can about Davey.'

Martin looked at her in silence for a moment. 'And you'll tell him?'

'He needs to know – I suppose.'

'I did say to you that I don't really know anything. The only thing I can think of is that we root out that warden who found him. Someone will know, Edie. Quite a lot of people will know if we ask. Sometimes I think we should have asked years ago, but now we've left it so long . . . It depends on you being ready.'

Edie gave a long, unsteady sigh. 'I'm ready.'

Thirty-Four

Martin parked his car in a side road, opposite St Matthew's church. The wrenching sound of the hand-brake seemed to twist Edie's nerves even tighter. She clasped her hands together and stared out through the windscreen at the branches of a tree. Its sharp twigs seemed to point accusingly at her. There was a silence and she knew Martin was looking at her, seeing how pale, how daunted she looked.

'Are you sure you want to do this?'

Edie swallowed. 'You think I should have done it ages ago, don't you? That I might have deprived David of his real family?'

'No.' He spoke calmly, assuredly. 'I think it's very unlikely now that there is anyone. You did everything you could, Edie, you shouldn't feel guilty. Look at all you've given him. He would have had to be fostered in any case, or gone to an orphanage.'

She looked round into his eyes, feeling like a child who wanted him to tell her everything would be all right. Martin touched her hands for a moment. As he did so she realized they were clenched so tight that her arm muscles were beginning to ache.

'Don't worry,' he said.

She followed him to Bristol Road and they stood looking around them in the weak, January sunshine. The wind made her eyes water. Martin stood with the collar of his coat turned up, looking back and forth along the road.

'Where on earth do we start?' It felt hopeless to Edie suddenly. There were so many roads and houses.

'I'm just trying to get my bearings. That night, we must have been ... Goodness, it's hard to tell. It felt almost like a different place. I think the warden stopped us – the ambulance – up there.' He pointed in towards town. 'We'll start along there, shall we?'

Edie walked beside him, her own mind full of memories of that night in 1940, so terrible for a great many people, but which ended with her holding Davey in her arms.

A little way along the main road, three streets ran off it and they stopped.

'Right,' Martin said. 'Where shall we start? My hunch is, it must have been Wellington Road.'

'We might as well stay on this side,' Edie said. 'We can do Wellington and cross over if there's no joy here. Do you remember the warden?'

'I think I'd know him if I saw him again. Thing was, he stepped out into the road and suddenly he was there, slap bang in front of the ambulance. Could have killed him. Moustachioed sort of chap. He was getting on a bit – let's hope he's still alive.'

They turned down Wellington Road. Edie was dismayed to see that it stretched on so far that she could not see the end of it. But then her attention was taken by the gaps in the long line of houses, the gaps from bomb damage common to almost every street within a mile or two of the centre, still not rebuilt, providing a playground for the games of local children and a breeding ground for weeds and rats.

The street was quiet, except for a gaggle of children on

the corner of an adjoining street and an elderly lady approaching them in the distance. People were resting after their Sunday lunches.

'I suppose I should ask in one of the pubs,' Martin said. 'They'd know who the wardens were.'

The elderly lady drew level with them. She was dressed in a black coat which almost reached her ankles, a black fur hat, and was walking with surprising energy for someone bent over a walking stick. She turned her head, peering from under the hat and said, 'Afternoon.'

'Excuse me!' Edie cried, on impulse. She had to repeat it, louder, before the woman stopped, turning her whole body round to speak to them. Her hand, holding the walking stick, was a waxen yellow, her veins a dark mesh across the bones. Two alert grey eyes peeped out from the folds and wrinkles of her face.

'Are you trying to find yer way?' she shouted. 'You'll have to speak loud if yer want my help, deary!'

Martin took over. He asked if she remembered who had been the ARP warden for the road. For a moment the woman stared ahead looking so blank that Edie decided it was hopeless. Then she seemed to leap into life.

'Oh now ... well, one of them was Bob Ryman.' She swivelled a little and pointed her walking stick towards the Bristol Road. ''E was up and down this end of the road. I live just up there, see, so I remember. Then down there—' She revolved sharply and aimed the stick again. 'They 'ad a lady doing it ... I forget 'er name. Madge ... no, Maud ... Let's see ...' She pulled a large hanky out of her pocket and wiped her nose, and during this pause, Martin said, 'I don't suppose you know what number Bob Ryman lives at?'

'Ah—' She looked downcast for a moment. 'Oh!' Her

eyes brightened and the stick came into action again. 'I do! Number twenty-eight!'

It all seemed too easy, when so many years had passed. The door of number twenty-eight was opened by a plump, elderly woman in slippers who listened with sympathy and said she'd take them through to 'my Bob'. They followed her down a long, tiled hall to the back room.

'Bob – some people to see you!'

The room was simply but cosily arranged. Two chairs, obviously his and hers, were drawn up by the fire and in one sat a man of about seventy, with a grey, trailing moustache. Edie thought of a picture book Davey had as a child containing 'The Walrus and the Carpenter'. Mr Ryman's moustache made him look rather like the walrus.

'I'm Martin Ferris and this is Edith Weale.' Martin held his hand out and Bob Ryman shook it, charmed by Martin but obviously bewildered. 'We have met before,' Martin went on, 'though you probably don't remember.'

'No.' Mr Ryman had a low, rumbling voice and spoke with slow deliberation, looking from one to the other of them. 'Can't say I remember yer.'

'Would yer like a cup of tea?' Mrs Ryman said. 'It's no trouble.'

'No – it's all right, thank you.' Edie smiled, nervously.

Martin helped bring across two wooden chairs from the table and he and Edie settled on them. Mrs Ryman sat and picked up her knitting.

'We've come because we need your help,' Martin began. Edie was very grateful that he was there. 'It's about the time you were an ARP warden.'

'Oh ar?' Bob Ryman nodded, still cautious, filling the bowl of his pipe with tobacco.

'One of those very bad nights in 1940 – November the nineteenth . . .'

'Ah – terrible.' He shook his head. 'Just terrible.'

'Well, I was driving an ambulance that night. And Edie here was working in the rest centre at St Matthew's . . .'

They had his attention now. He watched Martin, thumb still pushed into the bowl of his pipe.

'You stopped an ambulance – my ambulance, and you'd rescued a baby.'

'Oh ar—' Mr Ryman pointed the pipe at Martin excitedly. 'That little wench from up the road here. Oh, I'll never forget that – one of the bloomingest things I saw all the war that was.'

He stopped abruptly, and to Edie's frustration spent what seemed like an eternally long time with the pipe in his mouth, struggling to light it. The sweet smell of smoke crept round the room.

'Come on, Bob,' Mrs Ryman urged, knitting furiously. 'They ain't come to watch you puffing on that – they want to 'ear.'

At last the pipe deigned to behave itself.

'It was one of the houses down here, had a direct hit, like – at the back. Killed the lot of them – except that babby. She must've been blown out through the front, somehow. When I got to the 'ouse, it was dark, of course, and there were that much mess . . .' He made a pained face. 'Oh, you've never seen anything like the state of it. I mean, I daint know anyone was in there then, but of course the neighbours said they must've been and when the lads came and cleared it . . .' He looked down, shaking his head.

Edie and Martin exchanged glances. The night was being conjured up for them again, the sadness of it.

'But the babby – I mean it looked almost as if some-one'd put her there, deliberate like. She was lying out the front in the road, in this wooden cradle – only the side had come off of it. She was crying of course ... And covered in dust,'

'Shame,' Mrs Ryman murmured.

'Anyroad, I thought, well you can't stay lying down there, bab – let's get yer to safety. I carried her down the the main road and I was going to take her to the rest centre – only I saw the amb'lance coming ...' He indi-cated Martin. 'And Bob's yer uncle, as they say!' He gave a chesty laugh.

'Well,' Martin smiled. 'This is a great help, Mr Ryman.'

'Where was the house?' Edie asked, her heart thudding hard. They were getting closer every second. 'Did you know the family?'

'It were a way along the road – down on the right. I daint know 'em, no, and course they was all killed. Must've stayed on in the 'ouse.' He shook his head again. 'Terrible.'

They explained to the Rymans why they wanted to know, and they were very interested to hear about David.

'You must've brought him up very well,' Mrs Ryman said as they were leaving. 'He was a lucky lad, I reckon. Look – I'll point yer at the house.' She came out in her worn old slippers and showed them where to go. 'See along there? It was the first out of those two.'

They gave their thanks to the Rymans and went to stand and look at the remains of what had once been David's home. The damage had been so severe that though a mass of rubble had been cleared away, there was little left to see except the low remains of walls, a sad shell. At the back of one room Edie could see the blackened remains of a fireplace. She stood trying to rebuild the house in her mind, to imagine who might have lived there.

'Let's find out all we can,' Martin said. 'I'll try this side first.'

There was no reply when they knocked at the neighbouring house on the left. The door of the house to the right was answered by a hard-faced woman in her fifties, grey hair scraped back into a bun. Her folded arms hugged a baggy brown cardigan round her against the cold wind. Martin, once again, explained what they wanted to know.

'That lot?' She sounded irritated. 'All killed, they were. Made a right mess of our roof but we've fixed it up now – you can hardly see the damage. Bowles the name was. Funny sort of people – you know, never dressed right some'ow – and they were conchies. I don't hold with that sort of thing when all our lads were out there getting shot to pieces. I lost my son, you know – Arnhem. Tell that to the conchies. Anyway – didn't get them anywhere, did it?' She nodded viciously at the remains of the house. 'They'd taken in some Kraut woman and her child an' all. Refugees, they said. I had words with that Mrs Bowles about it once, said I didn't want Hitler's spawn living the other side of the wall to me and she said they were victims as much as us. Huh! What d'yer want to know for, any'ow?'

'I'm afraid it's rather a long story,' Martin said.

'Oh.' The woman was uninterested, began retreating inside. 'That's all I know, anyroad – killed, they was, all of 'em. Can't say any more than that.'

They stood out in the road, the wind harsh on their cheeks. Edie felt the woman's words hammering her, the loathing in them. It mirrored her own feelings. Germans ... Hitler ... *Some Kraut woman and her child* ...

'D'you want to ask anywhere else?' Martin said. His

voice was very gentle. Even in her stunned state, Edie thought how considerate he was, at his best when people were in distress.

'I don't think so. Not today.' They walked slowly back, all they had heard sinking in gradually.

'Does this mean . . .?' Edie spoke suddenly. 'What does it mean? That Davey's German, that his family, his mom, were German?'

'It sounds like it. When you fit it all together. Some of the neighbours might know more – people who were closer to them. But by the sound of it they were refugees from Germany.' He stopped and put his hand on her arm. 'It looks as if Davey was rescued more than once if they'd escaped over here. I would think he might really be Jewish after all.'

They drove back to Linden Road, talking in snatches, trying to fit together the little information they had. Frances's face was anxious as they walked in, especially as Edie's own expression gave away the fact that they had plenty to tell her.

They found themselves whispering in the hall.

'Where's Davey?' Edie asked.

'Upstairs. Busy with something or other. Come through to the kitchen – I'll put the kettle on.' Frances limped ahead of them, tutting at the pain in her hip.

As the water boiled they sat at the kitchen table and talked in low voices. Martin told Frances about Mr Ryman, and when it came to the lady next door, Edie took over. She described the remains of the house.

'The lady didn't like them – she was horrible about them really, wasn't she, Martin? Thing is, Frances, she said they were conchies . . .'

'Were they?' Frances exclaimed.

'She said they were called Bowles and they'd taken in a German woman and her child – so that must've been Davey.'

Frances sat up very straight.

'Bowles? Where was this?'

'Wellington Road,' Martin said.

'Bowles ... Bowles – of course! But they were Friends! The ones whose house was hit! Of course, she was a CO. She'd evidently been a pacifist even in the Great War. I mean Serena Bowles was getting on in age. I didn't know her very well, but I know she'd been a widow for years. And they were bombed out, d'you remember me telling you? She was one of the ones who'd taken in refugees. There was a whole family first of all, until they found somewhere else to live. And then she evidently took in a young Jewish woman from Berlin.'

They all looked at each other, struggling to work out the implications of this. The newsreels from the Nazi concentration camps had come to them on the cinema screens – snatches of an unimaginable hell. Was that the fate from which the young woman from Berlin had escaped? Edie felt an immediate, poignant sympathy for her. And who had she left behind in Germany, and what had become of them?

'Oh, Frances,' she whispered. 'How will it help my Davey to know this? Does he need to know?'

After a silence Frances sighed. 'Yes, darling. In the end, I think he does.'

Thirty-Five

Edie was dreading Janet and Martin leaving for Africa, far more than she could admit to them. She wanted to hold on to every day of the last weeks before they went, but the time spun past, and of course the Ferrises were busy with their preparations. Though she had joked about it at New Year, with all the sudden upheaval among her friends, Edie had suddenly begun to feel stuck and restless, and added to this was her dread of having to speak to David.

The Monday before Janet and Martin were due to leave she walked to work feeling very low. On the Sunday Janet had cooked a lovely joint of roast pork and asked them all over. 'Not to say goodbye,' she said tearfully. 'Definitely *au revoir*.' On Saturday they'd board the train to Liverpool, then the boat, to sail all those miles across the water to somewhere impossibly far away that Edie could barely imagine. They'd write, of course they would, but it wasn't the same at all. She felt that a long, happy phase of her life was ending, irrevocably.

Turning in through the factory gates, amid the other workers coming on shift, her heart sank even further at the thought of Ruby going away to see the Sorensons in July.

Overall on, she made her way to her work station. In this time of change Cadbury's felt more than ever like her family, the thread of stability in her life, but even at work there had been changes. After the war the extended sugar shortage kept rationing going on and off until only two years ago. There were more new lines, like 'Fudge' – a particular favourite of Davey's – and Edie had worked on some of the 'Vogue' chocolates which had gone into the displays for the Coronation, and this was the line she was weighing out today in preparation for packing. She settled herself rather disconsolately into her place on the line, her autumn leaf hair tucked under the white cap. In front of her was a large white scale and beside her the belt with the chocolates in tidy rows, cooled after passing through the enrobing machine which draped the fillings with a warm layer of brown sweetness. She tried to concentrate, but her mind wandered immediately.

Here I am again, day after day. I wonder if I could've gone to the grammar school like Davey and gone on to better things? Anyway it was far too late for that. She'd done well in her eleven plus, but Nellie said she wasn't having her swanning off to the grammar school, demanding posh uniforms and getting above herself. She'd been a bit disappointed, but then she'd gained her place at Cadbury's and had been very content here, especially when she had Ruby and Janet. They'd been such good pals here for so long. She sighed.

I know Ruby's only going for a fortnight, she thought, but to *America*. I'd never even been as far as London until I went with Davey.

Her mouth twitched into a brief smile. He was so fascinated by machines. They'd gone to the Festival of Britain in Birmingham, not London. Aged twelve he'd been the one to lead her round Bingley Hall, completely dismissing some areas of the exhibition and lingering for ages in front of the huge gas turbine and the other machines in the 'Discovery and Design' and 'People at

Work' sections. Seeing his deep delight, the next year she took him to the Motor Show at Earls Court, though for herself she would rather have made the journey to London for the Coronation to wave a flag in the Mall. Instead they watched on a neighbour's television, with everyone crowded in to see. But now Davey was growing up too – up and away from her. And how much more might he distance himself from her when she found the moment to tell him what she knew about his background? She kept putting it off and, as ever, when this thought occured to her, it seemed to wash over her like a freezing wave.

Saying goodbye to Janet and Martin seemed one of the hardest things she'd ever done. Dr Weller had promised to drive them to the station.

'I had to think hard what to wear,' Janet said, pushing her hair back from her face as she checked the catches on her suitcase. She stood up, flushed. 'I mean I'm wearing my warm coat today but will I need it again? Let alone stockings!'

'Never mind,' Frances said. 'You'll need it when you come back for visits.'

Edie heard her determination to be cheerful and calm, but she knew that if this was difficult for her, it was infinitely more so for Frances. Robert came round occasionally with his children, but they had nothing like the closeness that she had with Janet.

'My arms feel like pincushions after all those injections!' Janet chattered on, trying to cover up her own turmoil of feelings about leaving. 'And I haven't been at all sure what to pack: a few shirtwaister dresses and some sensible shoes ... That sounds rather like a missionary's wardrobe, doesn't it?'

'Well, I suppose you are a missionary,' Edie said. 'Sort of.'

'Yes – but I don't have to *dress* like one!'

'Stalwart underwear,' Frances said, laughing.

Martin, who had been gathering last-minute things together, came up and put his arm round Janet's shoulders.

'Ready?' he asked softly. 'Jonathan's waiting.'

Janet nodded determinedly.

'It'll be a tremendous adventure,' Frances spoke briskly and held her arms out. 'Goodbye, my love. Write to us as soon as you can. We'll be dying to hear.'

In her mother's arms, Janet said moistly, 'Oh, I will, I will!'

Edie, who didn't have Frances's self-control, sobbed as she hugged her friend.

'I wish you weren't going, but I hope you have a lovely time all the same.'

'Oh!' Janet was crying in earnest now. 'Edie, I'll miss you so much! But I know you'll look after Mummy and that's a great comfort.'

Edie found herself caught up in Martin's arms and he kissed her cheek.

'All the best, Edie.' He smiled fondly.

'You look after her,' Edie sniffed, trying to smile. 'That's my best friend you've got there!'

'Oh, I shall – don't you worry.'

David, awkward with adolescent shyness, was also hugged emotionally by Janet and Martin shook his hand.

'Bye, old chap – and you take care of your mother now, won't you?'

And a few moments later, with the suitcases stowed, they were driving off along Valentine Road, waving madly. The car turned slowly right into the Moseley

Road and suddenly they were gone. As Edie moved away she saw Frances still staring after them along the street, and knew that her thoughts were travelling with them in the car, to the dock, to the wide blue sea.

And the Cadbury girls were down to two.

It didn't seem any time before she was waving Ruby goodbye as well, with Marleen and Greta both in a state of high excitement about going on an aeroplane for the first time, and of being spoiled rotten by the Sorensons when they reached America.

'Greta's hardly slept the last few nights,' Ruby told her as they parted outside the factory gates shortly before they left. Ruby was looking very bonny, her plump white arms protruding from a sleeveless summer frock and bright green high-heeled shoes which she'd slipped on after work, along with the lipstick. Edie was struck by how mature she looked. We're both thirty-four, she thought, but I still look like a girl who hasn't grown up properly. I know I've filled out a little bit, but Rube looks so mature! Fondly, she wished them all a good trip.

'You going to bring back another nice Yank with you, eh?'

'Ooh, I don't know about that!' Ruby chuckled, backing off down the road. 'Don't know as I'll have time for that sort of thing with the girls around, or my "in-laws"! More's the pity! See yer, kid!'

'See yer.' Edie waved.

She walked off into the warm evening, hearing the carillon ring out its sweet chime in the distance. The sun was setting and the light was soft and golden over Bournville Green. She stopped for a moment, breathing in the scented summer air and smiling fondly at the sight of the

Continuation Schools where she and Ruby had begun their working life together. There had been so much laughter and happiness, and yet tonight she felt melancholy. So many years, gone so fast. And those intense years of Davey's childhood when he had wanted and needed her had slipped away. Now he had long surpassed her, in knowledge and in his understanding of things. He was so intelligent, his teachers said. He should think of going to the university, would be sure to go far.

Far, she thought wistfully. Why does everyone have to go far? Why can't they be content? I wonder if he'll have gone so far one day that he'll never want to see me?

Thirty-Six

The train chugged its way at an unhurried, rocking pace through the Welsh countryside. Outside its windows, the sun appeared dazzlingly every so often between foamy piles of cloud, shining on sheep nibbling the sparse hillside grass. Every so often they stopped at a small country station. They had the compartment to themselves, Edie sitting opposite Frances and David. Frances had begun the journey from Shrewsbury by reading the newspaper, but after they had eaten some of their ham sandwiches and the day grew even warmer, her grip on the paper grew slack and now she was sleeping, leaning on the headrest by the window. She had not woken when the ticket collector slid the door open and asked to see their tickets. Edie looked across at her, feeling protective. In repose, Frances's face still kept much of its rather noble beauty, but it was undoubtedly slacker, more aged. Her skin had lately acquired a more fragile quality. Edie sometimes felt afraid looking at her. Janet's departure seemed to have added years to her all of a sudden.

When she turned her gaze away from the window to look at David, though, her emotions altered from tenderness to nervousness and tension. He was oblivious to her looking at him. Nose in a book as usual, she thought. Shutting me out. She tried to see what he was reading but couldn't make out the title. She didn't like the uncomfortable, bitter feelings she found in herself sometimes these days. Was she jealous of his books, for goodness sake? It was ridiculous! But so often now he seemed to be walled round by the pages of books, and when he did emerge from behind them he could be so distant and moody, sometimes very sarcastic, when Frances wasn't within earshot. He was never intentionally rude to Frances. She had always commanded his respect and affection. Edie was most ashamed when she realized that sometimes she was even a bit jealous of Frances. Was it because he knew she wasn't a blood relation? Why was Davey only so cruel to her, his mother?

What're you reading? She might ask. A book. What's it about? Sometimes he would tell her, but more often he would just sigh and say, oh, you wouldn't really want to know. And the trouble was, he was right, she didn't really want to know what was in his book, she just wanted him to look up and talk to her.

Edie shifted in her seat. In the distance she saw a man in a cap striding across a field with a dog. She had decided to have a talk to Davey this weekend. They had organized the trip, she and Frances, partly to enable this conversation to happen. Frances thought it might be better done at a distance from home. And with Janet and Ruby away they felt rather desolate and wanted cheering up.

'We'll treat ourselves to a weekend at the seaside,' Frances said. 'I used to go to Aber when I was a girl – and I went with Robert and Janet once or twice. It'd be nice to see it again.'

They hadn't heard from Ruby, of course, but there had been several letters from Janet. She wrote to them both with her usual wry cheerfulness, though Edie sensed the homesickness that lay behind her excitement at settling in a new place. She described landing on the west coast of Africa at Matadi, the long train jouney to Leopoldville and then a steamer ride up the Congo River to Stanley-ville. The rest of the journey was a boneshaking three hundred miles by truck to the mission station.

'What an arrival!' she wrote in her first letter. 'They had all the schoolchildren out to greet us, playing all sorts of bugles and drums and singing, all dressed up to the nines. My hand was shaken so many times I'm surprised it's still attached to my arm!'

She loved the place, the tall palm trees and red roads, but in the next letter there was news of constant rain, of suffering from bites and skin infections. And Martin was of course kept very busy.

'What I need to do first,' Janet wrote bravely, 'is work on learning the language. Then I shall feel much more at home.'

Edie hoped so, for her sake, though in a private part of her mind she hoped the venture wouldn't work and they would come home. She wondered if Frances felt the same.

Within another hour the train eased its way into Aberystwyth station and they climbed out into its long, echoing space. Edie and David carried the luggage out to a taxi and they drove to their guesthouse, one of the tall, pastel-painted terraces along the front facing the sea. As the blue water came into view Frances said, 'That's a sight which always lifts the spirits, isn't it?' and Edie nodded, truly feeling lighter and happy on seeing the sea stretching away, flecked with white. Even David was smiling.

When they went inside and the landlady took their names, Edie suddenly saw their little party through her eyes and wondered what the busy, grey-haired woman made of them. Frances, stooped yet elegant, with her well modulated voice, Edie, petite, auburn-haired and freckled, and David, lanky, with his dark curling locks. What a funny lot we are, all thrown together Edie thought. She'll think Frances is my mom and I'm Davey's – when we don't share a drop of blood in common!

The guesthouse was terribly clean and neat. Edie and Frances shared a room, with David next door. Edie flung the window open and breathed in deeply. The sun had come out and its light reflected blindingly off the sea. The fresh air and distant cries from the beach filled her with expectation and she felt like jumping up and down like a child. They must go straight down to the beach and paddle! And it was only Friday – they had two whole days ahead of them.

Frances, rolling down her stockings at the edge of the bed, looked hot and tired.

'Are you all right?' Edie asked, suddenly concerned.

'Oh yes – just a little weary. But it's lovely to be here. I was just thinking – I should bide your time with David. Don't say anything today. Give him time to unwind as well.'

'I will,' Edie was saying, when there was a tap on the door. David's head appeared.

'I thought I'd go out,' he said.

'I'll come too!' Then Edie hesitated. Why was she so nervous of her own son these days? 'If you don't mind.'

David shrugged. 'No. Course not.'

'I'll rest for a while first,' Frances said. 'You two go along.'

'Don't unpack, will you?' Edie said. 'I'll do it when I get back.'

They passed the next twenty-four hours very companionably. Edie and David strolled along the beach that first evening, gently dodging the frothy edges of the waves which, on that languid summer day, barely seemed to have the vigour to break on the sand. They looked back at the attractive curving seafront, its hodge-podge of pink, pale blue and yellow houses. At the far end, up the cliff, ran the electric railway. Later the three of them ate a meal of fish together and as the sun went down, strolled out along the front and through some of the winding streets of the town. David walked slightly ahead of them, in his own world, but seeming relaxed and as if he was enjoying the place. They slept in beds with thick, well-stuffed eiderdowns and Edie woke the next morning to the sound of gulls. She stretched her limbs contentedly under the soft covers. If only they could come and live by the sea for ever!

Saturday was almost miraculously hot and fine, though with more of a breeze, and the waves curled and broke more briskly. They picnicked on the beach, and even went sea bathing. David ventured in first.

'Come on, Mom!' he called, jumping about with his arms outstretched, water up to his waist.

Edie watched him from the edge, suddenly longing to go in herself. She was a good swimmer from her training at Cadbury's, and after all the good times there and at the Rowheath Lido she associated swimming with happiness. Running up the beach she changed under a towel, with Frances's help, into her old black costume. It looked rather old-fashioned compared with the bikinis some of the young girls on the beach were wearing, but she didn't care, so long as she could plunge into the water.

'I'm coming!' She ran joyfully to the sea. She heard David laughing and saw in his face that he was surprised by her sudden girlishness. Not liking to get into cold water slowly, she kept running, legs slowed by the water, until it was deep enough to plunge in head first. The cold water raked through her hair and she emerged laughing and screaming.

'Oh my word – it's cold! But it's lovely!'

They swam back and forth, playing and splashing, and when they decided to get out Edie felt that she and David were more at one, closer than they had been for a long time. Not wanting to lose it, she said, 'We'll get dry, then go and get an ice cream, shall we?' Eyeing Frances, she added. 'And maybe go for a little walk?'

They dressed quickly, Edie in a print frock with shells on and David in his short-sleeved shirt and shorts. Unlike Edie, with her mother's pale Irish complexion, David tanned easily and his skin already had a healthy glow. They fetched ice cream cornets, bringing one back for Frances, who looked nicely settled midway up the beach, and Edie and David set off to walk along the prom.

'We must go on the railway before we go,' Edie said. 'You'd like that. And they say the view's marvellous.'

They strolled along, away from the Electric Cliff Railway, pointing out boats, the antics of a dog barking frantically and running in and out of the sea. All the time Edie could feel the nervous fluttering in her stomach growing worse until she felt sick, and she gave David the last of her ice to finish. They reached the end of the prom and leaned against the railings, looking out over the sea. Edie was glad to see that the only other person close by was an elderly man with a small dog. For a few moments they stood listening to the waves breaking gently against the wall below.

'Look, love—' Edie turned towards him and her blue eyes met his dark ones. He could hear from her tone that something was different. 'I need to talk to you. To tell you something.'

A flash of unease passed across his thin face, then he

looked away, down at the water, curls falling over his forehead. She saw his hands grip the rail very tightly, and he was moving restlessly from one foot to the other. 'What?' he said.

At that moment, for all her attempts to rehearse the situation, Edie suddenly had no idea how to work up to what she needed to tell him. She had to remind herself to breathe.

'Davey . . .' She risked using his baby name and for once he didn't protest. 'You're going to be sixteen soon. You're nearly grown up. And there are things you need to know.'

He gave a gruff laugh. 'You mean about girls?'

'No – well, yes, of course you need to know about all that. But that's not what I'm talking about . . .' She took his arm for a moment. 'This is going to be a shock and there's nothing I can say that can prevent that. I've put it off long enough, God knows, but I've got to tell you.'

She had his full attention now.

Awkwardly, she began, 'I love you, David, you know that, don't you?'

'Yes.' His tone was surly. She knew he was repelled by this opening up of emotions.

'Well – you know your birthday's November the nineteenth?'

He frowned. 'Yes.'

'Well . . .' Another deep, trembling breath. Say it . . . 'Davey, I don't know if that is your birthday. I don't know for sure when you were born.' He didn't speak, just stood very still. 'It was the day you were born for me because it was the day I first saw you. You were given to me, if you like. As it happens, the person who brought you to me was Martin Ferris. He was driving an ambulance that night.' She explained briefly about the rest

352

centre, about his escape from the bombed house. 'They think you must have been blown out through one of the windows. It was a miracle you weren't killed, like everyone else in the house . . .'

David was shaking his head, as if to throw off her words. He stepped back out of her reach.

'I don't understand—' His face creased. He was her little boy again, on the point of tears. 'You mean you're not my mom? Is that what you're saying? So who is? Why're you telling me . . .? I don't want to know!'

'Sweetheart . . .' Oh, this was terrible, worse than she'd feared. Her legs felt liquid, no bones to hold them straight. She forced them to move towards him but he retreated again. 'Your mother was killed when the house was bombed that night. That's what I'm trying to tell you. They told me she was a refugee . . . She must have loved you so very much because she came to England to save you and herself.' She could tell him now: they knew for certain. Frances had talked to a friend of Serena Bowles. 'The thing is, Davey – she was German. We think she was a German Jew. She came here to escape from Adolf Hitler and all the terrible things his people did to the Jews.'

He was turning, walking away from her. Not caring who heard now, Edie followed, calling after him.

'But when they brought you to me I loved you so much that I wanted to be your mother. And there was no one else – no one ever came to find you . . . Oh Davey, tell me I'm your mother . . . I've been a mother to you, haven't I? Don't go! Please don't . . .'

But he was already striding off into the distance. She watched his tall, thin figure striding upright and tense as a wire, through the crowds along the seafront until he vanished from view.

Alone, she turned away to face the sea. He knew now. The magic circle she had built so carefully containing herself and him, devoted mother and son, was broken open. Gone. There might be other people now, to be let in. Even if those people were dead, David belonged to them by the ties of blood. And they might not all be dead. Somewhere, there might be another family for him ... Leaning on the railing, her body began to shake with deep, wrenching sobs.

David felt he was going to explode. He strode along the prom, weaving in a fury between the leisurely Saturday afternoon trippers, wanting them all to vanish out of his way. What did they know about anything, ambling along, licking their ice creams! He was smouldering, bubbling up under the surface, almost ready to hit out at people who got in his way. Not knowing where he was heading, he walked on and on, needing to expend the burning energy which seemed to roar in his veins. It did not take him long to reach the far end of the prom, near the entrance to the electric railway. He stopped for a moment, then headed for the path which twisted up the steep hill in front of him. He didn't want to ride, he needed to climb! He almost threw himself at the incline, gaining some small satisfaction from the hard pull on his muscles and the pumping of his heart and lungs. Some walkers coming down the other way looked at him in surprise as he tore upwards, hitting out at the tough coastal grasses and plants when they brushed against his shins.

I'm not your mother ... I'm not your mother ... The words battered round and round in his brain. He kept seeing her face, his mother – *no, not his mother* – Edie's face, wounded and desperate as he pulled away from her, and he felt some satisfaction in giving her pain in those moments, feeling as he did, so hurt and bewildered himself. When no one could see, he beat his fists against his chest like King Kong, trying at once to release and hurt himself.

David often felt he was near to exploding these days. He couldn't understand his own moods. Sometimes he was full of ecstatic happiness, laughing with his friends, seeing or reading about things which interested him, or even sometimes just staring for hours out of the window. But there was also the sudden feeling of anger as if he might burst open with it, the upset and cringing embarrassment he felt at times. It was worst when that stupid Marleen kept looking at him with her cow eyes. They'd played together as children of course, but now he could always sense her watching him when the families were together, or sidling up to him, and he would take refuge behind a book, or leave the room. But this now was something far more extreme. In a few words his mother – *no, not mother* – had turned the basic things he thought he knew about himself upside down. It was as if the world was spinning and, dizzy and sick, he couldn't stop it.

He climbed up and up. The path was quiet. Most people were enjoying the beach and the rest who came up here did so in order to ride the railway and reach the Camera Obscura at the top. But he didn't want any of that, the people or entertainments. He soon reached the top and joined the cliff path. At last he found a solitary spot, tucked between two bushes of bright yellow, sweet-smelling broom and flung himself down. It was only then that the glory of the scene burst in on him and he sat panting, looking out, forgetting his confusion for

355

a second. In front of him spread the blue expanse of Cardigan Bay, the line of the coast brown and crinkled against it, like elephant hide. Frances had said you could see Snowdon from up here. He looked round and could indeed see mountains in the distance, against the powdery blue of the sky.

He lay back in the prickly undergrowth and looked up at the leaves and sky, hearing the blood pulsing through his sweating body.

I am a foundling. A little calmer now, he thought over what Edie had said. It was as if a whole collection of tiny details and incidents began to fall into place. Things he had never questioned swirled round in his mind. Chief among them was a sense of being different. He had always thought that was because he had turned out to be brainy and gone on to the grammar school. People remarked on that – it separated you. But that would have been the same if Edie really was his mother, wouldn't it?

But there were the other things he began to wonder about. Was that why Grandad Dennis had never shown any interest in him? Barely a word to him? He just thought that was how the old man was. But perhaps it was because he was not really his grandson. Why did they live with Frances? And why . . .? He sat up abruptly as something more solid than the odd look or remark clanged to his attention. That first day he had come home and cried after the boys teased him about his circumcision, he had seen real shock on Edie's face. At the time he thought she was startled and upset by the teasing, the boys' nasty behaviour, but of course it was far more than that. *She hadn't been the one who'd had him circumcised . . .* Something so private, so intimate about her child, yet she had barely been able to think of an answer to give him. And they all must have known she wasn't his real mother – Frances, Dr Ferris, Janet – all the people who surrounded him. Another wave of fury passed through him, a kind of frustration at being cheated of something, and suddenly he was sobbing, tears running down his cheeks. He sat curled tightly, hugging his knees. The crying began to drain some of the tension out of him, and after a time, unable to think any more, he lay down, curled on his side, exhausted and drowsy.

When he woke the air was cooler. He sat up and looked around, his left ribs hurting from pressing against the ground. The evening was very beautiful, the sea a rich sapphire tinged with purple, the bowl of the sky pale blue and gold as the sun went down. The sounds seemed to have changed, distant voices carrying differently in the late afternoon.

David stood up stiffly. He felt muzzy and his thigh and calf muscles were stiff, but he was calmer. It felt, for the moment, as if he had dreamt the last few hours and all was as normal. He could go back, have dinner with Frances and his mother, forget all that had happened.

But as he began to scramble back down the hill, the awkwardness returned. How could he be with her? How was he supposed to behave now? He loved her, of course. She had brought him up as her child, had always been kind to him. But he no longer knew how to feel. He was a cuckoo in the nest. Nothing could be the same again.

He went into the guesthouse and crept up the dark stairs to his room. He could hear that Edie and Frances were next door, talking in low voices. They'd be worried. They didn't know where he'd gone. Well, hard luck, he thought, lashing out again. But when he got to the door of his room he turned back and steeling himself, tapped on their door.

Edie had obviously been crying, and he saw how

worried Frances looked as well. They stood quite still as he came round the door, as if frightened of him, of what he might say.

'I'm back,' he said, tersely. Then he went to his own room.

Thirty-Seven

'Marleen – come 'ere, your bow's not straight,' Ruby hissed.

She and the girls were standing outside Frances's gate in Linden Road, decked out in some of their new finery from America, and she wanted them all to look perfect. Marleen tutted and stood with her head pertly on one side as Ruby fussed with the scarlet bow fastened round her swinging ponytail. Marleen and Greta were dressed in identical frocks, brilliant white with red polka dots and full, swirling skirts. Ruby's own outfit was similarly bold, bright green leaves on a yellow background with a drawstring neck and sleeves.

'Right – that's better. Now keep yourselves clean.'

She pressed the doorbell, waiting in anticipation. What news she had to tell! She looked proudly at her girls. At least she could show she could do something right. She always felt like the one who'd been trouble, when Edie lived a quiet, mousey life and had everyone's approval. Now she was going to show she could come up trumps!

The door flew open and Edie's beaming face appeared. Ruby took in that she'd changed her hair. For years she'd worn it long, tying it back for work, sometimes coiling it, plaited, round her head. But now she had had it cut and it hung, waving prettily round her face.

'Ruby! Oh my word, look at you all! Oh, we've missed you!'

'We've only been gone a fortnight,' Ruby laughed as the two of them hugged.

'But it felt longer! Come on in and see Frances.'

Ruby was gratified by Edie's excitement. She felt very worldly, now she'd crossed the Atlantic. As soon as she and the girls trooped in, David made for the stairs.

''Ello Davey!' Ruby called to him. He smiled back shyly as he moved away, ignoring Marleen's pert, 'Where're you off to?'

Frances greeted them warmly, and Edie brought tea through to the sitting-room at the back. The window was open and bright oblongs of sunlight lit up the crimsons and blues of the old turkey rug. Frances sat in her chair near the window, a white, crocheted shawl over her frock, listening intently to Ruby's news while Edie poured tea and fussed round the girls, giving them cake and offering them the old Ludo board to keep them occupied. Marleen looked disdainfully at it, and said, 'In *America*, everything's new.'

'Don't be rude, Marl,' Ruby said.

'Lucky old America,' Edie said, ignoring Marleen's tone. Greta, who was more placid, with a broad, blue-eyed face very like Wally's, got the board out and set it up. Marleen rolled her eyes, but settled down to play, even if the game was babyish.

'So you got back last night, did you?' Edie sat down with her tea. 'Seen your mom yet?'

'Yes – she came round this morning. No stopping her.' Ruby looked round at everyone and sat up very straight, unable to contain the news any longer. 'Oh, I've got so much to tell you! But I've got to say it – guess what?'

Edie grinned. 'Go on – what?'

Ruby watched their faces. 'I'm engaged. I'm going to

360

get married and we – the girls and me – we're going to live in America!'

She was gratified by the explosive effect of this announcement. Edie cried, 'No! You're having us on!' and even Frances almost dropped her teacup.

There was no stopping her then. All the news poured out. How good Ed and Louisa Sorenson had been to her, so hospitable and generous. They adored Greta, who was their only grandchild, but they'd been very good to Marleen and treated her equally well. Their store on one of the main streets of St Paul was flourishing and instead of living over it they now had a nice big house in the suburbs, which was where Ruby had been introduced to a neighbour, Carl Christie.

'He's an ex-serviceman, like Wally. He fought in the Pacific. And he's so handsome and kind. He's got a good business selling parts for farm machinery – doing well with it.'

'Has he never married?' Frances asked, struggling to keep up with all this.

Ruby saw her doubtful expression. Why did people always have to think the worst and look for snags? She so wanted them to be pleased and impressed.

'He was,' she said. 'But he said the war drove them apart and his wife left him – five years ago. She's gone to live in Minneapolis or Duluth or somewhere.' She enjoyed dropping the names of places in. She was a woman of the world, familiar with America – it was going to be her home!

'Oh, Rube,' Edie looked dismayed. 'It's all a bit sudden, isn't it? Are you sure about him?'

'Course I'm sure,' Ruby laughed. 'I wouldn't be marrying him if I wasn't, would I?' He was nice-looking and had a good living and it meant they could live in America, that was the main thing. And he'd learn to get on with the girls in time. These things always took a while to settle down. It was going to be marvellous – a whole new life!

She talked and talked about the Sorensons' shop, the clothes they'd given them, the trips they'd made in Ed Sorenson's big Buick, once as far as Lake Superior, with Canada just across the other side, and how she'd been to church with them and Carl and they were Presbyterians.

'But you never go to church!' Edie laughed incredulously.

'Well, I do now,' Ruby retorted. 'They were all very nice to me and the girls. Some of the families even invited us for tea. Americans are *so* hospitable.'

'And what do you think of it all, girls?' Frances turned to Marleen and Greta, who had given up pretending to play Ludo and were sitting listening. 'Carl Christie – that's the name, isn't it? He'll be your new father.'

Greta said, 'It'll be nice to live near my Grandy and Grandma,' and Marleen made a face but nodded resignedly. 'Well – if it means we can live in America.'

'It won't be all trips and new frocks all the time,' Frances pointed out gently. 'That's only on special holidays.'

'But we'll have holidays, won't we!' Ruby laughed, stroking Greta's fair hair. 'We'll have to learn to call them vacations like they do over there! Carl says we'll soon all be talking with proper American accents!'

She chattered on, bringing, as she saw it, a new world to Frances's hearth, to liven her and Edie up a bit. Bournville suddenly seemed so cramped and dull. You could almost fit Frances's house into the Sorensons' living-room! She and the girls left in a flurry of colour and excitement, saying that the plan was that as soon as she could make the arrangements she would be leaving and would marry Carl in St Paul. They'd be American citizens. She remembered just as she left to tell Edie she liked her new hairstyle and to ask after Janet.

'Well, in the last letter she said she hadn't been too well . . .' Frances began. But Ruby wasn't listening, she'd just noticed that Greta had dropped a blob of jam from the cake down her new skirt.

The three of them stepped out into the warm afternoon and waved goodbye.

'Come on, girls,' Ruby said, triumphantly. 'We shan't be living in our poky little house much longer, shall we?'

The next few weeks were full of unease for Edie. She felt as if her life was like a table and someone was sawing the legs off one by one until the whole thing was in danger of collapse. Ruby's announcement had dismayed both her and Frances, though all Frances said by way of comment when they left was, 'Dear, oh dear. She's such a hasty one.'

With Janet gone, Edie was even more appalled by Ruby's announcement – for herself, losing another friend overseas, as well as worrying for Ruby and what she was rushing into this time. But over and above all this, somewhere in her thoughts at almost all times, even when she was trying to concentrate on something else, was David.

That afternoon when he had disappeared along the seafront at Aberystwyth, Edie was filled with the most terrible anguish. His anger and apparent rejection of her felt like the worst moment of her life, worse even than losing Jack or her first child. Davey had been hers now for fifteen years, and now he knew the truth he didn't want her! She wept for a long time at the end of the prom, oblivious to everything around her. She was so frightened David would just keep walking and never come back. If he was really my child he would come, she thought wildly. He would be tied to me, the bond would draw him to me. But now, why should he come back?

Of course Frances was much calmer, and reassured her. He won't leave – he loves you. You've been his mother. Give him time for it to sink in. When he did come back, sullen, but calm, they ate their evening meal together, almost as if the conversation on the prom had never happened, except that Edie felt so churned up inside she barely touched her lamb chops. They avoided the subject. David even talked about where he'd walked to, about the beauty of the sun setting over the evening sea. But he seemed distant, over-polite, as if conversing with strangers. Edie couldn't bear to go to bed without trying to speak further to him.

When they had all gone up for the night, she tapped on his door, then cautiously opened it. He was leaning on the sill of the open window in his pale blue pyjamas, looking out at the sea. Laughter floated up from the street.

'Davey – David?' she corrected herself quickly.

He turned and looked at her but did not move away from the window. She could not read his expression. It was not hostile, just neutral, waiting for her to speak.

'I'm sorry.' More tears came then. She wanted him to come close, wanted his forgiveness. 'I'm sorry I've given you such a shock. I didn't want to tell you really – I was worried . . .' She couldn't finish.

He looked away out of the window and she felt rejected again, as if he couldn't stand the sight of her and her emotion. But when he turned back to her after a moment she saw he was struggling to contain his own tears. She held herself back from running to comfort him, knew he would not want it, not tonight.

'I do know a little bit more. When you want to know. We could find out . . .'

'Her name,' he said in a choked voice. 'D'you know what I would have been called?'

Softly, Edie said, 'I don't know what she called you, but her name was Gerda Mayer. She came from Berlin.'

David nodded slowly, and turned back towards the window. 'OK,' he said.

That week since they'd been back he had not spoken of it at all. Edie expected questions, outbursts, but he had been more or less his usual self, as if the weekend in Wales and what he had learned there was something separate from his normal life. He went out with his friends, built his models, read his books. She heard his wireless set playing in his room as usual. As the summer holidays passed and nothing more happened, Edie tried to talk to him about it several times and he brushed her off, though not aggressively. But she could not relax about it and several times Frances found her crying to release her constant tension and anxiety.

'I can't believe he's just going to leave it at that,' Edie sobbed one evening. 'I feel so wound up because I don't know what he's feeling – he won't say.'

'He probably doesn't even understand that himself,' Frances counselled. 'You know what he's like – he finds it hard enough to say what he feels normally. I'm just so sorry to see you getting yourself in such a state over it. I'm sure that when he's ready, he'll want to know more.'

David went back to school in September. He had excelled at his School Certificate and was now free to concentrate on his favourite subjects – mathematics and sciences. Two of his best friends were also studying the same subjects and he seemed very happy. But after a fortnight, when Edie came in from work, Frances said he had been quiet and withdrawn. Edie went up to David's room. She found him doing his homework, frowning over a maths problem, and he looked round at her.

'Have a nice day?' She kept her tone light, as if not expecting anything.

'Yes . . .' he said vaguely. And after a pause, 'Mom?'

Edie waited.

'I don't want . . . I mean, I don't want to upset you, that's the thing . . .'

She suppressed her immediate feeling of panic and let him finish.

'You're my mom – you always will be.' He raised his lovely dark eyes to her, full of need for reassurance. 'I just want to know where I came from.'

'Oh Davey—' She put her hands on his shoulders and kissed the top of his head. 'Of course you do. I know that, my lovely. And I'll help you do that any way I can.'

It was Frances who started them off, helping as she had done on so many occasions.

'So far as I remember there was a Committee for Refugees based at one of the synagogues,' she said as the three of them sat round the tea table the next day. Frances frowned into her teacup as she tried to recall the details. 'My memory just isn't what it was. The thing to do would be to ask some of the Friends. They'll know. '

Edie and David accompanied her to the Meeting House that Sunday. When the meeting was over Edie felt calmer, somehow more solid in herself after sitting still, listening in the silence, and sure, despite her fears of what it might cost her, that David had to do what he was doing. Frances talked discreetly to a Miss Jenkins, who had been a particular friend of Serena Bowles, the woman who took in David's mother.

'She doesn't know much about the refugee committee itself or who was on it,' Frances said as they walked home. Edie and David measured their pace to fit Frances's. One of her hip joints was causing her pain and she had taken to walking with a stick. 'But it seems our first step might be to get in touch with a Mr and Mrs Leishmann. Miss Jenkins seems to know them personally. They own a tailoring business near Five Ways.'

David was listening intently and Edie felt a strong impulse to try to silence Frances and ask her to repeat what she had learned when he was not about. It was as if she needed to hear the information first and allow herself to come to terms with it before allowing him to hear anything. Once again she felt panic – no, more than that, she realized, as she identified the unpleasant emotion that was stabbing inside her. How could she be jealous of a dead woman? But she was, and she tried to push the feeling away. David must be allowed to hear. He was almost grown up now, not a child.

'They attend Singers Hill Synagogue and of course they know all sorts of people. But she said they also used to help out at the club that was run there during the war to help refugees feel more at home. They'd be very good people to start with at least.'

'So when should we go and see them?' David asked earnestly.

'Maybe Saturday?' Edie tried to sound encouraging.

Frances paused for a moment, leaning on her stick to get her breath back. 'I can't imagine Saturday would be the best day for an Orthodox Jewish couple. I'll find out their telephone number and enquire.'

'D'you think they might have known...?' David began, then stopped himself from saying 'my mother' in front of Edie.

Frances eased herself into walking again. 'Oh,' she said gently. 'I expect they knew all sorts of people.'

Thirty-Eight

Leishmann's Bespoke Tailors was a fusty looking establishment, which announced its trade in gold scrolled lettering on the black paintwork above its dark windows. When Frances had spoken to him on the telephone, Mr Leishmann had been most kind and welcoming. The three of them were invited to tea on Sunday afternoon, but Mr Leishmann had asked if they would first meet him at the shop, where he had some work to finish, and they would walk together to his house nearby.

'Miss Jenkins told me the shop is deceptive,' Frances said as they stepped out of the station at Five Ways. 'It looks small and quite unassuming, but apparently the Leishmanns do some of the very finest work.'

When they pushed the door open there was a mellow-sounding 'ting'. It was gloomy inside, but as Mr Leishmann appeared from the back he clicked a switch, filling the room with light. The floor was covered with ancient brown linoleum. A yard from the back wall stretched a long counter with a brass tape measure screwed to the top, on which were lying a large pair of scissors and several reels of cotton. On a shelf to one side were stacked a number of bolts of cloth, and a huge dresser was arranged to one side of the room with a great many small drawers in it. There was a tailor's dummy in one corner.

'Good afternoon – hello, hello! Pleased to meet you. I am Joe Leishmann!'

They could hear him before he appeared, bustling in through a door at the back, and shook Frances heartily by the hand. He was tiny, round-faced man wearing thick, black-framed spectacles. His greying hair, despite his attempts to slick it back over his head as he greeted them, kept springing back up again in dense tufts. Edie guessed he must be in his mid-fifties, and his German accent was very strong. For a second she felt an instinctive inner recoil. In her life she had only ever heard German spoken in the newsreels of Hitler's hectoring voice at his Nazi rallies. But Mr Leishmann was quite different. He was smiling broadly and she felt immediate liking for him.

'So this is young David!' He hurried over and seized David's hand as well. David said a shy hello. Mr Leishmann peered at him for a moment, suddenly serious, and said, 'Oh yes ... Yes, yes,' then recollected himself and turned to meet Edie. Shaking his hand, she smiled into his twinkling eyes.

'Now, in a moment we will go to my home and drink coffee – or tea – and have some nice cakes.' Mr Leishmann's enthusiasm and his rounded tummy both testified to the fact that he was rather fond of cakes. 'But there is first one thing I have to do. Come—' He beckoned them like a traffic policeman. 'Through here – I will show you.'

At the back was a workroom with several sewing-machines. Bent over one of the long tables, a woman was working in the light from the window.

'This is . . .' Mr Leishmann started to say, then, making all of them jump, he broke into an anguished cry. 'No! Not like that! *Mein Gott*, how many times must I say it?'

He leapt over and started to adjust something she was doing to a garment being created out of a rich, sea-blue satin.

The woman pushed her chair back and got to her feet. Edie saw a strong-jawed, sullen face, black hair pulled back into a stylish bun, and full, plum-coloured lips. She was wearing a green dress which was nipped in at the waist and hugged her curvaceous figure.

'OK!' she roared back at him. It took Edie only a couple of seconds to discover she was Italian. 'You want to do it that way, you do it yourself! That is not right. How can I work with you when you know nothing about how to make it properly!' She slammed the fabric down. 'I fed up. I go home. You want a slave to work for you, a stupid person who know nothing, you find her somewhere else.' She turned to the three of them as if they were advocates brought in specially to defend her. 'Look, you see? He tell me one thing. Is no right. I do it the right way – the way I always done it. I am a woman – I know the way I making clothes for the woman. But no – is always wrong ... He is impossible ...'

'Nadia ...' Mr Leishmann tried to interrupt the flow with little success. 'She is my assistant,' he told Edie and the others. 'She thinks she knows everything ... Nadia, will you STOP zis shouting! Whose shop is this? Whose business, eh? This is Joe Leishmann to whom you are shouting!'

Nadia was silenced for a second and stood pouting, hand on hips. 'I do it my way. The right way,' she said with a smouldering expression. She gestured towards the door. 'Or I leave. I go now ...'

There then followed a long technical altercation at high volume and with much arm-waving about the way the dress was supposed to be tailored, during which Frances took the opportunity to lower herself on to the chair closest to the door. Each demonstrated to the other why their own way was the only possible method by which a sane person could fashion a garment of this quality and pattern. Mr Leishmann mopped his brow with his handkerchief. For a moment Edie thought he was showing signs of surrendering. But suddenly, in a quiet, steely tone, he said, 'Nadia, if you can't do what I ask you to do, I will give the dress to Esther to be finished.'

Nadia looked up at him, abruptly silenced. Pouting still more and giving an abrupt shrug, she said, 'OK, you win – this time. I do it your way. Don't blame me if she look like a bloody horse in it.'

'Good,' Mr Leishmann said cheerfully. 'My God, you make everything such hard work. Nadia – these are some friends of mine.'

Nadia looked round at them and, almost as if the last minutes of bickering had not taken place, gave a broad smile and nod. 'Nice to meet you.'

'Now – we are going home to take tea with Esther, but—' Mr Leishmann wagged his finger at her. 'I will be back later to see what you have done.'

Nadia scowled, subsiding back on to her chair. 'Jews,' she grumbled. 'You no working Saturday ... Now you go have tea and cakes. I'm a bloody Catholic, ain't I? I ain't s'posed to work Sundays!'

'Bye-bye Nadia,' Mr Leishmann said, ushering the three of them out into the front of the shop.

'You would never believe how much I pay her,' Mr Leishmann remarked, with a resigned air. Edie glanced round at Davey, who had been watching the proceedings with wide eyes. To her surprise she saw a broad grin spreading across his face.

The distance to the Leishmanns' house did not take many minutes. Mr Leishmann walked beside Frances, offering her his arm which she politely declined, and they made their way talking quietly togther.

'You all right?' Edie whispered to David. She reached out and squeezed his arm.

He nodded and gave her a nervous smile. But she could see the anticipation in him. And she found herself feeling excited too. For all her vulnerable feelings about David's origins, she too wanted to know, and now they were getting closer to finding out more.

The Leishmanns lived on the upper floor of a house in Frederick Road, a broad street of stylish Edgbaston houses, all set back from the road with well-tended front gardens. Edie felt rather intimidated when they turned in at the gate of the imposing Georgian house, newly painted white, its windows shining in the hard October light.

'Of course, it would be nice to occupy the whole of such a house,' Mr Leishmann said with a wry expression, as he let them in through a side door. 'But there is quite enough for Esther and myself to do already, and living up here we do not have to concern ourselves with the garden. If it was for us to do, it would soon be like the jungles of Africa.'

They climbed up a back staircase and along a short corridor which led them to the upper landing, from which the main staircase had been blocked off. Edie found herself walking on a thick, crimson carpet.

'Esther? I have brought our visitors!'

Like her husband, Esther Leishmann could be heard talking before she appeared.

'Ah, hello, good afternoon, come in, you are very welcome.'

She came out of one of the side rooms, very petite, dark hair fastened back in a neat chignon, and dressed in a beautifully tailored suit in a woollen bouclé material of soft browns. She shook each of them by the hand, greeting Frances warmly. She was an attractive woman, with fine, black brows, face softly powdered, her features accentuated by lipstick and a hint of rouge. As they shook hands Edie felt gold rings pressing against her palm. She realized Esther Leishmann was even smaller than she was.

'So you are Mrs Weale,' she said. She did not rush to release Edie's hand.

'Pleased to meet you,' Edie said. She felt the woman candidly scrutinizing her, but she saw sympathy in her eyes.

'And this must be David.' She took his hand, seeming to do so with a special carefulness, and her eyes lingered on his face, but she said no more then.

'Now – please come in. Everything is ready. I have been waiting for you.' She led them into their sitting-room, a rather grand parlour with a marble fireplace and long windows overlooking the garden. Once again the floor was covered by a luxurious carpet, mossy green this time, and the mirror over the mantlepiece, the tables and glass front of the china cabinet all gave off the shine of loving elbow grease. She settled them on brocade chairs. 'What took you such a long time, Joe?'

Mr Leishmann shrugged. 'Nadia.'

Esther Leishmann looked fondly at him over the tea-cups and made a scornful sound. 'You will never learn how to handle that woman. You know—' She turned to Edie and the others. 'He is really like a child when it comes to business.'

'But you make very beautiful clothes,' Frances said. 'Your suit – did you make that yourself? It's very fine.'

'You like it?' Esther Leishmann stood up and turned

round to show her. 'It's very easy when you know how.' She gave a conspiratorial smile. 'From one of the new Dior patterns. I can make one for you if you like.'

'Oh, I think I'm a bit old to keep up with fashion,' Frances laughed.

'No—' Esther Leishmann looked appraisingly at her. 'You have style. You know how to dress. I can see that.'

Frances raised her eyebrows at this directness. 'It's nice of you to say so. I have always rather enjoyed clothes,' she admitted.

'Of course – why not? Now – let us take tea.' Esther buzzed around energetically, pouring tea into bone china cups on the low table in front of them. There were platters loaded with pastries and cakes, and little plates and cake forks.

'Come,' she commanded David. 'You are much too thin. You must eat. Some of these I made, some are from Drucker's cake shop.'

They settled with their tea and Esther pressed cakes on them. Edie had a delicious slice of spiced apple sponge. She enjoyed sitting in the splendid room with its long brocade curtains, the cabinet full of china figurines and its view out to the garden. But as they talked for a time about the Leishmanns' business, David's schooling and her own job at Cadbury's, Edie began to wonder how on earth they were going to get round to the subject they had really come to talk about. She hoped Frances would take the lead for her.

But there was no problem. Edie admired the Leishmanns' directness, because as soon as tea was cleared to one side, Mr Leishmann sat forward in his chair and said gently to David, 'So – I understand that you have come to us to discover something of your mother?'

David blushed, but Edie was moved as he sat up

straighter and said, as if he had rehearsed it, 'The only mother I have ever known is here.' He gestured towards her. 'But I'd very much like to learn about my blood relatives and where they came from.'

Tears came to Edie's eyes and, agitated, she looked down to hide them. How grown up Davey was!

The Leishmanns both smiled at the reply, and Mr Leishmann said, '*Gut*. Well – we can give you a little help, and perhaps it will be possible to discover more.' He spoke carefully. 'Esther and I remember your mother, David. In fact we also remember you, as a small baby. Now – let me see, where do I begin, Esther?'

'You should tell the boy first about his mother,' Esther sat composedly, feet together in her smart black shoes. 'That is what he wants to know.'

'Well – firstly, Esther and I were involved with the Social Club for Refugees at Singers Hill Synagogue. Of course many of the refugees also went to the Central Synagogue. We had left Germany ourselves ... Ah, but that is another story. At that time, more and more accounts were coming out about how bad things were for the Jewish people. Sometimes as the war went on we could not even believe our ears ...' He stopped, shaking his head. 'We could not accept such things we were hearing ...'

'You are wandering, Joe,' Esther reproached him.

'Well, one story is always part of another story. Your mother, David, she was a young teacher from Berlin. I can't pretend I knew her very well, but we first met her when she arrived in the autumn of 1939. I think she was about twenty-four or twenty-five years old. Her husband had sent her away from Berlin, they had somehow procured a student permit for her. Things in Germany were very bad and by the time she left she was also expecting a child – you.' He laid his hand on David's knee for a second. 'He wanted her to be safe even though he could not leave himself. She said he was a chemist, an employee of the government?' He looked at Esther, who nodded. 'She was a quiet, demure girl. Very kind, very intelligent. You have her look, David. Now, from what I remember she had been in England a few months . . .'

'She was in London,' Esther said. She gesticulated with her hands as she talked. 'She told me she had first obtained work as a housemaid. They treated her like a slave – very bad food, working, working all hours of the day and night. And very harsh and rude. Of course she was getting big—' She held her hands out in front of her body. 'With the baby, and she was very unhappy. Then she met a social worker who helped her and I think sent her to Birmingham – to the home of your friend . . .' She nodded at Frances. 'She said the people were Quakers and they were kind to her – even though her English was poor and she had a baby coming. She was very affected by the kindness she received, from Mrs Bowles, I remember that.'

'When she came here,' Joe Leishmann went on, 'she came to Singers Hill and met with others like herself. I have to say it was hard for them – not everyone was so welcoming. I am ashamed to say that our community did not always greet them with its arms open. But of course some people were very kind. And we owe a special debt to the Quakers, and to the Christadelphians – those communities took in many people. Anyway, her life here was not so bad. We did what was possible, they came to *Shul*, there were social evenings and the religious festivals and we gave them whatever help we could. After all, it is not so long ago that Esther and I arrived on these shores and we know that everyone needs a little help.'

Edie watched David. He was completely rapt, waiting for details to fall from Mr Leishmann's lips like a dog waiting for scraps.

Joe Leishmann's brow wrinkled. 'I wish I had more to tell you. You know your mother's name was Gerda Mayer? She was a sweet girl. Once you were born she brought you to Singers Hill and they arranged your circumcision. But more than that, I don't think we know anything else, do we, Esther?'

'Yes, yes, Joe, I talked with her more than you. I know that her husband's name was Hermann and he had been a chemistry student, but Gerda did not mention to me where he was working. Or if she did I don't remember. And they attended the Fasenenstrasse Synagogue in Berlin, off Kurfürstendamm. She had taught for two years in one of the Jewish schools and she and her husband had not been married for many months. She wanted to stay with him, but then the pogrom came on 9 November 1938, the night the Nazis called *Kristallnacht*. They make it sound something pretty, no? They attacked the Jewish businesses, smashed the windows, and set fire to the Fasenenstrasse Synagogue. The roof was all burned, it was basically destroyed. So, of course, everyone was *very* frightened. After that they hurried to make arrangements for her to leave. Perhaps he hoped to join her here, I don't know.'

There was a silence, then David said, 'And my father?'

Esther Leishmann's face tightened as if she had dreaded the question. 'I'm sorry, David. We do not know what happened to him.'

Gently, Mr Leishmann said, 'It is possible that he survived – even if he went to one of the camps. Possible – he was a young man. But you have to understand it may not be so. So many thousands were taken from

Berlin, and so many were lost. You know, it may be possible that we can try to find out, if that is what you would like.'

David nodded, hesitantly.

'You need a little time to think, *ja*?'

Frances leaned forward. 'Were you from Berlin yourselves?'

'No,' Esther Leishmann said. 'We are from Hamburg. So unfortunately we do not know well the Jewish community in Berlin. We left Hamburg and came here in 1934 – we could see the direction in which things were going, the laws being passed. Already our children faced restrictions in which schools they could attend. We did not want this for our son and daughters. Just months after we left, the Nuremberg Laws took away the German citizenship of all Jews. We did not know then so clearly as we know it now – but we were saving all our lives when we came here.'

Edie shook her head slowly. Her own fears and feelings seemed petty at that moment against the enormity of what had happened to David's family. She felt Esther Leishmann's hand on her arm.

'This must be a difficult thing for you. We understand that – that you have loved David as your own. You have been a mother to him – and see, what a fine boy he has turned out to be.'

Edie accepted the proferred comfort with a smile. 'I just want him to be happy – to be settled in his mind.'

'We can help him,' Esther told her. 'And you must not worry. He may find the remnants of a new family. It does not mean he wishes to give up his old one.'

When they showed Edie and the others out later that afternoon, the Leishmanns parted from them with great warmth.

'You are welcome any time, any time,' Joe Leishmann said, shaking their hands. 'And David, you must come ... Call in at the shop soon and see us.' Still holding his hand, he pulled David a little closer. 'And I will find an address for you. I think I know to where we should write.'

Thirty-Nine

One weekend the following January, David made his way to Leishmanns' Tailors along snow-covered pavements, his coat collar turned up against the freezing wind. He stamped the snow from his shoes on the icy step. Hearing that gentle 'ting' as he pushed open the door, he felt his usual mixture of anticipation and slight nervousness at spending time with the Leishmanns – a result almost entirely of his shyness – a young lad with two middle-aged people. Even their son Sam, whom David had met several times, was ten years older than him. At sixteen, feeling his way into adulthood, David often felt gauche and awkward.

Mostly, however, meeting the Leishmanns had been one of the greatest experiences of his life. Closing the door behind him now, he could hear Mr Leishmann's voice carrying from behind the inner door, then some sharp retort from Nadia. He smiled to himself. The sparring matches between the two of them were a fact of life at Leishmanns'. While he had been a little alarmed at the ferocity of the first disagreement he had seen, he knew that this loud conflict was routine, and that if a chill silence fell over the workroom, that was something far more disturbing.

'Shalom, shalom!' Joe Leishmann's head appeared gleefully round the door. 'Nearly finished. Then we can go home and have tea!'

'Tell him to come in here. I want to have a look at him!' Nadia's voice boomed from behind him. 'See if he's putting any flesh on those bones!'

Mr Leishmann winked. 'You're not going to get away today!'

The Leishmanns invited him over now on a regular basis for Sunday tea, after Mr Leishmann was finishing up for the afternoon. With the shop closed on Saturday, their Sunday morning was often busy, though in the afternoon customers were only admitted by appointment, and it was a time when they tried to catch up on the work. David could have gone straight to the house, but he loved to call in at the shop. There was always a sense of something going on – it was so different from home and the quiet gentility of Bournville. It had colour. That was what it was. Somehow he had walked into a more colourful life.

Nadia was standing unrolling a bolt of navy cloth with a thin white pinstripe through it. She wore a swinging black skirt with a tight scarlet jumper tucked into it, a wide black belt accentuating her waist. David was mesmerized for a moment by the sight of her large breasts straining out under the woollen garment and he blushed and tore his eyes away.

''Ello there, sunshine!' Nadia greeted him. 'Oh, isn't he a lovely boy? He's going to have the girls swarming round!'

David blushed even more deeply, though he was getting used to Nadia's earthy observations. He had learned that she was in her mid-thirties, had married an English soldier she met in Italy during the war, and that she was not a woman of hidden depths. She said more or less whatever came into her head, very often at high volume. She was haughty, hot-tempered and warm-hearted all at once, and despite all their disagreements, she told David that no one could hold a candle to Joe Leishmann for tailoring.

'But don't you go telling him I said so!' she added threateningly.

As Mr Leishmann tidied up his work area, Nadia announced petulantly that she had a home to go to as well and would be leaving at the same time. They locked up the shop and headed out into the snow. The house felt cosy inside, and Esther Leishmann greeted them with the usual spread laid out for tea. David had barely missed a week coming here over the last two months. And he thought about it a great deal of the time. He had begun to find a whole new dimension to his life, to who he was.

On his first visit without Frances and Edie, he had felt uneasy, disloyal to them. Not that the visit was a secret. But it was the extent to which he *wanted* to go that bothered him. He could hardly contain his excitement all week at the prospect of being back with these people again. He didn't want Edie or Frances to know how he felt for fear of hurting their feelings. He knew Edie was struggling to be brave about it. Had she expected him to find out the few crumbs of information available about his past, then walk away? None of them could have predicted the strength of his attraction to what he had found, and as the weeks went by this became even more powerful than his feelings of guilt or disloyalty.

That first time they were alone, Esther Leishmann was very direct with him. As they sat with their cups of tea and the cakes with seams of nuts and cinnamon running through them, she sat up straight in her perfectly fitting suit, placed her feet tidily together and said, 'So, David. You know a little about your mother. You know that she was Jewish. When your mother is Jewish, that makes you

Jewish. You understand that, don't you? You are a Jewish boy.'

The way she said it made David feel as if he had found himself a member of an exclusive, magical club. He felt proud, chosen, at that moment, because these people seemed to want him to feel proud of what he had discovered about himself.

That day, also, she said to him, 'You know, I did not want to say this in front of your ... mother. In front of Edith. But your real mother, she called you by a different name. You want to know, David, what is your name?'

Heart pounding, almost as if something terrible was about to be revealed, he nodded.

'You were called Rudi. I do not remember if she chose a second name for you – perhaps after your father, Hermann. But your name for the first year of your life was Rudi Mayer.'

David swallowed. Rudi Mayer. 'Do you know when I was born?' he asked.

Esther stirred her tea, considering. 'Not for sure – Joe, do you have any idea about this?'

Joe Leishmann shrugged. 'I'm afraid women remember these things better.'

'Let's see,' Esther mused. '1939 ... Ah, now, yes! At the time of Hanukkah she had you with her. You were not newborn then – you were perhaps six weeks, two months old? I don't clearly remember. As I told you, I didn't know her so well.'

Since then, David felt as if he was living a secret life inside his head. If Hanukkah was early December he must have been born some time in October. What day though? That night when he was alone in his room, he sat at his desk in a small pool of light from his lamp and wrote over and over again on a sheet of paper, *Rudi Mayer, Rudi Mayer, Rudi Hermann Mayer*. He wrote the names of his parents, Gerda Mayer, Hermann Mayer. He stared at the frayed edges of the lampshade in front of him on the desk. Who am I? he thought. David Weale felt like one person, and Rudi Mayer quite another. David Weale was born on 19 November 1940. It felt as if Rudi Mayer had been born that day, last October, 1955, when he had first met the Leishmanns, leaping into the world fully grown yet utterly bewildered. The conflict burned inside him through those weeks, a combination of acute pain and pleasure which sometimes made him weep in the privacy of his bedroom.

This afternoon, sitting in the cosy room as the wind rattled the windows, Mr Leishmann looked at David over his glasses, with unusual solemnity.

'I have some news to tell you, David. One moment.' He got up and left the room for a moment, returning with a letter, which he held up solemnly and said, 'From Berlin.'

He sat down beside David on the couch, and exchanged the spectacles he was wearing for his half-moon reading glasses, tucking the others into the breast pocket of his jacket. David's heart began to thump so hard he laid his hand over it. Mr Leishmann had been given the address of a rabbi who had, as a young man, survived the camp at Theresienstadt and returned to Berlin. Few Jews had stayed in ruined Berlin, but the rabbi was one who decided to remain and help unite the remaining community, and to answer just such inquiries as theirs from scattered survivors. David had asked Mr Leishmann to write to him. Although he was quite good at German, he felt Mr Leishmann would do a better job of addressing a rabbi. He had not truly expected a reply though. People said that six million Jews had been killed during those years, as well as all the upheaval and deportations. How could they possibly expect to find one man? And Mr Leishmann had written the letter nearly three months ago. It seemed like a dream that there should be a real rabbi in Germany who might know something about his father!

'Now,' Joe Leishmann said gently. Esther sat still, watching David's face with a kind of knowing protectiveness. 'Rabbi Litthauer has written to us. I will read it to you, eh?' He laid a hand reassuringly on David's thigh for a moment. Haltingly, translating as he went along, he read:

Dear Herr Leishmann,
    I hope you will forgive my tardy reply to your letter. I receive still many enquiries of this kind and it can be a long and frustrating process, and full of painful reminders of the bitter fury which was unleashed upon the House of Israel.
    You asked me to try and determine the whereabouts, or verify the survival, of a Hermann Mayer, born in approximately 1912 and a member of the Fasenenstrasse Congregation. You informed me that his wife left the country in 1939. I am not able to tell you the events which followed this, though it is almost certain he was later deported to one of the concentration camps. I am happy to tell you, however, that according to a number of people to whom I have spoken, a Hermann Mayer made *aliyah* from here in 1946 and is now residing in the State of Israel.
    Through my enquiries I also discovered that a sister of Hermann Mayer, one Annaliese Mayer,

survived the war as a nurse in the Jewish Hospital. She is also now resident in Israel.

I do not have further information concerning their whereabouts, and I suggest that you address further enquiries to the authorities in Tel Aviv.

May the peace of Almighty God be upon you.

Rabbi Samuel Litthauer.

David's pulse began to race as Joe Leishmann read the letter and by the end he felt he was going to burst from the mingled feelings inside him. But he contained himself and listened with absolute attention.

'So—' Joe Leishmann folded the letter and handed it to him. 'This is yours now. You know what it means, to make *aliyah*?'

David shook his head. He knew nothing about anything. He was a complete ignoramus!

'It is when a Jewish person makes the journey to live in Israel, to the land of our fathers. All of our ancestors, David, yours and mine. And now, that is to where your father has gone.'

Unexpectedly, and to his enormous embarrassment, David burst into tears.

Forty

Ruby was to leave the country at the end of January. All through the months before, she was full of nothing else, as were the girls. Marleen though, having nearly given up on getting David to take any notice of her, was indignant at his complete lack of interest in the new life ahead of them.

Edie, whose mind was also elsewhere, preoccupied with David, found Ruby's one-track obsession rather trying, especially as she was the one being left behind – by everyone, it seemed.

'You can come out and visit us,' Ruby told her, during one of the dinner breaks at work. Some of the other girls in the factory were all agog to hear Ruby was moving to America. But then they weren't going to miss her as much as Edie. Especially as they were working together for the time being, putting Milk Tray chocolates in with the Easter eggs. Ruby's job was to slip the eggs into their bright display cartons. 'You've got to come. I want you to meet Carl and you'll love America!'

'Oh I don't know about that . . .' To Edie, the thought of flying across the Atlantic was almost beyond her imagination.

'Go on with yer! You can save up the fare and come and see me and the girls. Course—' Ruby stood up, brushing down her overall, 'Carl's paying for me and the girls. He might be able to pay for you as well, later on.'

Edie went back to work, heavy-hearted. She couldn't help resenting this Carl Christie whom Ruby thought so much of, for taking her friend away from her, however much Ruby seemed happy.

What's up with me? she thought. I don't like the way I'm carrying on at the moment. I can't seem to find a good word for anyone. She could barely admit to herself how jealous she was of the Leishmanns and all the time David was spending with them, especially that dressed-up mannequin Esther Leishmann. She knew perfectly well Esther Leishmann was a kind-hearted person. And they had been so good to Davey. But they had started taking him off to the synagogue on Saturdays as well as his visits to their house every week. And he seemed so excited, so full of life these days. He talked very little about it though, she couldn't draw him out on the subject, and she felt excluded and angry. What was it the Leishmanns could give David that she never could? And now here was Ruby full of her new start. Edie was feeling insecure and jealous. And now these emotions even extended to Frances!

A few days ago, a letter had come from Janet from Ibabongo. They had been intending to come home ' "for a furlough" as the missionaries call it', Janet wrote. 'But Martin is so busy, and there is so much to be done that we still can't see how we can get away for a break of more than a few days.' Both of them were working flat out, with the maternity wing, the leprosy hospital, the school. Would Frances perhaps consider coming out to visit them in the Congo instead?

Edie's first reaction was to think this a preposterous idea. From Janet's descriptions of the journeys she and Martin had made to reach the village, how did she think Frances could possibly manage at her age? But Frances seemed quite taken with the idea.

'I think I could cope,' she said. 'I shouldn't want to have to walk for hours at a time, but I don't imagine I should have to. It would be marvellous to see them and the work they're doing, and it doesn't sound as if they're going to manage a trip here.'

So even Frances was making plans for a future which didn't include her! Oh, I'm so silly, Edie thought, hating the bitter feelings which rose up in her. A few days before, she had met one of the volunteers from the WVS whom she ran into from time to time.

'Still here, are you?' she'd said. 'Still in the same place?' The words seemed to taunt her.

The night before Ruby's departure with Marleen and Greta, they all gathered at her house in Glover Road. Her suitcases were already packed and lined up in the back room and the house looked bare and rather sad. Ethel and Lionel were there and they all drank Ruby's health and wished her luck.

'You get yerself settled in, bab, and I'll be over!' Tearfully Ethel grinned round the room. 'We're not letting a chance like that slip by us, are we, Lionel?'

As they left that night, Edie and Ruby hugged each other tight.

'I wish you weren't going,' Edie said miserably. 'I really do. I wish everything could stay as it was.'

Ruby laughed through her tears, holding Edie tight. 'You can't ask the world to stop turning, Edie. You have to move with it. Now you get yourself a passport and get over to see us, eh?'

With final kisses and good wishes they left for home. Walking up Oak Tree Lane with Frances and David, Edie went on ahead of them in the winter night, lit by a slice of moon. Even the night air felt suddenly different, as if she was breathing in the scent of change. She had thought things would just go on, year after year. She had clung to the security of Frances and the home she had offered them while she was bringing up David. She had thought the three of them would always work at Cadbury's, always be there together. That she and Ruby would always be Ginger and Cocoa. And in months it had all changed. Her friends were scattering and she had watched her son fall in love in front of her eyes with something she could barely understand. He was moving ahead in his life. She was the one who had stayed still.

She was full of poignant thoughts that evening. How many years would Frances live for? How long would David be at home? All this time she had lived in the comfortable certainty of other people, barely looking at her own life. Still here. Yes – still here. So what do I do now? she thought, as they reached the brow of the hill in the moonlight. What can I do with my life now?

1957–9

Forty-One

'So – have you got everything, d'you think?'

They stood in the front room of Frances's house, David's suitcase and shoulder-bag waiting by the door.

'You'll never manage with just that, will you? What about that jersey – did you put it in?'

David tutted fondly, shrugging into his coat. 'Yes I did – I know Israel's cold in January. But I'm only going for a few months – not for ever!'

That was not how it felt to Edie.

'You will be all right, won't you?'

He came up and put his hands on her shoulders. Her long, thin boy, much taller than her now. How she loved him! They had eaten a farewell meal together last night, just the three of them, and it had felt so good-natured, so close at last, after all the turmoil they had passed through.

'I will. Don't fuss. And I'll write very often. You know I like writing letters. I'll miss you, but I'll be back very soon.' Seeing the tears welling in Edie's eyes, he hugged her. 'Look . . . Mom. It'll be OK.'

She could hear the emotion in his voice too and he pulled away. He has to do this, she told herself, forcing herself, as she had done so many times over the past months, to understand, to let him be.

'Mr Abrahams will be here in a minute,' he said, going to the window to hide his own moist eyes.

Frances limped into the room on her stick and said her

goodbyes with great affection, and there was a flurry of activity then, when Mr Abrahams's car drew up outside. He was a friend of Mr and Mrs Leishmann from the synagogue, and had offered to drive David all the way down to London Airport. Edie had decided not to go. She wouldn't have felt comfortable travelling with them, and preferred to say her goodbyes in the privacy of home.

'So, you are ready, young David?' Mr Abrahams boomed cheerfully as they opened the door.

Edie held David in her arms for one more snatched embrace.

'Goodbye, love,' she said softly.

''Bye, Mom.'

'Go safely,' Frances said.

Then he was waving through the shiny windows of Mr Abrahams's car and a moment later was gone.

Edie stared at the empty space where the car had been. He had been carried into her life, and now he had been carried out of it, that was how it felt.

'He won't come back,' she said, with flat certainty.

'Don't be silly, dear,' Frances said, sharp in the face of this melodramatic gloominess. 'Of course he will, in a few months – he's got his place at university.' She turned on the step, surreptitiously wiping a tear from her own eye.

'Let's get in out of this cold wind.'

There had been times over the past two years when things had been so bad that Edie could not have imagined David would ever again give her the sort of fond hug with which he parted from her before his flight to Tel Aviv. For a long time it had felt that they were enemies.

She had struggled from the start with his attachment to the Leishmanns, because she sensed that it was about so much more than his fondness for the couple. They were, as she saw it, stand-ins for his real parents. They had actually seen, touched, spoken to his real mother, Gerda Mayer. They were German and Jewish, the nearest he could get. And for a time, suddenly, she seemed to count for nothing. She had had great difficulty controlling her feelings. First of all it had got worse when David started attending the synagogue. Going to *Shul*, he started calling it. His language became peppered with Hebrew and Yiddish terms which she had never heard before. David was excited about learning them, about his new identity, and would have taught her if she had been willing to hear. But the sound of these guttural words made her feel immediately agitated, enraged even. The new language was going to turn David into someone who spoke differently, thought differently. Someone she didn't know.

It meant that she scarcely saw him at weekends. On Saturday – *Shabbat* as he insisted on calling it – he spent much of the day with them. *Them*, they had become in her mind. The enemy, tearing her son away. On Sundays, sometimes, he still came to the Friends' Meeting House, but while she had been influenced by the Friends to be suspicious of ritual and set words, David bemoaned the lack of it. He said Quaker prayer was all very well, but he needed something more. He wanted words, gestures, music. After lunch he was off again, to his cosy afternoon tea with the Leishmanns. Many times Esther Leishmann, hearing from David of Edie's difficulties in accepting what was happening, invited her to go as well, but she always refused. They didn't really want her there, Edie thought bitterly, and she would have felt uncomfortable.

'Can't you stay in for once and have tea with us?' she complained sometimes. 'We hardly ever see you.'

'But I promised I'd go,' he'd protest. 'You know what Mrs Leishmann's like – she'll have been baking.'

Usually Edie had to accept that, but once or twice she had lost her temper and shouted at him. 'Oh, go on – go then. You've always got summat better to do than spend any time at home, haven't you? Go on – go and see your Jewish friends – they obviously mean more to you than we do.'

And then she felt awful afterwards, ashamed of her bitterness, and sad because she knew, if she carried on, she would drive him further away. And she was aware that he was in turmoil too. Amid his excitement about the discoveries he was making was confusion, tension about who he was and how he should feel. Mostly it was locked up inside him. Now and then it poured out in explosive bursts of temper. She wanted him to talk to her about it, yet at the same time she didn't want to hear. It seemed as if there was no way to make things go right again. When she was angry she accused him of being secretive. In a calmer state she realized that he didn't know how to talk to her, and also that he was trying to protect her.

Despite herself she found herself searching his room when he was out, but all she ever found were books. He spent hours reading. Some of the books were about the Jewish religion, some on Zionism. Names jumped out from pages at her, *Jabotinsky, Herzl, Ben Gurion*, fathers of Zionism, names she had never heard before and which seemed harsh and alien.

The worst time had been the six weeks Frances was away visiting Janet. She had finally gone during the spring of 1957, as the first rainy season ended. The plan had been to go earlier, but Frances had not been in good health the summer before. Edie thought she was crazy to make the journey, but Frances was determined, and as it turned out, coped very well. She came home looking quite refreshed, despite the long journey, and full of Janet and Martin's work in Ibabongo.

But during that time Edie really touched bottom. Being alone in the house with no Frances to offer a consoling ear, she felt desperately alone and cut adrift. There was no Janet, Ruby's first excited letters dwindled into complete silence, and David was either out or in a world of his own. Of course she knew plenty of people in the factory in a day-to-day sort of way, but she had never needed to try to make deeper friendships when she had Ruby, Janet and Frances. Now the silence of the house filled her with sadness. Her life seemed to be full of absences.

David was studying hard. One evening she went up and tapped on his door. He was hunched over his desk, left hand raking through his dark hair, the other writing furiously. She ventured closer, awed by his intense concentration on things she could scarcely understand. He was working on maths problems, pages of his quick, sprawling figures. To her it was as comprehensible as a knitting pattern written in Chinese.

'You busy?' she said, though it was obvious he was.

He finished writing something, then looked up at her. She sensed him suppressing his irritation at being interrupted. Edie sat on the bed next to him and he straightened up in his chair, accepting her presence. His face was solemn, tired-looking.

'Don't work too late, will you?' she offered. 'You'll be falling asleep in the classroom.'

He smiled faintly. 'I've nearly finished.'

'Is it hard? It looks it to me.' She fiddled with the pleats of her skirt.

'Quite,' he said, rubbing his eyes with the heels of his hands. 'But we did it in the lesson. I've got the hang of it.'

'Got your big exams soon, haven't you?'

'They're called A levels,' he said, a touch impatient now.

'OK.' She got up. 'You'd better get finished. 'Night, love.'

''Night.' He was already leaning over his work again.

It was a few days later, while Frances was still away, that he made his announcement. The day before, he had been to tea with the Leishmanns, and he'd stayed late. He went to school as usual, but when Edie came home, instead of finding him in his room, deep in homework, he was waiting for her. He'd even started heating up their shepherd's pie. It made her so happy, that he was spending time with her of his own accord, and she laughed with him, telling him about her day.

'I went to the staff shop,' she told him, laying the table. 'I got you some misshapes – fudge mostly. And some Milk Tray.'

He smiled and thanked her. But when they were sitting over their meal, he put his knife and fork down and looked across at her, his long-fingered hands resting on the table.

'I have made a decision.' His voice was quiet, but sure and his eyes steadily held her gaze. 'I am going to go to Israel. I want to work on a kibbutz.'

Edie stared at him. What madness was he talking?

'What d'you mean?' she brought out, finally. It felt

like hearing news of a death. 'Israel? You can't go to Israel! You want to go to the university! All your plans!'

'I'll put it off for a year,' he tried to soothe her. 'I just want to go for a few months, to experience the life there.' He leaned forward. 'I want to know how it feels to be part of Israel – to be part of building something. It's a new state – not like any other there's ever been, built on ideals! – and the kibbutz is like one of the foundation bricks. People have their possessions in common, they work the land together, build villages where everyone's equal and their work counts equally. Not like here where everything is based on your class or how much money you've got. It's something completely different and it's the Jews who are building it!' His eyes flashed at her. He was afire with intense enthusiasm.

'I can't bear the thought of never being part of it. I want to go and join them. I can work for a few months to earn some of my fare and Mr Leishmann said they will give me the rest – that I should go and come back to tell them what it's like. They've never been there.'

Edie blazed with anger. 'I might have known they'd have summat to do with it. Always taking over, controlling you – putting these ideas into your head. I don't want you going. You've worked hard all these years because you wanted to be an engineer and go to university and now you'd let them just mess that up and have you . . . farming or whatever it is they do over there!'

'But I'll come back and go to university the year after!' He stood up, wild with emotion. 'I don't understand why you're so against me all the time, against everything I do. I can't help being who I am! You talk as if all I should ever do is sit here with you year after year. Men younger than me were soldiers in both the wars and no one stopped them going, did they? You can't own me, Mom. Sooner or later I have to go.' He stopped and looked at her in silence for a moment. Then, quietly, with great intensity, he said, 'I want to go and I want you to agree. But I shall go. You're going to have to accept it.'

He took his plate and went to finish eating in his room. Edie sat for a long time, her meal forgotten, staring at his empty chair. His words, those quiet, measured words sunk deep into her. *But I shall go.* And she knew then that she had to summon all her strength and courage. She had to fight her jealousy and resentment towards the Leishmanns, the synagogue, all the people who she felt were taking him away from her, and try to enter his new world. Because if she didn't move with him, she was going to lose him.

When spring came, he invited her to come to the synagogue for the annual *Seder* – the Passover celebration meal. He had invited her the year before but she had refused then, abruptly. What place did she have doing something like that?

But this year, hands clammy with nerves, she accompanied him as his guest. The occasion was strange to her. She had never been to anything like it before. When they arrived at the hall of Singers Hill Synagogue, she thought they must have strayed into a wedding by mistake. The tables were laid out round the hall and decorated beautifully with flowers, sparkling glasses and small dishes of food. On a table to one side stood a huge candelabra which David told her was the *Menorah*, and alongside it a tray covered with small dishes of food for the *Seder* ritual.

Mr and Mrs Leishmann greeted Edie with enthusiasm,

and when she saw Esther Leishmann again after such a long time, Edie found that she liked her better than she remembered. She had somehow built the woman up almost into a demon in her mind through her own fears and jealousy, and she felt ashamed. Proudly, David introduced her to some of his other friends, some his own age, others older. She tried to remember names – *this is Ruth, and this is Werner, this is Lily* ... She was made to feel very welcome. They sat together at the table and the *Seder* began with the lighting of candles and the blessing of the wine. As it progressed, Edie forgot most of her unease and became interested instead. She couldn't understand all that was going on, but she watched the questions and answers given by the people, one by the youngest person there, a tiny girl of about five years old with wide eyes, but who spoke her question like a tiny adult. 'Why is this night different from any other night?' There were many smiles as she did so.

David kept whispering to her throughout. 'That's the bitter herbs, and we dip them in salt water to represent the tears of the people who were in exile in Egypt. And that nutty stuff is *charoset* – it's supposed to look like the mortar they had to use for the bricks. And it's delicious.'

David passed her some of the unleavened bread. 'That is called a *matzah*,' he told her. They drank far more wine than Edie had ever been used to, which made her feel woozy but happier as well, and after there was singing and dancing. David's eyes shone with pride all evening at showing her, sharing it with her. And she smiled back and responded to the people who were friendly towards her. She understood that David somehow needed to bring the two sides of his life together.

Forty-Two

While Frances was away visiting the Congo, Edie had received the first letter she had had from Janet which was addressed only to her. Before, Janet had written to the two of them together, but this time she was able to write with a frankness she had never allowed herself before.

> 'Doctor's House!'
> Ibabongo
> 19. 1. 1957

Well, mother's here and I think she's doing marvellously. She does have that stiff old hip but she bore up amazingly well throughout the journey here, which can be really punishing. Martin was amazed at how well she's coped with everything, although she does keep fretting about her malaria tablets and what she should or shouldn't eat or drink. But I suppose that's to be expected. After all, she's barely ever been anywhere before! I'm full of admiration for her.

She's worrying about how you and David are getting along! I must say, I'm so glad of a chance to write just to you, Edie. I've missed you so much since we've been out here. It was odd when Mother came because as I was showing her round, telling her which plants are manioc, which plantains and rice, which of the red roads leads to the lepers' area and

which out of town, I saw all the trees and flowers
and the children coming out to greet her through my
first-day eyes again. It all came back to me, those first
weeks, how despite all the excitement of a new start
with Martin, how desperately homesick I was.
Especially as I was so ill and had all that horrible
trouble with my skin!

Edie frowned on reading this. She just about remembered these details. Janet must have made light of it in her
letters.

I'm cutting down on a few of my hours in the
hospital and school while Mother is here. The work
has been a godsend though, to fill my time, and of
course there is such suffering, you couldn't not help.
Leprosy is a terrible disease in all it does to the body
and the mind, and many of the people feel honoured
if someone so much as touches them to show that
they don't regard them as unclean. I shake hands, on
the quiet, as often as possible with people, against
medical advice! My friend Chrissie, the evangelical
missionary, does the same. The lepers certainly help
to relieve any self-indulgent bouts of self-pity. I am
thinking I should really stop playing about doing my
bits of volunteer work and take the bull by the horns
– train as a nurse myself so that I could be more use.
I do feel I should be of use to someone at least!
I do so miss you, Edie – your kindness and good
sense – and wish I'd confided in you more, though it
would have felt disloyal to Martin. I don't know if
you really knew how bad that patch was for us over
children, or rather the lack of them. I suppose I'm
over that now, but he is still the work obsessive he

ever was. He seems to feel he's not living fully unless he goes flat out at it. So I don't always see much of him and life can be lonely at times. I understand it, and he's very good to me, always has been. BUT . . .! Thank goodness for Chrissie! She's quite quaint in some ways but very passionate about everything she does and she's been good for me. But I'd like to see *you*, and sit talking away the afternoons like we sometimes used to! I can't help wishing things could have been different – that we could have had a family and not had to live all the way across the world for Martin to feel happy with himself.

Still – Chrissie says I am bound to have been brought over here (by the Lord, she would say) for a reason and sooner or later I'll find out exactly what it is!

With more affectionate greetings she signed off.

Her letter had allowed Edie to write back with more candour concerning her feelings about David at that time, which was a great relief. Janet replied, gently advising her to 'give him a long rope', as she put it. He needed time to adjust to his new sense of himself. Ever since, their letters had been closer, more confiding, and Edie found comfort in this with David gone.

She waited with great expectation for letters now. They heard from Marie Falla occasionally. Marie and her husband had settled in Walsall and had three children, but Marie usually wrote when the family visited Guernsey on holiday. But Edie heard nothing from Ruby any more, though she wrote to her from time to time, and though a little hurt, took this to mean that Ruby had settled into American life as if born to it. However, it was David's letters to which she looked forward most. When the first one arrived she was trembling with impatience as she opened it, and after reading with pleasure and surprise, handed it to Frances, saying, 'How is it I never noticed before how *funny* Davey is?'

'Yes, his sense of humour comes out in letters.' Frances peered at the closely written lines. 'You'll have to read it to me. I've left my reading glasses upstairs.'

As Edie read, she and Frances laughed at his light-hearted depiction of Kibbutz Hamesh, which meant Kibbutz Five, near Tiberias, and his tedious, back-breaking work of clearing fields, strewn with rocks and scrubby bushes, for cultivation. He described his workmates, especially a girl called Gila, a year his junior, whom he portrayed as an utterly terrifying Amazon.

> She's not very big but she still seems to be as strong
> as several horses. A proper Sabra. (That's what they
> call the native-born Israelis – the same name they
> give the prickly pears, because they say both are hard
> and spiny on the outside and soft and tender inside!)
> She strides about in dusty grey trousers with a scarf
> round her hair and keeps thrusting an army canteen
> at me and barking, 'Water – you must take water!'
> When she saw me rubbing my sore back the first day
> she looked at me with absolutely no pity at all and
> said, 'Is good you come in springtime, David' (she
> pronounces it Daveed). 'In summer, you die.' Then
> she strode off with a bucket of stones in each hand.
> So – I can hardly wait 'til summer now!

And he wrote about some of the linguistic misunderstandings that kept cropping up in a community peopled with occupants from all over the place.

'I have now been enrolled on an Ulpan,' he told them.

'I've heard so many languages here – Polish, Russian, German, French – so this is the course used all over Israel for immigrants to learn Hebrew. It's not too difficult, and especially as we're all trying to struggle on and speak it together. But life is full of mistakes. We have big breakfasts here – bread and cheese, yoghurt, salad. This morning at breakfast I asked someone to pass me a cucumber and had evidently asked them for a screwdriver instead!'

'Well,' Frances said at the end. 'He sounds happy, doesn't he?'

'Yes,' Edie sighed. 'He does. And I suppose I'm glad!'

Forty-Three

David went to search for his father for the first time at the end of March. Back in the winter, Mr Leishmann had entered into a brief but tantalizing correspondence with the authorities in Tel Aviv, and after a delay of some months, during which time his letter must have passed through a number of different hands, they received a reply. Of course, more than one Hermann Mayer appeared in their records, but there was one who appeared to fit, given the details of age and former place of residence, and who had spent the required number of weeks in the Absorption Centre for new immigrants in Tel Aviv. There was a forwarding address in Haifa.

On reading this letter, David had felt pulses of strange emotion. Part of it was like the excitement of a hunter tracking an animal. Haifa! So he knew which town the man had gone to. Perhaps he was getting closer to finding him ... But there was also a chill of fear. Was this Hermann Mayer his father? And if so, would he ever be able to meet him, find out about his blood family? Supposing it all felt wrong – that the man didn't feel like his father at all? In part, he wanted to run away and hide from all this. Sometimes he didn't want to know his name was Rudi Mayer. It would be far easier to remain plain English David Weale.

He had not told Edie, then, that he had discovered the possible whereabouts of his father, and when he and Joe

Leishmann composed a letter to the address in Haifa and waited in anticipation, there was no reply. Perhaps Hermann Mayer had died or moved house, or didn't want to know about a son who he had never seen. David asked himself why he should pursue this stranger and insist he take on the role of father.

But as soon as he had been in Kibbutz Hamesh for just a few days, had met other kibbutz members who had lost most or all of their families in the Nazi death camps, he knew for certain that he must go and search for Hermann Mayer. There were so many dead, so many families destroyed and lost to one another. His father and aunt were very likely to be alive and living somewhere in this small country. How could he stay here and not try to find them?

He looked out with intense interest from the smelly, rumbling old bus as they left Tiberias and travelled west. They passed through small towns and villages of square little houses where dogs and chickens scattered out of the bus's path and children stood staring. He saw young plantations of date and banana trees, bare stony fields where rows of women bent over hoes, tilling the earth. As they left Nazareth clouds piled in the sky and there came a harsh downpour, rain beating the windows and, for about twenty minutes, making it impossible to see anything outside at all. Eventually the clouds passed, leaving watery sunshine and the smell of the wet earth blowing in through the windows. It felt strange to be out on the road again after the enclosed, intense life of Kibbutz Hamesh, and he welcomed a chance to be quiet, away from the raucous, argumentative kibbutzniks.

When they reached Haifa he drank in the sight of it. In fact it was quite a disappointing prospect: a sprawl of industry surrounding the port of Haifa, its scooped-out bay formed by a little protuberance of land in the otherwise straight Israeli coast.

It was early afternoon when David climbed down from the bus, and the sun was shining. Amir, the land foreman, had given him a day and a half off to make the trip, when David told him what he needed to do. When he'd left, after that morning's chores, the tanned, wiry-legged Amir had said, 'Shalom – and good luck, Daveed,' with unusual tenderness.

Standing in the blast of blue fumes as the bus moved off again, David realized foolishly that he didn't even have a map of Haifa. He took out the slip of paper he had pushed into his pocket. He would have to keep asking until he found it.

Setting off along the busy road, he asked directions several times and was guided by pointing fingers and the usual Israeli mix of languages. It seemed that the address was in the old city, close to the industrial zone. He started to feel hungry and thirsty, hot now the sun was out, and rather jaded. Haifa was mainly a Jewish city, he had been told. Most of the Arabs had left when the State was established. In his idealistic mind that had made it sound fine, a jewel of a place, but in reality it seemed like a large, cacophonous building site. There was the oil refinery, and all the cranes and industrial buildings of the port, and on all sides blocks of sandy-coloured apartments were going up, spare and hollow-eyed without their windows in. He stopped at a café on the busy Allenby Road, with lorries roaring past, for a drink of coffee and a sticky slice of apple cake which put him in a better humour. By the time he found the address, in a crumbling, ochre-painted building in the old city, it was already three o'clock.

As he stood outside the heavy brown door in the

shade of the buildings, the situation seemed absurd. Here he was, some English boy, with a light tan and stronger muscles from a few weeks' work on the land, standing at a door he had never seen before and expecting to find his father behind it. A father he had written to but who had never replied to his letters at all, let alone with enthusiasm! He felt incredibly foolish and vulnerable.

He forced his hand to take the old brass knocker and banged it hard, twice. There was a long silence. The house felt deserted. As he looked up he saw that the paintwork was in a far worse state than the houses around it, all the shutters were closed and the ones near the top seemed to be covered in bird mess. Perhaps the place had stood empty for years? He pictured inside the hallway, filling up with letters that were never answered. Perhaps his letter was there, in a deep drift of lost correspondence? But then he saw there was no letterbox: instead there was a metal container attached to the wall, with a slit in it. He thought about trying to look inside it, but before he could move, the door of the adjoining house opened and he saw an old woman looking out at him. She was tiny, clad completely in black with a shawl round her shoulders, her grey hair in a bun, tiny black mules on her feet. Her face was as lined as a desert wadi.

'You want someone?'

Her voiced had a cracked note but the Hebrew was quite clear. She did not leave her own doorway though, hovering as if ready to scuttle back inside, and David went over to her, arranging his newly acquired Hebrew sentences in his mind.

'Is anyone inside?' He pointed up at the other house.

'*Lo.*' She shook her head emphatically. 'Not now.' She made signs to indicate that the inside of the house was very bad. It seemed one of the floors had collapsed. 'Who you want?'

'I am looking for a man called Hermann Mayer. I think he lived here when he came from Germany.'

'Hermann Mayer?' She did not have to think for long. Although she appeared so old she was completely alert. '*Ken!* Yes – he was here.' She nodded, but without much animation. 'Hermann Mayer ... *Ken, ken* ... I remember him.' He expected her to be more curious. In England people would be nosey and want to know what you were about. He supposed that here most people's lives were disjointed. Everyone was looking for someone.

'There was a lady,' she added. 'Miss Annaliese. Two, maybe three years they were here.' The woman saw he was a beginner in Hebrew, and explained slowly, with accompanying gestures, that she had been a sort of concierge for both the houses for many years, but now, given the state of the other place, for only one.

David felt his blood pulsing hard round his body. They had been here – they existed! He was so close!

'I wrote to them,' he said. 'Did you send letters to them?'

'Ah—' The old lady made a sorrowful gesture. She drew a line back and forth in the air with her hand. '*Lo.* Herr Mayer was a bitter man. He said no letters. Nothing good could come to him so to throw anything which came. He thought there would be nothing.' He saw her respond to the pain in his eyes as she spoke. It was lost, he was thinking. He'd never find him now. 'I'm sorry,' she said. 'You know him?'

It was his turn for an emphatic, '*Lo.*' He shook his head. 'But I believe he is my father.' Sadly, he asked, 'Do you know where he is now – *b'vaka'sha*? Please?'

413

'I have not seen him,' she said. Her tone was gentle. 'But I think they went to live on the Carmel. Michaelangelo Street. I do not know which house.'

David smiled, renewed in hope. 'Thank you – you are very kind. What is your name?'

'Mrs Spielman,' she told him. 'And yours?'

He hesitated. 'Rudi Mayer.'

She reached out and for a moment he felt her warm, wizened hand on his wrist. 'Perhaps you should not expect too much of your father. But I wish you good luck, my boy.'

I can't go tonight, he thought. The day was waning, and already seemed to have gone on a long time. He was tired and felt stirred up and unready, needing time for these new fragments of information from the old lady to sink into his mind.

The kibbutz had given him the address of a very cheap hostel he could stay in at the foot of Mount Carmel. It was rudimentary but clean, and he was to share a dormitory with five others. He gathered from them that the hostel was used mainly by Israelis on trips to look round the country, and idealistic young people, often American, on their way to try out life on a kibbutz. Keeping his canvas bag containing his few possessions with him, he went out again to explore further. Not far from the hostel one of the steep, zigzagging roads led up the Carmel and he began to climb. The evening was cool, scented with flowers and pleasant for walking, and when he had climbed a good way up he was at last rewarded with views that provided the sense of pride and exhilaration he had hoped for. Panting, he stood at a bend in the road and looked down over the gold dome of the Bahai shrine and the chaotic sprawl of the city where evening lights were coming on, twinkling in the dusk. Beyond these lay the wide sweep of the bay, lamps strung along the coast road like a necklace, and beyond them the dark sea. David smiled. Excitement welled up in him. *Eretz Yisrael.* He formed the words with his lips, proud of the feel of Hebrew. It seemed to require more energy and fire to speak than English, forcing out those sounds from the throat and teeth. And he would learn it until he was fluent like Amir and the others. Like Gila! The thought of her excited him, even though she seemed untouchable, almost another species. He took a deep breath of the sulphurous evening air. What a place this is! he thought. Our land. My people. What we can make here!

And behind him, somewhere on this hill with its apartments and gardens, were some of his family. For those moments of exhilaration he chose not to think of the old woman's words: *perhaps you should not expect too much of your father.*

He breakfasted on hard-boiled eggs with pure white shells, cucumbers and yesterday's stale *pittot*, the pockets of bread into which he stuffed the eggs, and with it, weak black coffee.

Refreshed, and nervous, he was ready to leave at an hour far too early to call on anyone. The day was warm, with hazy strips of cloud, and he decided to use up some of the time by walking up the Carmel once more instead of looking for a bus. It was Saturday tomorrow, he realized, the Jewish Shabbat. The religious Jews would go to *Shul*. He felt a pang for a moment. Had he been wrong to disappoint the Leishmanns and not to go to a religious kibbutz? Gila and the others at Hamesh showed no sign of wanting to go to *Shul* or anything else involving a synagogue. 'In Israel we are free to be Jews,' he was told. 'We have the land – we do not need a synagogue.' And he knew that he was finding a sense of his belonging as a Jew in this way as well. Here he could stop being Davey, an odd, trying-to-oblige mixture of Quaker and Jew, beloved son yet cuckoo in the nest. He could learn to be himself.

David climbed and climbed, physical exertion a distraction from the fear of what lay before him. Unlike last night, the old woman's warning now nagged in his mind. What exactly had she meant? What had happened to Hermann Mayer? There were so many horrible possibilities that he could not even bear to guess.

I must do this, he thought, pushing down hard on his legs on the steep road. I must see him and offer myself as his son. I need to know him – and perhaps he needs to know me, that I exist. But if he doesn't want me I mustn't be disappointed. At least I will have seen him for myself. After all, I already have a family . . .

Michaelangelo Street was high on the central Carmel, a quiet side street lined on one side with eucalyptus and bushes of pale blue plumbago flowers. On the other were sandy-coloured apartment blocks of two or three floors in the traditional style with stone steps running up the outside. They made David think of the pictures of Bible villages he used to draw as a child. From somewhere he could hear the low humming of an electric generator.

Mrs Spielman had not been able to tell him the number of the apartment, so he had prepared himself to ask. When he went to the door of the first apartment block, however, he saw that the name of the occupants was written above the bell. Kauffman. He wouldn't need to knock on doors! He climbed the stairs. Hirsch, Aron. On to the next block: Weisz, Eisner, Perlmann. He moved quietly up and down the stairs, absurdly nervous in case anyone came out and challenged him on the doorstep. Would he ever find his father like this? It seemed too ridiculously simple to suppose the name would just be there, among these others. Perhaps he had even changed his name?

He reached the fourth block: first floor, Rubenstein, second floor, another Hirsch, third floor, Mayer. There it was, in neat black letters, in front of his unbelieving eyes. MAYER!

From inside the apartment he could hear a voice, then realized it was too fast and fluent to be anything but a radio. He was standing trying to take in the implications of what he had to do next, when he heard someone coming up the steps behind him, the slapping tread of someone wearing mules. A broad-faced woman in her thirties appeared, hair tied back in a scarf. She gave David a curt nod and immediately rang on the Mayer doorbell. David, unable to get past without rudely pushing her, shrank back into the corner.

Forty-Four

The door opened. Over the sound of the radio David heard a guttural female voice say *bocker tov* (good morning), in a tone which suggested the visit was expected, and the woman in the scarf disappeared inside. The door began to close, but the occupant evidently caught a glimpse of him standing out there. It swung open again and David saw a middle-aged woman, her greying hair pinned softly up in a bun. She was scarcely taller than five foot, and dressed in a frock made from a rather shiny mauve material, a cream cardigan and low-heeled black shoes, a little scuffed at the toes. There was something smart, imposing, about her, though her clothes were obviously not new. Her face was very lined, the eyebrows plucked thin and their shape retraced by brown eyebrow pencil. Her demeanour was kind and intelligent, though her expression was temporarily clouded by suspicion. In Hebrew she said sharply, 'What do you want here?'

David was paralysed. He simply didn't know where to begin, and what he felt like doing most of all was running away. But he forced himself to move closer.

'I . . .' Stumblingly he organized some Hebrew words in his mind, then reminded himself to greet her. 'Shalom . . . Are you Annaliese Mayer?'

She frowned. '*Ken . . .*'

Oh, God help me, David thought. *This is it.*

'I am from England,' he said slowly, his gaze never

leaving her face. 'My mother escaped to England from Berlin in 1939. Her name was Gerda Mayer. The name she gave to me was Rudi. I am Rudi Mayer.'

The woman just stared at him, eyes wide. Seconds passed. He could almost see the functioning of her mind. Then one hand went to her mouth, the other groping for the doorframe, and she took a step backwards, shaking her head.

'*Nein . . . Mein Gott, nein!*'

His schoolboy German was still better than his Hebrew, and like her he reverted to it.

'It's true,' he said. 'I have come to look for you, and for my father.'

She stared at him still. 'But how . . .?' She shook her head. 'You died! *She* died . . . The place was bombed. We made enquiries after the war and they said everyone in that house was dead.'

'They thought so. But I did not die. I was rescued.'

Annaliese's face had gone pale. He could hear her short, sharp breaths. She moved towards him, cautious as if he might vanish at her touch like a soap bubble, eyes fixed on him in wonder. She reached out her hand and hesitantly David took it, feeling its cool, fragile skin.

'You are truly the son of Gerda? Gerda's little baby . . .' She just couldn't seem to take it in. David nodded, feeling a lump rise in his throat.

'My father —' His voice was husky. 'Hermann – is he here?'

Her face crumpled for a moment, and, still holding him with one hand, in a guarded way she reached round and closed the door of the apartment.

'Rudi,' she whispered. 'Little Rudi. She wrote us so very much about you. Gerda's darling child.' All at once he was clasped in her arms, and both of them were weeping. Annaliese kept pulling back to look at him, her tears flowing, reaching up to cup his face in her hands, to wipe his tears away, stroke his cheeks and hair, his strong arms and shoulders.

'You are so tall, such a grown-up boy. I should have known when I saw you standing there,' she told him through her tears. 'You are so very like her – the eyes, the hair.'

David struggled to keep up with her German, but he understood from her gestures. 'I have been told that.' He tried to smile. This felt unreal, as if he was acting in a play.

'Who told you this?'

'The Jews who knew her in Birmingham.'

Annaliese nodded. 'She told us that many people were kind to her.' It took her some time to collect herself. At last, wiping her face with her handkerchief, she said, 'You think I am strange not taking you inside. But Elena is doing a little cleaning, and Hermann, he is ... Ah, but in fact, this is a good time now.' She opened the door, cautiously and beckoned David inside. 'He is listening to his radio programme. Come in. Come! You must tell me everything!'

The apartment was cool inside, and smelt of stone, rather like an English country church. David found himself standing on a small landing with doors leading off it. The sound of the radio came from a room to his left, and from somewhere else, probably the bathroom, he could hear water swishing and realized it must be the cleaner. The stone floor was partially covered with a red rectangular rug, and on the one available wall space was a painting in a gold frame of a beautiful building, its roof topped by three ornate domes.

'Beautiful, *ja*?' Annaliese said. 'This was painted by

my uncle in the 1920s – it is the Synagogue Fasenen-strasse, a place your mother knew very well.' She gave a painful sigh. 'It was burned in the *pogrom* in November 1938. All the beautiful roof – gone.' She touched his back gently. 'Come into the kitchen – you will have coffee and some cake?'

The kitchen was small and quite bare, with a sink, two metal chairs pushed under a table topped with pale yellow Formica and a very large refrigerator. Annaliese ordered him to sit at the table while she made coffee.

'We have a while yet – his programme will end at eleven o'clock.'

The kitchen clock said twenty to eleven. David was feeling increasingly uncomfortable about the kind of reference he had heard so far to his father. The thought of coming face to face with him seemed frightening.

Annaliese paused for a moment, in the middle of spooning coffee. Her agitation was obvious.

'I wonder if you should go away. If I should take a little time to prepare Hermann. His health is not so good, you understand? Could you come back tomorrow?'

David explained that he had to return to Kibbutz Hamesh that afternoon.

'I see.' She poured boiling water. 'Then we shall do our best.'

Sitting opposite him she handed him the rich coffee and offered a plate of *lebkuchen*.

'So you speak German?'

'I learned a bit at school – I am not good at it, as you can hear.'

'No – you speak very well. And Hebrew?'

He took one of the little cakes from the plate. 'I am on an Ulpan. Just a few weeks. So German is easier.'

'OK. *Gut.*' She smiled and caressed his shoulder. 'Rudi

'. . . Little Rudi . . . I will speak simply so you can follow.'
She eyed the clock on the wall above them. 'Soon Hermann's programme will finish and he will want coffee. But I have to tell you about your father so that you understand.' As she talked she fiddled with a gold ring on the middle finger of her right hand. 'Hermann – he is my younger brother. He is now forty-eight years old, though you will be surprised because he looks much older. This is because of what he suffered in the camps. He is not the man he was before the war. Not at all. Hermann had a scientific training. Because of this he stayed in Berlin longer than many Jews because he was employed in the armaments industry. But even those Jews who were of use in this way were deported in 1943. He left in summertime. Soon after, the Nazis declared Berlin to be *Judenfrei*. No Jews left, they said. This was even a lie because they let some of us stay. I was a nurse in the Jewish Hospital all through the war. And of course there were others in hiding. Hermann was taken first to the camp at Theresienstadt. We heard nothing from him from that day. Later, they started to move groups of them to Auschwitz-Birkenau. You know what is this?'

'Of course.' David felt himself tightening inside.

'He was working for some months at Birkenau – in fact in one of the laboratories. Then he fell foul of one of the capos – some official – who sent him to the work parties outside. It was the Christmastime of 1944. Already his health was not good and after some weeks he fell ill. He was fortunate in this way: a few months earlier and he would have been sent straight to the gas chambers. Just a fortnight before, I heard, they had used the gas chambers in the camp for the last time – for a group of two thousand who had come on a transport from Theresienstadt. But the British and Russians were coming closer

– they did not want their crimes to be seen. Many of them – even the sick, the starving – were made to leave the camp. They were to march to their deaths – through the rain and snow, day after day. But Hermann was sent with some others to the transit camp at Bergen-Belsen. You have seen pictures of Bergen-Belsen, *ja*? I do not need to tell you. At that time the camp was full of typhus, and Hermann caught it. When the British came into the camp in April 1945 he was very ill. A few more days . . .' Annaliese shrugged, palms up. 'Even then it was not finished. They moved him when still he was quite sick, to another camp on the Dutch border. I think this totally finished him – really.'

David saw her examine his face, checking that he was understanding everything.

'Hermann was still quite a young man of course. He should have been in the prime of his life, but his health was broken. I am worried at his seeing you . . . But at the same time – such joy!' She beamed, wiping her eyes again.

'Have you been with him ever since?'

'*Ja.*' She spoke the word on a sharp intake of breath. 'What could I do? Our parents and our sister died in Auschwitz – even before Hermann was taken there. I was never married. When we found each other we were the only family we had left, except for one uncle who was in the United States. We already knew that Gerda was dead. And you.' Annaliese ran her eyes over him again, as if to confirm to herself that he was real, and gave a faint smile. 'All we could think of was to leave. The very soil of Germany was stained with the blood of our people. We applied to come here, before the State was declared. Finally we arrived in 1947.'

In the pause when she finished speaking, both of them became aware of a new silence in the apartment. The radio had been switched off. In the hallway, a door opened. Annaliese gave David a meaningful look.

'Your father does not speak of these things now. Nothing, ever. Just be calm, David. Let me talk to him.'

'Anna? Annaliese?'

A shuffling, bedroom-slippered tread was heard on the landing.

Annaliese stood up. 'I'm here, Hermann,' she said soothingly. 'In the kitchen. I have someone here I want you to meet.'

David got to his feet as well. His hands broke out in a nervous sweat and his heart was thumping like a drum. *Don't expect anything of him*, he kept saying to himself. *Just be calm.*

The door squeaked open and Hermann Mayer shuffled into the room. David saw a thin man with wispy white hair standing on end like an aura round his head, face furrowed with lines and wide blue eyes, slightly rheumy, wearing a bewildered expression. He had a shirt on, buttons unfastened at the top to reveal a pale, almost hairless chest, the bones protruding, and no trousers, only a pair of long, sagging underpants. Pushed into the slippers were scrawny legs, the ankles discoloured and swollen. David boiled inside with pity. All he could think in that moment was not, this is my father, but, this man looks seventy-five – and he's forty-eight years old.

'Annaliese—' Hermann said querulously. 'I don't know where is my newspaper.'

'I'm sorry, Hermann.' She spoke gently. 'I have not been out yet. I will get your newspaper. But first . . .' She went to her brother and took his arm between both her hands, caressing him, speaking in a low voice. David only managed to make out some of the words. 'I have a surprise for you. A happy surprise . . . You must prepare yourself . . .' After further gentle murmuring, from which David, trembling now, caught the words *Gerda . . . Rudi* he saw Hermann Mayer's eyes drift towards him as if it was the first time he had noticed there was anyone else in the room.

'Hermann—' Annaliese led him forward. Smiling tenderly she told him, 'This is your son, darling. This is little Rudi, Gerda's boy. *Your* boy. He has been safe all this time, and he has come from England to find us.'

David saw the tremor in his own hands mirrored in those of the man before him. Hermann stood looking at him, helplessly. His face remained expressionless for a time, then for a second it contorted and David thought he was going to weep. But the spasm passed. Eventually, he held out his hand, and very formally, as if David was perhaps a new business associate, he said:

'I am very pleased to meet you.'

Forty-Five

Dear Mum and Frances,

. . . Every day seems to get hotter here! Today is already 31°C and they say it will get even worse by August! I wonder what it's like at home . . .

. . . I've got a new job though and am 'lucky' to be working inside. I'm not sure which is worse in this weather, inside or out. But the digging of the swimming pool is coming along gradually. I don't know that I'll be here to see it in action though! I've moved on from working in the hen house (believe me, you can have too much of the company of chickens) and am now being trained up in machine maintenance, which as you can imagine is close to my heart and I'm told I have a 'flair' for it! Some of the farm machinery here is very old and a real challenge to keep going . . .

. . . Last week I was able to go to Haifa overnight again. My father seemed even more unwell than before, though Annaliese says he is often like this. I asked her whether my visits upset him. I was frightened that it might damage him – more than he is damaged already. She says there has been some change but she believes it to be temporary, and there has not

426

been any repetition of the upset on my first visit, when his emotion was so overpowering it was hard even to watch it. I think he is getting more used to me coming now. He is very dependent on my aunt for his day-to-day welfare and sometimes it seems he is more like her child than her brother. This time there was an outburst – not obviously connected with me but over something he had mislaid, which is the sort of thing which makes him very agitated. It was a terribly sad sight, seeing a man in such a state over a lost pair of spectacles. He does not talk about the camps at all, or what happened to him. The little information I told you was all from Annaliese. From what she says, he has never been able to have a normal life since he came here. He worked for a time as a postman, early on, but even that used to fill him with so much anxiety that he would come home early, weeping. Eventually he broke down in the street and couldn't move. He was taken home by the police and he did not work again after that. He has talked to me sometimes about my mother and their life together in Berlin, and when he talks about her he weeps, very suddenly, tears gushing from his eyes, and is very affectionate to me. Later he can be more distant. It feels as if his mind is divided into completely separate compartments which barely touch each other.

Evidently their family lived in an apartment in Charlottenburg. As he describes it – and Annaliese too – they must be rather grand houses not too far from the Fasenenstrasse Synagogue. They had big stairwells, the stairs winding up and up, and the inside was quite ornate with heavy furniture. (They don't live like that now. The apartment in Haifa is very simple.) They also had a house *meister* and a maid and cook. Now they just have Elena, a Christian woman who comes to clean the apartment! Apparently when Gerda and my father were courting they used to meet after work on a street called Kurfürstendamm for coffee and cakes. The Germans seem to like their coffee and cakes!

Since my last visit, Hermann has been talking a lot about someone he met in one of the camps. It's obviously preying on his mind. He does not mention what his connection is with this man except it is obvious he must have been in the British Army which went into Bergen-Belsen. He remembers the man's address from the time as if he is reading it from a piece of paper, and says he meant to write to him after he arrived in Israel, but never did. I asked him why he does not write now but he avoided the question. Often when I ask him anything direct his gaze drifts away towards the window as if he has not heard what I said. I have to be very careful – he is so fragile. But he has spoken of this man several times now. I know it is a very big thing to ask you, Mum, but I wondered if you would perhaps write to this address for me and see if he is still there? His name is Anatoli Gruschov. I know that is a Russian name, but he was definitely in the British Army. Perhaps we could even meet him one day?

Anyway, things are going well here otherwise. Gila says I am beginning to look like a Sabra so I must be doing something right!

With very much love to you both. I will write again soon!

David xxx

Frances watched over the top of her spectacles as Edie folded up the letter. Edie looked across and smiled. She had read it through several times.

'His friend Gila seems to be getting a lot of mention,' Frances remarked. 'I wonder if our David is having his heart stolen away by this fierce Sabra!'

'Well,' Edie said non-committally. 'He's only going to be there for another two months.'

'What an interesting letter.'

'Yes—' Edie was barely listening. After a moment she took the letter and went out into the garden. It was evening and there were birds singing. She took a deep breath of blossom-filled air. Reading David's letters from Israel had been tough at first, especially when he found his father and aunt. But abiding by her decision that she had to let him go where he needed to go, she wrote to him and said that she would like him to share his experiences with them, not feel he had to hide away his discovery of his family for fear of hurting her feelings. Tears in her eyes, she wrote, struggling for every ounce of generosity she could muster:

> There is more than one way of being a mother or a father. I have always known you were not my flesh and blood and I understand that you need to find out where you came from – I'm sorry if I have made it difficult for you. I was so frightened of losing you. But whatever happens, you're my boy and I will always love you. The kind of mothering I have given you is the sort made of all the time we have spent together, all the memories we have collected and the love we've shared. I know that you value this and you always will.

She was quite surprised at herself writing all this down. They were a household which didn't normally go in for outpourings of emotion. Still, she thought, sealing the envelope, you can spend your whole life not saying things, and then it's too late.

Standing in the garden, she thought about David's request that she write to the Russian man. For some reason she felt resistant towards doing it, but she knew this stemmed from the old jealousy of all these people David was associating with now. And increasingly she trusted David's judgement. He hadn't just danced to every tune the Leishmanns played, had he? They had wanted him to go to an Orthodox kibbutz in the Negev desert, but David had said that felt 'too much' and had chosen a secular kibbutz for himself. And all she had to do was find out if the Russian man still lived there – that wasn't much to ask, was it?

The same evening she dropped a little note of enquiry into the post to the London address at the bottom of David's letter. She only put in the barest explanation of the connection with Hermann Mayer in Israel. After all, this Mr Gruschov had most likely moved on years ago anyway.

Forty-Six

Edie had a reply from Mr Anatoli Gruschov almost by return of post, written on pale blue paper in a beautiful copperplate hand. The letter confirmed that he was still residing at his address in Wimbledon and that he did remember a Hermann Mayer from his brief time in Bergen-Belsen. The letter was very courteous, but concise to the point of curtness.

'Well,' Edie held it out to Frances. 'That's short and sweet. I'll send it on to Davey.'

Frances read the note. 'I'm surprised he even remembers Hermann Mayer – or any names. Think what it was like – thousands upon thousands all in a desperate state.'

Edie decided that now they were sure of the address, if either David or his father wanted to pursue it further it would be up to them. But before she had even got round to sending Gruschov's note to them, the next day another letter arrived.

Dear Mrs Weale,

    I hope you will forgive me for troubling you again. When I received your letter I was rather surprised and replied instantly and in too much haste. You do not explain the exact reason for your inquiry, but I am assuming you have some personal connection with Hermann Mayer. When I encountered him in the Bergen-Belsen camp he was in a most pitiful condition. Now I have had time to reflect on this painful period I wonder what news there is of him and feel it callous of me not to have enquired when I wrote to you yesterday.

I wonder if you would do me the great honour of calling on me? I am now working again so it would only be feasible for me on a Saturday or Sunday. It would be a great delight to welcome you to my house and to spend some time in your no doubt charming company.

Let me know a date at your convenience.

Yours sincerely,

Anatoli Gruschov.

'What a blooming cheek!' Edie exclaimed on reading it. 'Didn't he notice my address? Does he seriously expect me to go trekking all the way down to London to see him? He sounds a bit of a case!'

'Actually,' Frances contradicted her. 'I think he sounds rather nice. Gentlemanly. And rather melancholy. Perhaps he's lonely.'

Edie was just about to retort that if someone was lonely then maybe they needed to ask themselves why, when she remembered that lately she had felt increasingly lonely herself. That didn't make her barmy or dangerous to know, did it?

'He might think it rude to invite himself to visit us.' Frances looked thoughtfully at Edie. She had long been concerned about her, always cooped up here. She was a young woman still – she ought to get out and about!

'May I make a suggestion? How about buying yourself a ticket for a very early train on Saturday – or the one after? You could spend the morning looking round a gallery – there are all those marvellous paintings down there that you've never had the chance to see. Think of that as your main reason for going – and you could go and see Mr Gruschov afterwards and get a train back in the evening. How about that? And David will be delighted, since he asked you specially to find out.'

Edie looked up, astonished, shaking her coppery locks back from her face.

'You seriously think I should go?'

Frances smiled. 'Go on – for goodness sake, treat yourself to a day out.'

It suddenly became ridiculously important what she was to wear that Saturday. Persuaded by Frances, Edie dropped a line to say she would come a week on Saturday if that was convenient, and Anatoli Gruschov wrote a very courteous reply by return of post to say that he would be honoured to welcome her. Beforehand, Edie planned to visit the National Gallery, a thought which made her tingle with excitement. What a very grand thing to do!

'It's not as if I've got a wardrobe full of things to choose from, is it!' she said to Frances. 'I just feel everything's a bit drab.' She stood in front of her cupboard, looking at her three summer dresses. They all looked even more faded and unexciting than she remembered. She'd had two of them for years. 'And it might be cold when I set off.'

'Well,' Frances said. 'Go and treat yourself to a frock as well. You can always wear stockings to start off with. After all – what are you saving your money for? You can't take it with you!'

So the first Saturday she went into town and had a wonderful time trying on dresses and wondering why she

433

didn't indulge herself more often. She had still not broken the scrimping, make-do-and-mend wartime attitudes, even though they were no longer strictly necessary, as well as the simple Quaker tastes by which she was surrounded. But that afternoon she rediscovered the pleasure of buying something new and feminine. She found a pretty dress, cream with large sage green leaves all over it, and a full, flowing skirt. That shade of green looked lovely on her, setting off her eyes and hair, and the sleeves ended just above her elbows: long enough to hide her scar. At the waist there was a white belt, and to go with it she bought a pair of little white shoes with bows on the front, some sheer stockings and a white cardigan with three-quarter length sleeves. Togged up in front of the mirror at home in her whole new outfit she already felt better. She brushed her hair out and pinned it up, leaving the shorter strands at the front round her heart-shaped face, and smiled at herself.

'I s'pose you're not so bad,' she told her reflection, with a wink. She was so excited at the thought of the art gallery! She had been concentrating so hard and for so long on being David's mother, she had almost forgotten there were any other aspects of life.

The following Saturday in fact turned out very warm, and it was mild when Edie set off at seven into the quiet morning street, dew on the grass and the heads of roses in the front garden. She enjoyed the novelty of all of it – the journey down to London and learning how to use the Underground, the pleasure of stepping out into the sunshine in Trafalgar Square with its lions, the pigeons fluttering across it. But she eyed the grand frontage of the

National Gallery with some trepidation. Was she really allowed just to go in there and walk round for as long as she liked? But, once inside, she was completely absorbed for the rest of the morning, wandering the long, stately galleries, feasting on the sight of picture after picture. When she came out again it was as if she had woken up from a dream, and her heart thudded at the thought that now she had to go and see the stranger in Wimbledon. Why on earth had she said she'd go? She found a Lyons Corner House and sat down for lunch, suddenly exhausted. Until she'd had a rest and a bite to eat she couldn't go a step further!

Anatoli Gruschov's house was one of a line of suburban brick villas in a featureless Wimbledon street. By the time Edie arrived it was three o'clock, she felt tired and sticky and the soles of her feet were burning in the heat.

She stood in the porch with her cardigan over her arm. There was nothing at all distinctive about the place except that it had a rather run-down look. The windows were not very clean, the paintwork desperately needed attention, and blown into a corner of the porch was a gathering of leaves and litter, the scruffiness of which increased her sense of misgiving. What on earth was she doing here?

No point in giving myself time to get any more nervous, she thought, and rattled the dull knocker, which had obviously not been polished for years. She jumped violently a moment later as the latch rattled. From the dark hall emerged a man of middling height, with a magnificent head of wavy hair of a pewter grey and liquid brown eyes which twinkled at her out of a wide, amiable face.

'Ah!' he exclaimed, holding out his hand. When Edie took it it felt warm and strong. 'You must be Mrs Weale. Come in – you are very welcome.'

'Thank you.' Edie stepped inside and he closed the door. She had expected him to sound different, more Russian, but though there was the slightest foreign turn to his voice, he spoke beautiful English.

'Come through to the back, my dear – it's more comfortable, even if not tidier, I'm afraid.' He led her along the hall.

The house may not have been distinctive from the outside, but Anatoli Gruschov's living-room had a very definite character of its own. At the back were glass doors, flung open on to a chaotic-looking patch of garden, through which the sun was streaming in, accompanied by a languid breeze. Inside, the room was the most cluttered Edie had ever seen. It's like a nest! she thought, almost laughing in astonishment.

Across the middle was a large sofa covered in a worn gold brocade, and several tapestry cushions. But there was no space to sit down because piled all over it were heaps of paper, chiefly sheet music. A table, the rosewood desk positioned in one corner, the other two chairs and the grand piano were likewise encumbered and papers spilled on to the floor, the lino and colourful old rugs. All along the side walls were shelves reaching up to the ceiling, sagging with books, many with faded brown and blue leather spines, as well as some newer editions and piles of old newspapers. Leaning against the books was a hotch-potch of photographs, letters and cards, icons with burnished gold backgrounds and flat-faced saints, a pair of brass candlesticks and, inserted in a couple of places, pot plants which trailed strands of ivy down as far as the floor. There were pictures on the remaining walls in old gold frames and on the piano, along with the music, lay two violins with their bows alongside them, lumps of rosin, and several china cups minus their saucers. The violin cases were on the floor, along with an assortment of all kinds of other things: umbrella, straw hat, dog lead and several empty jam jars. The room did not smell of neglect, but rather gave off a whiff of old paper and camphor. The whole effect was of a jumbly, busy, rather attractive cosiness and Edie found herself smiling.

'Now—' Anatoli was saying, busily clearing the settee of heaps of music scores. 'I have been tidying up, but as you see there is still some way to go...' She watched him with amusement. He was a compact, quite powerful-looking man, dressed in soft-looking grey flannel trousers and a baggy jumper, knitted in a black and brown blend of wool, which looked excessive for the weather. 'There!' he exclaimed in triumph as the seat of the settee made what was clearly an unusual appearance. 'You can sit – and I will make tea,' he said with enthusiasm. 'Would you like tea? The kettle should be boiled by now. I have cakes!'

'That'd be very nice.' Edie perched on the settee and smiled up at him. 'Thank you.'

He disappeared for a few moments and Edie sat looking round and wondering what on earth the kitchen must look like. She was just thinking that Mr Gruschov must be a bachelor when she caught sight of a number of photographs on the side table. Quickly she got up to look. In an ornate silver frame was a wedding photograph, very clearly of Anatoli, standing up straight and proud, his hair then black and swept back from his strong, handsome face. On his arm, veil lifted back from her face, was a woman of a beauty fit to match his, with a distinctive, dark-eyed face. Both of them looked solemn for this momentous occasion.

'That's my wife, Margot – our wedding day.'

Edie jumped back, embarrassed.

'I'm sorry – I'm ever so nosy.'

'Of course. That's quite natural. You know nothing about me.' He seemed genuinely unbothered by her curiosity, and laid the tea tray on top of the papers on the low coffee table.

'Is she Russian as well?' Edie asked.

'Margot? No. She was English. She is not with me any more, I'm afraid to say – she died two years ago.'

'I'm so sorry,' Edie said. 'That's very sad.'

'Yes,' he agreed, sounding almost surprised to hear this fact identified. 'It is. But she was suffering. I am happy that she does not suffer any more. It's terrible to watch. I have two children: my son is in Canada, and my daughter married last year and lives in Brighton.' He leaned forwards and rubbed his hands. 'Now – I hope you like chocolate éclairs.'

On the tray, alongside a large brown teapot which must have held enough tea for ten, was a tiny plate of Rich Tea biscuits and another large serving dish, in the middle of which he had ceremoniously laid two enormous chocolate éclairs oozing with cream.

'Ooh yes,' Edie said, beginning to feel she had joined in a kind of Mad Hatter's tea party and quite prepared to enjoy it.

He poured cups of strong tea, handed Edie a plate with an éclair on and a fork and leaned back to his savour his own. They were seated at each end of the sofa.

'It is important to have treats – as often as possible, don't you think?'

Edie smiled. She could hear Frances in her head saying that if you had treats too often they weren't treats any more. 'Yes – I think that's a lovely idea,' she said, watching his intense enjoyment as he forked up a mouthful of choux pastry and contentedly chewed and swallowed.

'So, do you like to be called Edith Weale? Or Mrs Weale?'

'You can call me Edie. And I am Mrs Weale, but my husband died nearly twenty years ago.'

Anatoli's fork wavered above the éclair. 'No! You cannot have been old enough to have married twenty years ago!'

'That's nice of you – but I was nineteen. He died in an accident only a few months after we were married.'

'Good heavens. Well – that is sad too,' he pointed out.

'Yes, it was. But it's a long time ago now.'

'You never remarried?'

Edie looked down at her plate. 'No.'

'I'm sorry. Now I'm the nosy one.'

They both ate in silence for a few moments, then he said, 'And you have a son?'

Edie nodded, finishing her last mouthful. 'That's why I wrote to you. He is in Israel at the moment.'

Anatoli gave her an appraising look, putting down his empty plate. 'I would not have guessed that you are Jewish.'

Blushing, Edie looked down into her lap. If only she didn't have to explain her tie with David – if she could just say, I'm his mother and that could be that.

'I'm not.' She put her plate down and turned to Anatoli. 'David was not my husband's son.' Briefly, she explained how David had come into her life. 'He is Jewish, though I am not. Hermann Mayer was his real father. When David's mother escaped to England, Hermann stayed in Germany. It is only quite recently that we found out who David's real family are.'

Anatoli listened with deep attention. He leaned forward, resting his elbows on his knees.

'How extraordinary. How, well, *fitting* that we should meet. I have to confess that when I got your letter, I wanted just to throw it away. My reply the first time was abrupt and too hasty. I apologize for it.'

'It doesn't matter.'

'Well, in a way it does. That time, in that place, it is something you try to forget. The truth is, I was only there for a few days. They tried not to let many of the forces stay in Belsen for too long. It drove people mad. It was beyond any inhumanity that you can imagine. And the risk of disease was acute. But even a few days there . . .' He shook his head and was silent for a moment. 'Hermann Mayer was only one of so very many in the extremity of suffering. Typhus was killing the camp inmates like flies, on top of all the suffering they had already endured. The place was . . . Well, the smell—' His face twisted. 'I can still taste it in my nostrils when I think of it . . .'

He lapsed into silence, so Edie said, 'He lives with his sister, Annaliese, in Haifa. From what David has written to me, he has never been able to lead a normal life since.'

'I'm not surprised,' Anatoli said. 'Many survivors have managed to make a life, I know, and they are to be much admired. But others . . . Well, who knows? People disintegrate for far less reason. God knows, relief workers broke under the strain . . .'

He stopped again for a moment, then spoke more briskly. 'Look – really the details are too much to tell you . . . But the thing about Hermann was – well, of course he saw us and we were the British Army. And he wanted to tell me that his wife had died in England. I didn't really understand what he meant and of course I was busy – the work was overwhelming. We were burying thousands every day. He had typhus and I took him to the hospital. There was no bed for him but when I put him down in a space on the floor, he grasped the collar of my coat. I could easily have pulled away – he was weak as a straw. He could barely speak, but his eyes were begging me . . .' Anatoli paused for a moment, then went on. 'I saw that he wanted me to embrace him. I stayed kneeling and I did my best to wrap my arms round him again. The man was a bag of bones. He said he would never forget me, and that was when he made me tell him my address. He made me say it three or four times . . .' Anatoli stopped speaking for a moment and Edie was moved to see that his eyes were full of tears.

'He must've remembered your address all this time.'

'Yes—' He took out his handkerchief and wiped his eyes. 'And yet I never heard from him. I thought he had probably died.'

The two of them talked and talked for the rest of the afternoon. It grew dusk. Anatoli made more tea and Edie told him about bringing up David, and about Frances and Janet and working at Cadbury's. He told her that he had been born in St Petersburg in 1906 but his parents had emigrated to England a few years later, so he had only the very dimmest memories of the place.

'My father made musical instruments,' he told her. 'One of those violins there, on the piano, was made by his hands.' He got up and laid the instrument in her lap and Edie admired its lovely curving shape, the rich sheen of the wood.

'It's beautiful,' she said. 'So are you a musician?'

'No.' He put the violin back on the piano. 'I am a

pharmacist! But of course I play. Margot was a fine pianist and we used to spend many hours playing together. I was brought up to live and breathe music, the violin especially of course. It's just part of life – I have never made my living by it.'

'Will you play something for me?' She was surprised how relaxed she was with him, that she felt she could ask anything.

'Oh – well, let's see.'

He shuffled through some scores, stood one on the piano stand and picked up his instrument. A second later, music was pouring out round the room. He did not seem to need the music after all and closed his eyes and Edie, knowing she was unobserved, gave all her attention to the music with its high, minor-key melancholy. The violin seemed to touch the notes of all the lingering sadness in the world. By the time he had finished there were tears running down her cheeks.

'Yes—' He appeared undisturbed by her emotion. 'It does that. That is why I can only play occasionally – not all the time.'

She wiped her eyes and smiled at him through wet lashes. Anatoli laughed suddenly, giving a bow. 'Thank you. I have not had an audience for some time!'

Edie noticed suddenly how late it was. 'My goodness, what time is it? I must go or I'll never get home tonight!'

Anatoli told her it was six o'clock.

'I will take you to your railway station,' he said.

'Oh, you don't need to do that – it's all the way to Euston.'

'That's all right. What else should I do this evening?'

Edie gathered up her bag, unexpectedly delighted by this offer, finding herself reluctant to leave this cosy room, his conversation.

442

'Well – that's ever so kind of you . . .'

He smiled, with his mischievous twinkle. 'Madam – it would be a pleasure. In fact this entire afternoon has been a pleasure.'

Forty-Seven

The week after Edie met Anatoli Gruschov, their letters crossed in the post. Edie wrote a polite note to Anatoli thanking him for the afternoon they had spent together. She had been glad of his company back to Euston, and he had been very gentlemanly, taking her arm as they stepped in and out of the trains on the Underground.

'You must be careful of yourself,' he said.

When they parted he kissed her on each cheek and stood watching as she walked towards the train. She waved and saw his arm, clad in the woolly jumper, raised in reply. With a pang she got on the train. She had never had a day quite like it. But she did not let this feeling show in the letter. She told herself that Anatoli would show the same warmth and interest to anyone who crossed his path.

But his note arrived the day after she posted hers, thanking her also for taking the trouble to make the visit. She felt her heart beat faster as she read the rest.

'I have not spent an afternoon that has given me so much pleasure in a long time and on my return to my house, which felt sadly empty in your absence, I thought it a great shame that we have no other reason or excuse to meet. Even at my age I'm looking to justify myself with excuses! But perhaps you would not find it too forward of me if I were to suggest that I might visit you in Birmingham one day?'

'What does he say?' Frances asked. She had already had the full story from Edie.

'Oh – just thanks for the visit.' She folded the letter and put it away. Should she reply? If she did, what was she getting herself into? But then, she reasoned, he might not ever come. He was just being polite. She wrote back, briefly, saying that if he was ever up in Birmingham she would be very happy to see him again and left it at that.

She didn't spend time dwelling on this, though, because two other letters arrived which both took over all her and Frances's thoughts. The first, at the beginning of August, was from Janet and its tone was breathless:

You must've wondered what had happened to us, as I've not written properly for so long. Don't worry – we are all right, but I have hardly had time to eat or sleep this last fortnight, let alone write a proper letter. An extraordinary thing has happened – Martin and I are for the present the proud parents of twin girls! We were woken, early one morning, before sunrise, by their mewling. We went down in the dark, hearing their little cries – we thought they were kittens to begin with! – and there they were, tiny mites who had been wrapped up together in old strips of cloth and left at our door. They were newborn and the umbilical cords had just been cut and knotted. No one knows where they came from. We are fairly sure they are not from Ibabongo – all pregnancies and babies are accounted for! Martin thinks it most likely that they were left by a mother from one of the other villages around, most likely a leper woman who is not part of the colony here, who saw this as the best hope for them. Whoever she is, poor soul, we feel so

445

much for her. What a desperate act, but meant for the best, I'm sure.

For now, we are going to look after them. It's exhausting and very demanding but I have to tell you I am absolutely loving it! The girls are so beautiful. We have called them Ruth and Naomi. Ruth is the bigger of the two and is thriving, and Naomi is tiny and a little more delicate, but she should be all right with the care we are giving her. I feel very soppy at the sight of them cuddled up asleep together like little puppies. All I can think of is that they are a special gift to us from God. (Chrissie, of course, is utterly convinced of this!) I never expected to become a mother like this, and if they are to stay with us there may be all sort of problems and challenges ahead of us . . . But all I can do for now is love them. The future will have to look after itself!

Edie and Frances spent many an hour discussing this new development. They both knew how much Janet had craved children and they were glad to hear she was so happy.

'The only thing that really bothers me,' Frances said, as they sat out at the back of the house one warm evening, 'is other people's reactions and prejudices. You know what people can be like. If they wanted to bring them home, I can well imagine people saying all sorts of awful things about Janet and how they come to have coloured children.'

'Hmm.' Edie looked round at her. In the half light she saw how fragile Frances looked. It was another painful reminder of her growing old.

'Well, I suppose if they won't believe the truth when

446

they hear it, more fool them. You've never been one to take any notice of people gossiping.'

'No, I know.' She sighed. 'We'll cross that bridge when we come to it. It would have been so much more straightforward if they could have had their own.'

Edie was touched. She had never heard Frances openly expressing this regret before.

Then the letter from David arrived. Edie read it on the way in to work. It was quite short – he promised he would write again soon to fill them in on all the news – but he had something to say which could not wait.

> I have made a big and very difficult decision this week, but now it is done I feel at peace. I know this will hurt you and I wish I was with you to explain. I have decided that I am not going to come home and go to Imperial at the end of this month as planned. Instead, I am going to apply for a similar course at the universities in either Jerusalem or Tel Aviv. I am investigating the possibilities now and even if it is too late for this year, I have good qualifications and should be able to take up a place next time round. Studying engineering is something I have always wanted to do and here I can also see how much value it has in the life of the Kibbutz and in contributing to the building up of the state of Israel.
>
> I would much rather have told you this face to face. I know it will come as a shock. Two other things have influenced my decision to stay. One is that I feel truly at home here. The other is that I have found someone with whom I am very deeply in love

447

and in due course I hope that she will agree to be my wife. Her name is Gila Weissman and I know that when you meet her you will love her too.

After more expressions of love and concern for her feelings, he signed off.

Edie stopped at the corner of Bournville Lane, quite oblivious to anyone around her, and read the letter through twice more, trying to take in what he was saying. That he wanted to live in Israel. That he was never coming back ... The thing she'd feared most. And that he was thinking of marriage ... Marriage, already! Edie stood trying to breathe properly as she slipped the letter into her bag. She felt an anger, and a hurt too deep for tears to surface yet. Oh, she had thought she was letting go of David, allowing his life take its course, but she had not been prepared for this. For all that he had found his father and was so involved with all these people in Israel, what she had held on to was the thought that come September he would return to her, to take up his university place in London. But now he was making a break far more radical and final than she had ever dreamed of. Settling down in Israel! How had all this happened so quickly? In those moments of panic she felt certain she would never see him again.

She said nothing to anyone, but it was a desperate day at work. As the hours passed on the line, checking and assembling the little trays of chocolates, she passed through her darkest emotions yet of hurt and rejection, and of fear for her own future: that she would spend all her life now abandoned and alone. In the evening she broke the news to Frances, trying to be as calm and matter-of-fact as she could so as not to distress her. She was even more protective of Frances these days. Frances was of course also upset but tried to be comforting and positive. But to Edie it felt as if the whole of her world was crumbling and she needed to be alone. She went up to bed early that night and finally allowed the tears to come, sobbing out her pain and anguish for her boy, who always seemed to have to move further away from her, over the horizon until she could no longer see him. She knew he was a good boy, that he did not want to hurt her, but this didn't help to take away the agony of it.

When she was calmer, she lay looking up into the darkness, wondering if she would ever get to sleep. She longed for someone to talk to apart from Frances. Someone who she could open up to completely. If only Janet were here, instead of the other side of the world!

A thought struck her. A longing. She got up again and put the light on, searching in her drawer for a pad of notepaper.

Why not? she decided. I have to do things for myself now. That's how it has to be. She wrote her address at the top of the paper, then began, 'Dear Mr Gruschov . . .'

Forty-Eight

Edie stood at New Street Station as a cool breeze blew along the platform. The summer's definitely over, she thought, buttoning up her mac. She kept nervously smoothing her clothes and touching her hair, which was loose today, falling in soft waves round her face. Every few seconds she looked at the clock. The platform was very quiet, although the train was due in two minutes.

Why on earth did I say he could come? she groaned inwardly. Writing that letter when she was feeling low – what had possessed her! Pouring out her feelings about David to a man fourteen years older than her whom she'd only met once! What must he have thought of her writing him such an emotional letter? And now she'd said yes to him coming to see her dull little life. How on earth were they going to pass the time?

The seconds ticked past. A train pulled in on a neighbouring platform. Edie was so nervous she couldn't bear standing still and started pacing up and down ... Two minutes late ... Four minutes late ... What if it didn't arrive? Perhaps there'd been a mistake and she could just go home and continue her quiet Saturday. She was startled by the sense of desolation that washed through her at this thought. Oh, she did want him to come! There were so many reasons why: his dark eyes, full of amiability, his comfortable, somehow comforting mode of dress, his sympathy, the way they had talked for hours, all rushed into her mind. At last she heard the train coming in the distance and her heart began to thump even harder.

She saw him, some distance along the platform, before he noticed her, and took in that he was slightly more smartly dressed than the last time they had met. He was wearing dark trousers and a jacket, and seemed both taller than she remembered, and yet somehow more vulnerable in this big echoing space. As he turned and caught sight of her she saw he was also carrying a bouquet of flowers. For her? When had anyone ever bought flowers for her before?

A delighted expression spread across his face as he came towards her.

'My dear! How very lovely to see you!'

'Hello, Mr Gruschov,' she said, shyly.

'Oh please – call me Anatoli for goodness sake. We are not strangers, after all, are we?'

Edie blushed. 'So you've arrived safely. How was the journey?'

'Oh, perfectly good, thank you.' Oblivious of the other people surging past from the train, rather bashfully he handed her the flowers, pink and white carnations. 'I thought you might like these. But I see I've judged badly. They don't match your hair!'

'Oh, but they're lovely!' Edie protested, smiling down into the little bouquet. 'It's ever so kind of you. They're beautiful – and . . .' She looked up at him, suddenly finding a lump in her throat. It was impossible to continue small talk with him for more than even a minute. 'I'm glad you could come.'

He saw that she needed a moment to collect herself, and he glanced away as if looking for the way out.

'I'm afraid we shall need to catch another train,' she

said. 'I wouldn't recommend staying in town at the moment – it's like a building site.'

'Ah—' he said regretfully. 'Of course – so many parts of London are the same.'

'I don't know what we're going to do all day,' she confided. 'I'm afraid it's not very exciting where we live.'

'Oh,' Anatoli laughed. 'I think the day will be much happier without too much excitement.'

On the short train ride to Bournville he was full of genuine interest, commenting on the bomb damage and rebuilding, the glimpse they caught of the university, of the canal in its long straight cut through Selly Oak.

'Aha,' he said as Bournville came into view, the huge works with CADBURY large and clear along the side. 'So there is your place of work. I should like to see, very much.'

'Would you?' Edie found herself quite chuffed by this. 'Well, I s'pose we could go for a walk round.'

'Oh yes – it's a nice day for walking. You must show me everything.'

Frances came to the door to greet them, leaning on her stick, dressed in a russet coloured velvet skirt and blue sweater. Edie, perceiving her as if through Anatoli's eyes, for the first time, saw how much she was still a woman of natural grace and charm. Her face lit up at the sight of them and to Edie's relief she saw an instant rapport between the two of them.

'I am delighted to meet you,' Anatoli actually kissed Frances's hand, a gesture which in most men Edie would have found rather suspect, but somehow it was part of Anatoli's old-world quaintness.

'You're most welcome,' Frances smiled. 'Come in and make yourselves comfortable. Shall we have lunch straight away? Then you'll have plenty of time to go out if you want to.'

Edie had laid the table in the back room. As they went to take their places Anatoli admired one of her pictures which they'd had framed and hung opposite the window. He noticed her initials painted in one corner.

'This is yours?' He turned, seeming surprised.

'Yes – it's the lily pond in the girls' grounds at the factory. I've spent a lot of time there over the years!' She had been pleased with how it had turned out, felt she had captured the light on the water and the clusters of pink-tinged flowers, and it was also one of Frances's favourites.

'It's a real beauty,' Anatoli said. 'You have a gift! You should not speak about your painting as if you just do a little scribbling with a brush!'

Edie blushed with pleasure.

Since they had a visitor Edie and Frances had decided to have a Saturday roast instead of a Sunday one. Edie had prepared all the vegetables to go with their leg of lamb and mint sauce. Anatoli was full of praise for the meal, in particular for Frances's gravy.

'You know – my wife used to make gravy almost as good as this,' he said contentedly. 'So far as I can see it is something only an Englishwoman can do. I've tried to do it myself – I did the cooking when she was too ill to manage for herself. Margot gave me instructions, but I never could get it right. Too thick, too thin, too lumpy, like the Three Bears' porridge . . .' He shrugged, despairingly. 'God did not intend Russian men to make gravy.'

Laughing at Anatoli's exaggerated woe, Frances asked, 'How long have you been in this country?'

'Oh – since the age of six. My father decided to move my mother and myself and my elder brother to England in 1912. Things were very restless in Russia at that time, as you know, and my father felt he would have a better chance elsewhere, in England or America.'

'So why not America?' Frances asked.

Anatoli thought about it. 'You know – I never asked him that! Perhaps because England was nearer, though they did not speak a word of English. We still spoke Russian at home, even though of course I learned English as a schoolboy.'

Frances passed him the potatoes. 'Do have some more.'

Anatoli beamed. 'You know, this is the best meal I have had in, well, years!'

Edie watched with delight, seeing how the two of them got on. Frances's reaction to anyone was an important indicator – she was such a good judge of character, and she had obviously taken to Anatoli straight away. Edie found herself relaxing more and more and just enjoying the day.

'My husband was very interested in Russia and all that was going on there,' Frances was saying. 'I think he had a spark of the revolutionary in him.'

'Ah—' Anatoli shook his head. 'My father was the opposite. A deeply conservative man, even though he could see the suffering and the injustices of the poor in Russia. And now – the price that has been paid for that revolution under Stalin . . . Ideology more important than the people, than reality – and look what happens. No, I am grateful to have been brought up as an Englishman – even if I have not quite mastered the language properly.'

'Your English is perfect!' Edie said. She liked the Russian edges of his English – it was completely part of his whole personality.

After a delicious lemon meringue pie and a cup of tea,

Frances began to flag, and said she wanted to have her afternoon snooze.

'I can't seem to get through the day without sleeping any more,' she said rather wistfully.

'Well, Edith said she would show me round a little,' Anatoli said. 'Shall we go?'

Strolling down Linden Road in the weak autumn sunshine, he said, 'She is a very impressive lady, your Frances.'

'She's been like a mom to me,' Edie said. 'More than a mom in some ways – a lot more than my own ever was.'

'You speak harshly of your mother. What was she like?'

'Not very kind.' She didn't want to go into it, not today, but she explained how she had come to live with Frances. 'My father's still alive – I see him from time to time. But I s'pose I've had a funny life really,' she said as they turned on to Bournville Green. 'I haven't had much luck with blood relations. I've had to adopt a mother as well as a son!' They stopped by the circular Rest House. A few brown leaves drifted down through the air.

'You must have good instincts for what is good for you,' he said. 'Or you would not have found these things.'

'Maybe – I've definitely been lucky.' Or I was, she thought, for a spell, before Davey decided to go off and leave me for ever. They stood looking round for a moment and he commented on how pretty the place was, how clean and orderly.

'It is truly a garden factory. I have never seen this sort of thing before.'

'That's the Continuation School,' Edie pointed. 'We all used to go there one day a week. The baths are over the other side. Come on, I'll show you some more of it.'

She took him round the edge of the works, pointing out the various blocks she had worked in, the dining block and the recreation areas.

'That little picture I did – it was done just over in there,' she pointed towards the girls' grounds.

Memories flooded back as they walked round, and she found herself chatting on, about Ruby and Janet and the war and all that had happened, and Anatoli encouraged her. They walked and walked on into Selly Oak and found a little tea-room. Amid the steamy air Anatoli described how he and Margot had met and married before the war. She was a schoolteacher, and they had been introduced in a church, after a recital of the St Matthew Passion.

'She loved music,' he said, with a half smile. 'She would go to listen anywhere – she heard Dame Myra Hess play during the war. And of course she was a good pianist herself.'

Edie listened to him, struck by the admiration he had had for his wife. Yet as she heard him talk she felt a pang of some emotion, a sense of deflation, sadness almost. No one could ever replace Margot in Anatoli's eyes! She told herself not to be so silly. He was a friend. Nothing more – and that was what she needed most now, wasn't it? A good friend.

'So—' He leaned forward, his worn black sleeves resting on the table. 'Shall I ask for more water to top up this teapot?' Once the waitress had obliged and he had poured more tea for her, Anatoli looked across at her. 'You are upset about your David.'

Edie felt very embarrassed. 'I don't know what you must have thought – me writing all that to you. I'm sorry – I got a bit carried away.'

'Edith . . .' He spoke in a low, gentle voice. 'Why are

you ashamed of telling me your thoughts? Umm? I felt honoured to receive them. You feel sad because your son has grown up and you feel he is growing further and further away. You are lonely . . .'

Blushing even more, she admitted, yes, she was lonely.

'So – what is wrong with that? Is it your fault you are lonely?'

'I don't know.' She looked directly at him. 'Sometimes I think it probably is.'

'Look—' He sat back, teacup in one hand. 'I was a married man for many years. Margot and I used to go out a great deal together, play music, we had many friends. I still see a few of those friends – but times change. When Margot was ill I couldn't get out much, so I lost touch with people. Then suddenly, when you are alone again, it is not the same to do things on your own that you used to do together. And some friends have died or moved away . . . Suddenly I am, yes – a lonely man too. It takes time to get over losing someone so close – but one day I looked up and said to myself, "Anatoli – you are really an old hermit crab these days. And you never really liked being like that, did you?"'

Edie smiled, disarmed.

'You know – that day you came was the best day I can remember for . . . I can't even think how long. I don't know what you thought of me and all my chaotic life but I thought to myself, this girl is too good to lose!'

She was amused at being called a girl.

'Then—' he frowned, pretending to be offended, and put on a mocking voice, 'she writes me one of those ever-so-British notes, a note with a stiff upper lip, saying that I will be welcome to visit – perhaps if I were to call one day and leave my card with the butler . . .'

Edie was laughing now.

Anatoli flashed a grin at her, then his expression sobered. 'So when I received another letter, *saying* something, sharing something true, and very eloquently too, then . . . It made me happy – truly.'

'I'm glad then.' Her cheeks were burning after all he had said.

'There is not time in life for only dealing with the surface of each other.' Anatoli turned his cup round and round in the saucer. He was very serious now. 'Especially at my age. You know – that is what Hermann Mayer remembers. It is why I remember him. To me it seems I did so very little for him that I feel ashamed that he remembers me so acutely. But we were together for perhaps fifteen minutes, and it was fifteen truly human minutes. I can never forget. After this, etiquette and formality are a tissue of nothingness.'

Edie looked back at him, moved. 'I'm sorry. I'm not used to . . . to this.'

'Don't be sorry.' His eyes were twinkling again. 'But we shared so much that day, you remember? It would be a pity to waste such a friendship.'

'I just didn't know if – if you talked like that with everyone.'

'No. Oh no. Most people don't allow it. So – tell me more about your David.'

She poured it all out. Another letter had arrived since. He wanted to stay, to become an Israeli citizen. He knew this would mean that he had to be an army conscript. He was in love with a girl called Gila Weissman and they were both planning to apply to the Hebrew University in Jerusalem. He sounded so very passionate and, yes, happy too.

'I suppose the worst of it is that it's made me feel that everything I've given him is what he doesn't want now.

He doesn't want to be English, to live here near me, he wants to be Jewish, and Israeli and go into the army. I mean, he was never that sort of boy! He wasn't tough – he never even liked games at school very much. And he wants to marry some girl I've never even met and probably never will ...' She drew out a hanky to wipe her eyes.

'But why should you never meet her?' Anatoli leaned towards her, surprised.

'Well—' Edie said angrily. 'It's the other side of the world. I can't exactly just drop in and see them, can I?'

'And why not?' Gently he reached across and enclosed her left hand in his right. His touch felt warm and comforting. 'Look, he's alive, he's well and happy. He writes you letters because he loves you. He sounds like the sort of boy who loves easily and it must have been you who taught him that. It will be all right, Edith. And you will see him. Of course you will.'

Forty-Nine

'I'm all right,' Frances assured her for at least the third time. 'Really, dear – I shall have a lovely quiet day tucked here.'

'I feel terrible leaving you,' Edie said. How long was it since Frances had taken to resting so much? And how long had she been so wrapped up in herself and Anatoli that it had taken her until now to notice?

Frances rallied herself and sat up straight. 'Oh, don't be so silly, Edie. It's only for the day! I've everything I need, and you'll be back tonight. I'll be the one feeling terrible if you *don't* go!'

After Anatoli's first visit to Birmingham they had parted promising to meet again the following month. Edie went to London in October, and they both said let's not leave it so long next time. Soon there was barely a weekend when one of them was not making a journey to see the other.

Still uneasy about Frances, Edie went to catch her train. It was cold, mid-November, but she wrapped up warm in her new winter coat and tied a scarf round her hair. Who cared if it was cold! They had planned to go to a lunchtime concert in St Martin-in-the-Fields, then visit a small gallery Anatoli knew not far away. The day stretched pleasurably ahead.

With each visit they made to one another, Edie found herself more and more impatient to be in his company. A fortnight became too long to wait, then a week. Every time she was with him she felt special: she loved the way he listened to her and shared his thoughts with her, the way he looked at her, attentively, as she talked, and the fact that they enjoyed doing so many things together. She felt a great tenderness for him and, increasingly, desire. She knew she was falling more and more in love, and the feeling was so new and heady she could scarcely think of anything else.

I'm more flighty than when I was nineteen! she thought as the train chugged – so slowly! – towards London. This is ridiculous – he's so much older than me and it's all so *strange*. But the thought of a time when she had not known him now seemed unthinkable.

When she arrived at Euston there was no sign of him, though he had promised to be there. Deflated, she walked off the platform. How dismal the place seemed without him beaming at her, very often over a bouquet of flowers, and pacing impatiently up and down! Surely she had not mistaken the day?

Her heart lurched. There he was, running, waving, an eccentric-looking figure, a fur hat perched on his head today. A joyful smile broke across her face.

'Have you been here long? I'm sorry – I misjudged how long it would take.' He kissed her cheek.

'It's all right – we've only been in a few minutes. But I thought you weren't coming!'

'Not coming! How could I not be coming, you foolish girl? Umm?'

She laughed and linked her arm through his. She was struck once more by the comfort of their friendship, as if they had known each other for years. And at the same time, when she looked round at him as they stood waiting for the Tube, his rather severe profile, the hat, she felt a sense of mystery and strangeness. How well did she know him really? She wanted to know how it would be to kiss him – really kiss him – not just the affectionate pecks they gave each other on the cheek.

He caught her examining him and gave her a quizzical look.

'You're wondering about me – umm?'

She laughed at having her thoughts read so accurately. 'Sort of.'

'You're asking yourself if I am really Jack the Ripper?'

'No, of course not!' Her reply was half drowned by the train clattering in to the platform.

They sat in the echoing space of St Martin's as the pianist rolled the magnificent notes of Beethoven sonatas round the walls, listening attentively, though it was cold and Edie could feel her feet growing more and more icy. After the music had gone on for some time, Anatoli reached for her hand, holding it between both his own, and looked searchingly into her eyes. Moved, Edie looked solemnly back.

They did not speak as they walked out of the church, glad to move about and get warm, but kept hold of each other's hands. After lunch, they walked to the little gallery off the Strand. The artist was a young Italian called Alessandro Peti and Edie enjoyed the bright, sunshine colours of the work. Some of the paintings were abstract, but one of the last in the exhibition, to which Edie felt particularly drawn, was a picture almost completely of sea, in rich mix of azure and mauve. Providing perspective, the artist had painted the thinnest, curving spit of land, at the end of which stood a tiny lighthouse.

'I'd like to be there,' she said.

Anatoli turned towards her, bringing his lips close to her ear. 'What I should like is to be alone with you.'

They left the gallery. Edie knew that a step had been taken, that he had let her see how much he felt for her, but what should they do now? It was so cold and there was nowhere obvious to go.

Anatoli looked at his watch. 'We can sit and drink cups of tea all the afternoon, or, if we want to be warmer, we could go to my house – at least for a couple of hours.'

Edie hesitated for a second. The house was a place of memories – it was where Margot had lived with him. Margot whom she could never replace, who seemed to overshadow her. But she was still drawn to it, to its cosy, violin-filled clutter. Otherwise they'd have to walk the winter streets.

On the train out to Wimbledon they held hands. There was a new shyness between them and it struck her that Anatoli was even more ill at ease than she was. He looked ahead of him, now and then turning to give her a nervous smile or make a remark about the journey.

'Is there anything wrong?' she asked.

'No – I'm just a bit cold,' he said.

The house felt quite warm inside. Anatoli switched on the lights in the sitting-room and a heater which blew out hot air, and made tea. Edie looked around her contentedly.

'I love your house,' she said, standing by the piano as he came in with the tray. The warm glossy wood of the two violins gleamed on top of the piles of music.

Anatoli put the tray down and came over to her.

'Edith—' he said hesitantly. 'I'm sorry if my mood has been a bit strange...' He looked beyond her, for a moment, towards the yellowed keys of the piano, and his expression was melancholy.

'What's the matter?' she said, worried. 'Is it something I've done?'

463

'No!' He smiled at this notion. 'Well, not exactly. The thing is, Edith – I have tried very hard not to push you into anything. Not to expect you to feel as I do. You know, we men who've been married, we miss it. We ache to be with a woman again. I know I am a good deal older than you – you are so very young and beautiful. But you have made every difference to how I feel about life. And each time we meet, when I see you . . . I just find it harder and harder to bear it when you go away again.'

In a tremulous voice Edie said, 'Anatoli – I can't be like Margot for you . . . I can't even play the piano.'

He shook his head, horrified. 'My dear – you mustn't ever think like that.' He moved a little closer. 'Edith – Margot was my wife for many years. She was a lovely person, she was part of me and I loved her. But by the end of her life she was suffering terribly. You know, at times she was very cruel in those last weeks. Almost a different person. She didn't mean it, I know. It was the illness, the pain she was in. She is dead and I have made my peace with that. But you . . . In coming to me you have literally given me new life. You have made existence not just possible for me – but also joyful . . . I don't really expect you to feel the same, except sometimes in your eyes I think I see – something. I don't know if I am being foolish and seeing what I want to see.'

'You're not being foolish.' She spoke softly.

They looked into each other's eyes as he took in what she'd said. She heard his breathing become faster and all she could think of was how much she wanted to touch him, hold him.

'Oh God – I must not make a fool of myself.' She didn't know if he had intended to speak the words or just think them. He held out his arms. 'May I?'

They stepped into each other's embrace, he with a cry

of relief and happiness. She smelt his familiar smell, a mix of hair oil, soap and his own individual, manly scent. 'Oh my lovely one,' he said into her hair. 'My dear sweet girl.'

Edie raised her face to look at him. 'You are so good to me, Anatoli. I want to make you happy again.'

She raised her lips towards his and she saw a muscle twitch in his cheek. For a few seconds he nuzzled her face with his lips, as if tasting her, delaying the pleasure, then their lips found each other's, arms gathering each other in closer, until they were locked passionately together.

When he released her for a moment she said in wonder, 'I haven't felt like this – I've never felt like this before.' Whatever she had felt for Jack all those years ago was a shadow of the longing she felt now.

Her words seemed to excite Anatoli further, and, eyes closed, kissing her hard, he pressed against her. Then, abruptly, he drew back.

'What's the matter?'

'You are so beautiful – you are all my thoughts, Edith. I want to enjoy every intimacy with you ... But I am pushing you, hurrying you. Doing things at the wrong speed because I want you so much. It would not be right.'

Much as she wanted him, she knew he was speaking the truth.

More calmly she wrapped her arms round him. 'Yes, my love. I love you very, very much – but you are right.'

He laughed suddenly, out of happiness. 'This is a dream – I shall wake up! Come – sit with me, as close as you can. I want to hold you for every second until you leave!'

Fifty

Edie stayed with Anatoli until the last possible moment and, parting, they kissed passionately on Euston Station like adolescent lovers. She spent the journey thinking about him, longing to be beside him again. Neither of them had talked in any definite terms about the future, about marriage, or anything permanent. At the moment that didn't seem to matter either. The present was too full of promise and love to worry about the future.

The next day Frances seemed a little more lively and Edie was relieved. She was well enough to go to the Meeting House, and Edie devoted the day to her, cooking lunch and sitting with her.

'We'll have a quiet afternoon in,' Edie said, even though she felt restless with love's energy and would like to have gone for a walk round the park in the crisp, cold day. 'Would you like a game of draughts?'

Frances agreed that she felt up to playing and they were setting out the pieces on the table when someone knocked at the front door. They looked at each other and frowned, puzzled.

At first Edie didn't recognize the person on the doorstep. A middle-aged woman, very plump, with pasty features and dyed blonde hair scraped back into a ponytail. Her grey coat, much too tight on her, was belted tightly at the waist and on her feet she wore scuffed navy court shoes. Her expression was dull and unsmiling.

'Ede? You still live 'ere then?'

The eyes began to look familiar then, the shape of the face despite the extra padding on it. But it was only the voice she truly recognized.

'Ruby?' Even then Edie wasn't completely sure. 'Cocoa? Oh my goodness, Ruby – is that you?' She couldn't begin to hide how appalled she was by the sight of her as she stood nodding, shamefacedly. 'What in heaven's name's happened to you?'

'Can I come in?'

'Don't be daft, of *course* you can!' She led her through to the back. 'Frances – I've got a surprise for you. Ruby's here.'

'Ruby?' The struggle was visible on Frances's face as she tried to put together the memory of the brightly dressed, ebullient Ruby whom they had last seen when she left for America with the person standing in front of her now. 'How lovely to see you dear! Do take your coat off and sit down.'

Peeling off her coat, Ruby revealed a loose, unflattering dress in a floral material. It was partly her clothes that made her look so aged, and the dyed hair against her pale face, dark roots showing.

'It's all I can fit into,' she said bitterly, looking down at herself.

'How long've you been back?' Edie said. 'Oh Ruby, we haven't heard from you for so long. Why didn't you write?'

Over tea, Ruby talked and talked.

'I've never been good at letter-writing – you know that, Edie. And after a while I hadn't got the heart. I made the biggest mistake of my life marrying Carl. It was all right for a few weeks – he'd been all charm, romantic, full of how well we were going to live with his business

467

going well and that. And then it started. He'd been just the same to his first wife – one of the neighbours told me later. Wish she'd let me into a bit of this before I married him.'

'What did he do?' Edie asked carefully.

'He's a madman. One minute he's all right – big blue eyes, full of it. The next he changes. Just like that.' She snapped her fingers. 'Covered in bruises I was. Couldn't go out some days – 'specially if he'd given me a shiner. He had to be right about *everything*. Every little thing he'd make a fight about it. I got so's I was frightened to breathe.'

'Oh, my dear . . .' Frances looked really distressed. 'And what about the girls – where are they?'

'He never hit them, I'll say that for him. It were only me he used like a punchbag. But course, they hated him, seeing what he did, and Marleen was right lippy to him. The first year wasn't as bad. I stuck that out. Then he seemed to get worse. He was jealous, always saying I was seeing other men when I was too frightened to set foot out of the house. We had six months of hell before I packed up and went to Wally's mom and dad. Louisa took us in. She was horrified to find what Carl was really like. They'd known him years. Everyone'd blamed Martha, his first wife, for deserting him. Martha'd told hardly anyone the truth about him. Then we tried to patch it up. I mean I'd gone all the way over there to be with him. I went back to him and left the girls with Mr and Mrs Sorenson. But then Marleen started playing up. She was out all hours, giving them lip, hanging about with lads. They're ever so strait-laced and they wouldn't stand for it.'

She paused to drink some of her tea. 'When I was back living in the house with Carl he started off again. Nice as pie for a week or two, then back to square one. I said to him in the end, "I'm not staying here putting up with this. Not any more." And I cleared out and went back to the Sorensons. I met someone else, soon after, a bloke called Larry, and we were getting on well but I'd get home and they'd be on at me. "You're a married woman. You're acting like a street-walker . . ." All that sort of thing. And then Marleen went missing. A week she was away – in August, this was. Went off with some lad and they were living in his car, driving round. Greta was OK – she's quieter, like. Did better at school, but our Marleen . . .' Ruby shook her head. 'I've got no say over 'er now. Anyhow she's stayed over there. Says she's engaged to Danny, the boy she's with, and she's staying and getting married. She's seventeen. Seems happy enough.'

'You left her behind?' Edie was horrified. 'And you're back for good?'

'I couldn't force her to come – and I couldn't stay on with Mr and Mrs Sorenson. Not any longer. By the end of it I couldn't stand them and they couldn't stand me. But they didn't want Greta to go – that's why they put up with me as long as they did.'

'Well, where is she?' Frances asked.

'At Mom's. Greta's fond of Ed and Louisa, and they're good to her, but she didn't want to stay there without me. As for Carl – well, he's not right in the head, Edie. He's a sick man.'

'Oh, I do wish you'd kept in touch, Ruby,' Edie said, horrified by all she'd heard. 'You never answered my letters. There was me thinking you were over there having the time of your life.'

'That's one way of putting it,' Ruby said bitterly. 'I know I should've, and I'm sorry. It's just – sometimes I got so's I could hardly get out of bed or drag myself about. I just used to stay in and eat to try to cheer myself up.' Her face puckered. 'I've let myself go, I know.' Tears rolled down her face. 'Oh Edie – I've been so miserable ... And now I've lost my Marleen as well. I've had enough of it all ...'

'Oh, poor old Ruby—' Edie got up and put her arms round Ruby's shaking shoulders. It was terrible to see her looking so beaten and sad. Through all the other bad things that had happened to her, she had always kept her spark, but this time, Carl Christie seemed to have knocked it right out of her.

When she'd calmed a little and they were talking over a cup of tea, Frances asked gently, 'What d'you think you'll do now then, dear?'

'Well—' Ruby said, resignedly. 'I s'pose the best thing to do is go and ask for my old job back.'

Within a few weeks, Ruby was back on one of the lines at Cadbury's and had rented a place to live. Greta, who had grown up into a round-faced, blonde fourteen-year-old, quite quiet and pleasant, was also planning to apply to the Cadbury works when she could leave school the next year. Very occasionally they received a note from Marleen, whose engagement seemed to have become a rocky business. Ruby predicted that she'd soon be home, tail between her legs.

Ruby's spirits did not stay low for long. She was still the optimist and Edie was delighted to be able to see her in the dining-hall at lunch and go for swims again. In fact, with Anatoli in her life – Ruby was endlessly curious about him – Ruby back, and Janet's happy letters describing her new-found family, Edie was full of happiness. The only shadow in her life was her concern about

Frances, who up until now had refused to see a doctor. Her face was drawn and there were dark shadows under her eyes, but she insisted that it was just old age and there was nothing wrong.

One Saturday in December, Edie went into town early before meeting Anatoli's train from London. She wanted to go to the Bull Ring, or 'chaos corner' as everyone was calling it. She found going into town unpleasant and disorientating these days. The centre of Birmingham was a building site, its landscape constantly changing. Roads were being carved across the middle of the city, tunnels, pedestrian walkways. Buildings vanished, were replaced.

'It doesn't feel like the same place any more,' she grumbled to Frances before leaving home. 'If I don't come back, you'll know I've fallen down a big hole.'

She was making her way to the Rag Market when outside St Martin's church she spotted a familiar face topped by a smart little hat, moving towards her through the other shoppers. Edie might well have pretended not to see her, but Esther Leishmann headed straight for her. She had seen nothing at all of the Leishmanns ever since David left for Israel.

'Mrs Weale! How are you? You are missing young David a great deal, I am sure. But you know, we are getting such letters from him!'

Edie bridled immediately. Did the woman think David wasn't writing to her as well?

'Yes,' she said. 'Oh, I hear ever such a lot from him.'

'He seems totally set on staying in Israel. He has told you this?'

'Well, of course,' Edie snapped. 'He was due home in August. He tells me everything.' She stuck her chin out. 'And I'm glad for him. He seems very happy indeed, especially with his fiancée, Gila.'

To Edie's satisfaction, Esther Leishmann looked stunned. '*Fiancée*, did you say? What is this fiancée? Of course he mentioned the girl to us, but he says nothing about marriage. I mean she is not even a religious Jew!' She seemed really upset. 'He was such a good boy – I don't know why he wouldn't go to a proper kibbutz where he could have studied. We have suggested to him several times that he move but always he refuses. In fact he has not been writing to us so often recently. We were afraid he had been ill, perhaps?'

'Oh, no,' Edie said, unable to prevent herself feeling some triumph about the woman's lack of control over him. 'He's in very good health so far as I know. And he has been so happy at Hamesh. Now he is going to marry, I'm sure he won't be moving. They are going to the Hebrew University.'

She spoke with pride, and when she had parted with Esther Leishmann she knew just how proud she felt. David had written to her recently, 'I think I have to stop running from one extreme to the other and try to accept both strands of my life. Yes, I am Jewish, but I am also in some respects a Friend in my thinking. However, I have had to struggle with this. My conscience tells me that, when it comes to it, I shall have to be prepared to fight to defend the State of Israel – otherwise how can I call myself a Jew and an Israeli? I am a strange mongrel, I know, a Jewish Quaker! And the two things do not sit easily together. But somehow, that is who I am and I suppose I have to live with it.'

The price for David growing up and beginning to come to terms with himself was his living so far away. But for the first time, Edie glowed inside with pride at his strength in being able to do that, and in all that he had achieved.

Fifty-One

February 1959

'Mrs Hatton – come in. Take a seat.'

The doctor was rather elderly, and with a kindly, though detached manner. Edie, accompanying Frances, knew, somehow, what he was going to say. She also knew that Frances knew, though they had both been keeping up a pretence over Christmas that things were all right, despite her lack of appetite, the episodes of faintness. Anatoli had spent Christmas with them, and it had been a quiet, happy time, but even he, who did not know Frances nearly as well, could see that something was wrong.

'It isn't good news, I'm afraid, Mrs Hatton,' the doctor was saying.

Frances sat very straight in her hat and coat, her hands in her lap. She looked composed, but as the doctor said the word *cancer*, Edie saw the bones move in her jaw, as if she had momentarily clenched her teeth. This barely noticeable reaction sent a deep pang through Edie. Poor, dearest Frances – she was being so calm, so brave! Edie found it hard to concentrate on what the doctor was saying because she was trying so determinedly not to cry. His tone was enough to tell her. As she helped Frances up, and in a daze they left the surgery, Edie had come away with the grains of information that it was cancer, that it had begun to spread to her liver, that Frances, her dearest friend, was dying, or would be soon.

They stepped out into the freezing street. There had been heavy snow that winter and filthy, icy mush lay along the edges of the road. Edie took Frances's arm.

'Well,' Frances said, because somebody had to say something. 'I must organize myself.'

'Oh Frances . . .' Edie said.

Hearing her heartbroken tone, Frances squeezed her arm.

'Come along, dear. Perk up. We've known really, haven't we? We'll go in and have a nice cup of tea by the fire together. Let's not be miserable.'

Somehow as soon as the doctor had confirmed to them all how sick Frances really was, she quickly became more so. Edie was full of worries.

'It's not that I mind looking after her,' she confided to Ruby as they ate their lunchtime bowl of soup together one day. 'I'd do anything for her. It's just – I'm frightened – I don't know if I can do it properly.'

'Well, you can't – not on your own,' Ruby said. The colour had come back into her cheeks a little bit since she'd come home, and though she was still very plump she looked better in herself. Now she was back at Cadbury's she had flung herself into the Bournville Dramatic Society with some of her old pals. 'What about when you're at work?'

'I know.' Edie chewed the end of her thumb, frowning with worry. 'Mrs Jones next door said she'll help out, but she can't be there all day . . .'

'Well, when the time comes, she'll need to go into hospital.'

'She says she doesn't mind,' Edie said. 'Only I'd feel I was letting her down if I didn't look after her.'

All that spring was taken up with Frances's illness. Edie found it heartbreaking to watch. She could eat less and less and her rounded, comforting figure was vanishing, the weight melting from her bones. She was very calm, very patient, but by the middle of March she was already sinking fast. Death was beginning to inscribe itself in every line of her pinched face. How long did she have left? Edie had received a letter from Janet saying that she was trying to make arrangements to come as soon as possible. But how long would she be? They had heard nothing since, and Edie began to wonder whether she would make it in time.

Throughout that period, Edie knew that while she had loved Anatoli before, now she felt even more deeply for him because she knew she how much she could count on him. Weekend after weekend he made the journey up from London, and instead of travelling back on a Saturday night he stayed over and helped, making no demands of his own.

'This isn't very nice for you,' Edie said one day, when he'd come up to stay, week after week. ''Specially when you've already been through it with your wife.'

'So I know what it's like,' he said, putting his hands on her shoulders. 'Look – all I want is to be with you. We don't have to be always out enjoying ourselves or living life like a party! It's enough just to be together.'

'I do love you,' she wrapped her arms round him. 'You're so kind to me.'

'And you are kind to a lonely old man,' he said with a self-mocking smile.

He was happiest when he was close to her. When she passed him he would touch her, stroke her arm or lay a hand on her shoulder. He'd been especially protective since he discovered the scar on her arm and asked her about it. As she told him some of the details of her childhood he could barely believe it at first. He was completely horrified. Edie had never seen him so angry. He was an enormous comfort to her as her old friend was fading before her eyes.

Once Frances was settled for the night, when he was staying over, they sat cuddled together, talking, reading, kissing. That weekend, in the middle of March, they sat in the back room, in the glow of the fire. Their cold teacups were on the table and they had not wanted to switch the light on. Edie sat, warm and contented, leaning against Anatoli's solid body, his arm round her waist. Every so often he caressed her with his other hand, her hair, cheek, breast. Then she heard him clear his throat.

'Edith?' Even in that one word she could detect a longing.

'Umm?' She was staring into the fire, and he leaned closer and kissed her neck. Solemnly, he said, 'I must ask you something.'

'Must you?' she teased, twisting round to face him. Her hair fell forward, light and soft on his face as she kissed him.

'I would like you to be my wife.'

She could not speak for a moment. She loved him so much, felt so safe and cared for by him, she could scarcely believe something so good could be offered to her.

'Have I made a mistake?' he said, carefully.

Edie swallowed. 'Oh no! I want to marry you – of course I do! You just took me by surprise, that's all.'

'You are saying yes?'

She moved her face closer to his in the firelight.

'Yes, Anatoli. I love you very much. Of course I want to marry you. When I can . . .' She rolled her eyes upwards.

'I know. Once you are alone. She is very sick, poor Frances. Of course, I understand that. There is no hurry. We are talking about sharing our lives, not catching a train. Although—' His hands gently caressed her breasts, over her soft wool jumper. 'Heaven knows, I find it so hard to have to wait for you.'

His touch sent longing burning through her.

'Stop—' She held his hands, moving them away. 'That's too nice. You'll have to stop!'

She knew what it cost him to pull himself away from her as they kissed goodnight, because she felt the same. Lying in her bed, restless, unable to sleep, all she could think of was Anatoli in the small room at the back of the house. Was he thinking of her? Lying awake as she was, full of longing?

Time passed, slowly. The clock on the landing seemed to tick louder than ever as she lay awake, able to think of nothing but wanting him.

This is so ridiculous, she thought. Frances's wasted body lay in the room next to her. Death would soon take her. All she and Anatoli could feel was a great urge for life, for love. What was wrong with that? They'd both been married before, after all. She thought she heard him give a cough from along the passage. Was he still awake?

She slipped out of bed into the cold and, clenching her teeth, opened the squeaky bedroom door. She knew Frances was unlikely to hear – she took a sedative now, to make sure she slept – yet she still tip-toed as quietly as she could. She stopped at Anatoli's door. Should she knock? She decided not, and turned the handle.

She heard rather than saw him sit up as she came in.

'Edith? Is that you?'

Without replying, she went to the window and boldly drew back the curtain. The moon was up, shedding cool

477

white light. She could feel Anatoli watching her, leaning up on one elbow and she enjoyed the sensation, knowing how much he wanted her. Standing in the pool of light she reached for the hem of her nightdress and lifted it over her head.

'Oh—' His voice came softly to her. 'My beautiful girl.'

She went to sit beside him on the bed and he stroked her bare back, looking up into her eyes. 'Edith – you're so lovely. You're a miracle to me.'

She leaned down to kiss him and as she did so he cupped his hand round one of her pendent breasts, the feel of it making him close his eyes, sighing with pleasure. Edie felt as if every nerve of her body was alert to him, desiring him, his caresses seeming to reach through every part of her.

'Let's not wait,' she whispered to him urgently. 'I want to be with you now . . . always.'

For a moment he managed to hold back. 'Are you sure, Edith?'

She pulled back the covers and lay beside him, pulling him close. 'Very, very sure.'

She woke early the next morning, cramped in the narrow bed beside Anatoli. The curtain was still open and the objects in the room, the chair, the heavy dark cupboard and dressing table, were lit by a filtered, unearthly light. Easing herself out of bed she found that outside everything was wrapped in thick fog. Anatoli was still asleep, and she smiled down at the sight of his face, the dark brows pulled slightly into a frown as he slept. For a second she touched his stubbly cheek, then crept out on to the landing. Peeping in at Frances, she saw she was still asleep. She made tea and brought it up to the bedroom, turned on the little bar fire in the room and climbed back into bed. It felt very cosy with the fog outside.

Anatoli stirred, stretched, opened his eyes. Seeing her, he immediately smiled, and Edie was moved by the delight she saw in his expression.

'Hello,' he whispered. 'You're still here.'

'Yes. Still here.'

They nestled into each other. Gently he lifted her arm, his lips gently exploring the scalded tissue of her scar.

'Poor little one,' he murmured, as if kissing it better.

There was a worry nagging at her mind. 'Anatoli – we . . .' This was awkward. It was much easier to make love than to talk about it! 'Last night – I mean . . . We didn't . . . take any precautions.'

'I know. I'm sorry.' His warm hand caressed her face his eyes troubled. 'It was very stupid of me. I wasn't expecting it to happen and you were too much for me! You do not want a child – at all, with me?'

'Oh goodness, I don't know!' Things had moved so fast suddenly. 'I'm getting on a bit to start all that now, aren't I? In a way, yes, I'd love to have a child with you. Our own child. Of course I would. But not yet! And you have your son and daughter already . . .'

'That is true – but you know, to have a child is the heart of a marriage. It is the natural thing for a woman to have a child. It's a proper family, isn't it? You are not so very old! You're still quite a young woman.'

Edie leaned up on her elbow. She was filled with excitement. 'Would you like to have a baby – really?'

He stroked his hand along her body and she felt herself responding to his caresses. 'The most beautiful sight in the world is a woman with her child. It would make me so happy to give you this.'

'Oh Anatoli—' Her arms clasped him, drawing him close as they began to make love again. 'Let's not delay getting married. What are we waiting for? Let's do it as soon as we can!'

The fog didn't lift until almost midday, and they spent a cosy morning inside. Frances was having a reasonably good day. She had not been to the Friends' Meeting House for some time, though many of them had been to visit her. This morning she was not up to it either, but she was cheerful, and said she would come downstairs. She got dressed, though all her clothes hung on her now, putting on plenty of layers to keep warm and sitting wrapped in shawls and rugs. Anatoli kept her company, and they did crosswords and read together while Edie prepared the dinner. When she came through to the back to lay the table she found both of them laughing, and smiled with surprise.

'What's tickling you two?' She put the cutlery down on the table.

Frances held up a copy of the *Bournville Works Magazine* which came from the factory. As well as news of all the clubs and societies attached to Cadbury's, there was a wide variety of articles on everything from cocoa production in Ghana or the Cameroons to foreign travel or news of the new block that was under construction.

'Listen to this,' Frances chuckled. It wrung Edie's heart to hear her. Even her voice sounded thinner.

'Someone is fuming with disapproval about *The Archers*!' Anatoli said, satirically.

'This is a letter received by one of the scriptwriters,' Frances said. 'Dear Sir, I always listen to *The Archers*. I am a Christian, a God-fearing man, and I shall not fail to mention you in my prayers, in the earnest hope that, following Grace Archer's death, something dreadful will happen to you and yours. Yours sincerely – et cetera!'

They were laughing over this when they heard a rattle and someone called, 'Cooee!' through the letterbox.

'Surely that's . . .!' Edie ran to open the door. Oh please let it be . . .

A taxi was just pulling away outside, and standing beside a large suitcase was Janet, holding, one in each arm, two bonny babies, with very dark skin and large, inquisitive eyes.

'Oh, my word!' Edie shrieked, her cry echoing back through the house. 'At last! Look at you all! Aren't they beautiful! Oh, come here! ' She tried to fling her arms round all three of them.

'Oh, Edie,' Janet laughed. 'We've made it! It's so wonderful to see you. Look – my arms are going to come out of their sockets. Take one of the girls, will you? This is Naomi.'

Cautiously, Edie took the smaller of the two children, the child's soft, plump arms dark and strange to her. Anatoli had come out to find out what the commotion was about and chuckled with surprise, seeing the two women, each with a baby in their arms. Edie introduced them happily.

'These two're staring at us as if we come from another planet!' Edie laughed at the babies' boggled-looking expressions.

'Well, you do, to them,' Janet laughed, smiling her thanks to Anatoli, who picked up her case. 'They're used to most people being black – even we're more tanned than you. They must think you're very strange!' Janet looked thinner, lean and brown and there was a glow to her face, of happiness as well as from the sun.

'Look who's here!' Edie led them through the house, and Frances gave a weak cry of joy at the sight of the little crowd in front of her. 'Oh my dear, finally!'

Janet kissed her and sat Ruth down on the floor.

'Why ever didn't you let us know you were coming?' Edie asked.

Janet seemed surprised. 'But I did. I've written twice. I mean I know I'm late – there were the inevitable delays. I thought I'd be here yesterday.'

'We haven't heard a thing – not for a good six weeks,' Edie told her.

'Where's Martin? Is he with you?' Frances asked, as if expecting him to walk in. She had been so mesmerized by the babies she had almost forgotten him to begin with.

'He's coming in a fortnight,' Janet said. 'And we can both stay until the end of June. Or longer, if necessary,' she added. There was a silence as the implications of her words sunk in. Edie could see that she was doing her best to hide her shock at the hollow-eyed state of her mother. It was obvious it could not be long before she became very ill indeed.

'Oh Jan – I'm so happy to see you!' Edie flung her arms round her friend all over again. 'And your little girls – they're absolutely beautiful!'

Fifty-Two

The weeks which followed were a bittersweet time. For the next fortnight, after Janet had arrived, she and Edie wallowed in being able to spend hours together, looking after the twins, whom Edie immediately fell head over heels in love with, and endlessly talking, making up for the years they'd been apart. Janet did look different, leaner, definitely older ('The sun ages you terribly!' she told Edie). She wore her hair long and fastened rather carelessly in a bun at the back, though with the usual wild wisps escaping at the front. But once they had spent some time together Edie found that Janet hadn't really changed very much at all. They settled straight back into their old friendship, completely easy in each other's company.

Janet was obviously much happier than she had been when she left. Having the twins to look after had made all the difference, she said. And Edie told her more about Anatoli and how happy he'd made her.

'You don't need to tell me!' Janet laughed. 'Anyone can see you're in love. And he seems so sweet, and very quaint somehow.'

'Yes – he is. And kind. And you should hear him play the violin!'

Janet had plenty of time to spend alone with Frances and look after her while Edie was at work, and it was a huge relief to Edie that there was someone in the house.

At the weekends they often wheeled the girls out in an old twin pram, borrowed from a lady down the road. Some people, seeing them with two black babies, looked away, embarrassed, not sure what to make of it. Occasionally women – often mothers of twins themselves – made a fuss of them, asking all the twin questions people always asked. Yes, they were both girls, yes, one was bigger than the other, wasn't she? To their amusement, not one of the people who stopped and talked commented on their colour, as if their blackness was invisible and it was perfectly normal for a white woman to give birth to black twins. Edie wondered if Janet would find the situation upsetting, but she shrugged it off.

'We'll soon be back home,' she said, 'and everyone there knows how I come to be bringing them up!'

Edie felt a little desolate at the way she spoke so comfortably of the Congo as 'home'.

With Janet back, she felt free to go and visit Anatoli in London, and they spent a couple of wonderful weekends. Edie fell in love with the London parks now the spring was coming. They were very passionate together, but Edie told Anatoli that though she was looking forward to conceiving his child she didn't want to be a pregnant bride.

'I didn't catch that first time,' she told him. 'But I'd like us to take precautions – 'til we're married.'

It was not long before they were planning to marry as soon as they could. With Janet home and Frances so ill, it seemed wrong to put it off.

'I'd like us to marry before Frances . . . isn't here any more.' They were strolling through Regent's Park on a cool, but bright and sunny afternoon, watching the ducks and geese. Edie's arm was linked through Anatoli's.

'My dear, I am happy to marry you as soon as you like – you know that,' he said.

All Edie's uncertainties came pouring out. Of course she'd have to leave Birmingham and move into his house, wouldn't she? Leave behind her friends and her job. Of course she liked London, and she'd do anything so long as they could build a life together. But still . . .

'Oh – wait now!' Anatoli stopped, steering her round to face him and putting his hands on her shoulders. 'Look – don't take things for granted! I don't expect you to want to move into the house I shared with Margot! That would be very unfitting. I am not even especially attached to London. How about I sell my house and buy a place in Birmingham? Umm?'

Edie looked at him in amazement. 'But . . . What about your job?'

He shrugged. 'I'll get another one. I'm a good pharmacist!'

'And . . .' She struggled to think of other objections to his generosity. 'What about your children?'

He laughed. 'What about them? One is in Brighton, one in Canada – what possible difference does it make to them if I live in Wimbledon or Birmingham?'

She still couldn't take it in. 'Would you really do that? You wouldn't mind?'

'No, I wouldn't mind.' His eyes twinkled. 'I am ready for a new start. You are making me younger every day!'

They began to make their wedding plans swiftly, but unfortunately other events moved even more quickly. Martin arrived from the Congo, looking bronzed and, Edie thought, actually more handsome with age. It was lovely to see him and Janet together, and see how devoted they were to the little girls. He and Anatoli also seemed to find a lot to talk about when they were introduced, and Edie and Janet smiled at each other and winked.

But within the week Frances began suffering a lot of pain. Neither Edie nor Janet were getting any sleep sitting up with her, and Martin advised them to have her admitted to Selly Oak Hospital. When Janet had been to take in a few of her things, she came back in tears.

'She'll be better off in there,' Martin told her, holding her, stroking her shoulders. 'I know it's hard, but they can keep the pain at bay better, and she has almost reached the point when she doesn't know where she is. You and Edie can't go on like this.'

'I know,' Janet sobbed, tired and distraught. 'I don't know if I'm relieved or horrified at her going in there! It feels as if we've let her down, packing her off like that.'

'She wouldn't think that, darling,' Martin said. 'That's what hospitals are for.'

'No – she wouldn't,' Edie added doubtfully. She also felt she had let Frances down. It had felt so final, seeing her being taken into the ambulance on a stretcher, her pinched face yellow against her white nightgown. She had barely been conscious. But Edie was exhausted herself, pale and wrung out with emotion and lack of sleep. She had sat up with her the night before. Early on in the night she had combed Frances's hair, the front parts which she could reach. It was so thin now. There were hollows under her eyes, and the skin seemed to have stretched tight round her jaw now she had lost so much flesh. Most of the time she slept, her energy spent. Edie sat in the chair beside her, dozing.

But in the small hours, Frances surfaced, her eyes

opening, still radiant lights of life in her face. For a few moments she was alert.

'What time is it?' she asked, hoarsely.

'Three o'clock – nearly,' Edie told her.

'In the afternoon?'

'No, the morning.' They left a sidelight burning in the room. It was hard even for Edie to tell whether it was day or night in her weary state.

Frances frowned. 'Why aren't you in bed then, dear? You'll be tired.'

'Oh, I just thought I'd sit by you for a while,' Edie said, taking her cool, bony hand.

Frances's eyes fixed on her face, looking deeply into her. Solemnly, she whispered, 'You know I love you, dear, don't you? I want you to be happy.'

Edie wanted to howl. How could she begin to say to Frances what she had meant to her? All the love and care she had given her and David when they had really had no one else to care for them. She'd been a mother and friend all in one. No words could ever be enough. Through the big lump in her throat Edie managed, 'And I love you too . . .' She was about to try to say more, but Frances nodded with a faint smile and closed her eyes again.

Edie knew now that Frances would not return home, and was not going to be at her wedding. The thought grieved her enormously. But Frances had now given the only sort of blessing she could manage.

Two days later, as soon as Edie walked in from work and saw Janet's face, she knew.

'We've only just got in.' Janet was blotchy from crying. The twins were on her and Martin's laps and they were feeding them fingers of bread and butter. 'She died this afternoon. I got in there just in time, but she didn't come round. They had her on morphine and she was quite peaceful. I would have sent a message for you – but it was too late. Robert didn't manage to get there until afterwards.'

Edie sat down shakily at the kitchen table, coat on, still holding the handles of her bag. Although they had known it was coming, it still felt like a terrible shock. Martin sat opposite her, looking serious, and sorry.

'I'm sorry, Jan.' Tearfully, Edie got up and kissed her, squeezing her friend's shoulders.

'I've contacted the undertakers. The funeral's on Friday. She'd only want it very simple.'

'Look, we'll postpone the wedding,' Edie said at once. It was due to be on the Saturday.

'No!' Janet protested. 'Don't do that. That would be awful.'

'But we can't have it the day after the funeral!'

Janet looked thoughtfully at Martin for a moment. 'No, I think you should carry on. Think what Mom would have said if you'd talked about putting it off!'

Edie smiled wanly, imagining Frances getting going on the subject of death being a natural part of life. 'Yes, I suppose you're right.'

Those two days – funeral, then wedding – felt to Edie like a see-saw of emotions. On the Friday morning, before the funeral, she received a letter from David. She was already dressed and ready when it arrived, in her best green and white dress that she knew Frances especially liked. David's letter had a slightly agitated air about it. He wrote partly to congratulate Edie on her marriage to

488

Anatoli, saying how delighted he was, what a marvellous thing it seemed that she had found happiness by meeting someone through the links which already connected him to herself. She smiled, tears welling in her eyes as she read his warm words, his attempts always to make her feel loved and appreciated. But reading on, her face sobered.

> I have some other news to tell you, Mom. I hope you will be pleased about it, though Gila and I are still having to come to terms with it. She is expecting our child. She only discovered this a few days ago and to begin with she has been very upset. She had so many plans to study, to become a dentist, and we do not know how this will be managed now. But we do know that we shall be together and that we shall do our best to support each other and work out a way. Gila keeps saying she does not want to give up everything and be a housewife in Jerusalem, but she is not sure either that she wants to stay on the kibbutz for ever instead. Our plan for the short term is that when I start my studies in Jerusalem, she will come with me and we shall find a little room or flat to live in. I know we shall be very poor and it will be a struggle, but we want to be together – we know this much. I hope you are not disappointed with me about this . . .

'Oh . . .' Edie let out a long, groaning sigh and handed the letter to Janet. Janet read it and looked across at her soberly.

'There's nothing whatever I can do, is there?' Edie said. 'I've very little money, although I'd give them whatever I can spare.'

Janet shook her head. 'Poor David. He's right – it is going to be a struggle. But we mustn't disapprove.'

'I just wish I could see him,' Edie said desperately. 'And her! I mean that's my grandchild she's carrying – sort of!'

Janet gave an ironic smile. 'The begetting of children is a real game of dice, isn't it?'

Edie found herself thinking about this as they made their way to Frances's funeral: all the ties she had in her life, her rag-bag family who were nothing to do with blood but everything of love and steadfastness. Ties with Frances, Janet, David, Anatoli. And in a way, with Gerda Mayer, and with the fragile German man who was David's father, Hermann Mayer. Now, with Gila's pregnancy, they would soon have a grandchild in common.

It was a grey, windy day, suitably desolate for death and goodbyes. The Friends gave Frances a peaceful goodbye, witnessing about her life, her goodness, in the Meeting they held for her. Then the family stood around the grave in the wind, holding their hats on, each parting with Frances in their own way. Edie scattered her bunch of freesias on the coffin, sweet-smelling yellows, purples and white. She followed behind Janet and Robert, with Martin and Robert's wife Marian, having said her goodbyes quietly, with love and gratitude.

The next morning they were all up early, decorating St Francis's church, on the Green, for the wedding. Anatoli's family had left the Russian Orthodox Church and joined the Church of England soon after they arrived in the country and he was keen to be married in church.

After all the events of the week, Edie felt very emotional when she saw Anatoli waiting for her as she walked up the aisle. How long ago her first wedding seemed! And how much deeper and more full her feelings now. Her dress was very pretty, in cream, calf length with lacy neck sleeves, her hair pinned up and a tiny veil fastened to it. Janet and Ruby, her two matrons of honour, each wore matching lilac frocks.

Edie had never seen Anatoli looking so spruce, in a black suit, hair trimmed and immaculately tidy. He stood very straight, his dark eyes searching her out along the aisle. Her heart full of tenderness for him, Edie walked side by side with her father, to join him at the altar. When she reached him he grasped her hand and they exchanged tremulous smiles.

She walked out beaming on his arm, into a day which was warmer and sunnier by far than the previous one. Ruby, Janet and the others showered them with rice and confetti and, tears wiped away now, Edie laughed and flung her arms round Anatoli's neck. They lined up for photographs, and afterwards all walked happily back across the Green to the house. Soon everyone was tucking into a good lunch. It was even warm enough to open the back door and spread out on to the grass. Mrs Jones next door had iced the cake, and Anatoli had insisted on contributing some champagne – 'They may have no pubs here, but I'm not getting married without a drink!' – and they all toasted Edie and Anatoli over the cake.

Edie was glad that her dad had come along, though she knew Dennis would have been happier with a pint in his hand. He and Rodney and some of the other guests drifted off after a decent interval, but the others stayed on, taking chairs out on to the lawn in the warm afternoon. Janet laid a rug on the grass and Naomi and Ruth sat playing with a few old toys.

'It's marvellous when they're too young to move

about, isn't it?' Ruby carried her plate over and sat with Janet, watching them. 'You wait – you'll be chasing them round everywhere in a few weeks!'

'Oh, I know,' Janet laughed. 'Look at their faces – there's just mischief written all over them! This is the calm before the storm!'

'What's the calm before the storm?' Edie came over, and they both smiled up at her.

'Ruby was saying I'll soon be run ragged chasing these two. D'you know, twins can move in six different directions at once!'

They laughed, and Edie settled herself carefully on the rug as well, tucking her dress under her . . .

'You look lovely, Ede,' Ruby said.

'Ta – so do you.' She finished arranging her skirt, then looked bashfully up at Ruby. 'Who'd have thought – eh?'

Ruby nudged her. 'I know. And he's a lovely fella, your Anatoli. So romantic.'

'I know—' Edie reached for little Naomi's plump, warm hand. 'I can't believe how kind he is. I keep thinking I'm going to wake up soon.'

'No—' Janet said. 'It's your turn now.'

'When's it going to be mine?' Ruby asked, lugubriously. 'Eh – where've the fellas all got to, anyroad?'

'Martin said something about making tea,' Janet said. 'At least that was when he disappeared about half an hour ago.'

'Oh, he's probably dozed off in a corner somewhere,' Ruby said. 'Anyway, Anatoli's gone off as well. What are those two up to, d'you think?'

Edie was puzzled by this as well, but then she caught sight of Martin coming out of the house bearing a large tray of tea cups. 'Look! Good for him, he *has* done the tea!' she cried. 'Ooh, I could just do with that.'

Martin brought each of them a cup and the three of them stayed chatting on the rug, playing with the little girls.

'I don't know how you can live all the way over there,' Ruby said to Janet. 'America was bad enough.'

'But you were unhappy there. That's probably why you didn't like it.'

'Yes – I s'pose so,' Ruby said gloomily. Then she grinned. 'Eh – never mind. There're always more fish in the sea! Did I tell you about Kevin . . .?'

'Oh Ruby,' Janet cried. 'You're unbelievable!'

'No, just unlucky!' she pulled a mock doleful face. 'Oh – it's nice to be with you two again. Nothing like old pals.'

'A toast!' Edie joked, holding up her teacup, and the others joined in. 'Wherever we are we must keep in touch – pals, eh?'

'Pals!' the other two agreed. And solemnly sipped their cups of tea, before erupting into laughter again.

'Where did you get to this afternoon?' Edie asked.

She and Anatoli were lying naked under the sheets in Linden Road. They were leaving for a few days away by the sea the next day, but had decided to celebrate into the evening with their friends and not to rush away on their wedding night. After all, Janet and Martin wouldn't be here much longer. Late that night, warm from love-making, they lay together in Edie's bed, in the soft light of the room.

'I was talking to Martin.'

'But you were in there for ages!' Her curiosity was aroused. 'What on earth were you talking about?'

'Well – we were making a plan . . .'

'*Plan?*' she said, rather huffily. 'What on earth d'you mean?'

'OK – promise me you will just be quiet for two minutes while I tell you – with no interruptions?'

Edie nodded, vigorously.

'Right. OK. It's very simple. Frances said we could live here for a time after we were married in any case. She has a tenancy with the Bournville Village Trust – so for the time being we can keep that on. I was having a few words about the details of this because now Frances has passed away we need to organize things. I am selling my house in Wimbledon. No, you said you'd be quiet!' he protested as Edie was almost bursting, wanting to ask questions.

'Soon we can look to buy a place of our own, *but* for the time being it means that we also have some spare money. So – what we will do first is to buy two tickets to Tel Aviv, and go and visit that son of yours.' He grinned, as Edie was pressing a hand over her mouth to try and stop herself exploding with excitement. 'What do you think of that, Mrs Gruschov? Umm?'

Fifty-Three

Israel – July 1959

'Edith, my love. Wake up now – we' re nearly there.'

Edie came to, aware of something hard pressing against the left side of her head. It was the windowframe of a clanking, ramshackle bus. Groggily she opened her eyes. She'd fallen asleep when she'd vowed she wouldn't!

'Drink.' Anatoli handed her a bottle of water. 'You must drink. You are not used to this heat.'

Obediently she swallowed, making a face at the lukewarm water which tasted as if it had come out of a swimming pool. Her head throbbed. The windows were open all along the bus but the breeze that blew in was so sultry it barely cooled at all. She was damp with sweat between her legs, and shifted her position on the sticky seat, trying to straighten out her skirt. She had bought it for the trip, a soft cotton, in sky blue.

'Bother!' she smiled at Anatoli, gradually reviving. 'I was determined not to fall asleep. I didn't want to miss anything.'

But the heat and rocking rhythm of the bus had been too much for her. The last twenty-four hours had been exhausting, and different from any other she had experienced, and she was already very tired from all the sleepless nights at home worrying about coming to Israel in the first place. She was going to see David – that thought in itself was enough to keep her awake! But she also had to contend with his fierce young fiancée Gila, and all the other people with whom his life had become entwined. And she had to fly! She had kept herself awake with terrible visions of disaster – opening a wrong door and falling out of the aeroplane ... Then the journey itself had been exhausting. Landing at Lydda airport to the hot, sulphurous smell of Israel. All the noise and clamour. Everyone here seemed to do everything at full volume – a cacophony of guttural voices, blaring horns of cars and buses as they were driven to a place where they could sleep for the night, along Tel Aviv's busy streets, between pale blocks of buildings. All night there was a humming sound somewhere close, perhaps a generator, but it did not keep her awake. She woke refreshed, in the cool of the morning, to soft, coppery sunlight through the slats and the echo of sounds from the city outside.

On the bus journey she wanted to take in everything. As the sun moved higher in the sky, the land appeared harsher. How dry it was, she thought, seeing dust rising from the wheels of the truck in front. How inhospitable the earth looked where it was uncultivated, scattered with white, sharp stones between scrubby plants. Even the sheep and goats appeared wiry and dried up, like the plants, and the little black hens pecking by the roadside did not look as if they had much flesh on them. Then they would pass irrigated areas, where the land sprang into green fruitfulness: tomatoes, aubergines, cucumbers, and plantations of date and banana. She was astonished at the verdant growth, especially as they moved further north. And what a mixture of people! She stared fascinated at the women she saw, who reminded her of a page in a childhood encyclopedia of David's entitled *Peoples of the World*. There were women working the fields in trousers like landgirls, the way David had descibed Gila.

Others pushed prams wearing frocks and cardigans. Some women were dark-skinned, some fair. Some wore short skirts, others long colourful ones, and scarves covering dark hair, long black bedouin robes, shawls, and there were even, as Anatoli pointed out when they stopped in a place called Hadera, women in saris.

She had spent the first hour drinking in every detail, but gradually she had grown more and more drowsy.

They were coming into Tiberias. Hazy in the heat, Yam Kinneret, the Sea of Galilee as she knew it from the Bible, appeared in glimpses of deep blue between the buildings of the low, jumbled little town.

Anatoli reached for her hand, and they sat with their palms sweatily in each other's.

'Are you all right?'

Edie took a deep breath. 'Terrified.' She smiled nervously. 'Ridiculous, isn't it? But it's been such a long time. I'm scared he'll have changed so much that we shan't have anything to say to each other.'

'I don't believe,' Anatoli teased, 'that I have ever known a time when you had nothing to say!'

His teasing exasperated her in her tense mood and he sensed her irritation.

'Look—' He squeezed her hand. 'It will be all right. Really, my darling.'

'I just feel . . .' She sighed, trying to find a word to sum up her feelings of inadequacy, of fear in the face of all that David had found here. But it was fear of the unknown and she couldn't put it into words.

The bus ground screeching to a halt, and abruptly everyone started getting up and trying to get out and there was a loud gabble of voices.

'Well—' Anatoli said, as if offering her something

routine and everyday like a cup of tea. 'Shall we go and find your son?'

David had told them he knew the times of the buses coming into Tiberias, and if all was going according to plan, he should be there somewhere, among the throng of people in the street.

Will I recognize him? Edie wondered, climbing down out of the bus. Her heart was beating painfully hard at the thought that she might soon see him, yet at the same time there was also a sense of unreality about it, as if her body had travelled on ahead and her mind still had to catch up. Was she really here, or would she soon wake up in her bed in Bournville?

Standing at the side of the road with their suitcase, they looked back and forth. Heat pressed down on them and the slight breeze just made her feel more damp. The bus took off again in a cloud of fumes. Two women, both middle-aged, stood beside them, arguing volubly about their bags. Motorcycles roared past on the road, one ridden by soldiers, a boy and girl, both in uniform, and Edie watched them go past, screwing up her eyes against the glare. The girl's hair streamed out behind and she was laughing.

'Perhaps we should find a spot in the shade,' Anatoli suggested.

They were moving into the shade under the awning of a shop which had a pile of yellow melons outside, when they heard his voice.

'Mom! Over here – Mom!'

Running towards them, dodging through the traffic, was a tall, deeply tanned, broad-shouldered man with a mop of curly brown hair. For a moment Edie couldn't

498

put together the familiar sound of his voice with the apparition she saw in front of her. She stood quite still as he ran over to them.

'My goodness!' she gasped. 'Anatoli – it's him. Oh Davey, look at you!'

Forgetting all her nervousness, she just flung her arms round him in her joy at seeing him, laughing, but with tears coming too. What a great big muscular man he was! In her arms he felt twice the size he'd been when she last saw him!

'Hello, Mom.' He sounded rather bashful, but he was grinning, and very pleased to see her.

Edie drew back and groped in her pocket for a hanky to wipe her eyes. 'Oh I can't believe how you've grown and filled out. Look at him, Anatoli! When he came he was a pale shrimp of a lad!'

'Hello, David.' Anatoli held out his hand.

'I'm very pleased to meet you at last.' Edie saw David examine Anatoli intently. 'And congratulations to you both, again.'

He had brought one of the kibbutz cars to fetch them. Edie was further astonished. So he could drive now! And a man came up and asked him something she couldn't understand, and David gave him fluent directions in Hebrew. She was so proud of him! He had learned and grown so much.

Edie sat beside him in the front of the car, with Anatoli behind. She watched David's brown, muscular legs working the accelerator and clutch. He was wearing loose khaki shorts and sandals.

'Gila was going to come with me,' he said, backing the car to turn round. 'Unfortunately she wasn't feeling too well this morning, so she decided to rest and save her energy for later.'

'How far on is she now?' Edie asked hesitantly.

'About three months. She's been very well up until now – it's a shame it happened today. Maybe she's nervous because you're coming!'

Not half as nervous as I am, Edie thought, wiping her moist hands on her hanky. It felt more humid here than it had in Tel Aviv. Sweat seemed to sit clammily on the skin. It was too bad about having to let her scar show in this heat. She had long ago taken off her cardigan. And it didn't seem important any more.

She wanted to ask David everything at once. What have you said to Mrs Weissman, Gila's mother? Do you get on with her? When are you going to get married? Where will Anatoli and I be staying? And above all, the thing David could not possibly answer – what will Gila think of me? But she stifled her questions and instead they commented on the view and David pointed things out.

'That little building – you see the minaret back there – that's the old mosque. Everyone has been here – Samaritans, Crusaders, Turks. And there was an earthquake in 1837, so a lot of it was lost.'

'How far away is your kibbutz?' Edie asked.

'Oh, not far – three or four miles. It is one of the newer ones. Back that way—' He pointed back south with his thumb. 'At the bottom end of the lake, south of Kinneret, is Degania Aleph – that's the oldest kibbutz in Israel, founded in 1909. Hamesh has barely been going for ten years, so it is still a little rough round the edges.'

They left the town, and to their right the water of the lake spread out in patches of deep blue and turquoise.

'It's very peaceful,' she said. 'And very beautiful.'

'Yes,' David said happily. 'It's wonderful. It's very good for swimming and there are lovely fish.'

Edie looked dreamily out of the window while Anatoli

asked more questions. She had known the two of them would get on.

'How is your father?' Anatoli said. Edie listened more attentively now.

'Well—' David sighed. 'His health is never very strong. He depends on Annaliese for everything. It does worry me that she will find it too much to look after him one day. But he knows you're coming.'

Within minutes they had arrived, driving through the gate and raising a swirl of dust on the unpaved track inside. Edie's first impression was rather disappointing. Ahead of her rose a series of concrete buildings, square blocks, functional but with nothing attractive about them at all. In front of them was one lawn which had obviously been watered and tended to, and the other side, another which had been seeded and was struggling to survive in the heat. A jet of water squirted intermittently over it from a hosepipe. From somewhere, as she climbed out, she could hear children's voices chanting something, perhaps a nursery rhyme.

'Now—' David lifted the cases from the back. 'We have a small apartment where you can stay. Come with me – we'll go and settle you in and get something to drink. That's the first thing.'

He led them along the dry path past the communal dining-room to one of the blocks. Outside the door a young date palm was growing in the scuffed earth. They climbed two flights of bare concrete stairs and Edie's head throbbed. She was longing for a drink of water and to be able to sit and recover with her eyes closed for a few minutes. The journey from home seemed to have gone on for ever.

But when David opened the door of the apartment, into a very simple living-room with a few pieces of plain, rather ugly furniture standing round it, there was someone sitting waiting for them on one of the wooden chairs. David greeted her in Hebrew, and slowly, somehow reluctantly, she stood up. Edie saw a slight, yet wiry-looking girl with long black hair, dressed in a dark blue sundress. She had deep brown eyes and striking black eyebrows, and Edie could see that she was beautiful, except that now the brows were pulled into a frown. David touched her shoulder, seeming worried, and speaking soothingly to her in Hebrew, asking questions, and her face puckered for a moment. Edie could not read what was going on and thought she seemed angry. She felt herself tense up inside. This must be Gila, but what was going on? Had there been a row between them? David had not indicated anything might be wrong.

After he had spoken to her a bit more, David led her over to Edie.

'Mom, Anatoli. This is Gila.'

She obviously had to force a smile on to her face and Edie caught a glimpse of little white teeth, and of the beauty that would be present when she looked happy. They shook hands.

'Shalom – welcome,' she said softly, adding in broken English. 'I am pleased to meet you.'

Edie nodded and smiled, saying Shalom and that she was pleased too, but the pained, sad look did not lift from the girl's face.

There was a further exchange in Hebrew, David looking quite concerned, and Gila said an abrupt goodbye and left the apartment.

'Oh dear—' David looked really upset.

'Whatever's the matter?' Edie was convinced the problem had something to do with their visit. She felt upset herself.

'There's something wrong – with the baby. She's been having pains since yesterday and now she says she's started bleeding. Does that mean she's going to lose it?'

'Oh dear!' Edie cried. 'It might mean that – oh the poor girl, how terrible!' She went to David and stroked his arm. 'Look, love – you must go with her – don't send her off on her own. Can she see a doctor?'

'Yes – there's one on the kibbutz . . .' He looked stunned. 'I'm sorry, Mom – and I wanted to make everything comfortable for you both. Look – I'll put some water on to boil and you can make tea – and there's melon and bread in there.' He was about to go into the tiny kitchen but Anatoli stopped him.

'We can make tea, David. Edith and I will be quite all right and we'll have plenty of time together. Do go after her and make sure she's all right.'

'Yes – go on,' Edie urged. 'Quickly – go and catch her up!'

'I'll be back as soon as I can!'

And he was off. They heard his sandals slapping down the stairs.

Anatoli came and put his arms round Edie. 'Not a very good start. Poor David.'

'I know. Poor girl – no wonder she looked so grim. It does sound as if she's losing the child. But oh, Anatoli, at least I've seen him at last! He looks so well and so grown up! And we've got two whole weeks ahead of us to spend with him!'

David appeared later in the evening, by which time Edie and Anatoli had had a drink and a nap and were ready to face life again.

'How is she, love?' Edie asked. She felt quite maternal towards Gila, even though she'd seen her only once.

David flung himself down on the hard, plastic-covered sofa beside Edie. 'She's got to rest for a day or two. The doctor says she's miscarrying – it's gone too far to prevent it. She's in the best place – she's gone to her mother's.' He rubbed his hands over his face, then looked up wearily at them. 'She was upset when she first found out she was having a child. It changed all her plans. She would have had to interrupt her studies. She was angry. But now . . . we'd adjusted to the idea and she's very sad.'

'Of course she is,' Anatoli said.

Edie laid her hand on David's arm. 'It's a terrible thing. Please tell her how sorry we are and wish her a speedy recovery.'

David smiled wanly. 'I will. It's just such a pity it's happened now as well. She's usually so happy. And she was going to come with us to Haifa.'

They reassured him that they were perfectly happy to fit in with any plans and were there really to see him.

Later, as she and Anatoli went to bed after the evening meal, which that night they had in the apartment, Edie said, 'It feels very strange, all this going on with the baby. I can hardly take it in that it was his child. Last time I saw him he was barely more than a schoolboy!'

Fifty-Four

For the next two days, David was expected to work, as he had asked for time off later especially to go with Edie and Anatoli to Haifa. So they had some hours to themselves until David's leisure time. Gila was still recovering and David said she was quickly on the mend, though still feeling groggy. Edie was impressed by her toughness.

Kibbutz life in itself was an adventure. They took their meals in the communal dining-room and David showed them the hut where he and the others slept. Edie was amazed by these spartan living quarters and the fact that boys and girls were in there together.

They felt very lazy being on holiday while everyone else was hard at work. Instead of acting as volunteers, David had asked if they could pay for their board instead, and as they were rather exceptional visitors, the committee granted permission.

By the time they were due to travel to Haifa, Gila was up and insisting she felt well enough to come. They all got up at four thirty in the morning and by five, David and Gila were knocking on the door of the little apartment.

'Oh – d'you think you're strong enough, love?' Edie said to Gila, forgetting she could barely understand any English. She still felt rather nervous of the girl. It would be so much easier if they had more than a few words of the same language in common!

But Gila obviously made sense of what she said, and nodded, holding out her hand. 'Shalom, shalom.' Edie smiled, pulled her close and kissed her cheek.

'Tell her how sorry we are,' Edie said, stroking Gila's hand, wanting to give comfort. The whole event had brought them all closer. David translated and Gila attempted a wan smile and said, 'Yes. Thank you.'

David had arranged for someone to give them a lift to Tiberias, and they caught a very early morning bus to Haifa in the cool darkness. Edie loved the feel of the summer nights here, the aromatic smells of the plants, the scraping sounds of crickets when they went to bed and the dark, silky air. Now, before sunrise, it was quieter, warm and tranquil, with a sense of expectation. As they travelled, the sun rose behind the bus. Gila fell asleep against David's shoulder almost before they had started moving, and Edie dozed for a time too, until woken with a jolt as they stopped at Nazareth, to see the sun, dazzling now, gradually turning the bare earth from grey to white. She looked at David and Gila in the seat in front, the protective way he had his arm round her, her hair very black against his white shirt. She had heard Gila call him 'Doodi' affectionately, marrying his names, David and Rudi. Yes, she thought, with a pang at her own loss of him. They were young, but there was something real between them all right.

Anatoli saw her examining the two of them.

'They're lovely,' he whispered.

Edie felt a glow of pleasure. 'Yes, they are, aren't they?'

They were in Haifa before eight in the morning, and stopped to enjoy a big breakfast together in a café from which they could see the sea. They ate warm, fresh bread, cheese and houmous, tomatoes, cucumbers and yoghurt. Gila began to look a lot better after she had had a good meal.

Anatoli questioned the two of them gently about their plans for the future, David translating for Gila. Edie was grateful to Anatoli. She watched him, his broad, friendly face already tanned, eyes expressive with sympathy, fatherly towards Gila. Edie could see that Gila liked him and was more relaxed now. She told Anatoli that she had wanted to be a dentist ever since she was a little girl and had had an aching tooth removed on the kibbutz. She had been impressed that the dentist could make her feel so much better and she thought it was a good job. A useful job. Work and usefulness were vital to kibbutz life. She smiled as she talked, her real prettiness coming out now.

'I suppose,' she said wistfully, 'I can go to do my studies now. I am free again. But I am very sad.'

They all got to know each other better over breakfast, through their halting, translated conversation. Gila said that now she was getting better they were invited to her mother's home to meet her properly. They had so far only had a brief introduction to Mrs Weissman.

When they emerged from the café it was much hotter outside, the sun moving up the sky, turning the water of the bay a rich blue, hazier in the distance where it met the sky.

'Shalom – welcome, welcome!'

The first thing Edie noticed about Annaliese was how tiny she was, standing at her door in her little black mules, slightly stooped, wearing a flower print dress. She spoke in halting English when they arrived, beckoning them all inside. Edie immediately felt at ease with her, and admired her for her cheerful demeanour. David had told her what a hard life Annaliese had caring for Hermann, how fragile, how unwell he often was, physically and mentally. Edie wondered how he would cope with their visit, but she felt Anatoli was the one who would know how to manage it. It was he whom Hermann most wanted to see.

They all stood in the little hall. Annaliese switched into Hebrew as she greeted David and Gila, kissing both of them affectionately, holding on to Gila's hand as she talked. She spoke in concerned tones to Gila, giving her stomach a fleeting caress. Though Edie could not understand Annaliese's words, she could easily make sense of her expressions of sorrow over the miscarriage. She stroked Gila's cheek and Edie guessed she was saying that she looked pale and why had she made the journey today?

Then she turned to Anatoli to greet him properly after their brief social handshake. Seeing her looking at him intensely, he gave a slight bow, and said something in German. Annaliese clasped his hand and let out a passionate burst of speech.

'You and David'll have to tell me what everyone's saying,' Edie murmured to Anatoli as they followed Annaliese into the sitting-room. 'Or I'm not going to make head or tail of today!'

The living-room was furnished with crimson velvet chairs, a small settee and a great many bookshelves. Annaliese announced that she would make coffee.

As they waited, Edie looked round at all the books on the shelves facing her, most of which had titles in German on their faded spines. David was speaking softly to Gila. After a short time there came the sound of a door opening across the landing and Edie saw David's gaze flicker towards the hall. A moment later they heard Annaliese calling urgently, 'Hermann? Hermann!' But he had already shuffled across the landing and was standing looking into the room.

Edie was deeply shocked by the sight of him, even despite David's warnings. She thought immediately of Mr Vintner, the man from Glover Road who'd never recovered from the Great War. His gait was so shuffling, that of an old, broken man, and from beneath his uncombed white hair, from the pallid countenance, looked out watery, disturbed eyes.

'*Abba . . . Vater.*' David stood up and went to his side. Hermann acknowledged his presence with a brief look, then his gaze wandered, searching the room.

Annaliese stepped in and took his arm. She leaned close to him, almost as if telling him a secret, speaking softly. Twice he said, 'Eh?' and 'Umm?' as if he could not hear, or understand what she was saying. Then Edie heard her say Anatoli's name.

Anatoli got slowly to his feet. He walked round the small table and went to Hermann Mayer. He had to tell Edie afterwards exactly what he'd said.

'Hermann?' He spoke slowly, calmly. 'I have come to visit you at last. It is Gruschov. Anatoli Gruschov. Do you remember me?'

There was a silence. Edie became aware of the thumping of her own heart. She glanced at David, saw his set, serious expression as he watched his father. Hermann Mayer stared for some time into Anatoli's face and Edie thought, oh no, he doesn't recognize him. He has no idea who Anatoli is! It seemed so wrong that they should not recognize each other, as if this recognition was needed to verify the past.

Slowly, Hermann Mayer made a move to shake hands, once again, for all the world as if he was meeting a formal business aquaintance, but as his hand moved towards Anatoli, Edie could see the violent tremor in it. As their hands met, in stumbling speech he said,

'Anatoli Gruschov ... I see you now. How could I ever forget you? You ... who brought me back from the grave?'

A second later the two men were clasped tight in each other's arms. Anatoli seemed almost to be supporting Hermann, who had crumpled forwards on to him, and in a moment, out of the tense silence, came the weak, retching sound of sobs. Lost in the distress of memory he clung to Anatoli, snatches of speech coming from him, exclamations which sounded almost like curses, howls of pain, then the same phrase, the only one Edie could distinguish, again and again ... '*Was ist der Sinn meines Leibens?*' What is the point of my life?

His anguish washed over them all. Edie saw that Anatoli was also in tears and her husband's emotion and Hermann's broken distress made her weep also. Hermann kept touching Anatoli, his face, shoulders, hands as if in blessing, and yet there was profound distress in his every speech and gesture, and sometimes the words, that question, were spat out like a curse, as if Anatoli was the only one who could give answer. *Was ist der Sinn meines Leibens?* Anatoli, tears wetting his cheeks, said nothing, just held him tightly and wept with him.

All their eyes were on the two men for many minutes, until Annaliese, to the side of them, raised her hand to wipe her cheeks and Edie glanced round the room, to see that there was no one who had not been brought to tears by the meeting of the two men. David, red-eyed, was crying silently, but it was Gila, sitting with her hands over her face, who sobbed and sobbed as if she was a conduit for all the grief in the room, so that both Edie and David went to her and held her. Edie stroked her back, feeling not only the wiry strength of her, but love for the beautiful girl whom her son loved taking root in her own heart.

They were on the bus back to Tiberias, riding through a sunset the colour of blood oranges as the bus pulled away, its rays touching the golden dome of the Bahai Temple so that it glowed with fire. David and Gila were in the seat across the aisle. Once again Gila seemed wrung out and exhausted, needing to sleep.

It was the first time Edie had had a chance to speak with Anatoli alone. For part of the day he had sat talking quietly with Hermann in his room, emerging at last only to say that Hermann was exhausted and needed to sleep. Then Annaliese had sat talking to him, seeming also to need to pour out her feelings. Gila fell asleep, her face pale and drawn. David gently made her more comfortable, putting a cushion under her head as she lay on the couch while he and Edie went for a walk outside, up to the *Merkhaz*, or market on the Carmel, looking round at the shops and stalls and coming back with peaches and watermelon, bread and roasted chicken which Annaliese had asked them to buy, and gave them to eat before they left to catch the bus.

They watched the streets of Haifa recede behind them in the glowing evening, then Edie took Anatoli's hand.

'You never really told me what happened at all, did you? With Hermann – in Bergen-Belsen.'

Anatoli sighed. He seemed spent with emotion. Edie felt very tender towards him. She wanted to hold him close and give comfort.

'Why didn't you tell me all of it?' She felt a little hurt.

'When we talked about Hermann that time, I had only just met you,' Anatoli said. He put one arm round her shoulders, resting it on the back of the seat, while the other hand loosely clasped hers. 'And what a day that was.' He kissed her forehead and she smiled, a little appeased. 'All the detail was not necessary. Belsen was ...' He shrugged. 'Well, you cannot easily say what it was like. Hell on earth – that is all.' He stopped for a moment, looking ahead of him. 'There were so many who suffered ... I suppose that was why it is easier to hold on to one, and my mind has remembered Hermann. But of course there were others we saved from death. Many of them died later though. I suppose I did not think that loading you with the details was necessary. Even though it must never be forgotten, it is not healthy to dwell on it. You know that until today Annaliese did not know exactly how we met, Hermann and me?'

Edie could hardly believe this. 'He's never talked to her about it? All this time?'

Anatoli shook his head. 'She says not. Not in any detail. It is too shameful.'

'*Shameful?* What do you mean? Was he a collaborator or something?'

'No, no – nothing of that kind. He was a victim. I mean that sort of shame. Being in the hands of torturers who have the power to destroy you.'

Edie glanced down at the scar on her arm. Yes, in a very small way she understood that shame.

'First he was in Auschwitz, then Bergen-Belsen ... You know that Belsen was not supposed to be a concentration camp? It was a transit camp. They were trying to move people away from the other camps when they wanted to hide their crimes. But most people who were supposed to "pass through" Belsen never came out again. By the time the camp was discovered the inmates had been left to die. There was almost no food. They were starving. You see in Auschwitz, if you were weak, they sent you to the ovens. In Belsen there was no quick end. When we entered the camp the dead lay everywhere ... Piles of them, literally, everywhere you looked. You have seen on the newsreels? Really, Edith, I don't even like to describe it to you ...' She squeezed his hand.

'Trying to bury the dead became such a monstrous problem that after a time they had to bring machines to collect the bodies. But in the beginning we had to dig pits and carry them one by one. For a whole day this was my work – to bury the dead. One man taking the ankles, another the wrists and lowering them – no, throwing them, the task was so overwhelming – into the pits. From the pile I threw another of these bags of bones on top of the others. We threw another across him. And then we heard him call out. I can never forget it. The starving have such small voices, thin as a reed, and he had had no drink for hours, days probably. This voice said ...' Anatoli's own voice cracked as he said the words, ' "I am alive! Help me!" '

Edie stroked his hand.

'We both stopped, the other fellow and me, and looked. We were both thinking the same thing, I am sure, for those first moments: we might as well leave him there, he'll die anyway. But, without looking at each other – we were also somehow ashamed – we climbed down into the pit and brought him out again. He weighed only about five or six stone and I carried him in my arms to the hospital. He was suffering from typhus: I thought he would not live. They found a small space for him on the floor because it was so crowded. And that was when he spoke to me, whispered to me for my name, my home address . . . When I think of Belsen the first thing to come to my mind is Hermann Mayer's eyes. His sockets were hollowed out. He had the face of death – I don't know how he lived.' Again, an enormous sigh. 'And you know, he doesn't know why he lived either.'

'What happened to him after that?'

'Well – I did manage to see him once more in the hospital. He was still alive the next day. After that, I never knew of course. Until you wrote to me I had no idea what had happened to him. He did not contact me. It seems that meeting David, his son, has opened the past for him again. Annaliese told me that by the end of May '45, when he was only barely recovered, a thousand Belsen inmates, including Hermann, were transported to a camp on the Dutch border, called Lingen. It was for displaced persons. From the little she knew, it was a disaster. Conditions were appalling. They were put back in huts just like those at Belsen but with roofs full of holes and with no beds, no electricity. There was very little food and even the bread was often inedible. They thought they had been sent back to a concentration camp. You can imagine the effect on them. And what was worse was that as well as the Belsen Jews there were a lot of others – Russians and Poles who were Jew haters, all together. It was a fiasco. You know, though—' for a second he smiled. 'Annaliese said that some of the best help in the camp came from a lady who worked for the Quaker Relief Team. Hermann has never forgotten her. She was called Jane Levenson, and she was one of the people who helped to get them out of there. They transferred to another camp called Diepholz, near Osnabruck, and then back to Belsen.'

'Back to *Belsen*! Why would they do that? How terrible!'

'Yes. Indeed. But there they could get help from the Central Jewish Committee. They advised Hermann to write and make enquiries to Berlin – to see if anyone had returned home. That was how Annaliese discovered he had survived. Actually, I don't know what would have happened to him had she *not* survived. I suppose he would have been put in an institution. He was in the most degraded state, mentally and physically. It was she who arranged their passage to Israel and she has cared for him ever since. They had no one else. He already knew that his wife had been killed in England. Of course he did not know he had a surviving son.'

Anatoli's hand tightened on hers as they both looked across at David. He was leaning back against the window, asleep, Gila resting against his chest. He looked so very beautiful to Edie, yet so young and vulnerable. Her miracle baby. All the sadness of events, thoughts of the chain of people which had brought him to her, washed over her and she felt her heart expand to take in all of it, all of them. She felt no jealousy, no need to possess or control. Just love. They were all family now.

Epilogue

August 1959

'Go on – are you going to read it to us, then?' Ruby said.

Edie was sitting out on the grass in front of the wide terrace at Cadbury's, a small circle of friends round her as they all ate their lunchtime sandwiches. She had their rapt attention.

'Oh – all right then,' she said, with mock reluctance. The letter had been tucked in her pocket all morning and she was sure she'd been able to feel it, warm against her leg as if it was glowing! She opened the crinkly blue pages of David's letter, written three days after she and Anatoli had flown home to England.

Dear Mum and Anatoli,

. . . Well, it's 4am and I'm writing this before work begins. Yesterday was the most extraordinary day, and I just have to tell you about it!

You remember that Amir suggested I go back to Jerusalem? He seemed to think it was important for me, and he unexpectedly told me to go yesterday! So I did as he said, and went to Har Hazikaron – the Hill of Remembrance. Next time you visit we must go to this place. I don't really have words to express the effect it has on you. Two years ago they opened a museum here called Yad Vashem, to commemorate the Jewish victims of the Nazis. The place stands on a rocky rise, out on the western edge of the city, and walking into it you enter a truly dark world. In the Hall of Remembrance, a gloomy, almost empty space, stands a metal sculpture in which a fire burns perpetually, sending a smoky thread of memory up through a hole in the roof. The floor around it is tiled, and in it are set the names of all the camps: CHELMNO, AUSCHWITZ, BERGEN-BELSEN, etc. The sense of the dead being present and of their suffering in life is almost overwhelming. Standing there in the quiet, I could think only of my father, how the person he used to be died in those places.

In another building there's a register of names of those killed in the 'holocaust', as they now call it. This was why Amir suggested I come. I went to the desk and said I wanted to register a name. I felt nervous, in case they didn't think she counted. But when I gave the name, Gerda Mayer, and explained how she died, the man there nodded. Yes, it was true. She too was a victim of the holocaust and her name would be added to all the others. When I went back out, the light was blinding and the heat came down on me like a weight, the rocks and cypress trees shimmering in the distance. I felt exhausted when I got back to Tiberias, but also that what I had done was fitting. It completed something for Gerda and my father.

And then I drove the car back to Hamesh. It was late, very quiet when I turned the engine off, except for the crickets. And then something incredible happened. I thought Gila would be long asleep by then, but as I was winding up the window I heard, 'Doodi! Doodi!'

I thought there must be terrible news of some sort and I leapt out of the car. She just came running at me – she'd been waiting – flung herself into my arms, speaking so fast I couldn't keep up with her Hebrew! Oh Mum, Anatoli, you'll hardly believe it: she'd gone to the doctor again while I was away because she couldn't understand why she still felt so ropey. He gave her a full examination, and, well – you're still going to be a grandmother! She did lose a child, but she was going to have twins, and she's still carrying the second baby! I can hardly begin to tell you how we feel. The first time, all we could see were the problems. Now, even though the problems are the same, we know that what we have is very precious. I have never seen Gila so happy.

After a few more details of news he signed off, 'It is lovely to see you both so happy. And we look forward to seeing you again *soon*. Your loving David xx.'

When Edie and Anatoli had read the letter that morning, both of them had wept for joy. Reading it again brought more tears, and she looked up into her friends' smiling faces.

'Well,' Ruby said, wiping her own eyes. 'I thought our Marleen'd be the first to make one of us a grandmother, knowing her. Not young David.'

'So, I don't s'pose you'll ever be going to Israel again, will you?' one of her friends teased.

'You just try stopping me!' Edie beamed. 'You don't think I'd miss seeing my new daughter and grandchild do you?'

Acknowledgements

Grateful thanks are due to the following: Gertie Cook, Sarah Foden, Andi Jones, Eike Muller, Leslie Wilson; to the Cadbury Archive, *Bournville Works Magazine*, Cadbury World and Selly Oak and Stirchley Libraries; to the written work of Dr Carl Chinn, G. Letitia Hayes and Zoë Josephs.

Apologies for any liberties taken with Birmingham street names, with the Meeting of the Society of Friends in Bournville or with Singers Hill Synagogue.

CHOCOLATE GIRLS by Annie Murray is sponsored by Cadbury. For further information on many of the locations discussed, and on the whole Bournville Village, are available at the Cadbury World exhibition in Bournville. Phone 0121 451 4159 for details of visits.

FOR MORE ON

ANNIE MURRAY

sign up to receive our

SAGA NEWSLETTER

Packed with **features, competitions, authors' and readers' letters** and **news of exclusive events,** it's a must-read for every Annie Murray fan!

Simply fill in your details below and tick to confirm that you would like to receive saga-related news and promotions and return to us at **Pan Macmillan, Saga Newsletter, 20 New Wharf Road, London, N1 9RR**.

NAME _____

ADDRESS _____

_____

_____ POSTCODE _____

EMAIL _____

☐ *I would like to receive saga-related news and promotions (please tick)*

You can unsubscribe at any time in writing or through our website where you can also see our privacy policy which explains how we will store and use your data.